W9-ARU-775

Thirty-four East

Other books by Alfred Coppel / **Night of Fire and Snow**

Dark December / **A Certainty of Love** / **The Gate of Hell**

Order of Battle / **A Little Time for Laughter**

Between the Thunder and the Sun / **The Landlocked Man**

Alfred Coppel

Thirty-four East

Harcourt Brace Jovanovich, Inc., New York

Printed in the United States of America

Library of Congress Cataloging in Publication Data

Coppel, Alfred.
Thirty-four east.

I. Title.
PZ4.C785Th [PS3553.064] 813'.5'4 73-20346
ISBN 0-15-189950-9

C D E

To Darwin and Hildegarde
for encouragement when it was most needed,
to Julian
for the best of guidance,
and to Elisabeth, with love,
for patience and "the willing suspension of disbelief"

Contents

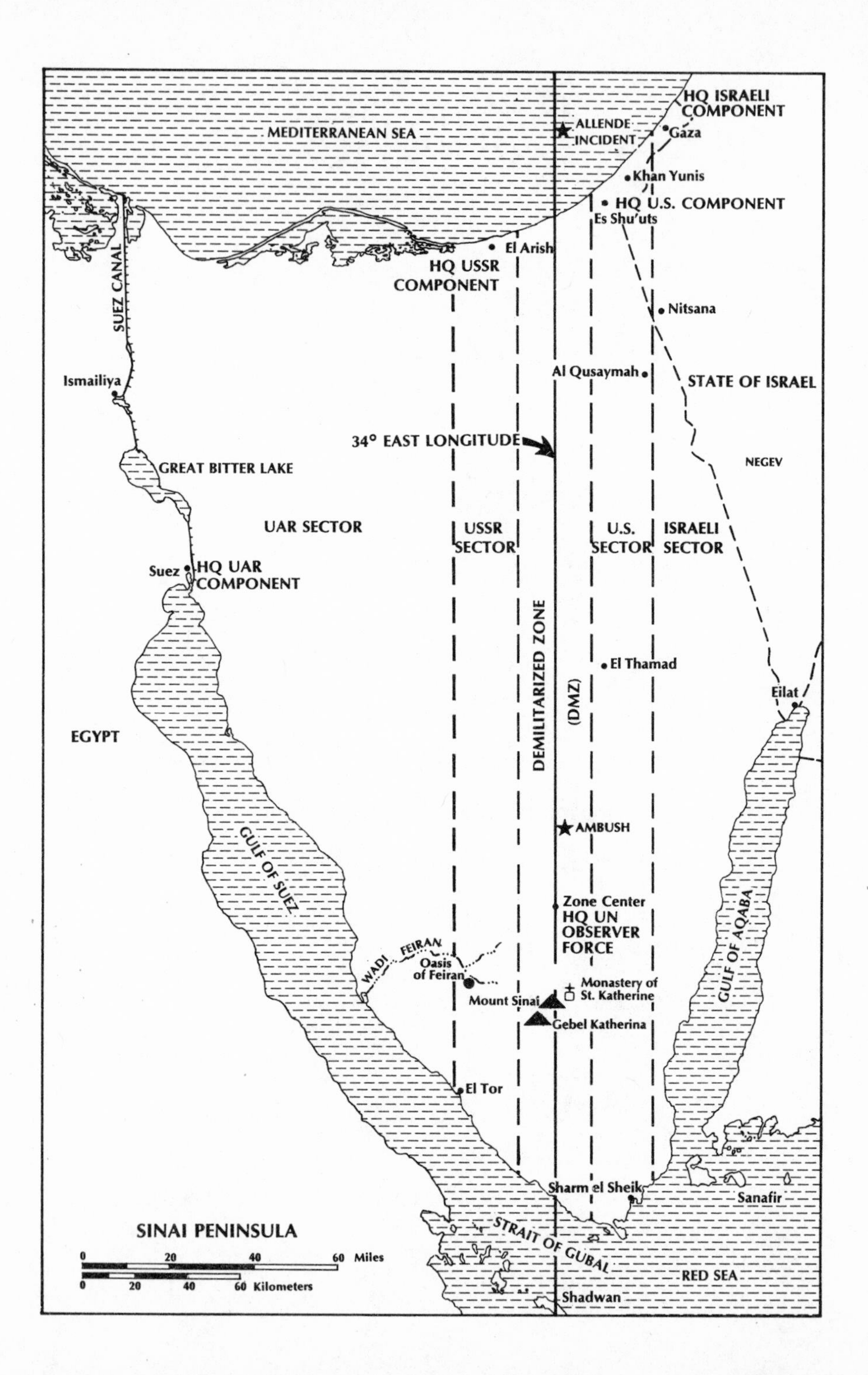

MEDITERRANEAN SEA
ALLENDE INCIDENT
HQ ISRAELI COMPONENT
Gaza
Khan Yunis
HQ U.S. COMPONENT
Es Shu'uts
El Arish
HQ USSR COMPONENT
SUEZ CANAL
Nitsana
Ismailiya
Al Qusaymah
STATE OF ISRAEL
34° EAST LONGITUDE
NEGEV
GREAT BITTER LAKE
UAR SECTOR
USSR SECTOR
U.S. SECTOR
ISRAELI SECTOR
Suez
HQ UAR COMPONENT
DEMILITARIZED ZONE
(DMZ)
El Thamad
Eilat
EGYPT
AMBUSH
GULF OF SUEZ
Zone Center
HQ UN OBSERVER FORCE
WADI FEIRAN
Oasis of Feiran
Monastery of St. Katherine
Mount Sinai
Gebel Katherina
GULF OF AQABA
El Tor
Sharm el Sheik
Sanafir
SINAI PENINSULA
STRAIT OF GUBAL
RED SEA
Shadwan
0 20 40 60 Miles
0 20 40 60 Kilometers

Part One

On the first day of a revolution he is a treasure; on the second he ought to be shot.

—Said of Mikhail Aleksandrovich Bakunin by an observer of his activities during the Paris revolt of 1848

1

Against the low sun, the mountains of the southern Sinai massif lay black and frayed-appearing in the morning light. The burgeoning glare of the white sky made the distance difficult to estimate, but Enver Lesh, with the American-made chart in his hands, knew that the hills lay no more than twenty-two kilometers from the sea at his back. He estimated that, assuming the rendezvous was accomplished on schedule, the commando could reach the foothills by late afternoon. Once there, the force would be clear of the Russian Sector and into the Demilitarized Zone, with only the United Nations patrols to trouble it. A power armed only with handguns and a treaty presented no threat to the operation: UN observers had been killed before.

Of the Albanian submarine that had deposited him on the lonely stretch of coast between Sharm el Sheik and El Tor, not far from the southern tip of the Sinai Peninsula, there was now no sign except a narrow slick on the waters of the Gulf of Suez. In any other place even this telltale clue would have annoyed Lesh, but in this oil-rich region of wells and tankers, drifting slicks meant nothing. Also, the inshore patrolling here was done by Egyptian Component gunboats, and the laxness of their crews was the primary reason for the selection of this site for the rendezvous with the guerrillas.

From the beach, where the waves lapped gently, the land

rose to a rock-strewn plain unbroken by even so much as a dune or a wadi. The lack of cover was compensated for by the easiness of the terrain. If Leila Jamil had done her job properly, obtaining the camels and clothing, an air observer would see nothing but a band of Sinai Bedouins trekking from the coast toward the oasis at Wadi Feiran.

This was the only moment of real danger: with six cases of weapons and supplies stacked on the sandy beach above the high-water mark and a single man in combat camouflage standing nakedly in the early-morning sunlight.

Lesh was in his late forties, of middle height and powerfully muscled. His pale-blue eyes were shaded by sunglasses that rested on the bridge of a thick, hooked nose that had been broken once and set badly. A drooping mustache accentuated his thin lips and strong, meaty chin. His teeth were long and tinged with yellow.

He was a colonel in the Albanian People's Liberation Army, though it had been years since he had served with a regular unit in the homeland. As a young man he had fought in Korea as a member of the Chinese People's Volunteers. In the 1960's he had served with the Vietcong; a napalm burn was a memento of that war. From Vietnam he had gone to West Bengal to help organize Maoist cadres, and when that was done he had been sent back to Indochina to fight with the Khmer Rouge. He had served on the military staff of the Albanian legation in Burundi, and as an instructor in weaponry in Libya, Syria, and Iraq. He was a professional irregular soldier, and it was in this capacity that he now found himself on this bleak stretch of coastline awaiting the arrival of the Abou Moussa Commando of the Arab Front for the Liberation of Palestine. He knew these guerrillas were irregular, too; he hoped they were professionals.

Lesh was a man without a private life, and with only one political ideal. A devoted Bakuninite, he was fond of quoting that nineteenth-century anarchist's dictum that the passion for destruction is also a *creative* passion. There was a savagery about that aphorism that satisfied him to the marrow of his being. Though ostensibly a sound Albanian Maoist, he actually had no interest in political systems. Russian revisionism, Chinese Chouism, American imperialism, Israeli Zionism, and Egyptian pan-Arabism left him equally unmoved. But the fanaticism of the Arab Front, which had gathered together the shattered remnants of the old Arab and Palestinian guerrilla and terrorist organizations, appealed to his Bakuninite passion for destruction. Men and women who could indiscriminately bomb, pillage, and murder to prolong a war beyond all reasonable hope of victory were suitable companions for Enver Lesh. The world was drifting into a sulky peace. But Bakunin antedates Marx, he had told himself wryly, and closely succeeds Cain. There was still killing to be done.

A fitting notion for a man standing alone on the shore of the Biblical Wilderness of Sin, he thought.

He saw them now, approaching out of the mirage from the south. There were fourteen of them, all mounted, and leading extra animals. He frowned. Leila Jamil had been told that fifty fighters would be required at a minimum; more, if the Russians and Americans took even rudimentary precautions.

He watched. The undulating pace of the camels gave them the look of oddly made ships on an ocean of shimmering sand and pebble. Behind them, the horizon lay flat as a ruler under a sky growing brassy with the morning light. They cast long shadows toward the beach, moving nearer in an eerie silence that seemed to smother the soft lapping of the waves.

At a distance of about a kilometer, the leader of the troop signaled and the riders fanned out to the landward side, forming a broad and ragged half-circle. Though it was manifestly impossible that he could be anything but alone on this exposed terrain, Jamil was not risking an ambush. Lesh approved of her caution. It was such attention to detail that kept guerrillas alive, and the Abou Moussa Commando had never been surprised by an enemy. He raised his empty hands above his head and waited. The troop closed in silently until he stood surrounded, his back to the sea.

He studied the dark faces, half concealed under the corded headcloths. Some of the men had thrown back their black Bedouin robes to expose their weapons, and what they carried proclaimed their military poverty. Once, the Chinese, and even the Russians, had willingly supplied the various Arab Front units with weapons. But this had not been so for several years now, ever since the Soviet Union had put its name to the Cyprus Accord and the Sinai Peninsula had thereby been divided.

What the guerrillas carried were captured weapons, mostly: some Uzi machine pistols made in Israel, some old-style Russian AK-47 assault rifles left from other times or stolen from the Egyptians, one old American Thompson, and three antique British Stens.

The commando leader rapped her camel with a rod, so that the beast knelt. As she dismounted, Lesh advanced to greet her. He had not seen Leila Jamil since the final planning meeting, held in a basement room in Beirut, two months and more ago. There in Lebanon the Mediterranean breezes were kinder than the listless, hot gusts he now felt from the Red Sea.

The guerrilla woman was nearing forty, Lesh estimated. She had been a beauty once, in the manner of Arab women, with fine features and large dark eyes. But endless skirmishing, flight, and the desert had hardened and desiccated that beauty almost to the vanishing point. Her eyes, so black that the pupils were lost in the circles of the irises, were hard as polished obsidian. Her lips were thin and compressed, and her straight nose was sharp as a blade. A cruel face, Lesh thought. The face of a basilisk.

One did not greet Leila Jamil with courtesies. "I told you we would need at least fifty men," Lesh said.

"I have more at Wadi Feiran. These are all I had animals for."

Lesh studied the tufted coats and wattled necks of the camels. He was not an expert on the condition of the ugly beasts, but he suspected that these were old animals, bought or, more likely, stolen from the native Bedouin, of whom there were still ten thousand or more ghosting to and fro across the peninsula.

"I have twenty men at Feiran," Leila said. "That should be more than enough. They are good men—men of sacrifice." She had been speaking in English, their common language, but for the last she used the Arabic *fedayeen,* which meant, as Lesh knew, something a bit more than its English equivalent. What she meant was that her men had made their peace with Allah and now desired only to die in the service of Islam.

Lesh understood this, for he was of a race with strong Islamic strains and undercurrents. The Moslems of Albania had been dying for savage and mystical causes for generations. He said, "Well. Thirty-four may do the work of fifty if they must. Tell your people to load the cases. We must get away from here at once."

"What have you brought us?"

Lesh strode to a wooden case and pried open the top. Inside, nested in tiers of four, lay new Russian Kalashnikov attack rifles. The standard weapon of Russian Guards and airborne infantry units. "As promised," he said.

"How did you get them?"

"With difficulty. The revisionists are not so generous as formerly," he replied. "Now we must go."

Jamil gave instructions for the loading of the cases onto the pack animals. From her own saddlebag she took a robe, headcloth, and agal, and gave them to Lesh. As he converted himself to a desert Bedouin, the woman watched him with steady interest. Presently she said, "In Beirut I had the impression your government was undecided about assisting us. Was I wrong?"

"No. But the decision was made."

"Why?"

Lesh favored her with a smile. "What does it matter? It was decided."

"We fight best when we know why and for whom, Lesh."

Lesh settled the dusty-smelling black robe on his large sloping shoulders and put the headcloth on his shaggy, graying hair. There were stains that could have been blood on the dingy cloth. He did not ask about the prior owner of the desert gear he was inheriting. He said, "The Russians and the Americans are making a love feast. Tirana wants them to love one another less. That is reason enough. It is hoped that our former Chinese friends will take proper note and react appropriately. But none of that matters. I would have come even without instructions from Tirana." His smile grew wider and somehow more threatening. "I have killed many things in my lifetime. But would you believe that I have never killed a dove? This will be a first."

He broke into laughter and mounted his camel expertly enough. Jamil was up beside him on her own mount. She gave a hand signal, and the troop moved out, angling away from the sea toward the northeast. Within a half hour they had vanished into the mirage, and when the next Egyptian patrol boat passed that particular part of the coast there was nothing to be seen but the shallow pad marks left in the sand by the feet of camels, a sight common enough there not to arouse interest or suspicion.

2

In Washington, a cold rain was falling. Through the high Georgian windows of the Oval Office, the President could see the wet gleam of lights on Pennsylvania Avenue, but the rain was misty and dimmed with lights beyond into a blurry twilight.

He turned from the window and sat wearily behind his desk, conscious of the fact that he was tireder than he should be and that his body ached more than was reasonable in a man not yet sixty. He rubbed unconsciously at the dull pain in his arm and marshaled his thoughts once again.

His visitor waited, primly silent in the chair across the desk. There was always about Talcott Quincy Bailey an air of moral superiority that his political enemies chose to call priggishness, and it was a fact, the President thought, that it was impossible to be around the Vice President for long without the uncomfortable feeling that one was being weighed and somehow found wanting.

Bailey was a New England aristocrat by birth, wealthy by inheritance, and a liberal intellectual by training and conviction. He would not have been the President's choice for a running mate; he had been forced on him by the extensive changes in party rules that had made the selection of a vice-presidential candidate a matter to be decided exclusively by the delegates to the national conventions.

Still, Bailey had been a running mate he could accept. He had proved his value by providing the margin of victory in a close election. He appealed to that coalition of intellectuals, pacifists, and theorists who vocally remembered the incredible disarray of American politics in the early seventies, the scandal of the Watergate affair, and even the spectacle of a Vice President ousted for corruption. These perennial protesters with the long memories were Bailey's constituents—and without them, the party would have failed at the polls. The problem was how to contain such a volatile coalition peaceably within an administration committed to moderation and reconciliation.

The warm light of the graceful room seemed to form an island of safety and comfort amid the frigid dampness falling on the city from the lowering sky.

The fact is, the President thought wryly, Talcott Bailey looks more properly at home in this gracious house than I do. The Vice President's face was narrow and ascetically handsome, lined only deeply enough to give it a touch of what the women of the news media called "a fine virility." During the campaign there had been more than one reporter who had commented on the generally held opinion that the bottom of the ticket outdid the top in "charisma." Bailey was tall, over six feet. The President was not. Bailey had a full head of ash-blond hair turning silver that curled fashionably over his collar and around his temples. The President was balding and still given to the personal style of his prairie-state homeland. The Vice President was an economist by training. He had served previous administrations in that capacity and had developed a number of rather startling programs for tax reform and welfare systems—none of which were found acceptable by the party conservatives, but which were appealing to the university and inner-city voters. These were the groups, heavily represented at the national convention, who had put Talcott Quincy Bailey on the ticket.

What most troubled the President, however, was not Bailey's economic radicalism. It was his deeply held conviction that the major cause of the nation's troubles over the last twenty years was the power and adventurousness of the military. Bailey was popularly known as the "Dove," and he earned the nickname almost daily by the outspokenness of his pacifism.

The argument that had kept them here in the Oval Office until almost midnight had been precipitated by Bailey's personal and acidly stated opposition to a supplemental defense appropriation requested by the administration to support a further three years of American commitment to the Peacekeeping Force in the Sinai Peninsula created by the Cyprus Accord.

The President broke the lengthening silence, speaking with authority. It was late and he was tired and he was increasingly impatient with the Vice President's resistance to anything and everything military. "I have considered your suggestions, Talc, and I have decided against giving them weight in this situation. The Peacekeeping Force is essential to our foreign policy. We can no longer simply allow those people to behave like children playing with matches in a powder magazine—and nothing will keep them from it but armed soldiers from the big powers. Everything else has been tried, Talc, even the pragmatic reasonableness of old Henry Kissinger. You know how every settlement has eroded until they are right back at each other's throats again. No, it has to be a long-term interposition, and the United States must continue to meet its responsibility. There can be no question of a reduction in the size of our component."

"If that's your final word, Mr. President—" Bailey said.

"It is. I've talked to Fowler Beal, and there will be no difficulty in the House."

"The Speaker is a very amenable fellow," Bailey said dryly. The point was a sensitive one, because Beal was an old political lieutenant of the President's, better known for his dumb loyalty than for any legislative intelligence.

The President's eyes, red and nested in wrinkled, graying

flesh, turned hard. "I wouldn't have it any other way, Talc. And to make certain there is no problem in the Senate, either, I want the bill moved up for consideration the day after tomorrow."

Bailey's quick anger was only barely suppressed. "But I will be in Sinai then, Mr. President. Or have you decided to go yourself—"

The President cut him off abruptly. "No, I have not. I most particularly want *you* to meet Rostov and sign the treaty renewal. You understand me."

Bailey composed himself with difficulty. What was wanted was the name Bailey on the Cyprus Accord, as insurance of approval of the treaty, and all it implied, by Bailey's supporters. What it implied, of course, was that the military remained a necessity to the nation. The United States, after the bitter experience of Vietnam, was still, with the Pax Americana-Russica, to play policeman to the world. "I understand you perfectly, Mr. President," he said heavily.

The President said, "Talc, I wish we could come to some agreement on this point."

"I don't think that's possible, Mr. President," Bailey answered.

The President's eyes sparked with rekindled anger. "You are such a bloody prig, Talcott. There's a world of moral arrogance in you."

"If you say so, Mr. President. Is that all for tonight?" He started to rise, but the President stopped him with a weary gesture.

"I'm sorry, Talc. I shouldn't have said a thing like that. I'm tired, I guess. My staff tells me I'm getting hard to live with. My wife and the girls are in Palm Springs. I should try to get away for a couple of days and join them. The desert air might improve my disposition. It could use some improvement, I think."

"A few days at the Palm Springs White House sound like a good idea, Mr. President," Bailey said.

The President grinned. It was his most famous expression, boyish and radiating warm charm. "I'll think about it," he said, dismissing the subject. "There's a personal matter I want you to handle for me in the Sinai."

"Of course, Mr. President."

"I mean besides not antagonizing General Tate and his soldier boys," the President said, smiling. "I will have a letter delivered to you that I want you to hand-carry to Judge Seidel. I want to see if we can get him back into the federal judiciary."

Bailey made no immediate comment. Jason Seidel had been a law-school classmate of the President's, had served four terms as a congressman and twelve years as a federal judge before taking the unprecedented step of resigning from the bench to accept a commission in the General Staff Corps and an assignment as young Tate's chief of staff in the United States Sector of the Peacekeeping Area. He belonged, as did the President, to the moderate wing of the party, and he was, Bailey suspected, the President's unofficial representative in the headquarters of the U.S. Component of the Peacekeeping Force. Now there was some talk that Justice Carmody would retire from the Supreme Court—the man was eighty and in poor health—and it was rumored that the President was thinking of appointing Seidel to the high court in Carmody's place. Bailey felt a surge of angry disapproval. To appoint a conservative like Seidel, a man with friendships in the military, in place of a grand old liberal like Carmody was an outrage.

The President said, "You are putting on your puritan face again, Talc. What is it? Seidel?"

"Are you seriously considering him for the Carmody seat?"

"It is a possibility." The President raised a cautioning hand. "Don't condemn what you don't understand, Talc. Seidel's brilliant—decent, too. It was a considerable personal sacrifice for him to go to the Sinai with Bill Tate."

"He's from the Middle West, so it would be a popular

appointment in some sections of the country, I suppose," Bailey said.

"I am aware that he would not be the favorite nominee in Cambridge or New Haven," the President said. "But in some circles that might be considered an advantage."

The Vice President flushed. "Are you going to make your meaning-of-moderation speech now, Mr. President?"

"No, Talc. Not tonight. I'm too tired and you've heard it before. You and I have fundamental differences of opinion on the functions of leadership in a democratic society. You believe the people elect us to do what we know is best for them. I believe they elect us to do, insofar as we can, those things they want done. You are an oligarch, at heart, Talc. I suppose, considering your birth, education, and experience, you've come a long way. But you are not really convinced that even a free people can be trusted to govern themselves."

"That's very interesting, Mr. President."

"Don't be too offended, Talcott. I admire your obvious quality. You are a moral, decent man. It is simply that when push comes to shove, you honestly believe that the people haven't the right to control their own lives. You know better than they how they should live."

"That's a cruel indictment, Mr. President."

"I don't mean it to be, Talc. For a good many years control of the people for their own good has been the essence of political practice in this country," the President said, depressed by the intransigent self-righteousness of the man. He said abruptly, "Well, it's late. Let's wind this up."

The Vice President stood, but paused before withdrawing.

"Was there something else, Talc?"

"What about the press?"

"What about them?"

"Taggart is still in Bethesda." The vice-presidential Press Secretary had entered Bethesda Naval Hospital for a gallstone operation one week earlier. Wags on the White House staff insisted that Taggart had suffered his attack deliberately, after attending a briefing on the climate and terrain of the Sinai Peninsula.

"Take Jape Reisman. He knows the area, and I won't need him—" a slow smile broadened into the presidential grin—"in Palm Springs."

"Very well, Mr. President."

"Good night, Talc. Have a pleasant trip."

"You, too, Mr. President."

As the Vice President let himself out of the Oval Office, the President caught sight of the ever-present warrant officer sitting in the hallway, the case containing the war codes on his lap. He saw the man, or one of his colleagues, nearby many times every day, but the sight rarely failed to move him. A man very like him sat just so in the Kremlin. Like the ghosts at the feast, they never allowed one to forget how tenuous a thing was peace, and how it depended so delicately on the rational behavior of practical men.

For my country's sake, and the world's, the President thought, I hope Talcott Bailey never has to carry such burdens.

3

Across the green-baize-covered table, the Soviet air commander, Colonel Yudenich, made a show of lighting a Turkish cigarette with a silver lighter. Colonel Novotny, the KGB chief, stared blankly out the dusty windows at the compound buildings, while Captain Zakharov, the naval commander, aristocratic and finely profiled, listened with patent disinterest to the interpreter.

This officer, a thick-bodied Ukrainian woman with the green shoulderboards of a KGB captain on her uniform, was reading aloud from the Forward Patrol Complaint Reports, documenting alleged violations of the Demilitarized Zone with tedious repetitions and badly printed photographs. The reports were a ritual for all Command Committee meetings, whether held here, at USSR Component headquarters in El Arish, or at the American headquarters in Es Shu'uts. They were read, denied, and finally sent to the United Nations Observer Team headquarters at Zone Center, to be filed and forgotten somewhere in the warren of new concrete-block buildings that had been erected in a desolate spot on the demarcation line.

The interpreter had been reading for almost an hour, and Major General William Tecumseh Sherman Tate felt himself running out of patience. His gaze wandered around the low-ceilinged narrow interior of the meeting shack. The wall at the far end of the room was dominated by a Russian military map of the Sinai Peninsula, acetate-covered and showing the five sectors into which the Cyprus Accord had partitioned the heart-shaped land mass between Egypt and Israel. The agreement had been the culmination of a frustration rooted in too frequent wars, resolutions passed and ignored, and constant incursion and reprisal. The slow crumbling of the tenuous peace of the seventies had finally forced the superpowers to do what they should have done long ago, Tate thought: interpose themselves directly between the combatants. But this did not automatically bring amity. Of that commodity there was little in this room.

The room was hot and stuffy, with the morning sun slanting through the unshaded windows. The Russians sat in full regalia, wearing blouses and medals. The old General insisted on it. He could be a tyrant, Tate thought. Once, the old man had even suggested to Tate that his officers, too, should approach these weekly meetings with more formality, a suggestion Tate had politely rejected, explaining that citizen soldiers, even professionals, tended to become restive when forced to wear full service dress in ninety-degree heat.

The General had accepted that, saying only that his own officers would continue to appear in dress uniform and medals in all weather, out of respect for the gravity of their responsibility to world peace here in the Sinai. His reproving manner made it clear to Tate that he thought the American attitude *nekulturny*—not cultured.

Lieutenant General Yuri Ulanov had every right to run his command as he pleased. He was, after all, a great soldier. He had been a company commander at Stalingrad when Tate was an army brat playing on the parade ground of the Presidio in San Francisco. If Ulanov chose to make his staff sweat under wool and a chestful of medals, he had the authority.

So the Russians sat and suffered while, outside, the honor guard paced and strutted in a stiff-kneed, arm-swinging show of discipline for a few apathetic Egyptian officers who waited in the blazing sun hoping to be called in by their Soviet allies to testify against the Americans and the Israelis.

Tate, reasonably comfortable in soft-laundered open-necked khaki, had brought no Israeli officers with him. He had long ago concluded that the Israelis and the Egyptians had no function at these meetings, and he refused to subject either Brigadier General Rabin or Captain Zadok to the humiliation the Egyptians were now undergoing by being forced to wait outside in the compound for a call that seldom came.

Tate's group included Captain Adams, his WAC military secretary; Colonel Seidel, his chief of staff—known to the troops as the "Judge"; Captain Beaufort, his pilot; and Sergeant Anspaugh, his crew chief and sometime driver. This morning he had carried the press, as well: Abel Crissman, of Reuters, and Tom Vano, of UPI. The newsmen had gone along to Truth House for cold drinks, a Russian breakfast, and Soviet propaganda handouts. Beaufort had remained with the helicopter at the helipad.

Lieutenant Colonel Dale Trask, the newly assigned commander of the tactical-air group, should have been included in the General's party. But Trask had scheduled himself for a familiarization flight in one of the component's VTOL Shrikes, and, with misgivings, Tate had decided against ordering him to postpone his mission.

Tate was unhappy about the new tac-air commander and intended to see if Seidel could devise some way to have him reassigned. On paper, Trask was a good choice to command the U.S. Component's airmen. His service and war record was outstanding. But as a second lieutenant in Vietnam, the only war he had experienced, he had been shot down and tortured by the Communists, and he made no secret of his hatred for his tormentors. This was understandable, Tate thought, but hardly a recommendation for assignment to a sensitive post eye to eye with Soviet troops. And Tate was further disturbed by the fact that the orders sending Trask to the Sinai came directly from Admiral Stuart Ainsworth, the chairman of the Joint Chiefs, who was, himself, possibly the foremost anti-Communist in the government.

Captain Adams had her recorder running and was taking notes on the tedious Russian complaints. A wisp of pale hair had fallen across her narrow forehead and clung to the damp flesh. Judge Seidel sat puffing his pipe, an expression of amiable boredom on his face.

Tate, surfeited with the interpreter's droning condemnations, said distinctly, "I think we've had enough of this for now."

The moon-faced woman stopped reading. Novotny, whose duty it was to prepare the accusations, frowned at the American officers. General Ulanov said nothing. He sat unblinking, his veiled eyes watering and bloodshot. He was almost seventy years old, and he disliked abrupt decisions.

Tate said, "I suggest we put this routine business aside and discuss planned security for the Vice President and the Deputy Premier now. We have tried to bring this up at the last two meetings, General, and you have put it off. Time is getting short."

"Deputy Premier Rostov is not yet in the Sinai," Ulanov said.

"I am aware of that," Tate answered. "But is it wise to wait until the last moment to co-ordinate our arrangements?"

"We can do nothing until the Comrade Deputy Premier arrives," Ulanov said.

As a student of Russian and Russians for most of his professional life, Tate realized that when this leaden tone was taken it meant that Slavic suspicion had been aroused. Co-operation with the Soviets was forever being made difficult to impossible by these psychological impasses.

He tried again. "Is the Deputy Premier arriving by air? If so, please supply us with a flight plan. We don't want to have an incident."

Vasily Yudenich, the most anti-American of the Soviet staff, said, "The Red Air Force is capable of flying from Moscow to El Arish without advice, General."

Tate suppressed an irritated rejoinder as Ulanov fixed his air commander with a stony stare. Presently the old man said, "Comrade Rostov is arriving in Alexandria late today. From there, tomorrow, he will fly directly to Zone Center by helicopter for the meeting."

Seidel spoke quietly. "To fly a helicopter—even the Deputy Premier's helicopter—into the Demilitarized Zone requires the approval of all the signatory powers as well as the United Nations, General."

"Is there any reason why it should be withheld?" Novotny asked.

"You'll recall," Tate said, "that the U.S. Component offered to fly an injured Swedish observer out of the DMZ last January and both the Soviet Union and the UAR refused to give their consent. The man died, Colonel, in case you have forgotten."

"This is a different situation," Novotny said.

"That may be. But the military forces within this peninsula are bound by their governments to abide by *all* the terms of the Cyprus Accord. The reasoning is sound, even if it inconveniences us. The world, Colonel, has had some reason to suspect the inviolability of demilitarized zones in the past."

"Socialist nations do not violate agreements, General."

"I'm delighted to hear it," Tate said. "And I am certain that Deputy Premier Rostov would not expect the strict rules set down in the accord to be broken simply because he prefers to travel by helicopter. There is no time to try to get the agreement of the occupying powers *and* the United Nations Cyprus Commission to a modification of the neutrality of the DMZ. The Deputy Premier will simply have to travel by surface transport—as the Vice President of the United States has already agreed to do."

He turned with scarcely a pause to Ulanov. "With your

permission, General, we will adjourn this meeting now. Major Paris, my security officer, will meet with the Swedes and his Soviet counterpart at Zone Center tomorrow to co-ordinate details and complete the necessary arrangements. General Eriksson is expecting them at 1100 hours." He turned to Captain Adams and said, "Please call Beaufort at the helipad and have him collect the press people. I want to get back to Es Shu'uts right away."

Elizabeth Adams noted the time on her recorder and stood to leave the shack. The abruptness with which her commander had terminated the meeting and the sullen reaction of some of the Russian officers disturbed her, but at the door General Tate caught her eye and smiled reassuringly. His expression warmed her, and she walked across the compound to the communications center lost in her familiar fantasy.

Captain Adams was in love with her commander. The slightly uneven features of his youthful face, the way his immaculate uniform clung to his strong athlete's body, and, above all, the skill and confidence with which he performed his duties in this most difficult assignment engendered something like worship in the Captain's virginal thirty-year-old heart.

Bill Tate had no inkling, of course, of his military secretary's fantasy, in which he nightly made love to her under the stark, brilliant stars of the desert and ran naked with her through the surf of the lonely beaches of northern Sinai.

Liz Adams was a finely bred, perhaps overbred, East Coast spinster, whose single act of rebellion had been joining the Women's Army Corps after obtaining a master's degree in sociology. She was afraid much of the time, though no one, except, perhaps, the perceptive Colonel Seidel, realized it. She feared the Russians; even the elegant and aristocratic Captain Nikolai Zakharov filled her with dread. Novotny, Yudenich, and old General Ulanov aroused hatred and loathing. To her, they were Asiatic nomads, only accidentally citizens of a twentieth-century nation. Sometimes they, too, invaded her fantasies—as Huns and Mongols hungry to destroy all that they had not the refinement to understand.

Between Liz and these imaginary dangers stood the strong figure of William Tecumseh Sherman Tate, wonderfully and remarkably (for she knew that the Army did not always reward such merit as his) the youngest major general in the armed forces of the United States. She described him in her frequent letters to friends at home as courageous, intelligent, and sorely tried by the political nature of his assignment and the boorishness of his Russian opponents. It was an evaluation of the American commander that, oddly enough, many under his authority would accept.

Bill Tate would have been touched but dismayed to see himself as Captain Adams saw him. He knew himself to be a good soldier, well trained and dedicated. He had fought in Vietnam and discovered that fear could be conquered. In an age when even soldiers tended to be cynical about conventional values, he was totally and unashamedly patriotic. He could be moved by the sweet sad notes of a bugle or the look of the national ensign fluttering against a cornflower-blue sky. But he was also a realist. He knew, for example, that if he had not been the descendant of a line of soldiers stretching back to the Revolutionary War, he might easily have been something other than a military man—a scholar, perhaps. His knowledge of Slavic languages and military history was evidence of an intellectual tradition common to his family. His forebears had fought in all of America's wars; his father had been a chief of staff of the Army. He knew, too, that if the President of the United States had not personally interested himself in William Tecumseh Sherman Tate, some other officer—equally qualified, or better—would presently command the United States Component in Sinai.

Tate also knew himself to be a fallible man, painfully so, in his personal life. He was a failed husband and, though he regretted it bitterly, a failed father. His wife had left him three years earlier. His son was a typically long-haired junior (and a strong partisan of Vice President Talcott Bailey) at Dartmouth. There had been no question of the boy's carrying on the family military tradition. It ends with me, Tate often thought, uncertain whether to be relieved or disappointed.

So Tate's view of himself was very different from Captain Adams's.

And then there was Deborah—Captain Deborah Zadok, of the Israel Defense Forces. This Israeli girl was all wrong for a man in his sensitive post. He was certain that it was now only a matter of time until Donaldson, the CIA station chief, or someone else in his headquarters sent a secret accusation back to the Pentagon saying that the commander was sexually involved with a Jewish woman officer of the Israeli Liaison Group, a woman suspected of being a Mosa'ad agent.

Yudenich recaptured his attention by saying, "Before we adjourn, General Tate, I wish to take special note of Incursion Number 542, the violation of the Demilitarized Zone and the Russian Sector's air space by an American Shrike aircraft overflying the coast between latitude twenty-eight degrees north and the Soviet airstrip at El Tor." The Shrikes, built by the new de Havilland-McDonnell-Douglas consortium, were a source of endless irritation to the Red Air Force people. The aircraft had vertical-takeoff-and-landing capabilities, Mach 3 speed, and carried a terrifying assortment of ordnance and intelligence-gathering devices. The Russians had nothing nearly as good, and their frustration took the form of a constant effort to get the machines banned from the Sinai.

Yudenich glanced at Ulanov. "With respect, Comrade General, I do not think we should put this incursion over to another meeting. The United Nations Observer Team should be notified."

Tate sensed something almost challenging in the airman's attitude toward his commander. When dealing with Soviet officials, one had to be alert constantly to nuances. Was this merely a sign of Yudenich's irritation, or had the fellow picked up some signal from Cairo or the Kremlin that the old General was on his way out? And what would such a change indicate about Soviet policy in the Peacekeeping Area, specifically just now, when the most dovish of American doves was coming to Sinai?

The men of the Politburo had long ago stopped seeking confrontations with American power. But did they see a chance to apply pressure for concessions from Vice President Bailey? Even after a generation of negotiating with Americans, Soviet leaders seemed incapable of understanding that American officials could not act purely on their own. One more quirk in the Byzantine Soviet mind, Tate thought, and a strange one when you considered that no Soviet leader since Nikita Khrushchev *ever* made a decision unsupported by his colleagues.

He glanced at the Judge to see if he had caught the tone of challenge in Yudenich's demand, but Seidel sat silently lipping his pipe stem.

Ulanov heaved himself ponderously to his feet. His face was sweaty damp, and his thick neck rolled over the collar of his blouse. There were dark stains under his arms. "At the next meeting, Yudenich. Not now."

Yudenich seemed unwilling to let the incident be closed, so Tate decided to close it for him. "Today's list of alleged violations by our side is unacceptable until such time as *our* list of Soviet and Egyptian violations is presented and filed," he said. "If there is nothing else of substance, we can consider this meeting closed." He shut his portfolio and stood, followed by Seidel.

There was a scraping of chairs on the other side of the table. Both Yudenich and Novotny were deliberately slow in rising. Ulanov, heat-worn and cross, scowled at his subordinates, annoyed by their lack of military punctilio. Tate suppressed an impulse to smile at the old General, who was, in his way, thanking him for breaking up the meeting.

The Russian interpreter gathered her notes. Tate placed his blue beret on his head and saluted General Ulanov with great formality. The Soviet officers returned the gesture, and the party filed out into the scouring glare of midmorning.

Ulanov touched Tate's arm and drew him aside. Seidel engaged Zakharov in polite conversation while Novotny and Yudenich signaled for the staff cars.

"I apologize for my officers," Ulanov said. "Some are too old to remember their manners. Some are too young to have any." His English was accented, but fluent.

"No offense taken, General," Tate said.

"We sometimes forget that we are not still adversaries."

There were streaks of innocence in the old man, Tate thought, that were almost touching when encountered.

"I have heard," Ulanov said, "that Peking is unhappy that the treaty is to be renewed. Not officially, of course. But Novotny's sources tell him that the militarists in Peking are opposing the official line."

Novotny had, of course, excellent "sources" inside the Communist nations. Tate asked, "Are they likely to interfere?"

Ulanov shook his head. "Not directly. But it is well to remember they still have cat's-paws and puppets." He glanced across the compound at the lumbering figure of the KGB commander. "Have you heard anything from your intelligence people?"

"Nothing. Even the Arab Front has been quiet on our side of the line," Tate said. There had been some reports of activity in Syria and Iraq, and of the disappearance of the Abou Moussa Commando from Lebanon, but he did not think it essential to share this information with the Russian, nor was there any reason to think it significant.

Ulanov lowered his voice. "Unofficially, William, I can inform you that Deputy Premier Rostov is arriving by sea."

"I surmised as much, Yuri Dmitrievich," Tate said, "but thank you for confirming it." He permitted himself a slight smile. "There was no reason at all to make a secret of it, you know."

"It is our way," Ulanov said. "We have grown very suspicious of you since we were allies in the Great Patriotic War."

"An understatement, Yuri Dmitrievich."

"Rostov is traveling aboard a warship. He met yesterday with the Syrians at Latakia."

Tate experienced a flicker of concern. Latakia lay on the Syrian coast north of Tripoli. Between Latakia and Alexandria lay the cruising warships of the United States Sixth Fleet, the submarines and destroyers of the Israeli Navy, and a whole lattice of air patrols. It would have been far wiser of the Russians not to be so secretive. Anatoly Rostov was said to have a volcanic temper and a prickly pride.

"Thank you for telling me," he said.

"Novotny will disapprove, but I thought it best," the Russian said.

Once again Tate felt the familiar exasperation with Russian secretiveness. There was absolutely no reason to conceal Rostov's itinerary. American or Israeli intelligence would disclose the fact that he had met with the Syrians en route to the Sinai—as he had a perfect right to do. It was a case of secrecy for secrecy's sake: always a risky business.

"Be sure you send a Swedish interpreter to Zone Center with your security man, Yuri. You know how confusing it can be to deal with Eriksson."

"I wish the Indians were in charge in the DMZ at this time," Ulanov said gloomily. "At least they patrol instead of sitting in barracks drinking." He paused. "Are you certain that you will not waive the prohibition against aircraft in the demilitarized area? Comrade Rostov dislikes motor travel. It would be an act of—" He made a Slavic wave.

"Kulturny?" Tate asked. "If it were my decision, I'd agree. But it is out of the question; you know that."

The old man made an effort to smile.

"Are you well, Yuri Dmitrievich?"

"Weary," Ulanov said. "Weary of dealing with Cossack hotheads, Libyan fanatics, Egyptian incompetents—and Yankee capitalists. I am old, William."

"Old? Kutusov was your age at Borodino."

"Other times, William. We could not survive a Borodino now."

No sane man could argue against that, Tate thought. There was peace and some *détente* now, but the world was still a nuclear powderkeg, and there were a dozen places on the planet that could supply the spark. Sinai and its demilitarized zone could easily be such a place. From where he stood he could see the Soviet and Egyptian flags moving fitfully in the rising desert wind. Between them stood the staff with the flag of the Peacekeeping Force, bearing the insigne they all, on both sides of thirty-four degrees east, wore on their uniforms: two half-circles, one red, one blue, forming a whole, the circle bisected by opposed arrows and surrounded by the word "peace" in four languages. An oddly hostile symbol, Tate often thought, for a force purporting to guard the peace.

The Egyptian officers who had been waiting hopefully to be called into the meeting now showed their disappointment by an exaggerated display of military courtesy. They stood at attention, buttoned up in their British-style tunics, fly whisks jammed grimly into their armpits. As Tate and Ulanov rejoined their officers at the waiting staff cars, they saluted grandly. Simultaneously, the honor guard of Russian soldiers went through their theatrical evolutions with much arm-swinging and foot-stomping in imitation of the guards at Lenin's tomb. Tate endured the ritual and returned the salute as the officer of the guard snapped his saber down.

Ulanov bade good-by to the Americans and walked wearily to his Zim turbocar. He was followed by Novotny and Yudenich. Zakharov and the woman interpreter rated only a Moskva, Tate noted with some amusement. The Navy was not highly regarded in the Russian Sector.

Sergeant Anspaugh appeared in the dark-green Dodge kept

at El Arish for the General's use. Beside him sat Captain Adams, and between them on the seat rested the black box the eggheads had provided Tate to jam whatever bugging devices the Russians concealed in the Dodge between his visits to El Arish. Tate followed Seidel into the rear while the honor guard and the Egyptians stood woodenly at attention.

"Go, Sergeant," Tate said. To Seidel he said, "Rostov is coming by sea from Latakia. As soon as we are airborne we'd better warn the Navy's bird farms not to play chicken with any Red ships for a day or so."

"Is that what Ulanov was whispering about?" Seidel asked. "He was making Novotny damned uncomfortable."

Tate stretched his long legs as much as he could and looked out the window at the bleak sandy wastes bordering the road to the helipad. "Judge, why in hell do they have to be so secretive? Something like this opens up all sorts of possibilities for trouble. It's so bloody unnecessary."

"You know them better than I do, Bill," Seidel answered.

"Nobody really knows the bastards. They don't know themselves. The old man is a great soldier, but he's not really in command any more. You saw that, didn't you?"

"I had that feeling."

"And Rostov's a Tartar, I hear. He's liable to eat Talcott Bailey alive."

"It's only supposed to be a renewal ceremony, Bill," the older man said. "The Vice President has no authority to make further concessions."

"Captain Adams," Tate said abruptly, "did Beaufort collect Vano and Crissman from Truth House?" He felt uneasy and anxious to get back to his own command. Too many small things seemed to be going vaguely wrong, and his combat instinct was warning him to be ready for some sort of action as yet undefined.

"They should be at the helipad by this time, General," Liz said. She reacted nervously to the General's tone, clenching her fists until the nails grooved her palms.

Tate frowned and said to Seidel, "Has Security or the Agency sniffed any Arab Front activity that's unusual, Judge?"

"Nothing you haven't been told about."

Tate compressed his lips in annoyance. The guerrillas were dangerous because they reacted to pressure like wild men. Major Paris said there were no terrorists left in the Sinai, but how could he be certain? There were thousands of nomads in the peninsula, roaming through and around the military lines in all the sectors. They ignored the Peacekeeping Force and the UN in the same way they had ignored Egyptians, Hyksos, Romans, Ottoman Turks, and the British. You could not detain them or interfere with their migrations. This was, after all, their country. But how many Bedouins were Arab Front guerrillas or sympathizers? They were an Arab people.

Tate regretted having brought the two newsmen with him. Both Vano and Crissman were decent men, but, being journalists, they simply could not be trusted to respect security. This meant that he could send no airborne messages. Which meant, in turn, that he could not even recall Trask from his aerial tour of the American and Israeli sectors without arousing their curiosity and suspicion.

It was barely possible that Vano, being an old hand in the Sinai and aware of some of the military problems Tate faced, might exercise some restraint—though eventually he would write some critical piece on the subject of the military's contempt for the First Amendment and the "chilling effect" of the Army's control of communications in the sector. But Crissman was a product of the London School of Economics and a doctrinaire leftist who would cheerfully refuse to cooperate with the occupying soldiers in any way.

No, he decided, it couldn't be risked. Nor could he use the cross-demarcation-line wire. It was not secure. To warn of Rostov's imminent appearance by sea would compromise General Ulanov to his KGB chief. The alert messages would have to wait until he reached Es Shu'uts—a matter of less than an hour, but even this small delay was troublesome.

"What's bothering you, Bill?" Seidel asked.

"Everything, Judge, a little bit. And no one thing in particular. Things *feel* wrong. I felt this way at Peng Lem, just before my A-camp was overrun by the North Vietnamese. There's too much secrecy and too much lying. Our intelligence is weak, and the Russians aren't helping matters much by acting like Russians." He paused to stare once again at the barren delta of Wadi el Arish. "I wish to God this business at Zone Center were over. And I wish they were sending someone other than the Vice President. He's trouble."

Seidel could not disagree with the General's judgment. He had some time ago written privately to the President along the same lines, questioning the decision to place Bailey, the Dove, and the professional soldiers of the U.S. Component into such an inevitably abrasive juxtaposition. His advice had been overruled for political reasons that he well understood. But he could not suppress the foreboding that for Bill Tate the Vice President would indeed be trouble, and he hoped that Tate would not forget that he was dealing with the man who could, at some time, become the commander in chief of the armed forces of the United States.

They rode in silence the remaining distance to the El Arish helipad.

4

At fifty-two thousand feet above Ras Kheitat, the midmorning sun had the harsh brilliance of polished steel. At the zenith, the sky darkened to a deep, misty blue, and a sliver of new moon could be seen with an etched clarity. Below, the mountains of central Sinai resembled folds in a blanket of mingled red, brown, and yellow. Only here and there, in narrow whitish bands, did wadis vein the barren land.

Directly over the Shrike's sloping nose Dale Trask could see the flat blue line of the Mediterranean Sea, almost two hundred and twenty-five kilometers to the north. Off his right wing tip lay the upper reaches of the Gulf of Aqaba, emerald green near the coasts of Sinai and Arabia, an unbelievably brilliant cobalt blue in the center.

Trask banked the aircraft slightly to the left and looked nearly straight down at the south end of the massive wadi—the multispoked ravine—that seemed to split the rumpled peninsula far below. At the end of that dry wash lay Zone Center, but from nearly ten miles up, the buildings and all works of man were quite invisible.

He could easily pinpoint all of Zone Center with his ground-search radar and image-enhancing cameras, but there was no need and he had no such inclination. He knew that he was on the eastern side of the boundary of the Demilitarized Zone. His inertial-navigation unit was functioning perfectly, and it was his intention now to fly straight north to the sea, examining the terrain of the DMZ and, with his high-angle view, the ground that lay under Russian and Egyptian control.

His speed was subsonic. The Shrike could loiter along at a mere five hundred knots over an extended range of more than three thousand miles, as now, or accelerate up to Mach 3 in seconds. Its hover and vertical-takeoff-and-landing capabilities made it, in Trask's opinion, the finest tac-air weapon the USAF had ever acquired. It would have been a pleasure to have used it in Vietnam, he thought.

He raised the sunshield of his helmet and studied the ground below with narrowed metallic-gray eyes. The misshapen jaw that required a specially fitted oxygen mask had been smashed by a kick from a North Vietnamese soldier, and the burned hands that sometimes ached inside his gloves were the work of North Vietnamese civilians. He flexed them on the flying controls as he remembered.

The hands had been first. Stunned and slightly wounded by splinters from an exploding SAM, he had landed in a village near Haiphong. The enraged peasants had rushed him into a recently bombed building and thrust his hands into the fire before he was even aware of what was happening to him. The shattered jaw and broken teeth had been received after he spit at a visiting American activist, who had stood by his bed talking treason while the dinks took pictures. He had been strapped to the bed to prevent damage to his hands, and when the activist and the photographers had gone, their propaganda spoiled, his North Vietnamese guard had punished him with a boot to the face.

Trask dreamed of it still. The pain, yes, but mostly the frustrated hatred and desire for revenge. He had been repatriated at the war's unsatisfactory end, leaving the bill unpaid.

He snapped the sunshade down once more and looked northeast. He could see Eilat, lying just beyond the armistice line that here formed the eastern boundary of the formal State of Israel Sector. On the outskirts of Eilat could be discerned, even from this great height, the runway patterns of an air base. The Israelis had concentrated their transport and bomber force there, a move necessitated by the terms of the Cyprus Accord. Neither Israeli nor Egyptian military aircraft were permitted within the Sinai Peninsula. The smaller pair of the four signatory powers had done their best to eliminate any disadvantage by moving their air units as near to the sector boundaries as possible. The Israelis at Eilat, Nitsana, and Gaza; the Egyptians at a cluster of Russian-built airstrips between Suez and Ismailiya. But if a clash ever came, Trask thought, it would be fought first by USAF Shrikes and Red Air Force MiG VTOL's. The idea of such a battle filled him with longing.

He nosed the Shrike slightly downward to pick up speed and watched the Machmeter climb swiftly through the speed of sound. At fifty thousand feet exactly he leveled the wings, checked to be certain that the ordnance pods were still safetied and capped, and then went into a series of level rolls, letting the brown earth and the blue-dark sky spin around and over him. His movements were precise, skilled. Pilot and aircraft were functioning in perfect unison, forming a kind of cybernetic organism meant for war.

He snapped out, his sharply raked wings level with the distant horizon, and let the speed build to Mach 1.5. Behind him lay a long, twisted contrail of ice crystals, white against the southern horizon.

"Spearchucker, this is Echo Sierra Control." The voice of the intercept officer on duty in the War Room at Es Shu'uts was tinged with a Texas drawl. He sounded bored.

Trask spoke into his voice-actuated microphone. "Echo Sierra, this is Spearchucker. Go."

"Radar has a water bogie inside the limits. Do you want to investigate or should I scramble a helo?"

Trask felt a flush of anger at the indolent tone and the lax procedure. He said, "This is Colonel Trask, Echo Sierra. Do not transmit again until you scramble. This is a direct order." He savagely punched the day's code key into his onboard computer. What sort of easygoing outfit was William Tecumseh Goddam Tate running in the sector? An unknown had violated the territorial waters of the U.S. Sector and the intercept officer offered the job of investigating as though it were an optional amusement.

When Echo Sierra Control called again, the Texas voice was chastened. "Sorry, Colonel Trask. We don't usually scramble routine intercept messages."

"You do from now on, Echo Sierra," Trask said grimly. "Now give me a vector."

"Spearchucker from Echo Sierra Control. Vector is zero five degrees. Bogie is possibly a nuke SS or a Guevara-class missile destroyer. They have just crossed the twelve-mile limit. Shall I back you with a helo?"

"Negative, Echo Sierra," Trask said. Backing a Shrike with a helicopter was a little like protecting a tank with a bicycle. He shoved the throttles all the way forward and lighted the afterburners. He nosed over into a long dive toward the coast, and the Machmeter swept past 2 and edged up on three times the speed of sound. At this rate he would cover the distance to the Mediterranean in less than four minutes, arriving there at zero altitude behind a massive shock wave. Whoever was aboard the bogie, he thought with cold satisfaction, would be treated to the grandfather of all sonic booms. "Echo Sierra Control, I want four Shrikes with full ordnance on the line and ready to scramble from Al Qusaymah on my command."

The intercept officer seemed to be having difficulty grasping the idea that a new regime was beginning for component tacair, Trask thought irritably, for the drawling voice said uncertainly: "Ah—Spearchucker—we—uh—we usually only keep two Shrikes on—uh—alert status. But I'll see what we can do—"

"You get your ass in the saddle, Echo Sierra, or you aren't

going to have enough to sit on for a week. You get those airplanes on the line right *now*."

There was the momentary soft hiss of an open carrier wave and then someone unknown, speaking in the background and against the muted sounds of the War Room, said: "Jesus—what's going on here?"

Trask said into the radio: "If I hear one more departure from procedure on the air, I'm going to put the entire intercept crew under arrest. Do you read me, Echo Sierra?"

The intercept officer's voice sounded awed. "Yes, sir, Spearchucker. Those Shrikes are coming on the line now, Spearchucker, sir." There was a momentary murmur of discussion before another voice came on the radio. "This is the senior intercept officer talking, sir. Four on the floor now at Al Qusaymah. Yes, sir. Your corrected vector is now zero four niner. The bogie is identified as a Guevara-class destroyer. They are inside fifteen kilometers."

Trask smiled grimly. All the bastards needed was a small rocket to shape them up. He noted with harsh satisfaction that the new intercept man was even using the proper metric terminology now, instead of the more familiar and traditional—but inaccurate—references to a "twelve-mile limit."

"All right, Echo Sierra," Trask said. "Now you people stay the hell on your toes down there, hear me? Keep the vectors coming. I want this kite aimed right down that Red bastard's throat when I make contact. Is his radar searching?"

"Navigational sweeps only, Spearchucker," the intercept officer said nervously.

Trask's deformed mouth twisted into an angry smile under the oxygen mask. The Commie crew of that Guevara was in for a shock. In a few seconds now the Shrike was going to hit them like its namesake—a tiny, cruel bird of prey. He angled more steeply, increasing his speed to almost Mach 3. He let himself imagine what it would be like to open the pods and arm the missiles and then press the button to grease the sons of bitches before they could even begin to back away from their snoop. His fingers ached for the feel of the triggers, and his heart pounded.

The Soviet missile destroyer *Allende,* having reached (according to the calculations of her navigation officer) a point exactly fifteen kilometers from the Sinai coast opposite Khan Yunis, now swung its blunt bow to a gyro heading of two hundred and twenty-five degrees true, to parallel the distant beach.

The *Allende* was the third of a new class of missile ships in the Soviet Navy. Nuclear-powered, with a low, clean profile, she hugged the water to make radar detection difficult. Most of her missile launchers and electronic gear were carried belowdecks for protection from weather and to improve her airflow at speed. In action, the launchers and missiles were raised to deck level forward of the high, narrow bridge. At a glance she could be mistaken for a large example of the older classes of Soviet nuclear submarines, but a closer inspection would disclose her unique virtues and differences. She had the characteristic flared bow of Soviet-designed warships, a raked fantail, and the lines of a racing yacht. To reduce weight, she carried no guns other than a pair of quad-forties on the bridge; her air defense relied on surface-to-air missiles. She was intended to trail American aircraft carriers and destroy them before they could launch nuclear air strikes. She was fast, beautiful, and altogether deadly. But she was vulnerable to air attack from within the minimum range of her SAM's.

The Guevara-class ships, all named for Latin-American revolutionaries, were a source of anger and envy for Admiral Ainsworth: envy because they were examples of a new and highly successful Soviet naval technology, and anger because the Senate, still heavily weighted with antimilitary sentiment, steadfastly refused to vote the funds needed to supply the United States Navy with anything nearly as good.

The low profile of the *Allende* made her difficult to locate and capable of great speed; but it also made living aboard her a cramped and confining business. Having in the ship the Deputy Premier of the Soviet Union and his staff increased the crowding and made Captain Sergei Bogdanov less than pleased that his ship had been given the dubious honor of carrying the Comrade Deputy Premier to Alexandria.

In the compartment that would have been called the wardroom on a capitalist ship, Deputy Premier Anatoly Borisovich Rostov and his two secretaries had been working through the morning on lists of the military supplies the Egyptians had requested from the USSR. The lists were long, expensive, and unrealistic. For the past few years the Egyptians had again been asking for increasingly more sophisticated weapons, machines that they were, in Rostov's opinion, completely unqualified to operate. Moreover, the last military mission sent by the UAR to Moscow had renewed Egyptian demands for purely offensive weapons—the latest-model MiG and Ilyushin medium-range bombers, intermediate-range ballistic missiles, and the latest versions of surface-to-air missiles. These demands arose on an almost yearly basis and were as often rejected. Rostov remembered when the Egyptians had expelled their Russian advisers in a fit of pique triggered by a refusal to supply long-range offensive weapons. The expulsion had been temporary, as almost every Egyptian policy seemed to be, but it had been an embarrassment to the Soviet government, and Rostov wanted no repetition. The Cyprus Accord made such a thing unlikely, of course, but Arabs were unpredictable, and they had never lost their desire for weapons that were too dangerous to be entrusted to them and too complex for them to maintain.

In Rostov's view it was wasteful to the point of lunacy to give the armed forces of an Arab nation anything but old and primitive machines. They had a long history of defeats at the hands of the Jews—and their record was unlikely to improve. Therefore, they must be prevented from fighting. The accord accomplished this. Arabs would have to engage both Soviet and American troops before they could reach their traditional enemy, and this made any further engorgement of their military quite useless. As long as the accord held, the Politburo could appease the Arab nationalists with old military garbage and not throw good rubles after bad. In spite of Zionist ambition and Arab bombast, Rostov thought, it was no longer these antagonists who would decide the future in the eastern Mediterranean. All that was now a function of Soviet and U.S. power. That was as it should be. The strong would decide. The United Nations, with its clutter of Graustarkian states, had been given the role it merited in the Sinai. It could play at policeman and observer, but without power or real consequence. Rostov was reminded of Stalin's scornful retort when asked if the Pope in Rome should not be consulted about some decision made by the allied powers during the Great Patriotic War: "How many divisions does *he* have?" Despite the old dictator's mistakes, which Rostov freely admitted were many, it was difficult for an ambitious man not to be a Stalinist at heart. The Americans, after all, understood only power.

The intercom on the wardroom table pinged, and one of the secretaries opened the circuit. Captain Bogdanov's voice said, "Comrade Deputy Premier, we are on the territorial boundary of the United States Sector. You expressed a desire to see and listen to them."

"I'll come," Rostov said.

He left the compartment and made his way through the ship toward the bridge deck. When he reached the bridge, he was pleased that the armored scuttles had been dogged open and a warm salty breeze was blowing through the crowded control spaces.

Captain Bogdanov, a tall, gray man whose angular thinness contrasted with the Deputy Premier's blocky, somewhat obese build, saluted and said, "We are fifteen kilometers from their coast, Comrade Deputy Premier. You can see the shore just there."

Rostov looked and was disappointed. He did not know exactly what he had expected to see along this American-occupied coast—radar towers and missile emplacements, he supposed. But there was nothing to be seen but a line of white sand, hazy with distance over the placid sea. Beyond, divided oddly by the mirage, lay the suggestion of faraway hills rising to a desert plateau.

Bogdanov sensed his vague disappointment and explained. "There is very little at Khan Yunis, sir. Nothing that can be seen from this far at sea. And at Es Shu'uts all the military installations are built inland—though we may see the United States Component building if the visibility remains good." He essayed a half-smile, knowing Rostov's contempt for the insubstantiality of American architecture. "They call it the 'Glasshouse.' "

"Do they patrol these waters, Comrade Captain?"

"Only irregularly by sea, in Hovercraft. There are air patrols inland, of course. But this area is the responsibility of their Sixth Fleet, and that unit has grown much smaller since the accord was signed, as you know."

Rostov leaned against the armored railing of the splinter shield. He had hoped, when it was decided that he should make this trip by sea, that he would enjoy the freshness of open decks and the sparkling autumn weather of the Mediterranean. But the *Allende* had no open decks, at least not for landlubber passengers. The areas forward and aft of the superstructure were cluttered with hatches and the tampons of the missile storages. There was a small flying bridge on the level above the control spaces, where he, Bogdanov, the helmsman, and the radar-navigation crew now stood, but it was no promenade deck. The ship offered only military advantages and was a poor transport. But it was one of the most powerful warships afloat and, as such, an object to be displayed before the envious Americans, Israelis, and Egyptians.

"We are taping the American radio transmissions, Comrade Deputy Premier, if you would care to listen."

Rostov nodded abstractedly, his mind far off now, considering the coming encounter with the American Vice President, whom he had never met. Bogdanov gave a quiet order to the combat-intelligence center deep inside the ship, and a stream of gibberish came from the overhead speakers, startling Rostov out of his reverie.

"What on earth is that?"

The Captain said, "The Americans are scrambling their transmissions. I don't know why."

"Is that customary?"

"They seldom bother, Comrade Deputy Premier, but they are doing it this morning. Possibly they are conducting some sort of exercise."

Rostov's small, sharp eyes studied the banked radar repeaters built into the scuttle in front of the helmsman. Only one was operating, and at a low level, outlining the featureless, almost straight line of the beach on their beam.

"Is there something wrong with your machines, Comrade Captain?" he asked. Rostov was, at heart, a landsman. It was from the MVD that he had come into the Politburo. The ships and men of the Navy remained something of a mystery to him, things and beings not completely to be trusted.

"We are operating only our lowest-power navigational radar, Comrade Deputy Premier. I have no wish to attract the attention of the American or Israeli naval units in this area." This last was said with some overtones of reproach, for Captain Bogdanov had been in favor of steaming directly from Latakia to Alexandria—avoiding this close approach to the American-held coastline. Rostov, his curiosity aroused, had overruled him.

"We are in international waters, surely, Comrade Captain?" Rostov asked.

"We are on the edge of the United States Sector, as you ordered, Comrade Deputy Premier," Bogdanov replied.

Rostov stared at the alien coast. How far one came, and to what strange places, in the search for—what? Power? Was it as simple as that, after all? He, Anatoly Borisovich Rostov, had been born fifty years ago on a collective farm more than a thousand kilometers from this place, in a time of near famine and at the beginning of the Stalinist terror. But he had always known that his horizon was not to be limited by the grainfields of southern Russia. The Komsomol, the party, the MVD—he had used them all, giving good service in return, and now he stood near the top of the gray hierarchy that ruled one-fifth of the world's surface and dominated the politics of two-fifths of the earth's people. Overweening pride was a prime sin in the Communist litany, but he could not find it within his heart to be modest about his achievements.

A thing appeared in the brassy sky: a tiny point of darkness. At first he took it to be a sea bird, indistinct against the high sun. Then with shocking suddenness the point sprouted thin wings, became cruciform, and grew larger and more menacing with its soundless approach.

A cry of alarm came through the intercom speakers from the combat-intelligence center, but before the sound could be translated into words and meaning, the dark cross became an aircraft, its underbelly pregnant with threatening ordnance. It was preceded by a thunderous, booming shock wave that was still pressuring the ears of the *Allende*'s personnel as it passed overhead, at near-zero altitude and with blinding speed. The ship had been taken by surprise. The bridge complement rushed across the deck to watch the plane vanish seaward, like an iris closing to a point of darkness. Secondary compression waves boomed across the *Allende*'s superstructure and through the bridge, fluttering charts and causing loose objects to chatter.

Rostov, startled, looked at Bogdanov for an explanation. The naval officer's face was flushed with embarrassed anger. The navigators jabbered in stunned surprise.

"Was that an American aircraft, Comrade Captain?" Rostov demanded.

"It was, Comrade Deputy Premier," the Captain said.

One of the younger officers of the navigation crew was foolish enough to say in an awed voice, "If that had been an attack in earnest, we would all be dead now."

Bogdanov spoke sharply, demanding silence on the bridge. The radar displays had come to life in a flurry of greenish light, and the voice of the combat-intelligence officer came from the speaker: "He's turning, Comrade Captain. He's coming back."

Trask's first pass over the Soviet ship had carried him far out to sea. Now he let his speed drop and banked in a wide turn to pin the intruder between the Shrike and the territorial limits of American-controlled waters. As he turned, he spoke into the radio. "Echo Sierra Control, this is Spearchucker. Message Accord Commissioners Cyprus as follows: Russian missile ship, Guevara class, discovered within United States Sector at—" he glanced at the chronograph on the instrument panel—"1147 hours local time. Copy that to Observer Team at Zone Center. Notify Sixth Fleet. Spearchucker is investigating."

The controller at Es Shu'uts responded uncertainly. "Spearchucker, Echo Sierra radar shows the bogie's track on the limit line. Shall we alert Kingpin?"

Kingpin was the radio code name for General Tate's helicopter, which might or might not be airborne at El Arish now. Trask frowned against the pressure of his oxygen mask. Ainsworth had warned him that Tate had a tendency to handle everything himself, not delegating to his subordinates. But this was a clear case of violation of U.S. Sector waters. The Soviet ship might be on the limit line now, but Trask was certain it had been closer inshore moments ago, and he intended to see that the snooping bastards didn't get away with it this time, as they did too often.

"Negative on Kingpin, Echo Sierra," he said. "I'll handle this."

"Spearchucker, do you require help from the alert flight?"

Trask smiled. They'd got those four Shrikes on the line on the double. All it took was a little jacking up. But he decided to let the pilots sit in their cockpits on the ground for the time being. At close range a Shrike was a match for any Guevara-class ship.

"Echo Sierra Control, this is Spearchucker. Negative the alert flight. Have radar record the tracks. I'm going in now."

He extended his speed-brakes, feeling the aircraft slough off excess speed. He could see the Guevara again now, its silhouette black against the dark blue of the sea. The water was arcing from her bow as she increased speed, heading away from the land. Not this time, you don't, you Red bastard, he thought. You don't snoop and run today.

He let the Shrike's air speed continue to drop. At two hundred knots he opened the hover-jets in the fuselage and let the airplane settle to an altitude of fifty feet above the calm water.

He closed the Russian warship and flew slowly alongside. On the bridge wing sailors were standing by the visual-signal equipment. Trask cut across the warship's bow, indicating clearly that he wished the vessel to return to her original course.

The officer of the watch was using binoculars, and there was a technician beside him operating a camera. Get a good look, Ivan, Trask said to himself.

He flew down the ship's port side, very close, and across the boiling wake. The Russian ensign snapped like a splash of blood on the jack staff. The colors were brilliant in the sunlight, the sea deep blue, shading to green toward the shore. Trask could see the glitter of gold braid on the uniforms of the officers rushing to the flying bridge. A signalman raised a lamp and began to flash code at the Shrike as it flew close alongside once again.

Trask read the message and smiled. They were sending "Keep clear" in International Code. He switched radio channels to the common frequency used by both Russian and U.S. Component units. "Aboard the unidentified vessel, hear this," he said deliberately. "You have violated waters controlled by the United States Component of the Peacekeeping Force. Reduce speed and identify yourself at once."

The Aldis lamp flashed again. The Russians continued to send "Keep clear."

Trask opened the fuselage gates to expose the television cameras and began recording the ship. If they had the proper detection gear aboard, they would know that their image was being transmitted back to Es Shu'uts control and to units of the Sixth Fleet via satellite. Trask suspected they wouldn't like it. The Russians most definitely did not want their new ships video-taped while under way at speed. The eggheads could learn a good deal from such pictures of ship, wake, and bow wave.

They had worked up almost to full speed, Trask estimated. It was time to put a stop to that. He banked across the warship's track again, and flew down the port side and across the boiling water behind the fantail.

"Vessel in view," he said into the microphone, "you have been observed violating United States Sector waters. This is a final warning. Identify yourself." His heart was beating heavily, with growing hope and excitement. Was it possible they would actually refuse to do as ordered? He flew parallel to the ship's track for a thousand yards, then turned and began to hover. He could see spray flying from the blast of the Shrike's hover-jets.

The ship came on. Sea water rose in a strangely transparent double arch at the stem, glistening diamond-bright in the sunlight. The flying bridge on top of the black superstructure was growing crowded with officers and sailors. Trask noted a civilian among the uniformed men on the bridge. Gunners began uncovering a pair of forty-millimeter antiaircraft guns —the only short-range weapons in sight. A signalman was still flashing angry messages.

The Shrike hovered on a column of jet exhaust, cupping the water below it. The warship came on, a giant steel orca moving at fifty knots.

Trask felt a delicious thrill as he lifted the red metal tabs on the panel beside him to arm the Shrike's ordnance. Small pyro-bolts blew away the fiberglass cones covering the warheads of the nested rockets under the wing. The plane carried thirty armor-piercing missiles that could turn the warship's upper works into a tangle of ripped and twisted metal.

The Russian ship reacted to the gesture like a galloping horse cruelly curbed. It heeled and turned sharply toward the shore. Water spewed and churned in great white explosions of spray at the stern as the screws were fully reversed. The fantail plunged more deeply into the sea, and the bull nose broached, rising like the head of a frightened whale.

Trask felt as though he could shout aloud for the pure joy of seeing this display of wild consternation. He had played a game of nerves with the unknown Soviet captain, and he had beaten him.

An angry accented voice shouted in Trask's headset: "This is a Soviet naval vessel in international waters! You are committing a breach of international law by this piratical interference with the freedom of the seas!"

As Trask maneuvered the jet to keep the ordnance pointed at the bridge, the ship turned in a half-circle, losing way. Communications gear was sprouting on her decks from hydraulically operated wells.

Trask felt the waves of adrenaline shock receding. There was a delightful weakness in his knees and shoulders. His mouth felt dry and his skin tight over tensed muscles.

"Soviet vessel from American aircraft," he said in a strained but steady voice. "You were detected in waters subject to United States Component control without permission. I am within my rights to detain you until you are identified. Respond at once. I wish the name of your commander, the name of your vessel, and the nature of your mission."

There was a long silence, and then a strangled, furious reply: "I am Captain Sergei Bogdanov of the Soviet Fleet, and I protest—"

"Name your vessel and mission, Captain," Trask said sharply.

The Russian's anger and humiliation made his voice hoarse. "This is the Soviet naval vessel *Allende*. My mission is routine patrol from Latakia to Alexandria. I warn you that I shall protest this banditry in international waters—"

"Your protest is noted, Captain," Trask said, more easily as the thrill of confrontation diminished. "You may now proceed. You are advised not to violate the waters of the United States Sector again. It could have serious consequences."

"With whom am I speaking?" the Russian demanded.

"With Lieutenant Colonel Trask of the United States Air Force and the United States Component in Sinai."

"You will hear more of this, Colonel Trask."

Trask indulged himself in a short, silent laugh. He felt spent, rubbery in the muscles of his back and thighs. No woman could have given him the satiated pleasure he was experiencing.

He wondered what he would have done if the Russian had refused his order to stop. Would he have attacked? He rather thought he would have: no authority was credible without the backing of a will to enforce it. In his mind he saw the rockets streaming from the pods, the white-hot flashes tearing at the black vessel, the bits of metal, flesh, and bloody bone flying, spinning, pocking the surface of the placid sea—

He shoved the throttles forward and banked the Shrike away from the wallowing ship. He circled once, then ignited the afterburners and headed back toward the low-lying land, the angry radio cries of the Russians sounding like music in his ears.

5

At seven minutes after noon, Nicosia time, in the old barracks of the Knights of St. John that now served as headquarters for the United Nations Commission for the Implementation of the Cyprus Accord, Public Information Officer Ravi Singh began to distribute mimeographed copies of Bulletin Number 12/137 to the assembled representatives of the press.

Bulletin Number 12/137 was a news release, and contained, in addition to a fact sheet on the Sinai Peninsula, the political and geographical cartography of the Peacekeeping sectors, and a short, emasculated historical summary of United Nations participation in the affairs of the Middle Eastern combatants, the following declaration:

"The long-awaited meeting between Vice President Talcott Quincy Bailey of the United States and Deputy Premier Anatoly Borisovich Rostov of the Soviet Union at Zone Center, Sinai, will take place at 1800 hours tomorrow as planned. There will be a short ceremony conducted by members of the United Nations Commission for the Implementation of the Cyprus Accord, after which the signing of the renewed Cyprus Accord will take place. Representatives of the United Arab Republic and the State of Israel will also sign the document, renewing the *status quo ante* in the Sinai Peninsula for a further period of three years."

Public Information Officer Ravi Singh then took pains to

explain yet again to the newsmen that the terms of the original accord made it difficult (if not impossible) to accommodate a full representation for the press at the Zone Center meeting, but that pool coverage, supported by an enlarged technical staff, would assure that the historic event would be fully reported. This did not please or satisfy the Western press, but there was little they could do but grumble.

At seven minutes after noon, local time, Father Anastasius, of the community of monks at the Monastery of St. Katherine, broke his fast with a sip of water. He rose from the rocky cave in which he had spent the night and morning and surveyed the glittering, russet panorama of the southern Sinai massif. His head ached and his seventy-year-old eyes watered from the sunlight, which struck him like a hammer blow. Slowly, with great effort, he began to pick his way down the rubbled path toward the Oasis of Feiran.

At seven minutes after five in the morning, Washington time, the President of the United States lay awake in his bed thinking about Talcott Quincy Bailey. His were the night thoughts that attack the unquiet mind in the bleak hours of the morning. He was reviewing the Vice President's political ambitions and attitudes and wondering if it was not, after all, a mistake to have given him the largely ritual task of signing the renewal of the Cyprus Accord.

The agreement to establish the Peacekeeping Force in Sinai had been a larger breakthrough in Soviet-American relations than the Nixon initiatives and the SALT treaties—larger even than the negotiations that followed the Yom Kippur War. All of those had prepared the ground for the Cyprus Accord, but the sense of the Nicosia conference had marked a turning point in history: when the governments of the superpowers decided to admit that despite differences of political systems they had more in common with each other than with their client states.

Talcott Bailey considered this cynical and possibly dangerous, for it committed the United States to maintain a military force in direct, isolated, close juxtaposition to a similar Russian force.

It was true, the President admitted, that the situation had within it the seeds of possible confrontation. But he and his predecessor, who had signed the original accord, were pragmatists. So were the Russians, he believed. The experience of Korea and Vietnam had shown all too clearly that client states can embroil great powers in their wars—wars unwinnable, except by unacceptable means.

The only alternative was clearly to place the directly controllable conventional forces of one's country in the position of absolute intervention, hence of highest risk. If the risk was recognized, the chances for a breach of the peace became minimal.

The President did not know what the eventual solution to the Sinai problem, and others like it, would be. It was quite conceivable that Russian and American, or Russian and Chinese, or American and Chinese forces would continue to face one another across arbitrary demarcation lines for decades to come. It was not the best or the cheapest solution to the world's distressing tendency to erupt into war, but it was the soundest, most *pragmatic* solution to the dangers inherent in the quarrels of small and angry nations.

In an age of nuclear arms and a hopelessly fragmented United Nations, it was the only option.

Bailey, however, belonged to that class of theorists who saw any reliance on military power as a threat to peace and to individual liberty. Because armies relied on discipline and nondemocratic forms and methods, the Vice President regarded them with deep suspicion.

The President recalled his conversation of the previous evening with Bailey. He had been rough on the man, he thought. Bailey, whose wealth was inherited and substantially protected by the astuteness of his New England forebears, believed that the expenditure of large amounts of public money could solve any social problem, but only if the nation's priorities were reordered. Foremost on the list of these priorities to be displaced was defense. To Bailey, money spent on weapons and soldiers was criminally wasted. Those within the administration who disagreed with him, the secretaries of Defense and State, for example, he scorned as old-fashioned "Cold Warriors."

The President lay wearily awake and considered the sort of world in which a nation governed by the theories of Talcott Bailey could survive as a great power. Such a world bore no resemblance to reality in the second half of the twentieth century.

Momentarily the President considered the possibility of canceling Bailey's trip to the Sinai and sending Ramsey Green, the Secretary of State, instead. He was tempted, but presently discarded the idea. The Russians might be offended, and Bailey certainly would be. Moreover, it was vital that the Israelis and the Arabs be impressed with the almost-top-level importance attached to the renewal of the accord by the U.S. government.

So Bailey it would have to be. But the President found that he did not envy young Bill Tate and his troops. They were undoubtedly in for a bad time at the hands of the Dove, who, the President was persuaded, would pass no opportunity to let them know exactly what he thought of them.

At seven minutes after 1800 hours, local time, the Soviet tracking station at Utata, on the Mongolian border, was receiving telemetry from Cosmos 623.

Five hundred and eighty kilometers above the Sayan Mountains on the USSR's southern border, the spy satellite hummed and chittered in the airless sunlight. It had made its last pass directly over the Red Sea, the Sinai Peninsula, and the eastern Mediterranean. Now it was disgorging the intelligence it had stored on its memory disks in a burst of high-speed, ultra-high-frequency transmissions. This intelligence consisted of infrared-sensing data, intercepted radio transmissions, and computer-coded high-resolution photography. This last was of excellent quality, for the area searched by Cosmos 623's cameras was almost totally free of cloud cover or atmospheric turbulence.

Utata's reception was good; the low-emission signals were recorded without distortion and fed routinely into the station's computers for preliminary decoding. The newly recorded tapes were then hand-carried to the land-line transmitter to be sent on to Baikonur for examination by space-intelligence evaluators. Due notice was taken of a transmission from an American Samos satellite whose orbit crossed that of Cosmos 623, of the position of the current Soviet-American Apollo-Soyuz III orbiting at eight hundred kilometers, and of the Mediterranean Telstar in synchronous orbit and relaying American civilian telephony and radio and television programs.

At Baikonur the bits of information relating to military intelligence were culled and sent, again over secure land lines, to GRU (Army Intelligence) headquarters on Arbat Square in Moscow, arriving only twenty-six minutes after transmission from Cosmos 623.

Normally, the high-resolution photography from the Cosmos satellites was processed in a routine manner by middle-rank officers of the Red Army's Intelligence Directorate of the General Staff. But on this day the technicians who translated the taped pattern of computer dots into photographs were surrounded by field-grade officers of both the GRU and the KGB. Shortly before, radio transmission from the missile destroyer *Allende* had been received at the Ministry of Marine and at GRU and KGB headquarters. A special meeting of the steering committee of the Politburo was being called, and the Premier himself had been alerted and was returning to Moscow from his *dacha* at Puskino.

As the photographs emerged from the printer, the technicians were shouldered aside and an angry, confirming babble of voices filled the heavily guarded room. The photography was excellent. From five hundred and eighty kilometers Cosmos 623's cameras were capable of resolving objects no more than two feet in diameter, and the pictures of the waters off Sinai showed with great clarity the deltoid shape of a Shrike jet hovering directly on the track of the *Allende*. One of the series had caught the plane's ordnance covers falling into the sea and the exposed warheads of the rockets protruding beyond the leading edge of the aircraft's wings.

There were mixed emotions around the photo table. Some of the officers (those who operated at the lower levels of intelligence gathering) were simply angry that a vessel of the Soviet Fleet carrying the second-ranking politician of the USSR had been arrogantly halted on the high seas. Others were less angry and more pleased that Soviet technology had produced irrefutable proof of an American misjudgment. And still others, among them Lieutenant Colonel Mikhail Sergeyevich Gukovsky, of the GRU, were engaged, less obviously, in planning.

Gukovsky was an officer of the Red Army's liaison with Department D of the Committee for State Security, the KGB. Department D was more familiarly known as "Dezinform," a shortened version of the Russian word for "disinformation service." The purpose of this department was twofold. In Cold War days it produced and disseminated false and misleading information intended to discredit the *glavni vrag*—the "main enemy"—in other words, the United States. With the coming of *détente,* however, Department D's primary function was to supply the United States with such carefully screened information as the KGB and the GRU might wish the United States to possess—without actually "sharing" intelligence with what was still, after all, the *glavni vrag*.

This objective was achieved by the relatively simple method of leaking intelligence into conduits certain to carry the desired material to the intended recipients. In the case of regular Cosmos material—which the GRU desired American intelligence to have in order to convince Washington of the efficiency of Russian technological surveillance—photographs were regularly supplied to a photo-intelligence clerk named Kamenev, who, with the approval of his superiors, sold them to agents of Mosa'ad, Israeli intelligence. Kamenev, a sergeant second class in the Red Army, was under the impression that his customers were Czechs.

Each third run of Cosmos satellite photographs of Sinai was delivered to Kamenev, who then turned them over to his "Czech" contact, who in turn put them in the pipeline that led, with commendable swiftness, across southwestern Russia, to Iran, and thence to Jerusalem. Dezinform was assured that the information was then promptly delivered into the hands of the CIA, and was also reasonably certain that the CIA was aware that the information was "tame" and *intended* to reach them, just as similar information was fed into conduits running in the opposite direction. But in this way it was possible to keep the *glavni vrag* aware of the extent of Soviet surveillance and technical capability.

The photographs from Cosmos 623 now being studied were not third series and would not ordinarily have been fed into Kamenev's pipeline. But the fact that the sequence showing the north coast of Sinai had caught the United States Component Shrike in a compromising position was reason enough to cause them to be rushed into the conduit.

In his haste, Gukovsky did not carefully examine *all* the photographs—most particularly those showing the southern part of the Sinai Peninsula. For a number of days the Cosmos cameras had been recording the seemingly aimless movements of a Bedouin band from the Aqaba shore south around the massif, then northwest toward the beaches of the Gulf of Suez. Since there were thousands of these nomads in the Sinai, and since their movements were almost always picked up by the supersensitive cameras of both Soviet and American satellites, there was nothing to make this particular band of any interest to the GRU. However, if Gukovsky had taken the trouble to plot this band's movements, he would have observed that they were now moving directly north*east* from the coast. He might even have noted that their number—which for many Cosmos passes had been stable at fourteen—had increased by one. And, finally, a microscopic examination of the almost miraculously fine-grained photographs would have disclosed the fact that the camel rider in the van—who had all-unknowingly raised his head to the sky as Cosmos 623 passed unseen overhead—was not an Arab at all, but a pale man with a heavy mustache whose photograph could easily have been retrieved by computers from the GRU and KGB files.

But the excitement caused by the American airman being caught so flagrantly on film in his act of banditry against the *Allende* possibly made Gukovsky a bit less careful and methodical than he would normally have been. He had come into possession of a piece of intelligence he did not know he had. Further, he allowed this bit to be included in the material handed over to Kamenev with instructions to "sell" it to his "Czech."

The Sergeant had never understood why his superiors wanted him to deliver secret materials to the Czechs. At first he had flatly refused to become involved in the operation; he had promptly reported it to his political supervisor—as a good Soviet citizen should do. The KGB officer investigated and assured him that he was not involved in any act of disloyalty to the state, but, rather, in a confidential *apparat* of Department D. To assure Kamenev's wholehearted co-operation, he was permitted to keep the relatively small sums the "Czechs" paid for the satellite material. Prices being what they were in Moscow, and a sergeant's pay being what *it* was, Kamenev decided to co-operate.

Now he left the building on Arbat Square and met his Czech friend on the Jauza Embankment. One hundred and fifty rubles and a packet changed hands, and the photographs taken by Cosmos 623 were on their way to Jerusalem. Lieutenant Colonel Gukovsky had committed the major blunder of his life.

6

General Tate learned of Trask's encounter with the Russian ship as his helicopter approached the pad at the airstrip west of Es Shu'uts. The message was delivered over a scrambled channel by a badly shaken senior intercept officer at Echo Sierra Control, where the radios were crackling with intercepted Russian messages between the *Allende* and Alexandria, and between Alexandria, El Arish, and Moscow. The effect of Colonel Trask's "investigation" of the Soviet missile ship had been very like that of a stick thrust into a wasps' nest.

Only Tate and Beaufort, who was flying the helicopter, were on the radio link. Anspaugh was riding in his accustomed crew chief's crouch between the pilots' chairs; Liz Adams and the Judge were engrossed in the minutes of the meeting with the Russians, and the newsmen, Crissman and Vano, were at the windows trying to look south into the restricted areas inland, where a forest of radio masts and radar dishes dotted the desert plateau.

As the full import of the message became clear, Tate felt the short hairs rise on the back of his neck, and a ball of hot anger began to form in the pit of his stomach. According to the radar plots reported by the intercept officer, the Russian ship had crossed the fifteen-kilometer limit once and possibly twice, though the depth of the incursion was far from clear.

The Russian was filling the radio spectrum with furious protests that could well be justified. So far, apparently, no mention had been made of the fact that Anatoly Rostov was aboard the missile ship. But it was dazzlingly clear that an Incident had taken place.

Beaufort looked across at Tate anxiously. Tate just perceptively shook his head and said, "Let's go down." He removed his helmet and ran a hand through his damp cropped hair. The fault was his own, he thought bitterly. He should never have allowed Trask to fly before giving him a thorough briefing on the delicately poised situation in the Sinai. Only a short time earlier, he had been considering how best to return Trask to Admiral Ainsworth with a minimum of military discourtesy. Now the problem was of a different magnitude. The least that could be expected from Ulanov and his people was a demand that Trask be instantly relieved and reprimanded—and this was a concession no commander facing Russians could afford to make. Long experience had taught Bill Tate that such an action would be taken as a sign of weakness and would provoke a series of probes and provocations.

He turned to the newsmen and said, "There's been some malfunction in the civilian satellite link, gentlemen. You'll have to file your stories on the committee meeting over the military net. The Security duty officer will give you clearance." It was a delaying tactic, and as soon as the newsmen reached the Glasshouse and learned of the incident offshore they would realize it. Their confidence in the credibility of the military in the sector would be compromised, but some time would have been bought. Time to do exactly what, Tate wondered. Trask, for reasons that Tate suspected were purely personal and subjective, had committed a military blunder. No, that wasn't right—Trask's blunder was political. His action, whatever his personal reasons, had been militarily correct and justifiable. But there was going to be hell to pay, nevertheless. If the Russians chose to do so, they could escalate the inevitable furor into an excuse for canceling the meeting at Zone Center. The U-2 incident and the humiliation of the canceled Paris summit meeting during the Eisenhower administration still haunted the White House.

Tate saw that the Judge was alerted to something out of the ordinary. Thank God for his quick mind, Tate thought. I'm going to need all his lawyer's artfulness before this flap is over.

The helicopter touched the pad, and two staff cars rolled up to meet it. Crissman and Vano were grumbling about the communications "problems" as they climbed into the first car. When they had gone, and only military personnel were present, Tate said to Liz Adams, "I want you to call the Communications Section immediately and tell them to break the civilian satellite link until further notice. Next, I want you to notify Major Paris that he's to clear all civilian traffic over the military net with me personally. And last, I want you to find Colonel Trask and bring him to my office *on the double.* Take Sergeant Robinson with you and tell Trask privately that he is to make no statement of any kind to any person whatsoever. That's a direct order from me. Give Robinson my personal instructions that he is to prevent Trask from speaking to anyone. He is authorized to place Trask under close arrest if necessary."

Liz nodded, wide-eyed. Tate turned to Seidel. "We have a full-blown bloody incident on our hands. Trask stopped Rostov's ship on the fifteen-kilometer limit. Their damned secrecy and Ainsworth's boy have put us in hot water up to our tails." He managed a thin smile at his secretary and said, "Go, Liz. Take the car."

He leaned back into the helicopter, where Anspaugh and Beaufort were filling out the flight forms and trying to hear what was being said on the ramp. "I don't think we'll be flying any more today," he said. "But stand by just in case."

Beaufort asked, "Should I call for another car, General?"

"Negative. I'll steal the Operations officer's jeep. Let's go, Judge. We have work to do."

In the Operations office the duty officer saluted and handed Tate a Telex message that read: VP AND PARTY DEPARTING WASHINGTON AIR FORCE TWO 1200 HOURS GMT ETA ECHO SIERRA 2030 GMT. FOR AINSWORTH JCS.

Tate handed the message to Seidel without comment.

"The Dove is going to want Trask's head, Bill," Seidel said.

"There's nothing I'd enjoy giving him more," Tate answered. "But I can't do that, Judge. Not now."

Loyalty, Seidel thought wryly. No military could function without it, of course. But sometimes one could wish soldiers were better politicians. Trask's rash behavior could well be the lever that would open the trap door beneath Bill Tate, and, by extension, the whole American commitment in the Sinai. He suppressed an urge to sigh heavily. It was going to be a long and difficult day.

Captain Deborah Zadok straightened her desk in the Israeli Liaison Group office and prepared to leave the building for the midday meal in the officers' mess. A few moments earlier she had seen General Tate and Colonel Seidel returning from the airstrip in the Operations jeep. It had struck her as only mildly unusual to see Tate traveling in such haste and with so little ceremony. Of all the American officers, it was the young commander who was most often discovered in improbable places, arriving unannounced and often unescorted at the outposts or in the bivouacs of the units training and maneuvering in the field. In this respect he behaved more like an Israeli general than an American one, and it pleased her. He was young to hold so high a rank among the Americans, and he was as strong and active as any of his infantrymen—as she had good reason to know.

She had hoped that he might stop at the Liaison Group office when he returned from El Arish, but she had not expected it. There was no reason for him to do so except to see her, and he was in no position to indulge in romantic gestures. Perhaps tonight, he had said. But even that wasn't certain. It depended on whether the American Vice President's party arrived today or tomorrow.

Something was going on in the American compound. There was an extremely heavy load on the communications net—the radio in the Liaison Group's monitoring office had not been silent for the last hour. A high percentage of the messages had been scrambled or coded, often both. The traffic was heaviest between the control center known as Echo Sierra and units of the Sixth Fleet, with a number of messages going to the formations stationed along the Demilitarized Zone. It seemed unlikely that all this could be connected with the Vice President's arrival. Rabin had briefed the Israeli staff extensively. As much as possible in a military area, the armies were to maintain a "low profile" during the Bailey visit. There were no plans for the Vice President to tour the Israeli Sector or to inspect the Americans along the DMZ. He would arrive, meet with General Tate and his staff people, then be taken by road to Zone Center tomorrow. There he would join with Deputy Premier Rostov and the United Nations observers, sign the renewal of the Cyprus Accord, and return to Es Shu'uts. After the completion of his task in Sinai, he would fly to Jerusalem for a purely ceremonial visit with the Premier of the State of Israel. There had been some ill feeling toward the Americans because the Jerusalem visit had been scheduled for *after* the meeting with Rostov. But the Americans (and, presumably, the Russians) were making it clear that the enforcement of the Cyprus Accord was, and would remain, a big-power matter. Rostov, Rabin had explained, was not visiting Cairo before going to Zone Center.

What the Americans and the Soviets were doing, Deborah realized, was attempting to simplify their relationship to each other and to their client states. The American-Israeli alliance was reasonably amicable and straightforward, as it had been since 1948. But Russian-Egyptian relations were complex, fragmented—primarily, Deborah thought, by the inconsistencies of the Arab character. The Egyptians on at least two occasions had come near to dissolving their partnership with the Russians. In 1972 they had temporarily expelled the Russian military and made overtures to Libya. There had even been some preliminary moves toward forming a federated state with their oil-rich western neighbor. But this, like the original United Arab Republic in Nasser's time, had come to nothing. Now the Russians were back and gave every indication of remaining indefinitely. The accord and their mandated mission in Sinai gave their presence in the Middle East a legitimacy they had no intention of surrendering.

Deborah opened a wall panel to expose a washstand, mirror, and air dryer. The building had been erected by an Israeli firm to American specifications, and the place was filled with gadgets: air conditioners and moisturizers, intercoms, washrooms, television circuits, polarized windows, and adjustable lighting. The Wilderness, she thought, is being Americanized. It will never be the same.

From her window she could see the new construction that had, since the Americans came, transformed Es Shu'uts from a sleepy Arab village—a place pocked and damaged by the 1956 and 1967 wars and damaged again by Egyptian raids in the Yom Kippur War of the early seventies—into a Yankee resort town. The tourists would not arrive until that distant day when the military situation changed, but the physical changes needed to accommodate them were already in place or under construction. To the west, on the seaward side of the coast road stood the Glasshouse, the steel-and-plastic slab of the United States Component building, ten stories high and glittering in the bright Sinai sunlight. To the southeast lay the headquarters compound, a complex of low concrete-block military buildings surrounded by green lawns and flower-bordered pathways. The American flag and the Circle and Arrows flag of the Peacekeeping Force waved gently in the hot wind rising from the mountains to the south. The Americans had installed a desalinization plant on the beach between Es Shu'uts and Khan Yunis, and they produced so much fresh water there that they could share it with the Israelis in Gaza, pipe it south to Nitsana, and still have enough left over to raise grass and flowers in their military compound. Across from the compound stood the Hotel Falasha, a winged stone-and-glass box facing the sea. It was owned by an Israeli-American consortium and at present housed all the American civilians who worked in and around Es Shu'uts.

When at last the tourists came, it would be expanded. The old town would be cleaned up and made into an attraction. The original Arab population had already been relocated. It was apparent that the Israelis had no intention of ever returning this part of Sinai to the UAR. What the Americans intended was something else again. Their substantial investment in the place seemed to indicate that they did not foresee a return of the eastern Sinai to Egyptian rule—but you could never be certain about the Americans. They were unpredictable. Vice President Bailey's views appeared to favor an eventual re-establishment of Egyptian sovereignty in the entire Sinai. He had said publicly on a number of occasions that the partition was a purely temporary military expediency. Needless to say, this was not a position that filled Jerusalem with joy.

Deborah dampened a comb and ran it through her thick black hair. The face in the mirror was, in her opinion, no more than pleasant. Certainly it was not beautiful. Her best feature was her eyes, almond-shaped and deep blue. Circassian eyes, Bill Tate called them, and perhaps he was right. There could be Circassians in the complex Zadok ancestry. The flat, high cheekbones looked slightly Slavic and gave a broadness to her face that accentuated the slightly prognathous mouth. It was a mildly distressing thing for a woman in her thirties to look so like a sulky child, Deborah thought, pulling at the comb.

The body, she thought candidly, was not bad. Not an American body, by any means. She hadn't the height of the American girls who lounged so like healthy animals around the Falasha swimming pool. Her breasts were good, her belly flat, her hips rounded but not too broad. She was a sabra. She had the strength and natural sexuality of her people, and she knew that it was this that had drawn the General to her.

She stood now, a secret smile on her face, thinking of Major General William Tecumseh Sherman Tate. What an odd, Yankee name he had. She thought of his lean face and his eyes, sometimes as blue as her own, sometimes the cold gray-blue of a winter sea. In his way he was an aristocrat, and for a long while this had seemed strange to her, because, never having visited the United States, she had not realized there could be such a thing as military aristocrats in that unruly country. She wondered, too, about his wife and tried to understand how she could become disenchanted with Bill and leave him, not wanting to share that portion of his life available to a woman. She must have been like the girls at the Falasha, those liberated but vulnerable women who took life's comforts as their due, but who would be helpless in a desert outpost with a Uzi machine pistol in their hands and a band of rape-hungry guerrillas just outside the wire. The differences between sabra and American girls were so great that sometimes she despaired of ever understanding any of them. Yet the General had come to her, to Deborah Zadok, rather than to one of the others—and he could have had his pick; there wasn't a doubt of that. She heard them talk about him.

The smile changed to one of thoughtful self-deprecation. No beauty, then. Could this fair Gentile from overseas be happy with this Jew? He could, and was—a happiness of a sort—provided only that she gave herself with desert-bred abandon, on a lonely beach or in the cool air-conditioned darkness of his quarters, wherever he chose to find the time and the privacy they needed. She thought of his rock-hard body, burned and scarred by the terrible inadvertences of his warrior's trade. The thoughts came quickly and with great clarity, and she remembered lying nude on a groundsheet, slick with sweat drying in the wind of the khamsin, and Bill using her, exploring her, making her moan with pleasure.

Perhaps it was not love, but what did it matter? It rocked the mind and turned the will to water. Did Mosa'ad take all that into consideration, she wondered. But what could the grim men in Jerusalem know about love or lust?

She shivered as the picturephone sounded. Closing the panel, she lifted the receiver. Dov Rabin's round, bearded face appeared on the tiny screen.

"Have you eaten yet, Deborah? I invite you to lunch at the Falasha."

All picturephone conversations in the United States Sector were taped for review by CIA Station Chief Sam Donaldson or his people. So this was not simply an invitation to share a meal, Deborah knew.

"In ten minutes."

"I will meet you in the bar."

"Yes. *Shalom,* Brigadier."

She left the building and walked through the harsh sun of early afternoon to the Falasha. Rabin was waiting, dressed as always in open-necked uniform shirt and rumpled trousers. The meal was quickly eaten, with only a minimum of conversation. Deborah noted that the dining room was remarkably empty of American officers; only the civilians seemed to have congregated as they customarily did. As she and Rabin left the hotel they exchanged casual greetings with Abel Crissman and Thomas Vano, the inseparable newsmen. These two had gone to El Arish with General Tate, she knew, but they seemed unaware of the rising tension among the military people. One piece of information, idly mentioned, Deborah found interesting. A malfunction had developed in the regular satellite circuits, and the routine press reports of the El Arish meeting had had to be sent over the military communication net. Considering the amount of coded traffic the net was carrying today, it seemed odd that the news people would be encouraged to use the military communications services.

Deborah and Rabin walked from the hotel grounds down to the beach. There were a few idlers there, those who had little work to do and who preferred the salt sea to the Falasha's filtered fresh-water pool. When they had left these behind, Rabin said, "I have received word that the Abou Moussa Commando might have crossed into Sinai from south Jordan."

The terrorists had lost much of their former popularity among Arabs, who, weary of the intermittent blood-letting, were turning away from their old heroes.

Ironically, the guerrillas, with their refusal to accept less than Israeli annihilation, had been instrumental in bringing the superpowers to the Sinai. Deborah knew a great deal about guerrillas and the Abou Moussa. Commanded by the legendary Leila Jamil, it was the best disciplined—and nearly the last—force remaining to the fanatics of the Arab Front.

"How fresh is your information?" she asked.

Rabin shrugged and pulled at his beard in a characteristic gesture of annoyance. "The information comes from an informer in Jordanian Aqaba, and you know how those people operate. There is no telling how long ago he saw the Abou Moussa—or, for that matter, if he saw them at all."

"I saw an intelligence précis that claimed they were without weapons."

"One of our patrols located their armory and destroyed it two months ago," Rabin said. "The Jordanians looked the other way. But they won't be weaponless for very long. There is no way to prevent some matériel reaching them as long as this half-peace continues."

Deborah looked steadily at Rabin. "Should I tell General Tate?"

Rabin essayed a thin smile. "And have him ask how you know?"

"Dov, he knows what I am."

"Have you told him?"

"Of course not."

"Then he cannot be certain."

"He isn't a stupid man."

"I'm aware of that. I am also aware that American interests

do not always coincide with ours. Therefore, I must remind you of who and what you are, Captain."

"That isn't necessary," Deborah said unhappily.

"I know," Rabin said. "We all do things we would prefer not to do. It is for the country—not for ourselves." He paused thoughtfully. "There is a conspiracy of silence here about you and the General. It is because almost everyone here is loyal to him. But the newsmen will—one day, perhaps soon, when they have nothing else to write about—begin to write about you and General Tate. You must be ready for that, and so must he. Of course we will deny that you have any intelligence function in the Liaison Group. But it won't be believed, and we will have to send you away. You understand this, do you?"

"Yes," Deborah said.

"You say he knows about you. Does *he* understand this?"

"When it happens," Deborah said bleakly, "it will not matter, because it will be the end of him—of his career as a soldier."

"I am sorry, Deborah."

"Probably you are."

"But we must use you as long as we can. There is no choice."

Deborah did not reply. She looked out at the empty sea, at the blue line of the horizon, and wished that she and Bill Tate could be somewhere beyond that distant, pure line of sea and sky—alone and free of all that divided them.

"There is some trouble," Rabin said.

She looked at him with alarm.

He shook his head. "Nothing to do with the General—at least not right away. That fire-eater Trask attacked, or stopped —something of that sort—a Russian ship this morning. I understand he threatened to fire on it because it was inside the fifteen-kilometer limit. Or he claimed it was. That point isn't certain. The trouble is that Rostov was on the ship, and now the Russians are making a tremendous uproar about the matter."

"That explains the 'technical trouble' with the civilian communications."

"The Americans are buying a little time and probably hoping the Russians will quiet down. Which they apparently have no intention of doing. There was even a suggestion this noon in Jerusalem that they might cancel the accord ceremony. I doubt they will go that far, but they have too good an opportunity to embarrass Tate and the Americans now to let the matter drop. They know perfectly well how unfriendly Vice President Bailey is toward the Peacekeeping Force idea. It gives them a lever to use in widening the American breach about the accord."

"The Americans would never withdraw from Sinai without our agreement," Deborah said.

"Wouldn't they? Not too long ago they withdrew 'with honor' in Vietnam." His eyes hardened. "I'm sorry, Deborah, but I must remind you that one should go carefully in the matter of trusting the Americans too far."

Deborah returned to the Liaison Group office with a sense of foreboding. The Telex copy informing her of the Vice President's estimated time of arrival in Es Shu'uts did not improve her mood. Until Talcott Bailey's party returned from Zone Center and departed for Jerusalem, it was unlikely there would be any private meeting between her and Bill Tate.

7

Throughout the afternoon the Abou Moussa Commando had made steady progress toward the mountains. Now, as the sun began its long fall into the western desert, the terrain over which they were traveling began to change from rock-strewn plain to a pattern of folds and hills and dry wadis. The camels, smelling water on the dry wind, raised their heads as they ambled, occasionally making snorting, grunting noises. Lesh had been riding in silence, deep in brooding thought. He was aware of Leila Jamil beside him and the men of the commando strung out behind in their ragged column of pairs.

"Beyond the next two ridges, Silent One," Jamil said. "Feiran."

Lesh nodded. He had been silent because he had been forming an opinion and a conclusion. The men of the commando were probably good enough fighters, but they lacked discipline. Their childlike behavior over the weapons had shown that, together with the unruly way they spoke to their commander. They badly needed a testing, and Lesh had been pondering the possibilities. Perhaps when they reached Feiran he would have to provoke some minor crisis to establish in their unschooled minds the need for absolute obedience—to himself, rather than to Leila Jamil, who obviously saw nothing wrong with their haphazard ways.

But at Feiran there would be more of them—twenty, Jamil

had said. Twenty—for whom no animals had been provided. Lesh was accustomed to these unforeseen difficulties. Every operation seemed to have its quota of them. The discipline problem he could handle, but the lack of transport was more serious. He was not sure of the exact time of the American Vice President's arrival at Zone Center. In order to ensure that the Abou Moussa Commando would be in position to intercept him, it would be necessary to cover about eighty kilometers in the next twenty-four hours. It would be necessary, as well, to find a suitable place to set the ambush—a place west of the boundary between the U.S. Sector and the DMZ, where only the Swedish soldiers of the UN Component had right of access. Alternatively, the attack could be made at Zone Center proper. But there, the Swedes might feel impelled to fight.

Lesh considered the possibilities dispassionately. If it became an operational necessity to fight the Swedes under General Eriksson, he would do it. He was willing to sacrifice up to one-third of the Abou Moussa to neutralize the Swedes, but it could get sticky if the Americans escorted their Vice President in force. It would be far better to bypass Zone Center and set his ambush somewhere along the Zone Center–El Thamad road. The UN Swedes, only a token in number and equipped lightly with side arms, would be most unlikely to join a fire fight near the line of the U.S. Sector, or even to patrol there on the day of ceremony. And the terms of the accord specifically enjoined the occupying powers from entering the Demilitarized Zone with aircraft—though it was to be expected that the Americans and possibly the Israelis, too, would violate the neutrality of the DMZ once the Abou Moussa struck.

There was also the possibility that the Russians might arrive early and cause a serious problem, but he considered this unlikely. It was the Russian way to arrive on time, or possibly late, to keep the Americans waiting. In any case, he doubted that they could affect the outcome of the first surprise attack. Talcott Bailey would be dead and the whole structure of agreements between the Soviets and the Americans would be badly shaken, if not destroyed. To accomplish this, Lesh was willing to sacrifice his entire force, and himself, if need be.

But there remained the difficulty of twenty men without camels and eighty kilometers to be covered in twenty-four hours.

"What troubles you, Lesh?"

The woman was perceptive, Lesh thought. Even on such short acquaintance she knew that his silence was due to something more than the undulating monotony of the camel's gait. But then, she would have to be perceptive, even intuitive, to have led a commando of Arab males for these eight years.

"Logistics," he said.

"There is a problem?"

He removed his headcloth and rubbed at the back of his neck. The slanting sun's touch was like fire, and the wind felt as though it had originated in some distant furnace. "Those twenty men you say you have at Feiran. Without camels."

"They can march."

He shook his head. "No time. They can't walk eighty kilometers in twenty-four hours."

"You know when the American will come?"

"Very nearly. The meeting is at 1800 hours tomorrow."

Jamil rode in silence for a time, listening to the voices of her men. Presently she shrugged and said, "We will find more animals."

Lesh felt a stirring of irritation. How like an Arab that was, simply to shrug and say: "Allah will provide."

He shifted in his saddle and peered off into the eastern mountains. They lay in rising scarps of bare rock, sheer cliffs, and rubbled, reddish talus. One saddle-backed peak rose above the others to a height of over twenty-six hundred meters.

"Gebel Katherina," Jamil said. "The holy mountain."

Lesh, who was as much at home with the writings of Felix Faber of Ulm as with those of Mikhail Bakunin, was aware that once these wastes had been heavily traveled by Christian pilgrims come to receive holiness from the bones of St. Katherine, beheaded after torture by the Emperor Maxentius, and transported miraculously to this highest peak in the Sinai.

He said ironically, "Perhaps we can move your twenty men the same way St. Katherine moved her bones."

"That is not as impossible as you think," Jamil answered.

"Miracles seldom happen around Marxists," Lesh said.

"The Monastery of St. Katherine is at the foot of the mountain just beyond, you know. Gebel Musa, or Mount Sinai."

"So?"

"The monks still feed the Bedouins."

"How does that help us?"

"The Bedouins herd goats for the monks. They do this on camelback. The herds are very large and they graze the western slopes of the range near Feiran, where there is water."

Lesh showed his long teeth in a smile. "I underestimated you, Jamil."

"At this season of the year there are always herds belonging to the monastery near Feiran. At night the camels are tethered in the oasis while the shepherds watch on foot."

"Twenty camels?"

"More."

"The Bedouins are Christians?"

"The tribes who range near the monastery are the descendants of converts who deserted Islam long ago."

"That would ease your conscience if it became necessary to kill some of them, I do not doubt."

Jamil's eyes were impenetrable above the tail of the kaffiyeh she had wrapped across her face to shield her from the desert wind. "Homeless men have no conscience, Lesh. But yes, it would be better if those whom we must kill are not of our faith."

Lesh replaced his own headcloth and continued to smile. Good. There would be no scruples, no squeamishness. Guerrilla leaders could not afford such luxuries. And in fairness to the Abou Moussa he had to admit that they were the pick—the survivors—of a dozen groups who had committed cold-blooded murder time and again, in such unlikely places as Munich, Khartoum, Paris, and New York, in the name of their cause.

He glanced at his wristwatch. It was nearing three in the afternoon. By this time the American would be somewhere in the air, hurrying to keep his fateful meeting—his legendary Appointment in Samarra. Perhaps, after all, there was something to the Arab notion of kismet. The idea that all was preordained was not strange to his Marxist mind. The Will of Allah or the imperatives of history—what did it matter? Every man had his rendezvous with death and spent his lifetime hurrying to keep it.

In the lounge cabin of Air Force Two, a heated argument was abating. The discussion had been between Secret Service Agent John Emerson and Colonel Benjamin Crowell, the Vice President's military aide, on one side, and the Vice President himself on the other. Given the relative ranks of the antagonists, there could be little doubt of the outcome.

Talcott Bailey had been saying, emphatically and with New England precision, that he had no intention of violating his own beliefs by arriving at the UN post at Zone Center with a large military escort. "This is a peace mission," he said, fixing the Secret Service man and his military aide with a cold and determined look. "I shall not compromise myself before Anatoly Rostov and the Russians by appearing with a battalion of Tate's warriors at my back." As he spoke, his long granite-hewn face took on an expression of such moral superiority and condescension that Crowell strained to contain his exasperated concern.

The Colonel was a black with twenty years of military service and he had the soldier's view of the need for sufficiency. Service in Korea and Vietnam had convinced him that it was rash to deal with Communists, under any circumstances, without ample power available. He had, however, expected his chief's decision. One did not serve Talcott Bailey long before discovering that his widely heralded dislike for all things military was genuine. Nevertheless, it struck Crowell as near lunacy for a high official of the United States government to travel through the Sinai without an adequate escort, and he had said so forcibly.

Crowell also knew that the Vice President's decision would be questioned by General Tate. This could easily precipitate a conflict between the soldiers and the politicians that the soldiers would, of course, lose. Tate had the authority to command in the U.S. Sector, but whether or not he could command the Vice President of the United States was a question Crowell preferred would remain untested.

He stared helplessly at Emerson, who looked sad. The agent's face was etched with lines set there by his responsibilities in an age of maniacal violence. As recently as a year ago, there had been a series of attacks on public figures in Paris, London, and New York in the name of the Irish Republican Army, the Iranian Student Front, the Japanese Rengo Sekigun, and the antiaccord Palestinians.

Knowing his man, Emerson spoke with care. "I know this is a peace mission, sir. The last thing either Ben or I want to do is compromise that spirit. But—" He rubbed a knuckle against a large nose and groped for the proper phrases. "But we are already understrength." He managed a thin grimace that was intended to remove the onus of criticism from his words. "You always travel light in the security department, sir. And I doubt the Russians, of all people, could regard the addition of a few soldiers to your escort as an indication of distrust. I beg you to reconsider, sir."

"John," Bailey said impatiently, "I appreciate your concern. But we are not planning a motorcade through crowded cities and dark alleys. This is the Sinai Peninsula. There are only some poor desert Bedouins living in the area."

"That's exactly my point, sir," Crowell said. "These are

desert people. We don't know them. We can't say what they are capable of—"

"I'm surprised at you, Benjamin. Are you suggesting there is something inherently different from us in these simple people whose land we have occupied?"

Crowell chewed his lip to hold back the retort that rose in him. Bailey could be infuriating when he moralized; it did not lessen the irritation factor that the man was completely sincere.

The Vice President said to Emerson, "I have confidence in you, John. And I want as little military around me as possible. So plan your dispositions accordingly." It was a command, and Emerson recognized it as such. He stood up and excused himself. "If you say so, sir." As he left the lounge to join his three fellow agents in the forward cabin, he shrugged imperceptibly at Crowell.

John Peters Reisman, the President's press secretary, on loan to Bailey, had deliberately stayed clear of the discussion of security measures. His private instructions from the President had been explicit. He was to do nothing that could antagonize Talcott Bailey or any of his people. He felt he could not interfere in this, to him, minor matter. So he sat, bulky and rumpled, a florid man running to fat as his forties progressed, listening to Colonel Crowell's failing arguments.

Bailey sat erect in his chair, giving every polite indication that he was still listening to his military aide. But Crowell and Reisman, as well as the Vice President's appointments secretary, Paul Bronstein, across the aisle, knew that any retreat from Bailey's stated position was extremely unlikely.

Bronstein, a youthful, black-bearded man from New York, stared out at the cobalt-colored water far below. Inwardly he agreed completely with everything that Ben Crowell had said: that it was risky, imprudent, and possibly even dangerous to travel in the Sinai without a large escort, and that the Russians would not find such behavior comprehensible in terms of good will, but would think it a subtle form of weakness and appeasement. He wondered why in hell they had to honor the terms of the goddam accord anyway, and travel by road instead of flying to Zone Center, the sensible, quickest, and safest way of arriving at the meeting site. Surely an exception to the prohibition of aircraft in the DMZ could be made for the Vice President of the United States.

But Bronstein had not the slightest intention of involving himself in any difference of opinion between the Boss and the bloody military. If Ben didn't drop it, he was going to get his black ass burned.

Crowell's presence tended to make Bronstein uneasy. He was too unlike the blacks with whom Bronstein was familiar. The New Yorker's rise to a position on the Vice President's staff had wound through certain of the accepted liberal establishments: the ghetto organizations, the affirmative-action university groups, the civil-rights movement, the antimilitary coalitions. Had Crowell been able to affect hip talk, even appreciate some revolutionary rhetoric, Bronstein would have felt at home with him. Instead, the Vice President's military aide insisted on being soldier first and black second. Bronstein found this disturbing.

"Sir," Crowell said in his flat Midwestern voice, "at least think it over after we get to Es Shu'uts. Let me talk to the intelligence people and find out what activity there has been in the field."

"The National Security Council is agreed that guerrilla activity is at a standstill in the United States Sector, Benjamin. That's quite good enough for me," the Vice President said.

Further discussion was prevented by the appearance of the air force master sergeant in charge of the airborne Telex. He delivered a message form to Bailey. "Personal for the Vice President from the White House, sir."

The men in the lounge watched Bailey read the President's message. As he did so, his face hardened with anger.

Presently he looked up and handed the form to Crowell, who read it and passed it on to Reisman.

Bailey said, "Well, this is your answer, Benjamin. We can scarcely put on a provocative show of force now."

Bronstein said, "Can I see that, Jape?"

Reisman looked at the Vice President, who said irritably, "Yes, yes, let Paul see it."

Bronstein took the form with a resentful look at Reisman, who ignored it and said easily, "The timing is unfortunate, sir, but it needn't become a matter for great concern."

Bailey said angrily, "One of Tate's war hawks stops the Deputy Premier's ship on the high seas and you think that's nothing, Jape?"

"I didn't say it was nothing," Reisman said in a mild voice. "I simply say that it needn't get out of hand."

"I wish I had your sanguine outlook," Bailey said. "The fool threatened to fire on Rostov, if you can imagine anything so stupid. I think there is a chance now that the Soviets may simply cancel the meeting."

Bronstein, reading the message anxiously, found himself hoping that the Russians would do exactly that.

"I don't excuse it, sir," Crowell said, "but apparently the Shrike pilot stopped the ship inside the fifteen-kilometer limit. It was there illegally, according to the terms of the accord."

"What possible difference does that make?" Bailey demanded impatiently. "The President says there will be a formal protest. The Soviets have a right to be furious."

"I don't get the impression the Old Man is too upset," Reisman said.

"No, that's easy for him." Bailey then flushed at the implied disloyalty in his own words.

"He says he will be in Palm Springs and temporarily unavailable when the protest comes," Bronstein, still looking at the Telex, said.

"He picks rare moments to improve his golf game," Reisman said, smiling. "That's the Old Man for you. He always handles Russian protests with a touch of benign neglect. He says it gives them time to cool down."

"I don't think that is funny, Jape," the Vice President said severely.

"I didn't mean it to be, sir. He is relying on you to explain to Rostov that no offense was intended."

"After one of his pet soldiers has embarrassed Rostov and the Soviet flag?" Bailey asked.

Reisman shrugged. "As I say, sir. It's a pity it had to happen just now, but I can't believe it will come to anything."

"What makes the President so certain I shall even see Rostov? Remember the U-2 incident and the Eisenhower summit?"

"The Russians will fuss some," Crowell said, "but there is no real chance they'll delay the renewal of the accord, sir. Their position in the southern Mediterranean depends on it."

"I agree," Reisman said, fumbling for a rumpled cigarette package in his rumpled coat. "The President knows they won't cancel the meeting. That's why that bit about Palm Springs. He'll take himself out of the way for a day or two and let them think things over. After all, this"—he tapped the message—"only happened a short time ago. The Russians are probably still conferring, trying to see how much they can make out of it. Remember—*we* can threaten to cancel as easily as they. Their ship was inside U.S. Sector waters, which is specifically prohibited in the accord, and—"

"So *we* say," Bronstein interrupted.

Crowell looked at him. "I don't think I appreciate your suggestion that the American command lies, Bronstein."

"It has been known to happen, Ben," Bronstein said. "Now and again."

Bailey interceded in the new quarrel, but could not fail to leave one small barb in his aide's flesh. "Regrettably, Benjamin, he has you there. But regardless of whether or not Tate's pilot can claim justification, the fact remains that he displayed shockingly poor judgment."

"Probably some kid lieutenant ready to save the Free World," Reisman offered.

"Nevertheless, it is inexcusable." The Vice President turned to the Sergeant, who was still standing by. "Has there been anything about this on the news?"

"Not a thing, sir. We did have a SigCom on some temporary malfunction in the Mediterranean Telstar. Maybe that's the reason for the silence."

"Thank you, Sergeant," Bailey said. "Acknowledge the Telex. There is no reply at the moment." When the airman had returned to the flight deck, the Vice President said to Reisman, "Do you believe that about the Telstar?"

Reisman said evenly, "Of course not. Tate's buying a little time, that's all. But he can't sit on the story for more than a couple of hours. There will be a leak at Es Shu'uts, or in Jerusalem, or the Egyptians or Russians will release the story."

Bronstein looked significantly at Crowell. "Another example of how the military doesn't lie, Colonel?"

Crowell remained silent, his rugged face set and angry.

"Benjamin, I'm sorry," the Vice President said. "You might have convinced me about the military escort to Zone Center, though it would have been against my principles and inclinations. But now, with this *incident* on our hands—" He shook his head positively. "I shall have to do everything I can to convince the Soviets of our good intentions and of our *trust*. There will be the barest minimum of military in the Zone Center party. You, of course, and I suppose I shall have to include someone from General Tate's staff. And I want it specifically understood that we are observing, *in every way,* the terms of the accord. No aircraft are even to approach the Demilitarized Zone on my behalf. I rely on you to arrange it exactly as I say."

"Yes, sir," Crowell said.

"Bill Tate won't like it, sir," Reisman commented.

"I'm sorry about that," Bailey said. "But I am not concerned with what young General Tate likes or does not like. I shall want to hear from him a very good explanation of how it is that he has allowed some fool pilot to compromise a diplomatic initiative the President thinks is important to world peace."

Reisman suppressed a sigh and turned his attention to the view outside. He felt sweaty and uncomfortable and oddly tense. He was sorry the President had sent him on this errand. He didn't like Bailey and he didn't like being the President's spy—though, as a practical matter, he would do all this and anything more asked of him by the Old Man. Still, he could be getting ready now to fly to Palm Springs with the President. Instead, here he was, listening to the self-righteousness of the Dove.

A man given to the sour habit of self-examination, Reisman often wondered how much his dislike of Talcott Bailey was reinforced by the invidious comparison between the Vice President's ascetic good looks and aristocratic *noblesse* and his own rumpled, often sweaty, obese raunchiness. Would I like him more, he asked himself, if his hair were less richly silver, his profile less Yankee classic, his goddam ageless body less lean and erect? Possibly. But at bottom it was Bailey's utter conviction that he was right—always, entirely, instinctively right—that made Reisman dislike him. What, he wondered, would it take to convince the Vice President that the world was not, as he saw it, a place where lambs and lions could gambol in innocent joy together?

Though he had not said so to the President, Reisman doubted the wisdom of sending Bailey into the Peacekeeping Area; it was not a climate in which he could be expected to thrive. He thought idly of some lines of Auden's he had once encountered:

> *Come to our bracing desert*
> *Where eternity is eventful,*
> *For the weatherglass*
> *Is set at Alas,*
> *The thermometer at Resentful.*

The trouble was, Reisman thought, looking now at the shores of that "bracing desert," one's priorities tended to get scrambled. As Air Force Two approached the barren land, he wondered if Roman civilians had suddenly found, as they came into the Wilderness, that they loved the legions more than they had imagined possible.

He felt an uneasy reprise of the half-forgotten emotions he had experienced entering a theater of war: a sudden distrust of politicians and an empathy with the poor bloody infantry, the soldiers. Yes, the men like William Tecumseh Sherman Tate, who did as they were told and were shat upon by the press, the politicians, and the electorate of the Great Republic, none of whom had any real idea of what it was the armed forces faced in the bear pit to which their duty consigned them. Small wonder if the thermometer was always set at resentful.

Reisman, who had seen rather more of life than most, hoped that events would not deal too harshly with Talcott Bailey. The education of men close to immense power could be very expensive. And one could never be certain how many human beings, all across the world, might have to pay the cost.

8

Seated grimly and officially behind his uncluttered desk, General Tate studied his unrepentant tactical air commander, standing at attention before him. Lieutenant Colonel Trask still wore his flying clothes, and the red marks of his oxygen mask showed on his twisted jaw. His eyes were cold and angry, but his manner was correct.

"The Red was inside the fifteen-kilometer limit, General," he said in a dry, harsh voice. "The radar tapes will bear me out."

Tate regarded Trask steadily, wondering how and if it would ever be possible to make him understand the situation his zealous aggressiveness had created. He knew Trask's record, and why anger against the Communists seethed inside him. He knew, too, that Trask probably resented the fact that Tate ranked him by three grades and stood immeasurably above him in the military hierarchy. Both he and Trask knew perfectly well that in all military organizations there were those special persons, chosen at an early stage in their careers for high command and armed with the approval and patronage of older commanders who were, themselves, selected by the same system of tacit aristocracy.

Bill Tate and Dale Trask were both products of this selection system, but something had gone wrong in Trask's career. His capture by the North Vietnamese and his vicious treatment at their hands had scarred him emotionally to such an obvious degree that some of his early sponsors had withdrawn their support, fearing to put one so psychologically damaged in a position of sensitive command.

Trask remained one of Admiral Ainsworth's men, but he was Ainsworth's in a particular fashion now. No longer destined for high command, he could still be useful to the Chairman of the Joint Chiefs as a specialized weapon: a private line into Tate's essentially political command.

Knowing this, Tate would ordinarily have welcomed any excuse to fire Trask. Yet he now found himself in the infuriating position of having to support Trask's lapse of judgment. The rising storm of protest over the buzzing of the *Allende* posed a greater threat to the integrity of the U.S. Component command than did Trask's divided loyalty.

Behind Trask stood Sergeant Major Crispus Attucks Robinson, immense and silent. His face seemed carved from some black wood, polished and highlighted into an ebony mask. The single pale-blue ribbon of the Medal of Honor on his chest probably intimidated Trask more than the Sergeant's formidable appearance. Trask, for all his faults, was a soldier, and to a soldier any man who wore the Medal was something unique.

Tate said, "I hope the tapes will bear you out, Colonel. The Vice President is certain to ask to review them, and I won't be able to refuse."

Colonel Seidel, seated by the General's desk, said, "I have run the tapes, General. Apparently the Russian was *on* the fifteen-kilometer line when the interception took place."

"He was inside our area," Trask said flatly.

"You knew that Deputy Premier Rostov was expected," Tate said, controlling his temper at Trask's near-insubordinate manner.

"I didn't know he was on the Red snooper," Trask said. "But it wouldn't have made any difference. They were intruding."

Tate looked at Seidel, who shrugged slightly and said, "The

tapes don't confirm that, General. They were on the limit, but not in our waters."

"He was in our territory," Trask said stubbornly. "Or so near it as makes no difference."

Tate suppressed a growing anger. "Colonel, that's a goddam stupid thing to say. We expect more common sense from members of this command. An officer assigned to the Peacekeeping Area should know how sensitive the Russians are to anything that touches their dignity."

"Screw their dignity, General. The Red was snooping and he got what was coming to him. He's damned lucky I didn't grease him," Trask said in a loud voice. "And it wasn't necessary to send your sergeant after me in front of members of my command—"

Tate's eyes hardened at the direct challenge to his authority. His voice cracked like a rifle shot. *"Colonel!* That will be all of that."

Trask hesitated, but his injured pride and outrage would not let him retreat. He stood pinned between a lifetime of discipline and a furious urge to tell this ground-gripping soldier boy that his command was lax and loaded with goof-offs and Red-lovers. "General," he said, blusteringly, "I do my job as I see it—" He was struck by what he considered a saving thought: "The way other people see it, too—"

Tate felt fury knotting in his stomach. The damned fool was throwing Ainsworth at him now. That had to be stopped—and at once.

"Stand at attention, Colonel," he said.

Trask's eyes widened. No one had spoken to him like that since his cadet days. He could not believe his ears. But the expression on General Tate's face convinced him that he had gone too far and that he had better obey. He straightened, eyes fixed on a point above the General's head.

Tate spoke with frigid deliberation. "Colonel Trask, if I ever hear you make such a statement again, I will relieve you and send you back to Washington under arrest. Is that clear?"

Trask worked the sudden dryness out of his throat and began, "General, I—"

"Is that clear?"

"Yes, sir."

"I want you to understand something, Colonel. So I am going to say it once. I didn't ask for you in this command. I was reluctant to accept you in this headquarters because I thought you might do something rash. This is a political command, Colonel, and we live with some very narrow margins. An officer of this organization is expected to have—*and use*—good judgment. You haven't been here three days and you have already justified my doubts. I am not going to relieve you, for reasons that concern the welfare of this command. But until further notice you are grounded. There will be no more personal patrols. All air operations are to be cleared with my chief of staff until I personally rescind the order. That is a direct order. *Do you read me, Colonel?"*

Trask's scarred mouth twisted with the effort of controlling his temper. In a half-suffocated voice he replied, "Yes, sir."

"You, personally, are restricted to the military compound, the tac-air post, and Echo Sierra Control. Is *that* clear?"

Trask sounded as though he were strangling. "Yes—*sir*."

Tate said frigidly, "You are dismissed, Colonel Trask."

Trask saluted, performed an about-face with military-school precision, and strode from the room, his face blank.

When the door closed behind him, Tate said to Robinson, "Did he give you any problems, Sergeant?"

Robinson's face remained impassive. "None I couldn't handle, General."

"I'm sure of that," Tate said. For a time he looked thoughtfully at Robinson, who stood at attention, his short-cropped hair seeming to brush the perforated ceiling tiles. Then he went on, "I'll want you to make the trip to Zone Center tomorrow, Sergeant. I can't say just now how large an escort will be accompanying the Vice President—that will have to wait until I see him. But I'll want you with the troops. Plan accordingly."

The black face remained formal. But Tate knew that the Sergeant was pleased. Was it because history, of a sort, would be made at Zone Center when the accord was renewed? Robinson was, in his fashion, a student of the times, and he understood clearly how vital to the American commitment in the Middle East tomorrow's ceremony would be. Or was it simply that he was pleased that his chief was, once again, acknowledging him as the best soldier under his command? The years Tate and Robinson had served together had not broken down the reserve of rank between them. In all that mattered, they understood one another perfectly and without a need for explanations, but there remained shadowy areas in their relationship that each respected and left inviolate.

"Yes, sir," Robinson said.

"Alert the Special Forces detachment. They will supply the escort."

"Yes, sir. I'll take care of it."

"Tell the men there are to be no political arguments with members of the Vice President's party."

"There won't be, General. I guarantee it."

"All right, Sergeant. That's all."

Robinson saluted, stepped back the correct one pace, about-faced, and left the office.

"What was that about?" Seidel asked.

"Over half of the Special Forces detachment troops are black, Judge. If a few of the Vice President's staff start digging for antimilitary complaints, they are apt to get one hell of a shock. They aren't the sort of blacks Bailey's people are accustomed to dealing with," Tate said ironically.

"I don't doubt it. And Robinson is one hell of an intimidating figure."

Tate's eyes turned cold. "He's one hell of a soldier. He not only knows how, he knows *why*. In his gut—without all the bullshit and propaganda."

Seidel could not neglect the opportunity to probe at the commander's convictions: the occasions came too seldom to be missed. "Does that mean he doesn't think about race, General?"

"Don't give me that crap, Judge," Tate said. "A black man can love his country without trying to be white." He paused, as though undecided about pursuing the subject further. Then he said, "My education on the subject of race was about what yours was. I didn't grow up in the South. I didn't really think about Negroes at all. Then the Army said I'd better start thinking about them and so I did. I spent a few years trying to be 'unprejudiced.' I thought that meant letting black soldiers get away with shoddy performances and near insubordination. Then I met Robinson and learned what a black soldier could be. My A-camp near Peng Lem was overrun by North Vietnamese shock troops. Robinson was my weapons man. There was one hell of a killing. He saved our asses—not by being black, but by being the best goddam soldier in Vietnam. It was a revelation, Judge. Because we were doing exactly the same thing—soldiering and trying to stay alive." Tate grimaced at the memory of that gray, deadly day when the gravid rain clouds lay low on the mountains and kept the Phantoms away. "This black and white thing that's been plaguing our country for a couple of hundred years or so didn't seem very important then. To either of us. Does that answer your question?"

"Is that why there are so many blacks in your command now?" Seidel asked.

"The Army is way ahead of the rest of the country in race relations, Judge. There are one hell of a lot of black regular soldiers. I picked good soldiers for this command. I didn't think about color while I was doing it."

"Robinson's Medal of Honor. You got it for him?"

"I wrote the citation."

"That day in Vietnam?"

"There were two hundred dead North Vietnamese inside our wire by nightfall. The rest of us—the team members who happened to be in camp that day, and the Mike Force Montagnards, thirty of them, accounted for half the enemy killed. The rest were Robinson's—" Tate recognized the look of suppressed civilian horror in Seidel's eyes and added, "Killing isn't a soldier's only business, Judge. But it's a big part of what we do, and we have to face it and live with it. It's all very well to talk about the blessings of peace, but remember this: when the war you never wanted comes, you'd better have men like Sergeant Robinson available to do your killing for you if you want to stay alive to try again. That's what it means to be a *soldier.*"

Seidel, a civilian at heart, despite his uniform, realized that he had been given an insight into an attitude unique to men-at-arms. The soldier believed—knew—that the race of man was not yet—if it ever would be—as the doves saw it, reasonable and yearning for peace. The soldier had to be able to see man quite differently: aggressive, contentious, and cruel, his heart filled with murder. Little wonder, then, that sometimes one caught a glimpse of something in men like Robinson—and Tate, too—that terrified. It was as though one had a fleeting vision of the world in flames. And the worst of it was that though it would be the Tates and Robinsons who used the weapons, they did so at the bidding of men like himself, like Talcott Bailey, who sought only peace.

In such a context, the rashness of a Dale Trask was frightening. Seidel, whose training and outlook were political and legal, found himself searching for some solution that would rid Tate and the sector of the man. "Will you convene a board of inquiry on Trask?" he asked.

"You should know I can't do that," Tate said curtly. "I can fire him or I can forget it. But I can't make a display of him. Not now."

"The Vice President may insist," Seidel said.

"That's exactly why I can't convene a board. It was a damned stupid thing Trask did, Judge. He let his personal feelings influence his judgment, and an officer of this command doesn't have that privilege. But I can't hand the Russians his head. I won't let this command be turned into a whipping boy for Talcott Bailey and his friends."

"The President may back Bailey if he demands action."

Tate looked curiously at the Colonel. "You think so, Judge?"

Seidel shook his head wearily. "No, not really. But you can't keep a command as political as this one out of politics. Either way, Trask has put you in a bad spot."

"What would you do?" Tate asked.

Seidel sat silent. He saw himself inheriting the task of political advocate for Tate, for his men, and, finally, for the entire concept of an American peacekeeping force in the Sinai. Which was, of course, precisely the post he was meant to fill. It was for this reason the President had put him here. Yet he wished with all his heart that he could avoid this duty. He was a principled man. As a congressman and as a judge he had tried not to evade responsibility. But he was still, he reminded himself, reasonably ambitious. He had taken this post in the reasoned expectation that the President would, in time, reward him. To embroil himself in a losing battle over a Red-hating light colonel, of whom Bailey would surely want to make an example, would leave scars that could be crippling to a man interested in politics.

"Is that a fair question, General?" he asked, temporizing.

"Of course not, Judge. I shouldn't have asked. It is my responsibility."

"You don't know, of course, that Bailey *will* want Trask up on charges."

"I think we both know the Vice President well enough."

Seidel said regretfully, "You mean to put yourself out on a limb for Trask?"

"I can't let current popular ideology affect a military decision."

"But isn't that what you will be doing by standing up for him? Letting ideology affect your decision—in reverse?"

"You have me there, Judge," Tate said. "But if I have to be influenced by political concerns, I have to believe that the integrity of this command and its job here are more important than appeasing the Russians and Bailey."

Seidel could not help remarking: "Admiral Ainsworth will approve of your decision, anyway."

"That may be. Though he may change his opinion after Bailey and his people go home and I send Trask back to a desk in the Pentagon."

"It sounds as though you have made up your mind to get everyone mad at you. Bailey, the Russians—and Ainsworth. Is that really wise?"

Tate stretched his legs and leaned back in his chair. "What the hell is wise these days? You'll remember that back in the seventies the Russians very kindly offered to intervene here on their own and set off one hell of a flap. So now—today—I am just going to do what I think is best for this command. Maybe sitting here glaring at one another over thirty-four east isn't the only way to keep the peace in this part of the world. But it's the way two presidents and the American people have decided to try it, and that's got to be enough for me." He regarded Seidel with an almost ironic smile on his lips. "That's the other part of soldiering, Judge. The part that goes with these—" He touched the two silver stars on his collar.

"You may never get another one of those, Bill," Seidel said with genuine concern, "and that would be a shame. Personally, I would like to see you one of the Joint Chiefs one day, and so would a good many others I know. Is it worth risking that just to buck Bailey?"

"You know better than that," Tate said. "If you didn't, you wouldn't be sitting where you are. I don't like Bailey. I don't believe—as he apparently does—that the lion and the lamb are going to lie down together. Not in the foreseeable future, at any rate." Tate looked at his chief of staff for a long moment, seeming to weigh a further response. Then he said, "But none of that is relevant to the problem we have here. No matter what that damned fool Trask has done, or come close to doing, I can't let the military integrity of this command be compromised. And it will be if I let Vice President Bailey force me into firing one of my officers to appease the Russians. It is just that simple. But then, Judge, I'm a simple man."

"Like hell you are, General," Seidel said with feeling. "Like bloody hell you are."

At precisely eight o'clock in the morning, Washington time, Admiral Stuart Ainsworth, chairman of the Joint Chiefs of Staff, sat down behind his Pentagon desk and prepared to begin his day. At five that morning he had been awakened by a telephone call from the duty officer in the War Room with an account of Colonel Trask's encounter with the *Allende*. Since that time he had received hourly reports on the Russian reactions. These reports came from Naval Intelligence, from the CIA, and from the Defense Intelligence Agency. In addition to these came others—from Ainsworth's own sources within the White House and the Congress.

It was characteristic of Stuart Ainsworth's regime as chairman of the Joint Chiefs that all Soviet-related intelligence came to him directly. It was an article of faith with the Admiral that the United States was largely unaware of the true extent of the Communist menace. He believed that the nation's danger stemmed as much from the liberals' misconceptions of Soviet intent as from Russian power. If pressed, he would sometimes say that the Cold War began not in 1946, but in 1917, with the birth of the Soviet Union. He believed that the USSR meant to destroy the capitalist world and, specifically, the world's most capitalist nation. In his view this aim was the one constant in Soviet policy; all else was dictated by expediency.

In a long military career, Ainsworth had seen many changes in American opinion. He had served through the days of the euphoric alliance of World War II, the angry days of Korea, the rabidly anti-Communist atmosphere of the McCarthy era. He had commanded a cruiser division during the Cuban missile crisis blockade and an aircraft carrier task force off Vietnam. He had viewed with misgivings the Nixon missions to Peking and Moscow and had spoken against the ratification of the Cyprus Accord when, as chief of Naval Operations, he had appeared before the Foreign Relations Committee. Three years later, his remarks were still being quoted by opponents of the American role in the Sinai.

As a junior officer, he had learned that it was risky to say what one believed in Washington among the doves and liberals. He had seen other officers ruin their careers by sounding warnings America did not want to hear. Yet his long experience convinced him that war between the United States and Russia was inevitable.

History taught how ungrateful democracies could be to military men. Athens disgraced and impoverished Miltiades, the victor of Marathon, and exiled Themistocles, who fashioned the Persian defeat at Salamis. America rewarded Billy Mitchell with a court-martial for his services and George Patton with a loss of command for his. It was the way of the mob, and Stuart Ainsworth had no intention of letting the American mob destroy him—or the nation. As he rose in rank, his political opinions became more extreme, but his caution grew. Since his unsuccessful testimony before the Foreign Relations Committee he had kept his opinions to himself, or had limited them to a small circle of friends within the government.

Ainsworth was without personal political ambition. His plans did not embrace any further career that must rely on popularity. He considered democracy a luxury that could be afforded only by those prepared to be utterly ruthless in its defense. It was this certainty that supported his conviction that a man in his position needed the moral courage to strike first and strike hard against his country's enemies.

An austere man descended from a family of Scottish Calvinists, the Admiral burned with the inner fire of the zealot. Those who served him either loathed and feared him or were overwhelmed and converted by the strength of his will and beliefs. He had enemies and disciples. He was a harsh disciplinarian and one of the most efficient chairmen since the post was created. The President disliked him and the Vice President loathed him. The men of the Congress, most of them, were awed by his frigid rectitude and computerlike mind.

And Fowler Litton Beal, the Speaker of the House of Representatives, who was at this moment approaching the Chairman's office for an eight o'clock appointment, admired the Admiral more than any man in Washington.

Fowler Beal, a soft, rumpled man who had reached his present eminence in Congress by seniority and a slavish loyalty to his party, was everything Ainsworth was not. Though he wished to think of himself as sternly principled and forceful, he wasn't—and he knew it. His personal life was untidy. He drank too much and worried about it. His political career had been undistinguished, even dull. In his home state he was regarded with a certain scornful tolerance. His constituents called him "Old Fowler." He was sixty now, but he had been Old Fowler to his supporters for the twenty-six years he had served in the House. He was a party hack, and he knew this, too. He was not brilliant, not charismatic, not much of anything except loyal and willing to take instructions. It was inevitable that such a man would stand in awe of the austere Chairman of the Joint Chiefs and be anxious to number him among his friends.

He was ushered into Admiral Ainsworth's office by a starchy naval commander in impeccable blues and wearing two rows of campaign ribbons. The young officer's bearing and looks made Fowler acutely conscious of his own wrinkled suit and flabby body. Before his elevation to the Speaker's chair, he had served for a number of years on the House Armed Services Committee, where he had gained a reputation as a good friend of the military. When he saw fine young officers like this aide he could congratulate himself on that much, at least.

It pleased him out of all proportion that Ainsworth rose from his desk to greet him and shake his hand as he came into the paneled office. He noted that one wall had been rolled back to display a map of the eastern Mediterranean and was delighted that the Admiral was, once again, going to take him into his confidence.

When the aide had gone, Ainsworth escorted the Congressman to a chair and said, "I'm glad you could make it on such short notice, Fowler."

After the Admiral's early-morning telephone call, which had awakened and excited Beal with its cryptic urgency, nothing could have kept him away. What he viewed as his personal relationship with the gray-haired Admiral was one of Beal's most valued social and political possessions, an ornament to an otherwise drab career.

"I realized it had to be important, Stuart," he said, waiting expectantly.

"I would have come to see you in your office," Ainsworth said, "but it's only a matter of hours before the press is onto this thing, and they'll be scribbling and talking about every move I make."

Beal's excitement grew. He had no idea what "this thing" might be. Last night, Washington had seemed its customary dull off-year self. The Vice President was en route to the Middle East. The President had spent two days in the countryside and was now back. Congress was in adjournment. Nothing remarkable had happened up to the time Fowler and his wife had retired to their separate bedrooms in their Georgetown residence. He had, in fact, been considering a visit to

Rockville, and a certain Miss MacLean who lived there at his expense.

Ainsworth gave the Speaker a swift précis of the day's events off the Sinai coast. He finished by defending Colonel Trask's actions as those of a dedicated and efficiently aggressive officer, and asked for the Speaker's opinion on what might now be expected in the way of retaliation from the Russians.

The simple truth was that Beal had not the slightest idea what could now be expected from the Soviets, who were so completely unpredictable and, to him, unknowable. He had some difficulty focusing his attention on what the Admiral was saying about Colonel Dale Trask.

"I expect I shall have a Telex from Bill Tate within the hour asking me to recall Trask," Ainsworth said. "I have no intention of doing that. But Tate may go directly to the President."

Beal forced himself to listen. He said, "Will he do that, Stuart? Can he?"

"Unfortunately, he can," the Admiral said. "The accord, you see." When he mentioned the Cyprus Accord, his voice turned colder. Beal remembered that Ainsworth had advised against ratifying a treaty that authorized a Russian presence in the Sinai Peninsula. He had been chief of Naval Operations then, during the last days of the previous administration. When the President, after his inauguration, had named him chairman of the Joint Chiefs—despite the known dislike of him—there had been raised eyebrows in Congress. But it was one of the President's characteristic political gestures: to balance the doves in his administration with so hawkish a chairman.

"The American protocol that implements the treaty," Ainsworth said, "places our component of the Peacekeeping Force directly under the orders of the commander in chief. I testified against the accord, you'll remember, for that reason—among others."

Beal forced his political mind to mesh. He was not a brilliant man, as many had noted, but he was a completely political one. "I suppose the Vice President will insist that Tate relieve Colonel Trask. He's sure to raise hell about this happening just before his meeting with Rostov."

"Actually, Trask isn't the problem, Fowler. He may have been a bit overzealous in stopping the *Allende,* but we can make a legal case for it if we must. What I am afraid of is that Bailey will take this incident as an excuse to make unauthorized concessions to the Russians." He rose and went to the map. "Look here," he said, pointing at the Sinai coast. "The Soviets claim to have only the allowed five thousand effectives in their sector. You remember that the treaty allows them another two thousand for logistical support. The Egyptians have three thousand and one thousand in their sector. Total strength, according to the treaty, is eleven thousand men for the Other Side." His long finger tapped the map at the head of the Gulf of Suez. "But here, just west of the peninsula, there are two Egyptian armored divisions." He touched the western shores of Great Bitter Lake. "Here there is a parachute division of 'volunteers' from Libya." He moved his finger to the north along the shores of the Suez Canal. "And *here* we have no fewer than five missile brigades of the Red Army, plus two bomber groups of the Red Air Force." He returned to his desk and stood framed by the gold-fringed national ensign and his personal four-starred flag. "If the Soviets decide to make a move, there are just four understrength brigades in our sector to stop them. The Jews have almost nothing in their sector—the treaty saw to that."

Beal thought vaguely that these dispositions did not exactly match the announced strengths of the four signatory powers in the area, but it was possible that his own information was not as up to date as Ainsworth's.

"I'm telling you about all this, Fowler, because you've always been a friend of the armed forces and you have a right to know what the situation is. The President has refused to let me reinforce the Sixth Fleet. I don't blame *him*—I'm certain it is the Vice President's influence. They don't call him the

'Dove' for nothing, after all." He sat down again, folding his hands on the bare surface of the desk and speaking more quietly. He had frightened the Congressman enough for now, he thought, with his talk of U.S. military weakness in the Peacekeeping Area. What he wanted from him was a statement of support for the battles to come: battles that had not been unforeseen, but that might be prematurely precipitated by Trask's imprudent action off the coast of Sinai.

"By noon today," he said, "the fact that an American aircraft buzzed Rostov's ship will have stirred up every left winger, peacenik, and appeaser in the country. A good many of them, as you well know, are in the Congress. The news media will have a field day with it. Our good friend Ambassador Kornilov will be beating down the doors at the State Department. No one was hurt, no one was anything but ruffled, you understand. And the Red ship was inside our fifteen-kilometer limit. But that will all be lost in the slather the Commie sympathizers will start pouring out." He stared fixedly at Beal for a moment, trying to calculate how far he could be pushed before his instinct for political self-preservation immobilized him. "It could be serious, Fowler. I don't think it will come to anything, but I feel it my duty to bring the armed forces to third-degree readiness."

Beal was startled. "Is that necessary, Stuart?"

"As a precautionary measure only. Samos Center reports that the Russians are already moving air units. They're bluffing, as usual, but we must show them we are not intimidated."

"What does the President say?"

"Third-degree readiness is well below Yellow Alert status. We call it for exercises two or three times a year. The President needn't be involved. I will notify him at the next National Security Council meeting. Which is not until Monday week. But the Russkis will know about it. They keep very close watch on us. They'll know and realize we mean business and can't be pressed."

Beal sat in silence, a spot of burning discomfort in the pit of his ample belly. He had an unhappy notion that he was out of his depth in this discussion. "What do you want from me, Stuart?"

"For the moment, Fowler, only your support in Congress when the word gets around about the *Allende* incident. Trask isn't important in himself, though he is a good officer and should be kept where he is. What is important is that there be a core of resistance to the movement to appease the Reds that is surely going to start up the minute the media get hold of what happened this morning."

"That's all?" Beal felt a small tremor of relief. Stuart Ainsworth could be a frightening man sometimes.

"I hear a rumor about the President planning to go out to the West Coast for a few days' rest. Is there anything to it?" Ainsworth asked. Actually, he had seen a copy of the Telex sent from the White House to Air Force Two. His sources were expectedly efficient in monitoring communications.

"I haven't heard anything like that," Beal said. "There is a congressional breakfast on Thursday. It hasn't been canceled."

"It will be," Ainsworth said. "But no matter. Can I count on your support?"

"Yes." Beal nodded. "Yes, of course, Stuart."

"Thank you, Mr. Speaker," the Admiral said formally, rising.

"I have always been a good friend of the military," Beal said. "You can rely on me to remain so, Admiral."

Ainsworth walked to the door with him, hand on his shoulder. As the Speaker of the House left the Pentagon and his car carried him toward Capitol Hill, he suspected that he had been manipulated, committed to something. But he was not sure what that something could be.

9

Air Force Colonel Ira Dayton, the President's pilot, was preparing to leave his Fort Meyer quarters for his monthly examination by the Flight Surgeon when the call came from the White House. Helen Risor, the President's secretary, was on the line to inform him that the President had decided to spend the next two or three days at the Palm Springs White House and that he wished to leave Andrews Air Force Base early tomorrow. The President's party would include two of the regular Secret Service men, plus Secretary of Defense Ames Dickinson and herself.

Dayton did not know the Secretary of Defense well. Dickinson was new in the post, having recently replaced a holdover from the previous administration. But two things were said about him: he would have a problem reining in the Joint Chiefs—in particular, Admiral Ainsworth; and he was a long-time political friend and golfing crony of the President.

After telling his wife that she would have to make their excuses to a friend who had invited them to a dinner party in Chevy Chase that evening, Dayton called the line at Andrews to alert the crew of Air Force One. The President's Flight, which he commanded, was a smoothly organized unit, and he was able to set matters in motion with that single call.

Air Force Two, carrying the Vice President to Es Shu'uts,

had left the previous day, commanded by the lieutenant colonel who customarily flew as second pilot on Dayton's trips with the President. Thus Dayton would be flying with two new men he was in the process of breaking in. Major Allan Campbell and Captain Edward Wingate were both highly qualified, with several thousand hours in the latest planes, but they were not intimately familiar with their commander. Dayton decided to spend most of the rest of the day briefing them.

But first he telephoned the Senior Flight Surgeon at Andrews to postpone his appointment. At his last session, Colonel Brady had warned him of a slightly elevated blood pressure and prescribed some changes in his diet. An electrocardiogram had shown no anomalies, but Brady had scheduled a complete chest survey for the next session. Since this would entail half a day with radiologists and the cardiovascular specialist on Brady's staff, Dayton was happy to postpone it. The doctor, a personal friend, asked how he was feeling.

"I feel fine, Ted." Actually, this was not strictly true. For the last forty-eight hours he had been feeling rather poorly, with a brassy cough and some hoarseness. But like many men who were almost never ill, Dayton found it impossible to believe that his athlete's body (he had been an All-American running back at the Air Force Academy) could actually be in the process of betraying him.

"You sound hoarse. Better take some antihistamine before you fly."

"Yes, I'll do that."

"You'll be on the schedule for next week, then, Ira. Better plan on spending the day out here. Check with the base hospital when you get back."

"Right, Ted," Dayton said, and broke the connection. He coughed, trying to clear the vague thickness from his throat. There was a slight feeling of constriction in his chest. He decided to let the new pilots do most of the flying and restrict himself to making the takeoffs and landings.

He next called the meteorologist at Andrews and asked for the Palm Springs twenty-four-hour forecast. He was told that the weather over all the southwestern United States would be clear and cold, with strong, gusty winds. He thought about the President, an eighteen handicapper, playing golf in the winds that swirled through the San Jacinto Valley, and smiled. His own handicap was two.

Dayton would never again set foot on a golf course, with the President or alone. Next to his beating heart, the distinct bulge of an aneurysm grew, thinning the walls of the pulsing aorta. Colonel Ira Dayton had begun the last full day of his life.

The vanguard of the Abou Moussa Commando reached the last low ridge before the Oasis of Feiran in the hot windy hour before sunset. The shadows of the mounted men stretched ahead of them in strange pillared patterns, and behind them a bloated sun touched a horizon made indistinct by a haze of blowing dust.

Enver Lesh raised his field glasses to study the land ahead and could just make out the stain of dirty green that marked the western limits of the oasis. Stunted palms grew there, twisted shapes sculptured by the wind, tamarisks, reeds, and rushes waving in the khamsin. Between the ridge and the oasis lay a few kilometers of packed sand dotted with rubble and rock. The low angle of the sun striped the plain with shadows, and among the shadows Lesh could make out the shapes of what were surely men, though they looked like rocks and dusty bushes of *spina Christi*. Stroking his heavy mustache, he smiled at the stillness of the pickets and wondered how many automatic weapons were being aimed at the line of men paused atop the low ridge.

"I can see your outposts, Jamil," he said to the woman behind him, meaning to let her know that he understood she had ordered her people who had remained at Feiran not to allow strangers to approach uncovered from any direction.

"Can you also see the ones behind you, Lesh?" she asked coldly.

He turned in the saddle to see that a line of men had risen from the ground the Abou Moussa had just passed: a half-dozen of them, holding automatic rifles at the ready, dark shapes with robes flapping like fluttering wings against the orange-tinted sunset sky.

"Very good, woman, very *good,*" he said.

"It is our desert, Lesh. It is all they have left us, so we have learned to use it well." She raised her arm to signal the silent men to close in. As they came, their dirt-colored robes streaming in the wind, Lesh had to suppress an uncharacteristic shudder. Now the Abou Moussa was complete, and it seemed to draw some power from its completeness. These men were the best of the remnant, Lesh realized, the last really useful contingent of a movement that had once numbered in the thousands. The Arab Front for the Liberation of Palestine consisted now mainly of politicians and talkers, plotters and skulking bombers who spent their time in the coffeehouses of Damascus and Baghdad, or in the safe gardens of the American University of Beirut. Once there had been El Fatah, the National Front for the Liberation of Palestine, the Black September Group. Of all those, only this remained available for action. The Jews and the friends of the Jews had worn the movement down.

Lesh watched the men approach and was struck by the thought that these were a physically handsome people, but their eyes were the eyes of wild animals or fanatics: black as obsidian and as impenetrable.

Jamil said, in Arabic, "This is Lesh, who has brought us the weapons we were promised."

One of the men on foot, thin and older than the rest, asked, "And will he also fight?"

Lesh said in careful Arabic, "Better than most, dung man."

Jamil laughed. "This is Rifai, Lesh. Once, he hijacked a jet airplane from London to Beirut."

Lesh showed his long teeth in a smile. "And lived to tell about it. My congratulations, Rifai. *Bis'mallah.*"

"This is Abdullah," Jamil said, indicating another of the men. "His brother was at Furstenfeldbrück."

Lesh nodded acknowledgment.

Jamil went along the semicircle, giving only single names, which was as it should be.

When she had finished, she spoke to the man called Rifai. "Are there monastery shepherds at the oasis?"

"The water carriers have arrived. They say the flocks are coming down from the mountain."

"And camels?"

"Some. I don't know how many."

She looked at Lesh. "We can still march."

Lesh shook his head. "When will the shepherds arrive at the watercourse?" he asked.

Rifai squinted at the reddening, darkening sky. His eyes were red-rimmed from the wind and dust. "Two hours, maybe three."

"How many?"

Rifai shrugged. "Perhaps a dozen. Perhaps twice that."

"Armed?"

The red-rimmed black eyes held Lesh steadily. "Some. Not many."

"With what?"

"Jezails. Knives. Slings."

"Nothing more?"

"There's no need. No one ever steals sheep from the monks of St. Katherine."

"It is not sheep we need, Rifai," Jamil said.

The wind buffeted uncomfortably at Lesh's back, whipping the tails of his kaffiyeh in front of his face. He said to Jamil, "Issue new weapons to these men and then let's get down to the watercourse. We will need some time to eat and then to get ready."

The woman said nothing, only turned and gave the needed

orders. When the new Kalashnikovs were handed out, the party, now at full strength, moved down the shallow slope toward the darkening shadows of Feiran. Lesh began silently to plan the ambush of the shepherds as he rode.

In the wardroom of the *Allende,* Deputy Premier Anatoly Rostov waited for the appearance of the shore party and Captain Bogdanov. Through the open scuttles he could hear the sounds of the port and naval base, crowded with shipping from the Warsaw Pact nations.

The Russo-Egyptian alliance had had its good moments and its bad ones. The troubles of the seventies—when the Israelis had seemed ready and able to march to Cairo and Damascus—had repaired somewhat the former coolness between the two countries. Friendship was now the order of the day. For this, one had to thank the Americans, Rostov conceded. If it had not been for the Cyprus Accord, the fool Egyptians might have remained hostile toward their sometime benefactors, nursing their Arab pride, injured by Russian reluctance to throw good rubles after bad in arming them for battles they habitually lost. Now the alliance was healthy again—or as healthy as it could ever be, Rostov thought—nourished by the Egyptian dream of coequality as a signatory nation of the accord.

Through the scuttles came the hot evening wind carrying the stink of the great sprawling, dirty city of Alexandria. Rostov's short and stubby nose wrinkled with distaste. He was of peasant stock and had no objection to honest animal and human smells, but this place stank of foreign rot and decay, centuries of it. He disliked Egypt and the Egyptians. He disliked all non-Russians, though he had learned to tolerate them in his many years of service to the state.

It had been an infuriating day, beginning with the insult to the Soviet Union delivered by the pilot of the American Shrike. Then there had been a series of messages from Moscow warning him privately that he was not to take any action on his own that might endanger his meeting with the American Vice President in Zone Center: messages that Rostov found gratuitous and demeaning, since he was perfectly well aware of the importance of the meeting without being told by the Politburo. He had been angered by the incident off the coast of the U.S. Sector, but he was too good a politician not to know that it could be used to embarrass Talcott Bailey and place him at a disadvantage during the negotiations.

On the quay he could hear the undisciplined chatter of the Egyptian honor guard waiting for his appearance. They could wait indefinitely, he decided, since he had no intention of making a formal arrival on the pier. Egyptian security was abominable.

Throughout the afternoon, as the *Allende* was approaching Alexandria, he had monitored the stream of messages flowing between Moscow and Washington. It seemed that the incident off the coast had been photographed by a Cosmos, and by this time Leonid Kornilov, in Washington, should have the graphic evidence of a violation of international law by an aircraft of the U.S. Component in Sinai. Kornilov had been instructed to seek a direct meeting with the President, but it appeared that the Americans were not completely asleep—the President was reported unavailable: something about a weekend visit to California. The Ambassador would have to content himself with the Secretary of State, it seemed, and this would take time. As much time as they could manage, Rostov thought. With the meeting set for the following evening in Zone Center, eleven in the morning in Washington, the Americans hoped to delay discussion of the incident until after the accord was renewed. Given the same situation, Rostov thought, he would probably do the same.

An hour later, the Egyptian honor guard was still waiting on the pier and the shore party had come aboard the *Allende*. The wardroom was now crowded with Soviet and Egyptian uniforms and filled with the smell of Bogdanov's lavish buffet, sweat, and the perfumed hair oil of the Egyptian officers. The Egyptian designated to accompany Rostov to Zone Center and to sign the renewal of the accord for the UAR was a general bedecked with even more medals than his Soviet counterparts had. He clicked and jingled as he moved, accompanied everywhere by an interpreter who spoke Russian badly.

"General Suweif would like to propose a toast," the smooth-faced interpreter said in Rostov's ear. "To Soviet-Egyptian friendship."

Rostov raised his glass until the Arabic gibberish had ceased and then drank. Bogdanov's champagne was Veuve Clicquot 1956 and excellent, but Rostov preferred vodka. He signaled to a naval aide and said in dialect, "Talk to these fools."

The young officer promptly began to express his admiration for Alexandria in fluent Arabic, and Rostov moved away from the Egyptians, seeking out General Ulanov.

He found him surrounded by his staff officers, only one of whom—Novotny, the KGB commander—was drunk. Navy Captain Zakharov stood slightly apart, speaking with Bogdanov. The Air Force's Yudenich looked unhappily bored. Still chafing from the Shrike incident, Rostov supposed, and regarding it as some sort of assault on his personal honor.

Ulanov seemed tired, Rostov thought. Perhaps his health would supply an acceptable reason to replace him as commander of the USSR Component in the Sinai. He was too friendly with the American commander, according to the security reports reaching Moscow. Coexistence was one thing; co-operation and friendship something else entirely.

Rostov glanced about the crowded, noisy compartment and said to Ulanov, "We must end this farce soon and get down to work, Comrade General."

The old General had eaten only sparingly of Bogdanov's spread, but he held a glass of iced vodka. Rostov studied him carefully and noted that he showed no sign of having consumed any liquor at all. The old man knows he is growing senile, Rostov thought, and is trying to hide it.

In the center of the room, Novotny stood surrounded by Egyptian officers. His face was flushed and sweaty, and his bemedaled uniform was stained with caviar. Rostov regarded him with distaste. Novotny aped the style and manner of the Old Bolsheviks, but he was far from convincing. He was not old enough, he was not ruthless enough, and, above all, he was not strong enough. He was a surrogate revolutionary, a bureaucrat more akin to Heinrich Himmler than to Lavrenti Beria. Rostov felt a momentary depression. That, it seemed, was what happened to the heirs of successful revolutionaries. They grew sleek with unhealthy fat—in the belly and in the head. He wondered if the Chinese were making the same discovery now that the Maoist doctrine was secure from internal attack. Or did they somehow manage to keep their revolution in ferment? To Rostov and others in the Politburo, the Chinese continued to be a deadly threat. Thus far, Rostov and his friends had managed to keep fifty divisions deployed along the Chinese border, and there were some who believed that it was only the *détente* with the U.S., such as it was, that prevented war. As to that, Rostov could not say. The Chinese, he felt certain, were still capable of being troublemakers. Though the Americans did not believe it, it was only the Chinese and the Albanians who supported the remnants of the Arab terrorist movement.

Novotny raised his glass and shouted for attention. "To Soviet culture!" he bellowed.

Everyone but Rostov and Ulanov drank dutifully.

"To the Soviet Fatherland and the struggle of the people against imperialism!"

Bogdanov and Zakharov looked vaguely pained, but drank their wine. The Egyptians did likewise.

"To our gallant allies of the United Arab Republic," Novotny shouted, his words half swallowed in laughter and self-approval. "To their victory against the forces of international Jewry!"

"Idiot," Yudenich muttered.

"Vasily Ivanovich," Ulanov said to the air commander, "take that fool out on deck before he says something worse."

Rostov stared at Novotny and then looked back to Ulanov. "Is he always like that?"

The old General shrugged. "He is uncultured, Comrade Deputy Premier."

Rostov frowned. Novotny had not only made a bad impression on everyone, but had also set the Deputy Premier to thinking about the quality of security in their sector with such a man in charge of intelligence. He said, "I do not envy you, Comrade General, being saddled with that one."

Ulanov said wheezily, "He was not my choice, Comrade Deputy Premier. But he does what he is told. There is not much work for policemen in an organization of soldiers."

Rostov's eyes narrowed. Had Ulanov forgotten that during the Great Patriotic War he, Anatoly Rostov, had served as a captain in the then MVD?

"It seems to me, Comrade General, that it is precisely in an organization of soldiers that vigilance is most essential. Professional soldiers tend to regard themselves as something separate from the masses."

"The Army is always loyal, Comrade Deputy Premier," Ulanov said stolidly.

"No doubt," Rostov said in a dry voice. After all, what other response could come from the legendary hero of Stalingrad? The man was old, possibly sick, politically naïve.

Ulanov said, "I have received a personal message from General Tate apologizing for the incident with the American airplane, Comrade Deputy Premier."

"A personal message?"

"Yes. A Telex addressed to me."

"He acknowledged that the pilot of the aircraft committed a criminal act and should be punished?" Rostov demanded.

"No. He merely expressed his regrets."

"And you attach some significance to this gesture?"

The old General's eyes looked hooded. "Only that he wished me to know that he was sorry it happened."

"He is frightened about the possible consequences?"

"Not frightened, Comrade Deputy Premier. General Tate does not frighten easily. I believe he regrets that the incident took place, that is all."

"That most certainly is *not* all, Comrade General. An official protest is being delivered to Washington—and the attack on this ship will be discussed at Zone Center." When Ulanov remained silent, he added, "You feel some friendship for the American, I think."

Ulanov said, "I would, Comrade Deputy Premier, if it were permitted."

Rostov was surprised at the implied insolence of the reply. It was not at all what one would normally expect from an old war horse like Yuri Ulanov.

"Tell me, Comrade General," Rostov said, "what is troubling you about this day's business?"

The old man hesitated, and then, Rostov thought, reached some decision within himself. "If we had informed the Americans of the *Allende*'s mission and movements, it would not have taken place."

"You think we should ask permission of the Americans to move about the Mediterranean Sea, Comrade General?"

"Of course not, Comrade Deputy Premier. I simply mean that the secrecy surrounding your arrival is partly to blame for creating an awkward situation. It could have been avoided."

"You are very outspoken."

"You asked me, Comrade Deputy Premier."

"Yes, I did," Rostov said. So the old man was not about to blame the Americans for an insult to the Soviet flag or any such psychologically useful event. Apparently not all professional soldiers were fools.

"Suppose your General Tate ordered the attack himself—for reasons of his own?" It was a probing, random thrust intended merely to sound the depth of Ulanov's professional regard for his opposite number on the other side of thirty-four east.

"He isn't *my* General Tate, Comrade Deputy Premier. But one can admire an adversary—"

"Ah, yes. The code of the professional warrior. One sometimes forgets that it lives on—even in the Red Army."

Ulanov ignored the interruption and the sarcasm. "I can think of no reason why any American should have ordered the *Allende* intercepted—" (Rostov took note of the General's refusal to use the word "attack" to describe the incident)—"least of all General Tate, who understands Russian psychology very well."

"It was purely an accident, then? Is that what you believe?" Such a thing, though possible, seemed unlikely to a man of Rostov's turn of mind. Little happened in the world that was not, in some way, planned. Rostov was certain of that much.

"It may have been routine, Comrade Deputy Premier. Even we intercept vessels within the fifteen-kilometer limit of the coast. It is specified in the accord."

"We were in international waters, Comrade General."

"Of course, Comrade Deputy Premier," Ulanov said wearily.

Rostov decided to change the subject. He would remember this conversation for the light it cast on Ulanov's opinions. The old man was too friendly with Tate and too disposed to think well of the Americans. Some changes would have to be made in the command structure of the component.

"After Bogdanov clears out this gathering of peacocks," Rostov said, "I want to discuss the security arrangements for my trip to Zone Center. Did I understand Yudenich to say the Jews will not waive the terms of the accord so that we can go by air?"

"That is so, Comrade Deputy Premier."

Rostov chewed his heavy lips for a time and considered the

consequences of ignoring the proscription of aircraft in the Demilitarized Zone. No, that would not do. The Americans would take it as a deliberate retaliation for the incident at sea, and he would lose whatever psychological and moral advantage he now held over Talcott Bailey, who worried about such things. Furthermore, it would probably encourage the Egyptians to risk aerial incursions into the DMZ and possibly even into the American or Israeli sectors. They were not to be trusted, nor would aggressiveness on their part serve any useful purpose. The trip, then, would have to be made overland. It would be long and uncomfortable, but for the time being it was essential that Soviet behavior be absolutely correct.

"Is that fool Novotny in charge of my security detail?" he asked, staring at the open hatch through which Yudenich and the weaving KGB man had vanished.

"I will take personal command, Comrade Deputy Premier," Ulanov said.

Rostov had a momentary qualm about subjecting this old, tired man to a long and trying journey overland through the Sinai wilderness, but he suppressed it. It would be well to have the Soviet commander in the Peacekeeping Area in personal charge of the escort. Perhaps he would have a chance to observe Ulanov and Tate together. Rostov believed he had an instinct for detecting disaffection—sometimes even before the disaffected one knew of it himself.

"Very well, Comrade General," he said. "The time of the meeting has been set, as you know, for 1800 hours tomorrow—the anniversary of the original signing of the accord. Make your dispositions accordingly."

Father Anastasius was still making his slow way down the rocky path toward the Oasis of Feiran. For fifty years he had lived in the community of monks at the foot of the mountain on which, Mohammed the Prophet himself agreed, God had appeared to the Jew Moses. He now resembled the parchment mummy of St. Stephanos that guarded the gates to the charnel house, where he performed his humble duties.

He had come to the monastery so long ago, it seemed to him, that he could scarcely remember a former life. He had vague memories of a childhood among the white rocks and bright sun of Macedonia, and of a father who offered him to the church as penance for who could tell what peasant sins. But to Father Anastasius life was limited in time and space to his existence in the ancient stone buildings below Moses' mountain.

The cloistered way in which he had spent his life caused him no regrets. He was devout, healthy, with the desiccated hardiness of the desert, and fulfilled by his religion. As one of the older members of the community, he was privileged from time to time to leave the monastery and retreat into the mountains to meditate and pray. Like the Hindu holy men of the East, he would spend days fasting among the higher crags and passes of the massif, alone with the sun and wind and, he had no doubt, God.

Anastasius knew very little about a great many things, but a great deal about one thing in particular. He knew all that could be learned from the old books and manuscripts about the Monastery of St. Katherine and the men who had served it. At times, he dreamed of martyrdom, imagining himself to be one of the pilgrims slaughtered by the Saracens in the Middle Ages, or (in moments of uncharacteristic hubris) a saint like Katherine herself, his holy bones destined to lie in the charnel house, watched throughout all time by St. Stephanos, sitting in his chair and dressed in the *megaloschemos*—the "angel robe" of the highest monastic rank.

Now, in this darkening hour, making his way down the unmarked path toward Feiran, he found his mind wandering. Two days of fasting and sun had made him lightheaded, but he felt exalted, as though near to some wondrous epiphany. With the more practical portion of his half-starved brain he was thinking that he would meet the monastery shepherds at Feiran and share their meal, and perhaps return to the monastery with them as they moved the flocks back across the mountain passes.

His sandaled feet trod the stony ground familiarly, and the evening wind pressed the rough cloth of his robe about him, outlining his emaciated form. In the distance he could see the palms and tamarisks, darkly waving in the deepening shadows cast by the ridges between the oasis and the red sky. He could make out beyond the invisible watercourse the lighter-colored shapes of the sheep the Bedouins herded for the monks, and he suppressed a nearly carnal desire for the taste of cheese and a bit of mutton.

Time passed swiftly in the wilderness, and Anastasius sometimes imagined that God used Sinai as a measuring rod against which the changes in the outside world could be judged. For the last few years there had been little contact between the monastery and the world. Tourists used to come to St. Katherine, to walk through the stone corridors and chambers and gape at the relics preserved there against time. But recently there had been no tourists, and few visitors of any sort, even pious pilgrims. Occasionally, men in khaki uniforms and blue berets would call at the monastery to speak with the Deacon, but the visitors from outside, the men and women who used to stand in awe before the mosaic of Christos Pantokrator, the Sovereign Lord of the World, whose serene and stern face had adorned the cupola of the apse since the time of the Emperor Justinian, no longer came. It was, Father Anastasius fantasized, the time of the Saracens all over again.

It was growing darker at the bottom of the wadi that formed the oasis; the sky, however, seemed to be redder than before, with long, still streamers of sunset burning across the vault of the heavens. The light in the sky turned the shadows to amber and gold, so that the air seemed charged with the blood of the Sacred Heart.

Anastasius, familiar as he was with the sunsets of Sinai, was moved and humbled by the ominous beauty of the transition from day to night. He could not help but pause and kneel on the rocky ground to chant a private Kyrie eleison.

He was on his knees in prayer when he heard the first rattle of popping noises. The peculiar sounds puzzled and disturbed him. Rising to his feet, he stood listening. The odd sounds came in chains, six or seven at a time, and from several sources. The ruddy light had begun to die swiftly, in the way of twilights, but within the grove of palm and tamarisk he could see flashes of yellow light, flickering pin points of fire. The pale shapes of the herd seemed to be milling senselessly and with growing panic.

The old monk began to walk toward the oasis, stumbling from time to time and filled with an anxiety not fully understood, only felt. In this land of miraculous happenings, where God burned a bush that was not consumed and where a holy mountain stood wreathed in mystical fire, was it possible that something akin to those ancient and arcane events was taking place now? He began to run, rockingly, because of his age. His breath came dryly into his lungs, and his heart labored.

From the oasis came a cry—a shrill, furious scream of pain and anguish. Anastasius heard it clearly and was filled with dread. No miracle of God would produce such a shout of pain from a human throat. If miracle this was, it was a black one, a work of the devil, unholy Lucifer, the fallen angel.

He could hear other voices now, and the cries were like the first, of pain, of fury and outrage. The strings of popping sounds continued, and the flashes of light grew in brightness as he approached the grove bordering the watercourse. He could hear men shouting in the Bedouin tongue, and other voices, commanding and angry.

A shape materialized before him, ragged and robed in darkness. The last red sunlight smeared the figure, which seemed hardly human to Anastasius. It came running, hobbling, loping in a broken gait. It was a Bedouin, one of the herdsmen. His headcloth was gone, his black hair flew out with his erratic movements, and his eyes were wet pits of darkness. The monk could hear the wind rushing in and out of him with a dreadful bubbling sound. The Bedouin came on, seemingly not seeing Anastasius at all, but seeking to run past him, through him. Then he fell and rolled onto his back, and Anastasius could see that the lower half of his face was missing. His cheeks ended at the upper jaw, wet and glistening red, so that the upper teeth, all streaked with blood, hung like pickets over a pulsing crater that ended above the windpipe. The eyes rolled, fixed, and finally glazed.

Terror-stricken, Anastasius crossed himself and murmured a prayer for the dead. His body began to tremble like that of a beaten animal, shivering in uncontrollable waves of horror. He steadied himself against the rocks bordering the path and then saw with disgust that his hand was slippery with the Bedouin's blood.

The nightmare grew. He could see others running, crawling. The explosions were louder, and it began to filter through his medieval mind that these were the sounds of weapons, firearms. Someone was slaughtering the herdsmen, killing them as they ran, as they fell, and even as they crawled into the watercourse or among the rocks.

Someone in the shadows shouted in Arabic: "Don't let the camels bolt, or it's for nothing!"

It took Anastasius a further moment to understand that the Bedouins were being butchered for their camels. Twenty-five or so human beings were being killed by marauders for two dozen camels.

He gripped his crude wooden cross, with the broad wings of the Greek Orthodox faith, held it aloft, and went stumbling into the confusion of running men and animals shouting: *"Stop! Stop in the name of God!"*

He had run only a short distance when he was knocked to the ground by a massive blow. The darkness seemed to explode into fire, and then he lay dazed on the ground among the reeds growing near the watercourse. He could hear them crackling and rustling in the wind, while the noises of the killing seemed far away. His left hand ached terribly. He wondered if he had injured it as he fell, but his thoughts were muddled and confused with images of wind and rock and sun. *Christos* forgive—he had lost his cross, a fixture of his life for fifty years— How could such a thing befall?

The popping noises of gunfire stopped, except for an occasional single shot. A loose camel loped by him in the darkness, crashing through the reeds and into the water. He heard it splash away up the slope of the spring. Suddenly he was terribly thirsty. The sound of the water was torture. He could smell it. The back of his throat was parched and foul.

In the distance he heard a woman's voice call out to someone to collect the animals. It was not a Bedouin voice. The Bedouin voices were all stilled.

St. Katherine, St. Stephanos, he thought, is this a miracle? He tried to think holy thoughts, humbly, because he was growing more certain that somehow he had been chosen for martyrdom. But, St. Katherine, he thought, I do not understand it. Have the Saracens returned?

There were a few more isolated shots, far off. The Saracens were killing the wounded. His sense of exaltation had vanished; now he felt feverishly angry with such wickedness. Curse them, St. Stephanos, he tried to say aloud—and found that he could not speak. His left hand began to throb, with great pulses. He had moved, and the movement lifted his slight weight from the bullet-shattered mess that was all that remained below his wrist. The soft-nosed Kalashnikov bullets had amputated his hand, and now his blood was leaking into the sandy soil of Feiran.

His groping fingers touched the mash of meat, bone, and blood, and he realized that the Saracens had taken his hand away. It should have horrified him, but in the face of what else had happened it seemed a small thing. I am not a complete martyr, he thought with uncharacteristic giddiness, only a single hand's worth.

With a great effort he rolled onto his back and gripped the

mangled wrist, but the blood still flowed from the twisted, knotted veins and arteries. He knew that he must stop the sticky flow or die. Actually, in the face of such wickedness, it was difficult not to choose simple death. But the monastery should be warned that the Saracens had returned to Sinai after a thousand-year absence.

A man less inured to hardships, less honed to leathery strength, would surely have expired within the next few moments. But Father Anastasius refused death's offer. He used his right hand to unfasten the coarse cord about his waist and wrapped it around and around his left forearm. The old fibers tasted bitter as he held them with his teeth and knotted the cord tightly.

The marauders were prowling through the dark oasis searching for survivors of the massacre with their electric torches. A single shot. Voices. Another shot. Laughter. Anastasius closed his eyes and lay still in the reeds. His mind began to wander again, and he seemed to be reading from the manuscript of Theodulus, the son of St. Nilus: ". . . *the Saracens had decided to sacrifice me and Magathon's slaves to their abominable gods . . . the altar had been built, the knife sharpened for sacrifice . . . the bowl, incense and wreath made ready. . . . I was expecting nothing but death, when God by a stroke of his almighty power prevented it. . . .*" Of course, that was as it should be. Where could God's power be greater in all the world than here, at the base of His holy mountain? Anastasius, parched and grievously wounded, lay for a long time listening to the Saracens, who were moving away to the north end of the oasis to make their camp, not wanting to lie asleep among the innocent Bedouins they had murdered.

Presently the old monk forced himself to move. The effort was agony, but he persisted. He had lost his sandals, but he dug his heels into the ground and shoved, inching himself along through the reeds toward the water. From time to time the trailing ends of the cord binding his mutilated wrist caught in the brush, and each slight tug was like a hammer's blow on the raw injury. He bit on his dry lips until the blood came, but he kept on.

After what seemed an eternity, he felt the blessed coolness against his head. He turned and pressed his gaunt cheek against the mud. Another push with his heels and the water lapped against his twisting, groping mouth and he drank.

He made a sound that was halfway between a grunt and a moan and rolled again, using his good hand to help himself crawl along the shore of the watercourse. Though he hoped that the Saracens had stopped their search for survivors, he knew that he must move away or die. Another heave, another convulsive effort, and he was sitting upright, propped against the trunk of a small tamarisk. He looked up through the branches and saw that the sunset was long gone. There were brilliant stars in the sky, a sky scoured by the wind that was now dying into a desert stillness. Far off, he could hear the voices of the murderers, quieter now, perhaps subdued by the wicked thing they had done.

He shut his eyes briefly and forced his right hand to grasp the remains of his left. The pain almost made him faint, but he forced the stump against the rough cloth of his robe and looped the loose ends of the tourniquet around his neck to make a crude sling. Breathing shallowly with the effort, he threw his water bottle toward the spring. It fell short. He pulled it to him on its cord and tried again, shoving at it with his gaunt and bony feet until it lay half in the mud, filling slowly. When that was done, he pulled it back again and looped its cord around his neck.

He felt weak, but he could not delay. Only night could save him. He reached above his head and pressed against the trunk of the tamarisk. Then he dug his heels into the ground once again and arched his back, scraping up the tree, his body quivering with pain and effort. His robe grew soapy with blood as the strain forced his wound open again, but he persisted until he stood on his feet, leaning against the tree and sucking air into his lungs.

Next he tightened the tourniquet, fighting against the sick darkness that threatened to engulf him. As he stood, head down, strings of bitter saliva drooled from his open mouth. He wanted water again, but he dared not yet use the little that had leaked into his bottle. There was sun and heat to come, and a rocky journey across the mountains that would tax the endurance of a saint—which he now knew he was not, for saints do not curse the wicked, and he, with all his heart, consigned the murderers of the Bedouins to the blackest pit of hell.

Something banged against his feet and legs and almost threw him to the ground—gray-white shapes, rank-smelling and wild. He stifled a moan of mingled pain and fright, but the white shapes were gone, panicky sheep seeking the scattered herd.

He began to move, quietly, he hoped, but any way he could. One naked foot ahead of the other, feeling the stones against the leathery skin of his soles, the reeds against his old ankles. One step. Another. And another. The aching throb of his wound seemed to thrust a trembling vibration through his entire body, but he did not hesitate. He walked, back, across an infinity of darkness and sun and heights and agony, toward his monastery—to give the warning that the Saracens had returned.

10

Deborah Zadok lay in bed in her quarters, an unread book open on the counterpane. The room was lighted by a single lamp, and the hi-fi set—a gift from Bill Tate—was playing a tape of the third movement of Beethoven's "Eroica," deep and sad and moving.

The music suited her mood: she was heavy with melancholy. Her affair was ending—must end, she knew. It had become a danger to Bill, a relationship that could destroy his career. She was not a person who could rationalize betrayal, and she could sense the conflicts rising around her.

She had been at the airfield with the official party to greet the Vice President, and in person he had seemed even colder and more self-righteous than his reputation indicated. He was apparently angry about the encounter between Colonel Trask and the Russian ship and seemed determined to establish authority over the American soldiers in the sector. This clearly would include Bill Tate, whom the Vice President and his staff had treated with almost open contempt. Though the General had, of course, offered the full military formalities of welcome, there had been an obvious lack of friendliness. This had undoubtedly continued into the private meeting that followed.

It was late now, nearly midnight, and it was extremely unlikely that the meeting was over even yet. Tomorrow was the anniversary of the accord, and the day designated for

Talcott Bailey to travel to Zone Center to meet with Anatoly Rostov.

The Vice President had been coolly correct with the Israelis in the welcoming party. Brigadier General Rabin and the rest of the Liaison Group had been polite, but it was clear there was no love lost on either side. If we face one another with such antagonism on this side of thirty-four east, Deborah thought, what hope is there for real peace with those west of the line? She was tired and felt like weeping. Instead, she closed her eyes and listened to the music, thinking that she was far too emotional to be any sort of agent, no matter what Mosa'ad expected of her.

Her impression of the American Vice President had been dismaying, and she wondered if such a man could ever grasp the realities of the chronic state of war that existed between Israel and her Arab neighbors. Bailey's pedantic idealism made him vulnerable to the self-delusion of his class. What hope was there for a realistic appraisal of geopolitics by one who seemed convinced that accommodation with one's avowed enemies could be brought about by the *noblesse* of reasonable men?

Before the meeting at the airfield, Rabin had told her in confidence that there had been a number of "incidents" in the Golan Heights. Syrian-based terrorists had infiltrated from the north and mined the secondary road between Haifa and Jerusalem. A busload of kibbutzniks had tripped the mines; two had been killed and a number wounded. That the Air Force or the Army would retaliate was as certain as tomorrow's sunrise. And the Russians, who had moved into Syria in force over the last few years, would protest. The renewal ceremony at Zone Center, already darkened by the affair of Colonel Trask and the *Allende,* would take place—if at all—in an atmosphere of deepening crisis.

Deborah had turned out the lamp and closed her eyes for a time, and might even have slept, when she heard the familiar authoritative rap at her door. She was suddenly fully awake, both astonished and concerned that Bill Tate had come to her so unexpectedly. His rashness frightened her, and yet her heart contracted with excitement.

She opened the door and stood aside. His dark shape blotted out the dim lights of the compound. Beyond him she could see the huge figure of Sergeant Major Robinson standing guard at the corner of the building.

"You," she said. In easier moments she called him by name, and sometimes, chidingly, by rank. But on occasions of stress (and there had been many of these recently), it was simply *You*. "I didn't expect to see you tonight."

He stepped inside and closed the door. She was overwhelmingly aware of him standing near her in the darkness. She could catch the faint smell of laundered khaki and strong soap and leather and the man scent that clung to him after the long day. The metal stars on his uniform caught an errant gleam of light from the drape-covered windows as he moved.

"I said this morning I would come."

"That was this morning. A hundred years ago."

"At least a hundred," he said. He reached for her, held her shoulders for a moment, then slipped her cotton nightdress down. He brushed her naked breast with the back of his hand. The warm metal of the Academy ring he wore touched her nipple, and her legs trembled. He held her against him, one hand spread on her back, the other cupping her head as he kissed her.

Presently he said, "I wasn't going to miss that. Not for Talcott Bailey or anyone like him."

"This is dangerous."

She felt him give a short, silent laugh. "Yes. I agree. The Dove will say I'm all balls and no forehead. The licentious soldier."

"Don't," she said.

"Sorry. I didn't mean that."

She drew him to the bed and began to work on the buttons of his shirt. "Yes, you did. It's all right." She could feel the tension in him. His muscles were taut with strain. She tried to make herself think sensibly, but all she could feel was her need to satisfy his maleness. The rest could come after. "Lie down," she whispered.

He did as he was told, silently. She searched his bare chest with her lips, opened his belt buckle. The brass jingled softly in the dark, and he said, "Damn."

She said throatily, "Don't talk." Then she took him in her mouth, rubbing her forehead against the oddly smooth skin of his inner thigh. He was thick, erect, fully aroused long before she touched him.

Suddenly he caught her hair and lifted her face. "No," he said, "not like that." He stripped off his clothes and hers with swift anger, pushed her onto her back, and entered her deeply.

They made love in silence; there was nothing to waste on words. The bed grew rumpled and damp, and Deborah stopped thinking. If she was aware that he was using her for more than love, she didn't care. The physical reality swamped any semblance of reasoned thought. They were more than sexual partners—they were two halves of the same thrashing, self-devouring organism.

When at last they lay still, slick with sweat and gasping, Deborah thought: Lust. My God, it's nothing but lust—

"No," he said, raising his head to see her in the dark. She knew then that she had spoken aloud. "No," he said again. "It's more than that."

She held him with all her strength, her arms trembling. She could feel wetness on her cheeks and didn't know whether it was sweat or tears. She often cried at these times.

He brushed her eyes with his lips and then rolled over so that she rested half on top of him, their legs tangled in the bedclothes. The tape player turned itself off with a snap, and the room was silent except for the sound of their breathing.

"You really shouldn't have come tonight," she said. "I would have understood that you couldn't."

"To hell with that," he said.

She drew a shuddering breath. "Not wise. Not wise at all."

He smiled mirthlessly. "There's no army regulation against it. Even for generals."

"I suppose everyone knows about us."

"Yes," he said, plainly not wanting to pursue this line of talk.

"Will you go to Zone Center with him?" she asked.

He sat up abruptly, angry again. "No," he said. "He specifically ordered me to remain in Es Shu'uts. He doesn't want any soldiers."

"No soldiers?" she said, perplexed. "I don't understand."

"Who does? He says it is a purely civilian occasion and he wants no military. His aide and one other officer, that's all. He had to accept military transport, though, so I intend to send one squad, no matter what he says. But that's all I can do. The man behaves like a lunatic." He fumbled in his clothes for a cigarette, lit it. In the brief flare of light Deborah caught his sullen expression. He was a man grown accustomed to command, and the Vice President had frustrated and angered him. She wondered if that was the real reason he had come to her, even though to do so at this time was so unwise.

"But he isn't a lunatic," Tate said. "He's an idealist, and that's a thousand times worse."

"Is Dov Rabin going to Zone Center?" she asked.

"Yes. He's been designated official representative by Jerusalem." Tate paused, stared at the glowing coal of the cigarette, then stubbed it out angrily. "And you," he said. "You are going."

Deborah held her breath.

"That's right. You. Rabin's idea."

"I see."

His voice was hostile. "I'm ordered to sit here because soldiers offend our Mister Bailey. But he has no authority over you Israelis, and your prime minister insists that there be an Israeli contingent present when the accord is renewed."

She had never heard him so at a loss. It did not fit her

picture of him. But she had never seen him faced with the maneuverings of politicians, either. He was actually a simple man, she thought. It was a revelation and it made her love him more—if love was what she felt for him. She was not certain of that.

"There is no danger, surely?"

"Intelligence says not. Intelligence is right about a third of the time. *My* intelligence, that is. What does Mosa'ad say?"

She felt shocked and cold inside at his tone.

He moved in the dark. "Don't answer that," he said. "Don't ever answer that."

She heard the acceptance of betrayal clearly in his voice and understood that he could never be certain that she had not given herself under orders. Feeling sick with self-loathing, she hunched her naked shoulders and huddled, weeping silently.

She knew him—and yet she did not know him. In this barren land of soldiers he had been—at least until today—supreme. One did not question the local gods, even when they shared one's bed. But it was something else to stand ready to inform on them, betray their trust.

For a long time he said nothing; then he reached out, touched her bowed head with a surprising gentleness. "It's all right," he said. "Don't cry, Deborah." He so seldom spoke her name that it was like a strange caress to hear him say it now. She held his hand against her cheek, feeling its warmth and strength. It made it easier, somehow, to believe that their affair was not near its end.

Tate was thinking that it was a bitter irony that having destroyed his personal life on the altar of his career, he was now in the position of risking that career for this feckless affair with an Israeli spy. And bitterest of all was the knowledge that he did not know whether or not he loved her.

The wind had died and now the night was clear and still, with the dark bulk of the mountains shutting off the blaze of stars to the east. The palm and tamarisk trees rustled with small desert vermin excited by the smell of blood. There were twenty-eight dead Bedouins in the oasis of Feiran. The guerrillas had robbed some of the bodies, but there was nothing really worth taking. The ancient jezails the herdsmen had carried were smashed and scattered. Water bottles and food were something else again. These the men of the Abou Moussa gathered at their campsite at the north end of the oasis.

At midnight, Enver Lesh made a tour of the outposts to ascertain if the sentries were awake and attentive while their comrades slept. Satisfied, he walked down to the watercourse, where the tethered camels stood hobbled. There were forty-five of the beasts now, enough to mount the whole commando and have some to spare.

It had been a reassuring business, the attack on the shepherds. He had ordered it for the animals, of course. But equally important had been the opportunity to watch the men kill. If they would murder over a score of Bedouins—Arabs like themselves—there was enough iron in them to accomplish the killing of the American.

Leila Jamil had assured him of the troop's determination, but one had to make certain. Acts of terror were never simple. Men balked at odd times and for strange reasons. It was necessary to be absolutely sure. Now, he was—as sure as one could be with these people.

He had also wanted to know whether or not they would follow his orders without the intercession of their own leader. Jamil had served her purpose by gathering the commando and delivering it into his hands. It would not have done to find that he could bring them onto the killing ground only to discover that he must give his instructions to her and that she must relay them to the commando. Fire fights were not won in such a manner—particularly those fire fights that must inevitably result in heavy casualties among the attackers. But the ambush of the shepherds had gone well; he was now reasonably satisfied that the weapon would not turn in his hand.

He walked back to the place by the watercourse where he had spread his sleeping bag. At a distance he could make out the dark bulk of the woman lying under a tamarisk. In the starlight he could see her eyes gleaming as she watched him. He went to her and squatted. "Tomorrow," he said. "You will show me the place on the map where we can intercept the Americans."

She said, "Are you satisfied?"

"With the men? They did well."

"They have killed before. Was it necessary to prove it again?"

"We needed more animals."

She rolled over, turning her back on him.

"What's the matter?" he asked.

"I'm tired. I need to sleep."

Lesh stared at the dark curve of her back. "You need something else."

"Not from you," she said. There was a slight movement, and he caught the gleam of a knife blade in the dim starlight.

He showed his great teeth in a smile, but said nothing.

"Let me sleep," she said. "Go away."

"In a moment. Did you know one of the Bedouins got away?"

She turned again to look at him. "We killed them all."

He shook his head. "Rifai says not."

"He told you?"

Lesh smiled again. "He told me."

"He should have made sure of him."

"I agree. But it doesn't matter."

"Rifai should have made sure of him," she said again.

"He lost him in the dark, he says."

The woman drew in a shallow, weary breath. "We are getting careless."

"That will change," Lesh said. "I'll see to that."

"*You* will."

"Yes."

"I see."

Lesh stood, stretching his legs. He did not feel like sleeping. The killing had stimulated him more than the others, and he wished that he could march through the night directly to the Americans' stronghold and attack them there; but that was, of course, only a fantasy. One had to act with pragmatic caution in war if one was to be effective.

While Lesh dreamed his dreams, Leila Jamil turned away and wrapped herself in her djellabah. The warmth of the day had turned to a bitter cold now that the sun was down. She closed her eyes and relaxed, but sleep would not come. She thought about Lesh. His grossness repelled her, as did his clumsy sexuality. Throughout the day he had projected his maleness at her in words and gestures and thinly veiled suggestions. The man might be an excellent guerrilla fighter, but in other matters he was a fool. How did he imagine that a woman like her had lived among rough and lonely men for so long? Was he so insensitive that he could not feel the difference in her sex?

11

It was after midnight when Colonel Jason Seidel said good night to the Vice President in his suite in the Falasha and returned to the military compound.

His interview with the man had been unsettling. Even a lifetime of politics, the law, and the military had not prepared him to cope easily with zealots. The man was sincere, well-meaning, and almost certainly wrong on every basic notion of the workings of American society. Americans were not the sullen children the Vice President seemed to think they were. Nor were they the plastic, selfish, insensitive, and greedy imperialists young Bronstein thought them. They could not, in Seidel's opinion, be forced into the life style favored by Bailey and his wing of the party. Two presidential elections had proved this beyond a shadow of doubt, and yet Bailey and his supporters not only refused to accept the people's decisions, but also refused even to admit the decisions had been made.

Bailey had delivered personally a letter to Seidel from the President. It was characteristic of the man's undoubted integrity that he did not know certainly what it contained. Though it had, with equal certainty, come as no surprise, when Seidel shared the information—as he had to—that the Colonel was under consideration for an appointment to the Supreme Court.

What the Vice President felt about such a possibility was

not difficult to guess. His political support, vocal and tightly organized, was rooted in the peace movement of the sixties; no man with Jason Seidel's record of conservatism was likely to win its approval. The best that could be hoped for—and apparently this was the President's opinion as well—was that its opposition might be muted.

Bailey, with a politician's sure instinct working, had quickly evaluated Seidel's potential weaknesses. "The President has his opinions and I have mine, Judge. I feel it only proper to warn you that whatever influence I have and how I use it for or against your appointment will be strongly affected by your performance here. I must say that my interview with our young Achilles was less than satisfactory. You, I expect to be more sensible. The Russians will almost surely demand that Trask be relieved and court-martialed. I would certainly do so in their position."

"General Tate would like nothing better than to get rid of Colonel Trask, Mr. Vice President. The Colonel was handpicked for this assignment by Admiral Ainsworth, and the General does not share the Admiral's view of how matters should be conducted in this part of the world. But the General will never relieve Trask under duress. He isn't that sort of man."

"It would be wise for General Tate to accept civilian judgments," Bailey replied. "Trask has created an incident that has made my task here more difficult. Quite frankly, Judge, I feel that this all tends to bear out my conviction that it is a mistake for the United States to be involved in this so-called peacekeeping operation. As you can plainly see, the possibilities of deeper and more dangerous involvements exist. Suppose that madman had opened fire on the Soviet ship? Suppose he had killed Rostov?"

Seidel conceded that the possibility was frightening. "But these are the normal risks in a sensitive military command such as this one. We minimize them by relying on intelligent and politically aware commanders."

"I don't share your confidence in Tate. He is only a soldier, after all," the Vice President said.

And there, Seidel thought, they had come to the pivot of the argument—the unresolvable conflict. To Talcott Bailey, steeped in his own sanctimonious ethic, no soldier could ever be trusted to make other than purely military judgments. Trask had provided an excuse for an open conflict between Bailey and Tate, but if it had not been Trask and the *Allende,* it would have been something else. Bailey would have found some reason to challenge Tate's authority in the sector—and Bill Tate would have resisted. The fact that Tate would personally have liked nothing better than to rid himself of Lieutenant Colonel Dale Trask and now felt he could not without compromising his authority only made the affair more ironic and bizarre.

"My point is," the Vice President had concluded, "that any man who hopes, as you do, to sit on the Supreme Court of the United States should have no doubts about where his sympathies lie in any conflict between the military and civilian authorities under the Constitution."

On that bleak note they had parted, and Seidel thoughtfully started on his way back to his own quarters. Bailey not only had raised a point of genuine concern to Seidel, but also had attacked his weakest flank: his ambition. It was well and hatefully done, he reflected.

He considered the day that had already begun. At midmorning the Vice President would depart for Zone Center to sign, at approximately 1800 hours, a renewal of an accord with which he was not in sympathy. He could expect, at the very least, a quasi-diplomatic tirade from Anatoly Rostov, thanks to Trask. From that viewpoint, one could understand Bailey's fury at Tate's refusal to bend. But the Vice President would have the last word. Of that there could be no real doubt.

Bailey had wasted no time in retaliating. He had declared unequivocally that he would tolerate only the minimum military escort to Zone Center. And he had specifically excluded General Tate from attendance. This had been a gross reprimand to Tate, and he had taken it in grim silence. In this matter there was no question of the Vice President's authority; he had the absolute and final decision on the make-up of the party accompanying him to Zone Center.

Seidel was considering this when he passed through the portion of the military compound housing the members of the Israeli Liaison Group. He noted, with a surge of strong disapproval, the tall dark figure of Sergeant Major Robinson standing at the corner of the building where Captain Zadok lived. Knowing something of the loneliness of Bill Tate's personal life, his failed marriage and all that it implied, he understood exactly what Robinson's presence meant. Had Tate been someone other than the commander, Seidel would have sympathized with him and would have accepted with good grace his infatuation with the Israeli. But the attachment was unwise and unseemly, and in the present circumstances to indulge it so openly was outrageous.

He hurried through the Israeli compound and into the area of concrete huts housing the senior American military staff. He was somewhat surprised to find Jape Reisman waiting for him there.

"May I come in, Colonel?" Reisman asked. "I'm sorry about the lateness of the hour, but I'd like to have a word with you."

Seidel led Reisman into his quarters without comment. Since the Vice President's arrival in the sector nothing seemed to be running in its accustomed track.

Reisman surveyed with mild surprise the austerity of Seidel's living arrangements. Seidel had been a widower for many years, and it was understandable that he might accommodate himself to a certain asceticism. But senior officers, at least those of Reisman's acquaintance, tended to use the privileges of their rank to ease the strains of military life. Apparently the Judge did not. The room was bare of comforts, furnished with a GI cot, a metal desk, some GI metal bookcases filled with field manuals and legal works, and little else.

"I'm afraid I can't offer you a drink, Mr. Reisman," Seidel said. "I don't keep the stuff around."

Reisman made a dismissive gesture and said, smiling, "You don't pamper yourself, Judge."

Seidel shrugged. "I don't spend much time here, Mr. Reisman."

"Jape."

"Yes, of course." Seidel offered the only chair and seated himself on the cot. "How can I be of help to you?"

"I hope it's the other way around," Reisman said.

Seidel waited curiously for Reisman to continue, but he seemed in no rush to get to the point of his visit. Instead, he said, "Major Paris's deputy took me on a tour of Echo Sierra Control. That's quite a set of toys the soldiers have there."

Seidel puffed his pipe alight with a battered Zippo. "Hardly toys, Mr. Reisman. You would find a similar control-and-command communications center on the other side of thirty-four east."

"The rubles and dollars flow, Judge."

"You have to balance the expense of the Peacekeeping Force with the alternatives," Seidel said. "What do you imagine World War III would cost?"

"Touché, Judge. I just get the taxpayer's twitch every now and then. Even when I'm talking to the next associate justice of the Supreme Court."

"Maybe," Seidel said.

"Justice Carmody is definitely retiring, Judge. You have the President's commitment—in writing."

"Don't think I'm not grateful to the President—but politics is a slippery game. I'm not counting on anything yet."

"Then I'm afraid I'm going to shake you up a little, Judge," Reisman said. "The President asked me to see you personally and privately to amplify what he couldn't risk putting in a letter just now."

Seidel puffed his pipe and waited. Reisman was an old pro and could not be hurried. He would say what he came to say when he was ready and after he had prepared the ground carefully.

"The President wants you to co-operate in every way with Talcott Bailey. Even if you don't agree with him. Even if it means some inconvenience to General Tate. Am I getting through, Judge?"

Seidel felt a pang of disappointment. Of course he realized that the President played for higher stakes than one soldier's authority within his command. But the President had personally put Bill Tate here in the Sinai, and it was saddening to realize that he considered him expendable. "You are getting through very clearly," he said.

Reisman stood and walked to the window. He looked rumpled and tired. "This business about Trask—it's unfortunate, Judge. But if it comes to a showdown, the President is going to need Talcott and his supporters more than he needs a bright young general."

Unless and until it came to the real crunch, Seidel thought, the soldiers were always expendable.

"The Vice President has decided to exclude General Tate from the Zone Center meeting," Seidel said.

Reisman nodded. "A rap on the wrist."

"A little more than that. It will make it difficult, if not outright impossible, for him to deal effectively with Ulanov and the other Russians once you people leave here."

"I know," Reisman said. "It isn't the way the President would like to have it, but this Trask business caught everyone unprepared." He turned and looked hard at Seidel. "And it *was* General Tate's responsibility to see to it that nothing like that happened—particularly at this time."

"Yes," Seidel said. There was no denying it.

"The President's had to—leave town for a few days because of it. He doesn't want to see the Russian Ambassador until after the Zone Center meeting. Secretary of State Green is contriving to be unavailable as well."

"Yes." Seidel said again.

"Does Tate understand all this?"

"Of course."

"He'll stick to his refusal to relieve Trask?"

"I'm sure of it," Seidel said. Then, with a slight edge in his voice, he added: "Just as I'm sure the President is counting on it. If Trask were relieved because of a Russian protest, the President would have Admiral Ainsworth and the war hawks on his back."

Reisman regarded Seidel appraisingly. "I see you haven't lost your political instincts, Judge."

"Politics isn't something you forget."

A thin smile touched Reisman's meaty features. "Like riding a bicycle."

"May I speak freely?"

"Please."

"I'm to do everything I can to convince Bill Tate he should give in to Talcott Bailey—knowing that he will not. I'm to do this to appease Bailey and his people because the President wants them kept—if not happy—at least quiet. Am I correct so far?"

"Please go on, Judge. Get it off your chest."

"And when the Vice President returns to Washington, the President will relieve Tate, perhaps retire him. Right?"

"Possibly."

"He'll do this even though Tate is within his rights to refuse to get rid of Trask. That way the President will have quieted both Bailey's doves and Ainsworth's hawks. The only cost will be Bill Tate's career. The fact that he is probably the best young commander in the Army isn't important."

"It's important, Judge. But not vital. If we were at war or

near to it, we'd have to play it differently. But you don't get something for nothing. What is important is that the accord will have been renewed—*signed by Bailey*—and the U.S. Component will stay in the Sinai. As a force for peace, the way two Presidents have intended, and not as a counterforce salient, as Ainsworth sees it. The President likes and admires General Tate, Judge, but what must be must be."

"Yes," Seidel said wearily. "The doctrine of interposition must survive—even if Bill Tate doesn't. It makes a dirty sort of sense."

"No one knows any better than you do that politics isn't a sporting game. The President has to ride two horses in the party, and one of them belongs to Bailey's organization. We can't have another party split now. Three years from now—after some solid spadework—our wing of the party will be strong enough to win an election even if the isolationists refuse to read the handwriting on the wall."

"I had hoped," Seidel said, "that domestic politics wouldn't influence decisions about the Sinai this early. I was naïve, of course. I've been away from Congress too long, I suppose."

"Yes, Judge. Naïve is the word. The people have repudiated Bailey's sort of isolationism at the polls every time it has been put to them. But the *party,* Judge— You know how important a working united party campaign can be. You saw what happened in the early seventies. The President doesn't intend to let the party split within itself. But we need time to consolidate positions and make certain that we have the support of most of the doves when the time comes to go to the people again. We need to make *sure* we have an electable candidate, Judge."

"I didn't realize the President was so uncertain about his popular appeal," Seidel said, the edge coming back into his voice.

Reisman silently studied Seidel's craggy face. "Judge, I'm going to say something to you—in deepest confidence. So that you'll see the need for all this—unfortunate business. But let me preface my statement by warning you that I am prepared to deny this conversation ever took place. Even under oath and the threat of an accusation of perjury. Is that understood?"

Seidel nodded slowly, a frown creasing his brow.

"The President is a great one for using the carrot and the stick. We agree on that, I think."

"Too well," Seidel said.

"And you are thinking right now that that letter in your pocket is the carrot. Right?"

"The thought occurred to me."

Reisman shook his head. "The President doesn't have to buy your loyalty. He knows that and so do you. He's old-fashioned in many ways. He thinks a president should be president of all the people. He's been a good president so far. We agree on that?"

"I know how good he is," Seidel said.

"Bear with me. And think about what I am saying very carefully, please. He believes that the people support the idea of Americans helping to keep the peace here in the Sinai. Do you?"

"Yes."

"Without qualifications?"

"The nation knows we can't ever be isolationist again, no matter what Bailey's constituents think. I agree with that."

"Do you think Bailey knows how the voters feel?"

"He's an intelligent man. He knows."

"But?" Reisman waited, as though the question were rhetorical—as, in fact, it seemed to Seidel.

"The Vice President belongs to that group who knows better than the people. Call them elitists, if you want labels. There are no surprises in this, Mr. Reisman."

"All right, then. Here is a surprise for you," Reisman said deliberately. *"The President isn't going to run for re-election."*

Seidel felt a cold shock. It was as though the very foundation upon which he had built his political thinking of the last years had just cracked and was about to shatter.

Reisman said, "He can't, Judge. There are good reasons. The main one is the question of his health. The President has Parkinson's disease. This fact is secret, but the diagnosis is confirmed. There just isn't time for him to do what he wants to do for the country."

"My God," Seidel said in a quiet tone. "I had no idea."

"He can finish his term, but he can't run again."

Seidel drew on his pipe and found it cold. He tapped the dottle into an ashtray with a distracted, mechanical motion. Presently he said, "It is difficult to come to grips with something like this. What about Talcott Bailey? Does he know?"

Reisman shrugged. "One can't be sure, Judge. Secrets aren't easily kept in Washington these days. We think this one is safe. If it leaked to the press, the least we could expect would be a campaign for a resignation and a Bailey takeover."

"That would be disastrous," Seidel said heavily.

"The point is that Bailey probably could not win the presidency at the polls, Judge. And if he should, by some miracle, squeak through, think what that would mean. The armed forces cut to almost nothing. Treaties abrogated. Allies lost. Ainsworth and his friends would call it outright treason. We'd explode internally. I don't question the Vice President's sincerity or his honesty. Maybe he wouldn't actually do what he has been saying should be done; maybe he wouldn't disarm unilaterally; maybe he wouldn't pull out of NATO and SEATO and the Sinai. But if he *says* it, I have to believe he *means* it. Talcott Bailey as president of the United States is an invitation to international blackmail. And the invitation would be accepted with glee by quite a few. I don't even like to think what it would mean to people like the Israelis, who have trusted us to stand strong as a restraint against super-bullies."

He paced the small bare room. Then he stopped and looked

hard at Seidel. "So it can't be Talcott Bailey now—or next time. It is as simple as that."

"Has the President made a firm decision about this?"

Reisman slowly nodded. "Always barring the unforeseen, of course. He has."

"Who?"

"Associate Justice of the Supreme Court Jason Seidel."

"You *can't* be serious!"

"It doesn't much matter whether or not I can be. Though, in point of fact, I concur with the President's opinion, for whatever that is worth. I assure you *he* is *quite* serious."

"Good God."

"Think about it, Judge. You are the right age, the right party. You have the brains, and God knows you have enough integrity for two presidents. Yet you understand the realities of politics. You've served in the Congress, and you will have served on the highest court. It's been two generations since a Supreme Court justice even made a try for the presidency—but the President thinks the time is right. Or will be, after you've been on the court for a year or two. Think about it. You aren't widely known now, but you will be by convention time. And be certain of this: *If he wants you, you're right for the job*. You are old friends, but if he didn't think you were the best choice, he wouldn't let you get near the White House. Believe me, Judge, he'd throw you, me, Bailey, or the Virgin Mary into the brimstone if he believed it was right for the United States. He's that tough, and you know it. What's happening here ought to convince you, if you should have any doubts on that score." His expression changed to one of mingled envy and pity. "I wish to God he trusted *me* half as much as he trusts you, Judge."

Seidel's thoughts tumbled. What words were adequate to reply to this? His life had been spent in politics and the law. For politics, it was customary to substitute the euphemistic "public service." But he knew, as all politicians know, that such a life isn't spent in pure service. Ambition was always there, prodding, urging. He had never looked as high as the presidency, but if the President thought it could happen, then it could. Jason Seidel could become president of the United States. The idea was numbing, exciting—in the end, humbling.

Reisman said, "Well, Judge?"

"I don't know. It will take time to get used to this."

"The President wants you to attend the Zone Center conference. Can you handle Bailey, or shall I call the White House and have him get the word direct?"

Seidel wondered briefly if this was some sort of test, a trial of his ability to deal with Bailey and his people. And with a stab of regret he realized that from this time forward each new task, each suggestion, would arouse suspicion in him. "I'll handle it," he said.

"Good." Reisman extended his hand, and Seidel took it. Then Reisman opened the door and stood for a moment against the starry dark of the desert night. "You've been touched by fate, Judge. See you in the morning—Colonel."

Captain Elizabeth Adams was finding it difficult to sleep. First there had been the oppressive heat all through the day, and then through most of the evening the khamsin had blown, raising a mist of fine dust and sand that sifted under doors and into the air-conditioning systems of offices and sleeping quarters. Now the night was still and cold, with the frighteningly brilliant desert stars burning like evil gem stones in a sky of absolute blackness.

Her mind was troubled by the events of the long day. The meeting at El Arish had seemed to promise that the day would be like any other meeting day in the Peacekeeping Area, and yet almost from the moment the General and his party left the Russian headquarters the day had begun to crumble into a confused and disquieting series of mishaps.

She kicked away the covers and lay in the darkness, thinking about the General. Presently she felt her own hands touching her thighs and belly through the thin cloth of her pajamas. She could almost imagine the hands were not her own, but his. She flushed and sat up abruptly. It was disgusting, she thought, to let her imagination run away with her that way. William Tate did not love her: he scarcely knew she was alive. No, that wasn't fair. But he certainly did not think of her as a sex object. He *respected* her—as a soldier and for her skills, her intelligence, her loyalty. But he didn't think about her as a woman at all. That was reserved for someone else.

She went to the door, opened it, and stood looking out across the compound at the silent buildings across the square. Even the town was silent. Sometimes, at this hour, one could hear, carried on the wind, the faint sounds of Arab music from the cafés. But in the stillness tonight there was nothing.

She shivered and turned back to her room, but the dark cubicle seemed oppressive. She slipped a greatcoat over her night clothes and stepped outside onto the grass of the square. Standing under the sky, the grass brittle against her bare feet, she wondered what Bill Tate would say if she suddenly presented herself at his quarters. The thought was so incongruous that it made her want to laugh and cry at the same time. The cold lawn against her feet and the night air against her legs made her feel peculiarly naked and deliciously vulnerable. She knew that she should return to her room, because within minutes some soldier doing interior guard duty would encounter her and she would feel the fool wandering about the compound in pajamas and greatcoat. But, instead, she made herself walk across the grass square until she stood at the corner of the second compound, from which she could see lights in the building where the Israeli officers lived. Now she knew why she had come out into the night, and the realization revolted her. Standing in the shadows she looked over at Deborah Zadok's quarters, and there was a dry taste in her mouth as she saw the tall, broad figure of Sergeant Major Robinson standing guard.

The General was with his Jewish mistress. The same sometimes out-of-control imagination that saw the Russians across thirty-four east as Mongol barbarians now created naked images of Tate and the Israeli girl. Liz's stomach griped with the nausea of raw jealousy. For just an instant she wished with all her heart that she could kill the Jew, disfigure her, claw her heavy Jewish breasts, and push nails into her Jewish belly—

The sound of a step behind her brought her reeling back into cold reality. She was trembling, frightened by the intensity of her feelings. Turning, she almost collided with a man wearing a flying jacket. It was a moment before she recognized Colonel Trask. She could smell the strong odor of liquor on his breath.

"What the hell!" he said. "It's Adams, isn't it?" His disfigured face was invisible in the starlight, and he reached out to steady Liz, who had stumbled as she stepped back against the building. "Easy, there, Captain," he said.

Liz retreated another step. She had to move around him to return to her quarters and found that she could not do it.

Trask said, "They closed the bar at the officers' club. Threw everyone out. Big day tomorrow."

Liz realized that he was drunk, but his voice was firm and tinged with anger.

"I came out for a walk. I couldn't sleep." Her remark sounded inane, but she felt the need to say something.

"I wouldn't go over there," Trask said. "That black bastard might make trouble."

She felt the blood rising to her cheeks. Did everyone around headquarters know what their commander was doing and how she felt about it? It was too degrading to believe. "I'm going back to my quarters. Good night, Colonel."

Trask's hand caught her arm and held her. "Tell me something, lady soldier. Am I supposed to be grateful to the big man over there for not sacking me?" He was drunker than Liz had thought, and his sudden violence frightened her. She pulled away, but he held her. "What's the matter, Captain? Can't answer that? Then try this one. What are we supposed to do with a commander who thinks with his balls instead of his head?"

Liz pulled free. "You're despicable, Colonel," she said in a trembling whisper. "Now let me by."

Trask stepped aside. "When you tell him about this, Captain, be sure you tell him where we were when it happened." He touched the peak of his cap in a mock gesture of salute and turned away, walking with a slightly rolling gait toward the bachelor officers' quarters. Liz watched him go, tears of fright and humiliation hot in her eyes. Hugging herself against the cold, which now seemed much more intense, she stumbled back toward her own quarters.

This was the Jewish woman's fault, she thought shakily. Because of her, Trask could say things like that about General Tate and laugh at him. Somehow, sometime, God or Fate or Liz Adams would find an opportunity to make Deborah Zadok pay for what she was doing to a brave and gallant man.

In a dingy office on the ground floor of an old building in Makhsus Road, near Tehran's Mehrabad Airport, an Israeli trader opened the door of his leather-goods warehouse to a traveler who had crossed the Soviet border earlier in the evening at the seldom-used post south of Ashkhabad.

The traveler delivered a roll of badly tanned and odoriferous leather and departed. The trader locked his door, unrolled the hides, and withdrew a plastic packet containing six photographs.

The prints meant nothing to the trader, who was, in fact, a legitimate businessman in Iran. From time to time he received such shipments and delivered them to the trade attaché of the small Israeli legation staff in Tehran. He was aware, of course, that he formed part of an espionage apparatus, but he was assured that he was not engaged in any activity that threatened Iran in any way, and he was reasonably certain that the Iranian police watched without intention of interfering. He suspected—correctly, as it happened—that much of the information coming out of the Soviet Union along the line of communication of which he was a small part was shared with Iranian authorities.

The lateness of the hour prevented him from delivering the plastic packet of satellite photographs to the legation representative. There was no indication that the material was other than routinely obtained, and therefore it required no special haste in handling. He locked the packet in his office safe, for delivery at the opening of the business day. He then turned off the lights, locked his establishment, and went home.

The high-resolution photographs taken that morning by Cosmos 623 were over halfway to Jerusalem. They would not begin to move again until nine in the morning, and they would arrive at Mosa'ad headquarters in Jerusalem only three hours before the time set for the Russian-American meeting at Zone Center, astride thirty-four east.

At Andrews Air Force Base in Washington, Air Force One was being scrupulously checked over preparatory to the President's takeoff early in the morning for Palm Springs.

In his stateroom aboard the *Allende* in Alexandria's harbor, Deputy Premier Anatoly Rostov slept fitfully, disturbed by the unfamiliar shipboard noises of a docked vessel.

In Ismailiya, KGB Colonel Grigory Novotny, working late because of his late start, finally put his signature to an order of the day to the full company of KGB troops assigned to escort Rostov to Zone Center.

Father Anastasius, now delirious from the pain of his shattered hand and tortured by hordes of devils in the night, stumbled through the tumbled boulders in the darkness. Lost, the old monk moved northwestward, rather than eastward. As the Abou Moussa Commando stirred and began to ride into the DMZ some few kilometers south of him, Anastasius—fleeing Saracens and demons—continued into the Russian Sector.

Behind him, the first hint of daylight limned the ridges of Sinai's central massif against the sky.

12

General Tate did not consider himself an introspective man, or one given to extensive self-examination. But he spent the early hours of the morning in fitful sleep with many wakings. The day before had been a day of near disaster. The events that had conspired to undermine his confidence had been of a sort that he could easily have handled singly, but in combination they filled the dark hours before dawn with an unfamiliar despair.

Love and politics had never been his primary preoccupations. He had never thought them to be suitable concerns for a professional soldier. Yet now he found that he faced a crisis in both—a crisis that he felt, suddenly, was beyond his capacity to resolve.

He had used Deborah Zadok in a way that angry men had used women since the beginning of time, and he was sick of himself. He had taken her last night, not in love or affection, but as an anodyne for the frustrated fury aroused in him by Talcott Bailey. He had made a camp follower out of her, and the act had degraded them both. Worse, it had opened the hidden chasm between them. To justify his behavior, he had allowed her association with Mosa'ad to surface between them, and his having done so made a continuation of their affair impossible. The thought of a future without Deborah seemed bleak beyond all expectation.

His interview with the Vice President had been worse than expected. He had been prepared for Bailey's anger over the *Allende* incident—he would have reacted the same way had their positions been reversed. But he had not expected the extent to which the Vice President was prepared to go to make clear his distaste for the military. Bailey had decided, against the recommendations of his own military aide and the head of his Secret Service guards, to limit his escort to Zone Center to a single squad of soldiers and a communications team. Tate would have thought this unwise in any case, but the fact that the decision had been made as both a political ploy and an overt chastisement of the commander of the U.S. Component he found almost insupportable. It angered him because it indicated contempt for sanity as well as for the armed forces. It worried him because it made it impossible to guarantee the Vice President's safety in an area under his command. And it embittered him because his own exclusion from the official party was petty and insulting. It would make his dealings with the Russians and Egyptians difficult in the future. And it suggested that the President, on whom the component relied for support and good will at home, had weighed an effective American presence in the Sinai against the approval of Bailey's doves and was ready to temporize. Once again, it seemed, politics and expediency had blindly triumphed over all-too-clear reality.

At first light Tate dressed and made an inspection of the vehicles selected for the Vice President's convoy. During the night a number of news people had arrived in Es Shu'uts from Cyprus with film and taping equipment. There were no facilities at Zone Center for direct ground-to-satellite transmission, so the ceremonies would be recorded and rebroadcast from Echo Sierra Control. Still, the amount of equipment the network technicians had unloaded at the airstrip was considerable and necessitated two eight-by-eight turbotrucks. Ordinarily all this gear would have been sent ahead, to be in place for the Vice President's and the Deputy Premier's arrivals at Zone Center. But the tight restrictions on travel of any sort in the demilitarized area by other than UN personnel had made it necessary to enlarge the Vice President's convoy to accommodate the newcomers. Paul Bronstein, Bailey's spokesman, had held an extensive press briefing at the Falasha late last night. Even this event had produced a small incident. Bronstein had refused to let the component information officers participate, saying that their presence would produce a "chilling effect." It had therefore been necessary to hold a second briefing by members of the component information staff to explain the peculiar military dispositions in the sector, the travel arrangements made by the component, and the expected accommodations at Zone Center. Sam Donaldson's CIA people had attended both briefings, of course, though Bronstein did not know it.

By 0700 hours the convoy was in readiness, the single squad from the Special Forces detachment was standing by, with Sergeant Major Robinson in command, the cameras and recording gear had been loaded. In typical army fashion, Tate noted, all preparations had been completed in plenty of time to keep the troops standing around in idleness for several hours before departure. For the first time that morning, he allowed himself the privilege of annoyance. He stood for a time regarding the convoy and the soldiers waiting in the main square of the compound. The sky was thinly overcast this morning, and the rising sun cast long, pallid shadows across the grounds. The American flag and the Circle and Arrows standard of the Peacekeeping Force hung limply on their staffs in front of the headquarters building. The last chill of the desert night was dissipating, and the morning work force was straggling from the cantonments and from the Falasha grounds toward the harshly glittering tower of the Glasshouse.

Tate called Robinson over and instructed him to dismiss the troops to the stand-by area, where they could smoke, talk, and drink coffee without disturbing the military decorum of the waiting convoy. Then he returned to his office to await the arrival of Seidel and the Vice President's staff.

At 0800 hours Tate received a visit from the Vice President's military aide. Crowell informed him that the Vice President wished Colonel Jason Seidel to accompany the official party to Zone Center.

"Permission granted, Colonel," Tate said. "I planned to send him, in any case—since the Vice President prefers me to remain in Es Shu'uts."

Crowell had the grace to look uncomfortable. "I am genuinely sorry about that, General," he said. "You realize there is nothing I can do."

"I understand, Colonel. I don't envy you your assignment," Tate said bleakly.

Crowell felt the need to explain his chief. "He isn't a petty man, General. Not really. He has some strong opinions about the defense establishment, that's all."

"Your loyalty is commendable, Colonel," Tate said in a dry voice. "The Vice President and I disagree on nearly everything except one point—that he *is* the Vice President. In the absence of specific orders to the contrary from the President, I will comply with his wishes in almost every particular."

"Yes, of course, sir."

Tate regarded Crowell appraisingly. He was a soldier with a first-class combat record, not a political soldier in any sense. That much was good, anyway. He said, "I am assigning Sergeant Major Robinson to handle the escort. As you may have gathered from the discussions at the Falasha last night, I think the escort is far too small. But since the Vice President wants it that way, I'm putting my best man in command of the detachment. There will be an air force officer assigned as communications specialist, but Robinson will be troop commander. He knows the country and the situation, Colonel. Please keep that in mind."

"Understood, General," Crowell said.

"Major Paris, my security officer, is at Zone Center now.

Ulanov's KGB man, Novotny, should be with him by this time. The UN constabulary commander is a Swede this month —they rotate command, as you know, among Swedes, Hungarians, and Indians. But they are short of personnel in the DMZ and they expect visitors from the occupying powers to handle most of their own security. Rostov will arrive with a full battalion of KGB troops, unless I miss my guess." He glanced through the windows at the thinly clouded, metallic sky. "I plan to fly cover on you until you move out of our sector. The Vice President made it clear he would prefer I did not, but he stopped short of giving me a direct order. So one of the helicopters you'll see will be mine. I think that covers everything, Colonel."

"Yes, sir." Crowell studied the man behind the desk, trying to judge the extent of his disapproval of the political manner in which this operation was to be conducted. The blue eyes were cold and noncommittal, the ordinarily firm mouth was set in a thin line. Major General William Tecumseh Sherman Tate was bloody angry, Crowell concluded. "If there is anything I can do for you personally, sir—"

"Nothing," Tate said. "But I thank you, Colonel."

When Crowell had gone, Liz Adams's voice came through the intercom. "Colonel Seidel is here, General. Can you see him now?" Her tone was flat, somehow strained, but Tate was too preoccupied to notice. He said, "Send him in, Captain. And when Rabin arrives, have him come in directly, too."

"Yes, sir," she said.

Seidel came into the office dressed in new and unfamiliar field kit: camouflaged fatigues and paratroop boots, webbing harness and blue beret.

"You look like a soldier boy, Judge," Tate said with a thin smile.

"I feel like a fool. Men my age shouldn't play dress-up," Seidel said. He was relieved to see that Tate had himself under control. This was a bitter morning for him, and possibly the beginning of a troublesome thirty-six hours. The responsibility for the Vice President's safety and the success of his mission rested on Tate's shoulders, but he had been seriously handicapped by Talcott Bailey himself.

"Look out for things, Judge," Tate said. "See that Robinson gets some co-operation from the civilians, will you?"

"Of course, General."

Tate leaned back in his chair. "Ulanov is going to ask you why I'm not with the official party. Keep explanations to a minimum. Those people are going to be tough to deal with after this is all over."

"I'm sorry. I wish there was something I could do."

Tate withheld comment for pride's sake. He was disappointed with the strength of the support he had received from his chief of staff. Somehow he had expected more.

Dov Rabin arrived with two officers of the Israeli Liaison Group. Deborah was not among them, and Tate was relieved. He had not been looking forward to seeing her this morning. When he did, he was not sure he could trust himself to keep his decisions impersonal and his attitude militarily correct.

Rabin, too, was dressed in field gear, and his two officers carried Uzi machine pistols slung over their shoulders.

Tate said, "The Vice President would prefer you don't make a show of weapons, Brigadier."

The Israeli smiled and said, "We will be as unobtrusive as possible, General. But since I understand we are traveling with a single squad of your soldiers, I thought it best to take some small precautions."

"Has there been any guerrilla activity Donaldson and Paris haven't heard about?" Seidel asked.

"The Arab Front has been very quiet. We have heard talk, but there is always talk among the Arabs, Colonel."

"Nothing more definite than talk?"

Rabin shrugged. "What do the satellites show, Colonel?"

"Very little," Seidel answered.

"We are expecting some Cosmos information from Mosa'ad, but it is not due at this end of the pipeline until this evening," Rabin said. "I have left instructions that it be forwarded to Es Shu'uts the moment we have it."

Tate felt a twinge of impatience. Intelligence work seemed fantastically and unnecessarily complicated to him. It was general knowledge at the higher levels of command on both sides of thirty-four east that Russian and American satellite information was routinely "stolen" and shared. But the very fact that it was so easily obtained made it suspect.

"Will the convoy have air cover as far as the Demilitarized Zone, General?" Rabin asked.

"Yes."

"I am relieved to hear it."

"Are you worried, Brigadier?" Seidel asked.

"No. But there is always the unexpected, isn't there, Colonel? And this movement will be largely one of civilians, as I understand it—the politicians, of course, and the news people with their equipment. Frankly, I would prefer fewer supernumeraries and more effectives. But the decision is not mine to make."

Everyone in the room knew that what Rabin meant was that the Israelis, with their experience with Arab guerrillas and the rugged Sinai terrain, would have handled matters quite differently. It was Rabin's way of stating his understanding of the situation in the Peacekeeping Area. The main responsibility for whatever happened in the Sinai was now Russian and American rather than Israeli and Egyptian. The superpowers had simply pre-empted the long confrontation in the Middle East; their own national interests demanded it.

When Rabin and his officers had gone to the assembly area, Tate said to Seidel, "There's one thing more, Judge." He seemed uncharacteristically reticent about speaking. Seidel, guessing what might be in his mind, waited.

"A personal thing, Judge," Tate said. "Look out for Captain Zadok, will you?"

"Of course."

"I'm uneasy about this mission. I don't know why. Maybe it

just goes against everything I've learned, to hang a plum like the Vice President of the United States out where the Arabs can reach him. Bailey could draw trouble between here and Zone Center." He frowned and stood staring at the Peace-keeping Force flag on the standard. "Hell, I don't expect anything to happen, Judge. But if it should—I won't be there. I don't like that. It makes me damned nervous. So—you'll do that, won't you? I mean about Captain Zadok?"

Seidel was touched. Bill Tate had never spoken so intimately to him, nor had he ever seemed vulnerable before. And until now he had never confirmed what Seidel already knew, that he was personally involved with Deborah Zadok.

He wanted very much to warn Tate that she was likely to be the lever with which his enemies would tip him into limbo. He wanted to give him some advice about the need to be, in this time and place, more self-interested. He was, after all, one of the bright young men of the Army, until yesterday a potential army chief of staff and eventual chairman of the Joint Chiefs of Staff. One didn't jeopardize all that for a Deborah Zadok. But he said only what Tate wanted him to say: "I will do what I can, Bill."

Dale Trask watched the departure of the Vice President's convoy with mixed emotions. He felt a perverse pride in the efficient and military way the departure was handled, though he was surprised by the weakness of the detachment assigned to escort the Vice President. This was a thing he would have to report in some detail to Admiral Ainsworth when he was sent back to Washington in disgrace (as he had no doubt he would be). But given the limited number of effectives, the motorcade managed to seem reasonably impressive.

In the first turbojeep rode four field-equipped Special Forces troopers. They were followed by an air force van containing the communications equipment that had to go wherever the Vice President went. Next came the Vice President's large car, in which rode Bailey, Crowell, Seidel, Bronstein, the senior Secret Service agent, and Reisman. The car, painted desert tan, flew a placard with the vice-presidential seal on one fender and another bearing the Circle and Arrows device of the Peacekeeping Force. No American flag, Trask noted. Typical of Bailey, that was, as though the sight of Old Glory would offend the Reds at Zone Center.

Behind the Vice President's car was a sedan with two more Secret Service men and two paratroopers from the Special Forces detachment. Next in line came a car laid on at the last moment to carry the news media people who had arrived last night, and this was followed by two trucks loaded with taping gear and cameras. Behind the trucks was a command car with the Israelis—Brigadier Rabin and Captain Zadok in back, two officers in front. The Israelis, at least, made no pretense of not being heavily armed. There were four Uzis in the car, and Trask could see the mounting for a heavy machine gun, though he had no way of knowing whether or not the gun was actually aboard. Behind the Israelis came a weapons carrier with more soldiers, and bringing up the rear was another turbojeep, carrying General Tate's black sergeant, who would take the point once clear of Es Shu'uts.

The sight of Robinson as troop commander for the convoy made Trask's scarred lips tighten in anger. He still smarted from the indignity of being, in effect, arrested by Robinson and marched like any stockade yard bird into Tate's headquarters.

The convoy had assembled in the compound square in front of the headquarters building. Tate had spent some few minutes in conversation with the Vice President and Seidel before moving down the line for a word with Rabin. Trask wondered whether or not Captain Adams was watching from inside the building. He had been drunk last night when he encountered her and he was vaguely sorry he had spoken to her as he did, but what was done was done, and it hardly mattered now, because it was likely he would not remain long enough in the sector to learn the results of his crude comments. He did not for one moment believe the headquarters scuttlebutt that Tate and Bailey had come to a tight-lipped disagreement on the question of relieving Lieutenant Colonel Dale Trask as tac-air commander. It was not possible that a political soldier of Tate's promise would risk his future over the relief of a light colonel of the Air Force with his ass in a sling—particularly since Tate had made no effort at all to hide his personal dislike.

Well, fuck you, my shiny young general, Trask thought. You've already half ruined yourself by screwing a Jew officer and by being so friendly with the Reds. I may get shot down, he told himself, but the Admiral will sure as hell not let Tate go on the way he was going here in the sector.

As the convoy had begun to move out, Trask stood at the corner of the BOQ and watched the lead vehicles clear the guard post at the compound gate and turn southwest, away from the town. Just past the Glasshouse the road veered more sharply south, and there was nothing but rock and sand for the hundred and twenty kilometers to El Thamad, where the motorcade would cross the DMZ.

Tate stood at salute as the Vice President's car rolled by and held it until the command car with the Israelis had passed. Trask noticed that only Rabin and the two officers in front returned the courtesy. Deborah Zadok looked away. Trask felt a stab of curiosity. Was something wrong there? Was Tate playing it safe, and had he brushed the woman off? It was the sort of thing one could expect a military politician to do. Convinced, as he was, that William Tate held his present rank because he was one of the chosen ones of the Army, a specially privileged creature from the day he first stepped onto the plain at West Point, Trask felt it secretly vindicated his resentment that Tate was doing something personally contemptible.

He watched until the last car reached the road and then returned to his quarters, closed the door, and poured himself a drink from the open bottle of Scotch on his dresser. He felt oddly aloof from the activities that had just taken place in the square. He had not felt this way since the strange days in the prison camp outside Hanoi. He used to listen to the bombs falling on the harbor and on the railhead near the camp with this same peculiar sensation of mingled apprehension and detachment. In those days his defiance and his hatred of the gooks kept him sane. Now, he supposed, it was his defiance and his dislike of General William Tecumseh Sherman God-dam Tate. It came to much the same thing, he thought, and finished his whisky.

Bill Tate watched Bailey's motorcade depart with very different feelings.

A voice at his side said, "Well, he does travel like a Man of the People, doesn't he? One squad and no fuss, thank you very much."

Tate turned his head. Donaldson stood beside him.

"It's his prerogative to travel any way he chooses," Tate said.

Donaldson ran a hand over his grizzled, crew-cut hair and grunted. "Rostov will arrive in grander style."

"Probably," Tate said. He watched the last vehicles of the motorcade pass the Glasshouse, shapes reflected darkly in the Lexan-and-glass surface. He turned away from the square and started for the helipad.

Donaldson kept pace with him. "Trask got loaded at the officers' club last night," he said. "What are you going to do about him?"

Tate suppressed a feeling of dislike for Donaldson, a dislike he instantly recognized as unfair. The Station Chief was simply doing one part of his job when he asked such questions, no matter how insinuating and impertinent they might seem.

"I haven't decided yet," Tate said. That was true enough, as far as it went. Trask would have to be relieved and sent back to Washington, but the timing of his dismissal remained to be worked out. Nothing could be done while the Vice President remained in the Sinai without its appearing to be a capitulation to political pressures.

"He had a word or two about you with Liz Adams."

Tate stopped abruptly and looked at Donaldson, his anger rising.

"I'm sorry, General. But you ought to know that Captain Adams was hanging around outside the Israeli quarters last night."

Tate's face whitened with the effort it cost him to keep his voice steady. "That's enough, Sam."

Donaldson's expression was mournful, but his eyes were cold and unblinking. "I'm sorry, General. I'm just doing my job. You are sitting on a land mine and it's my duty to tell you so."

Tate spoke with deliberation, accenting each word with frigid precision. "Limit yourself to keeping me informed about the opposition. I don't want to hear gossip about Colonel Trask, or Captain Adams, or anyone else. Do I make myself clear?"

Donaldson stared expressionlessly at Tate. At last he looked away and said, "If that's the way you want it, General."

"That's exactly the way I want it," Tate said, and strode off in the direction of the helipad. He was cold with fury, not least because he knew that he had just torn a strip off Donaldson for doing what he was paid to do: keep the commanding officer informed about everything taking place in his command. But what was that about Liz spying on him? That was absurd. Plain, honest Liz didn't spend her nights snooping on her commander's sex life. Or did she?

Damn, Tate thought angrily. The appearance of Bailey and his civilians in the sector was turning everything upside down. Reliable people had begun acting like fools. He reached the helipad scowling and in a filthy temper. Beaufort and Anspaugh alighted from the waiting gunship and saluted.

"Come on, come on," he said irritably. "Get aboard and

fire up. I want to ride shotgun on that convoy as far as Thamad. *Move.*"

The pilot and crew chief scrambled aboard the Huey, and Tate climbed into the right-hand seat by the open door. Anspaugh tried to help him fasten the shoulder harness, but he said impatiently, "Leave it, Sergeant. Let's get moving."

As Beaufort lifted the helicopter from the pad, Tate donned his helmet and fastened his harness. He was letting his temper get the upper hand, and he had better settle down. The wind and clatter coming in through the open doors gave him a sense of doing something, a sense of purposeful motion, and made him feel slightly better. But as Beaufort guided the Huey across Es Shu'uts and south toward the road to El Thamad, Tate could not shake himself free of the sense of angry foreboding that held him. Yesterday had been a bad day, and something warned him that today was going to be even worse.

13

The sky had taken on an odd hue, like that of beaten, tarnished silver, as the Abou Moussa Commando passed under the brow of Ras el Gineina. The mountain, which stood thirty kilometers from the UN compound at Zone Center, was over sixteen hundred meters high and barren. Its slopes, slashed and furrowed by eroded faults and draws bare of any vegetation, were steep. The Abou Moussa followed the ancient herdsmen's track three hundred meters below the rounded peak. Since the path was narrow, the guerrillas had fallen into single file, urging their stolen camels along between the escarpment and a deep ravine.

Enver Lesh had, with some difficulty, headed his animal into a small declivity from which he could see the entire line of march as it wound through the tumbled terrain.

Leila Jamil rode in the van, guiding the line of mounted men steadily northward. The *fedayeen* behind her seemed intent on watching the sky. Their vigilance was not needed, Lesh knew, because the terms of the Cyprus Accord expressly prohibited aircraft within the air space of the demilitarized area, twelve and one-half kilometers on either side of thirty-four east. The prohibition, he thought, was simply one more example of the incredible stupidity of the United Nations. No single nation would ever have agreed to leave a demilitarized zone undefended or unpatrolled from the air. Yet the nations of the General Assembly, acting in concert, had done exactly that—demanded it, in fact, as the price of their approval and co-operation with the occupying powers in the Sinai. Our strength, he thought, lies not in ideology but in the idiocy of others. What would Bakunin have thought of that? He would have relished it, of course. It would have delighted his nineteenth-century anarchist's heart.

Lesh studied his map once again. The commando was about sixteen kilometers from the Thamad road. He glanced at his watch and then at the sun, which seemed strangely pale today, dimmed by an almost imperceptible layer of thin, stratospheric cirrus. Figuring the time they would need, given the increasing difficulty of the terrain now that they were in the heart of the massif, he saw that they should have plenty of time to patrol the area and take up positions.

The Russians and the Egyptians were an unknown quantity, but they would be approaching Zone Center from the west, and, given any luck at all, the Abou Moussa—or what remained of it after the fire fight—would not encounter them.

The original plan, as conceived in Tirana, had made no provision for an orderly retreat to safety by the Arab survivors of the attack. Jamil and her men were totally expendable. Their usefulness, diminishing over the last years, would be utterly lost after they killed the American Vice President. In a matter of minutes they would become liabilities. It was therefore logical and proper that Lesh's orders were to separate himself from the survivors at the earliest possible moment and make his way alone to the southeast coast and there await the submarine that should even now be cruising off the Saudi Arabian island of Sanafir.

Lesh had been an irregular soldier too long, however, to be sanguine about his chances of ever making such a rendezvous. It was entirely possible that the submarine was nowhere near Sanafir. Simple common sense told him that an Albanian submarine would find difficulty in loitering in the northern waters of the Red Sea. Both the Soviet and the American navies cruised those waters daily, and Tirana would be unlikely to risk even a thirty-year-old ex-Russian sub on the slim chance of rescuing Enver Lesh.

But as he watched his force file past him, Lesh was exercising the inventive faculty that had kept him alive in Vietnam, Bengal, and Cambodia. Suppose, he asked himself, he were to modify the original attack plan slightly? Killing for killing's sake was all very well. As Bakunin said, "The passion for destruction is also a creative passion." The murder of the American and his party would serve Tirana and Peking most effectively, driving a wedge into the uneasy Soviet-American *détente*. But would it also serve Enver Lesh, who would dearly love to live to fight again some other day? It would immortalize him among revolutionaries (should anyone ever know of his part in the action—which was doubtful), but would it allow him to survive? The answer was clear. It would not.

He had less fear than most of dying, but he was unwilling to die if there was an alternative. And there *was* an alternative. Throughout the hours in which the commando moved north from the massacre of the sheepherders at Feiran, he had been pondering a third possibility, one that complicated his *tactical* problem but would immensely improve his *strategic* position.

Suppose, he asked himself, that by exercising great care (and taking commensurately higher casualties) it became possible to capture, rather than to kill, Talcott Bailey? What then?

The risks were enormous—greater by far than those entailed in simply murdering Bailey and his party, he felt certain. The Arab Front would, of course, take the major part of the blame. But it was unrealistic to suppose that the CIA, the KGB, Mosa'ad, and every other intelligence organization in the world would not ferret out little Albania's part in the crime. From Tirana, the path to Peking would be childishly simple to follow.

For a moment Lesh felt a thrill of sheer savagery. War would be a definite possibility. He could imagine the world's terror as the thermonuclear rockets came flaming out of their pits. The man who created that chaos would be greater by far than Bakunin!

But Lesh's mind, erotically aroused by pure destruction, could encompass a still headier thought. With the American Vice President as his hostage, he could very nearly dictate terms to anyone. The Americans, the Russians—even the Chinese, his ideological fathers—would be near to helpless.

He looked to the north, where Jamil was leading the file along a descending ridge toward the southernmost branch of Wadi el Arish, on the slopes of which Zone Center had been constructed. Jamil and her people—those who lived through the fight and all those others who sympathized with her cause throughout the Middle East and the rest of the world—would leap at the chance to take such a hostage as Talcott Bailey. With him alive in their hands they might open prisons in Israel and everywhere terrorists were held. They might even be able to drive the Soviets and the Americans out of the Sinai and back to their own borders. Lesh doubted this, but it was certainly worth attempting. It was better by far than dying here in these mountains, hunted down like beasts by raging Americans and frightened Russians.

He prodded his camel into a shambling run toward the head of the column. Jamil, he was sure, would approve of his change of plans.

An hour after leaving Es Shu'uts the Vice President's convoy was traveling the macadam track across the plateau of Al Qusaymah at a steady seventy kilometers an hour. The road, improved and rebuilt by U.S. Component engineers to carry military traffic between Thamad and the north coast, was today empty of traffic. Major Paris had seen to that. He had also ordered that while the party remained on the American side of the DMZ, there would be small detachments of soldiers stationed at ten-kilometer intervals along the route. He had instructed the troops to make themselves as inconspicuous as possible and to avoid disturbing the Vice President. But the convoy was to remain under surveillance until it crossed into the DMZ.

At Zone Center, the Major was now doing his best to persuade the UN commander, a fat Swedish general, that he should use the available troops in some more practical endeavor than the ceremonial parade he had planned for the arrival of the important personages. General Eriksson, who hated the desert and suffered from the heat and boredom of life at Zone Center, resented most Americans, and this American in particular. He did not like being told that he should disperse his men in the surrounding hills and wadis. He did not appreciate Paris's brusque American ways. He had called in all but the most distant UN patrols so that Zone Center might make a proper show when Deputy Premier Rostov and Vice President Bailey appeared, and he had no intention of revising his plans to assuage the paranoia of the Yankee intelligence officer at this late hour.

"I have been pulling in my patrols for three days, Major," he said loftily, "so that the Deputy Premier and the Vice President may see the caliber of the UN force here in the Demilitarized Zone. I have no intention of scattering my people over hundreds of square kilometers to guard against imaginary enemies."

"There are Bedouins everywhere in the DMZ, General," Paris said.

"A few tribesmen and their families, Major. Are you Americans frightened of them?"

The General's anti-Americanism presented Paris with an insuperable obstacle. It angered him, but he could do nothing.

"Be easy in your mind, Major Paris," Eriksson said in his precise school English. "This is, after all, UN territory."

Paris, standing on the low portico of the American-financed headquarters building under the Circle and Arrows and UN flags, looked across the American-built parade ground to the American-supplied concrete-block barracks and offices on the far side of the narrow valley. Citrus trees bought with donations from American school children lined the macadam streets paid for out of American voluntary contributions to the UN. "Of course, General," he said ironically. "I'd forgotten that."

In the Vice President's car, Jape Reisman sat quietly looking at the oddly metallic sky, the barren lunar desert of the north plateau, and the russet loom of the distant southern mountains. Talcott Bailey and Jason Seidel were involved in an increasingly acerbic discussion of the political situation in the United States. Paul Bronstein, sitting in front with the driver, occasionally turned to inject a comment or an opinion. The Secret Service man, Emerson, and Crowell rode in silence.

The Colonel's sharp eyes had picked out several of the temporary positions along the road, and Reisman could see that he approved of them. Thus far, the Vice President had made no comment about what were obviously security arrangements made without his knowledge or consent.

Seidel was saying, "I do not feel that there is general acceptance of isolationism at home."

Reisman suppressed a smile. The mention of the word "isolationism" was certain to make Bailey bridle. He did not consider himself an isolationist; though the distinction between Bailey and a real isolationist was difficult to define, he never failed to try.

"It is not isolationism to concentrate on our problems in the United States instead of on adventures abroad, Judge," Bailey said with an edge of irritation in his voice. "My constituency, as you call it, consists mainly of people who believe we should meet our responsibilities and commitments at home. You have been out of public service for a number of years now, and I suspect you are no longer in touch with the tides that are running very deep across the country."

"Perhaps you are right, Mr. Vice President," Seidel said.

But you very much doubt it, don't you, Reisman thought. Yes, the President had made a good choice of a potential successor in Seidel. With some seasoning, he might make one hell of a chief executive.

Bailey leaned forward and peered upward out of a side window. "Is that a helicopter I hear, John?"

Emerson craned to look, squinting against the thin, piercing light of the sun. Over the sound of the wheels on the macadam surface, Reisman could now hear the familiar whack-whack-whacking sound of a chopper.

"Yes, sir. A Huey gunship," Emerson said.

Bailey tightened his mouth.

Crowell said comfortably, "We have had air cover ever since we left Es Shu'uts, sir."

"William Tecumseh Sherman Tate marching through Georgia again," Bronstein said nastily. "He takes a good deal on himself, doesn't he?"

"Making sure the Vice President is safe, for instance," Crowell said, not succeeding in masking his dislike for Bronstein.

"I wouldn't put it past him to fly that thing straight into the DMZ," Bronstein said.

"I think not, Mr. Bronstein," Seidel said in a distant tone. "General Tate knows the terms of the accord as well as you do."

"I wanted our military presence kept to a minimum, Judge," the Vice President said.

"It would be difficult to reduce it further, sir," Seidel rejoined.

"We'll look mighty peaceable compared to what forces the Reds will have at Zone Center," Crowell said. He sounded disconsolate at the thought.

Bronstein glanced back through the car's rear window at

the command car carrying Brigadier Rabin and Captain Zadok. The girl was looking up at the helicopter, her dark hair blowing from under her cap in the dry wind.

Bronstein regarded the Israelis with suppressed resentment. In the ordinary course of events, he would have become, he supposed, a partisan of the State of Israel. He was a member of a large Jewish family, all of whom were heavy contributors of time and money to Jewish charitable and welfare organizations, including those whose purpose was to encourage and finance immigration of Jews from Eastern Europe into Israel. But he enjoyed his perversities, and the very fact that his relations and social peers were so dedicated to the Zionist position in the Middle East had been, long ago, enough to cause him to assume a quasi-pro-Arab stance. The incongruity of his position gave him a pleasurable contrariness, a bizarre satisfaction, so that, once taken, it was difficult to abandon.

His early intellectual development had been guided by a series of then-fashionable New Left teachers who had derived much satisfaction from the act of aligning themselves with all the forces challenging what they chose to call the "Establishment." Since the established American position on Israel had always been one of friendship, it naturally followed that their position must be critical of that stance.

While Bronstein was in college, his activist peer group had supported "liberation" organizations. That quite naturally expanded to include support for the various Palestinian refugee groups and, finally, for the then-active Arab terrorist organizations such as El Fatah, the Palestine Liberation Organization, and even Black September.

The Olympic murders of 1972, which took place while he was finishing his graduate work at Harvard, sufficiently shocked the young man to cause him to resign from organizations giving actual aid to the terrorists and the new coalition that became the Arab Front for the Liberation of Palestine. But an ingrained rationale for pro-Arabism remained very much a part of his political personality.

The bitter plight of the second- and third-generation Palestinian refugees, which he had seen firsthand as a member of the Vice President's staff, did nothing to change his predilection. To this was added the deep, if secret, inferiority he felt in his dealing with Israelis. Ghetto Jews he could accept, assured within himself that he had far surpassed them in freedom and power and authority and accomplishment. But the Sabras of Israel gave him no chance to feel superior. On the contrary, they often arrogantly appeared to demonstrate that he—like many American Jews—had lived safe and protected while they created a Jewish state out of the desert in the face of hostility from one hundred million Arabs.

He had managed, since joining the Vice President's staff, to temper his feelings and to hide the depth of his resentment of the Israelis. Talcott Bailey, for all his coldness and pedantry, was a fair man. He would never have tolerated an enemy of Israel on his staff in so sensitive a position as Paul's. Bronstein's attitude, as opposed to his statements, was assumed by Bailey to be the result of a devotion to even-handedness and a desire for equity for all participants in the continuing tragedy of the Middle East.

But now, looking back at the stocky Israeli general and the dark girl riding in the open command car, all of Bronstein's prejudices were close to the surface. Perhaps, he thought, it was this ancient earth—this wilderness of sand and rock—which had three times been efficiently, swiftly taken from its blustering landlords by Jews playing at soldier. There was something deeply moving about conquered land. It stirred his sense of outrage.

And on a somewhat lower emotional level, he resented the obvious fact that William Tate—the WASP golden boy, the chosen of the mighty in high places—got on so well with the Israelis. Which was natural enough, he told himself bitterly, considering how they strutted about, so *goyische,* the new Spartans. That Tate, who represented all Bronstein feared and despised in Gentile America, should regard these sunburned Jews with respect and affection touched a raw nerve.

Worse, he had just heard that it was common knowledge Tate was having an affair with the Captain. The idea revolted and angered him. He found it almost impossible to examine his reaction to this relatively unremarkable relationship. The idea of Tate screwing a Jewish woman affected him viscerally. He suspected the feelings were rooted in racial prejudice, but rejected the notion. He sincerely considered himself free of such flaws.

The object of Bronstein's concern, sitting beside Dov Rabin in the open command car, was looking toward the east, where the helicopter gunship had vanished on one of its sweeps ahead of the convoy. She was certain that *he* was piloting the aircraft, though it had crossed the track at too high an altitude for her to recognize any of its crewmen.

He had been disturbed and angered by being excluded from the party traveling to Zone Center. It was not possible to say with any certainty how much of his response had been due to the effect such a decision would inevitably have on the efficiency of his command of the U.S. Component and how much had been due to his concern for the safety of the Vice President. She knew that he disliked Talcott Bailey, that he disagreed with him on almost every point touching the American presence in the Sinai, and that he thought the Vice President an ideological disaster. Yet she was also sure that he had a deeply felt sense of duty and loyalty to those peculiarly American concepts that historically had subordinated their military to civilian control. It was an anomaly in one so arrogant—for he *was* that, she thought, arrogant and proud. In other armies, men like Bill Tate grew impatient and made military coups. In the United States Army, she thought, they accept their subordination and punish the women who love them.

Rabin spoke. "Is it he?"

"In the helicopter? I don't know. I think so," she replied. It was a measure of Tate's personality that there was no need for Rabin to be more specific.

Rabin indicated the desert to the west. The gunship had reappeared briefly, flying at low altitude over the rock-strewn plateau. It vanished again over a low range of hills ahead. "That is what I like best about General William—his trusting nature," he said with ironic approval.

Deborah looked bleak. "He trusted us, Dov," she said.

Rabin's dark eyes were understanding. "We have not harmed him, Deborah."

"Have you a mistress, Dov?" Deborah asked lightly.

"Several."

"And are *they* all spies?"

He grunted briefly. "I wouldn't be surprised."

"That's comforting."

"Don't dramatize the situation," Rabin said. "It is not as though we were his enemies."

"Oh, yes. There is that, isn't there." She turned from Rabin so that he wouldn't see the way her eyes glistened suddenly with tears. She was tired and overwrought, and last night had been her last time with Bill Tate. Somehow she was sure of it. Since morning she had carried a dead weight in her chest, a sense of unspoken and unacknowledged—but real—loss.

"I received further information on the Abou Moussa this morning," Rabin said.

"Are they in the Sinai?" she forced herself to ask, not really caring.

"Not according to our Jordanian source. It seems that they did not stay in the peninsula, but crossed back into Jordan and are moving south into Saudi Arabia looking for funds. I don't believe a word of it. I don't know where they are, but I'm certain our informer doesn't either. If he was any good, the Arab Front gunmen would have killed him long ago."

“God,” Deborah said, “I’m so tired of it, all the fighting and killing. When will it ever end?”

“Peace is coming, Deborah,” Rabin said. “Once the Russians and Americans came here, the price of war got too high. So believe me, peace is coming.” He drew a deep, weary breath. “All of us are tired. Even the Syrians and Libyans are worn out with fighting. There are only the guerrillas left, and they are dying out. It has to end, you see—one of these days.”

“But *he*—” Deborah lifted her chin at the Vice President’s car—“*he* wants the Americans to pack up and go home.”

“Fortunately for everyone, *he* is not president. It is not for him to say.”

Bleak comfort, Deborah thought, but what Dov said was true. As long as Russians and Americans, rather than Arabs and Israelis, faced one another across the thirty-fourth meridian, the price of war would indeed be too high for the world to accept. For a lifetime of cold and lonely nights, I will remember that, she told herself.

The group on the VIP ramp at Andrews Air Force Base, gathered to see the President off, included Admiral Ainsworth and Fowler Beal. A cold rain was falling as the President’s car arrived at the boarding steps of Air Force One.

On the flight deck Colonel Ira Dayton and the two new pilots, Campbell and Wingate, were completing the pre-takeoff checklist and preparing to start the engines as soon as the President’s party came aboard. Dayton decided that he would not make the takeoff. Campbell could use the practice, and, quite frankly, Dayton was forced to admit he did not feel at the top of his form. He had not slept at all well. “Take the left-hand seat, Major,” he said. “I’ll handle the radio.” He settled himself in the copilot’s chair and asked Andrews Flight Control Center for the final clearance. The center responded swiftly; one did not keep the President’s aircraft waiting for clearances. “You are cleared at three one thousand to Nashville Center, then three three thousand to Phoenix-Riverside. Palm Springs reports ceiling and visibility unlimited. Winds are from the north at thirty, gusting to forty. Temperature is fifty-one degrees." The voice grew less impersonal. "Cold and bumpy, Colonel. But there will be plenty of sunshine. Have a good trip."

Dayton acknowledged and looked out the flight engineer's window. The ramp lights were yellow in the murky, nasty light. Dirty water stood in puddles on the ferroconcrete surface, reflecting the barely lightening sky. The President and the Secretary of Defense had arrived with Helen Risor, some men from the White House staff, the Secret Service men, and the ever-present silent warrant officer who carried the "football"—the chained and locked case containing the nuclear-attack codes.

The President and Dickinson, both hatless in the rain, had stopped to have a word with Ainsworth and Beal. Presently the President left them and walked up the boarding stairs. Ainsworth and the ramp attendants stood at salute.

The intercom pinged, and Dayton picked up the handset. The first steward, a corporal, reported: "President is aboard, Colonel."

Dayton spoke to Campbell and Pete Craigie, the flight engineer. "Ramp is away. Wind them up."

With Wingate looking on from the third pilot's seat, Campbell, Dayton, and Craigie ran through the checklist of starting procedures.

The door to the flight deck opened, and the President's white head appeared. It was his custom always to exchange a few words with the flight crew before departure. "All set, Ira?"

"Ready when you are, Mr. President."

The President said, "New crew."

"Yes, Mr. President." Dayton introduced Campbell and Wingate, and the President said, "Don't get up, gentlemen. We'll have a chat later." He flashed his smile at the men in the cockpit and said, "Well, come on, Ira. Let's get out of this weather and find some sunshine."

"Yes, Mr. President."

Air Force One, its mirror-bright surfaces streaming mist, rolled to the holding area at the head of the active runway.

The Speaker of the House stole a glance at Ainsworth, whose face was stony in the rainy light; he seemed unperturbed by the President's decision to fly to Palm Springs so suddenly. "Of course he's ducking the Russian Ambassador," Ainsworth had said earlier, in that harsh, dry voice. "It doesn't matter. The Reds want the damned accord renewed more than we do. And why not? It legitimizes the bastards' presence in the Sinai Peninsula. He can afford to let State handle the *Allende* business. Please note that he is taking Dickinson out of range, too. That's good politics, wouldn't you say, Fowler?"

Beal wondered if he was correct in assuming, as he did, that the Admiral would give a great deal to be allowed to do more than buzz Russian ships. He would like to chase them out of the Mediterranean and up the Volga River at the point of a nuclear rocket. Beal tried to imagine what a confrontation such as that would mean to the always uneasy stability and peace of the world. It made him slightly ill. His mind, he had long ago decided, was simply not large enough to deal with the ultimate consequences of such concepts.

"Well, they're off," Ainsworth said.

Beal raised his eyes. Air Force One, anticollision lights flashing in the twilight, was moving down the runway, vaporizing sheets of spray from the puddles on the concrete as it gained speed. He had a moment's envy of the man in the airplane. In a few hours he would be away, in bright sunlight, walking confidently along a manicured fairway. He had the courage to depart, to take his pleasure while others remained in gloomy Washington to face the quarrels of the day. How marvelous it would be to so control one's own destiny.

Beal decided that he would not return home immediately. For years he had kept girls out in Rockville. First one and then another, but always someone who knew how to make a man feel good. The current one, Terri MacLean, would be sleeping when he arrived and would arise grumbling but warm from the bed. That would make up a little bit for having to stand in the rain and wish himself a bigger man than he was.

He looked at Ainsworth's grim face and then at the runway once more. The airplane gained speed, rotated into takeoff attitude, and left the ground. He watched it wistfully until its lights vanished in the murky, blue-gray sky above the nation's capital.

14

At approximately the time Vice President Bailey's motorcade reached the U.S. Component base at El Thamad, the diplomatic courier from Tehran appeared at the inconspicuous building in Jerusalem that housed the Russian Analysis Desk of Mosa'ad. Among the numerous items he delivered to the duty officer in the heavily guarded vestibule was the sealed plastic pouch containing the photographs taken of Sinai by Cosmos 623.

The material from Tehran was logged in, sorted, and dispatched to the appropriate destinations in the building. This process took about an hour and was completed somewhat after four o'clock. By that time the Vice President's convoy was rolling past the outposts of the First Para-Recon Battalion's southern perimeter, heading for the demarcation line of the DMZ, a half-dozen kilometers southwest.

At 1615, General Tate, flying his gunship at one thousand feet over the easternmost branch of Wadi el Arish, observed the convoy crossing into the Demilitarized Zone. He watched it until it turned south again along the road paralleling thirty-four east and terminating at Zone Center. He radioed his position and the position of the American vehicles to Echo Sierra and reluctantly turned north toward Es Shu'uts.

At this moment, in Jerusalem, the Cosmos photographs were being placed on the light table for examination. Earlier that afternoon, Major Avram Bar-Sharon, a paratrooper serving as military liaison in Mosa'ad headquarters, had assisted Moshe Greenblatt, the regular photo-evaluator, in an examination of the latest American Samos photographs of south Sinai. The Major, whose infantry unit had often come under fire in the occupied territory from Arab guerrillas masquerading as Bedouins, had been following with some interest the moves of a nomad band apparently foraging in the territory between El Tor, on the Gulf of Suez, and the edge of the southern Sinai massif. The American satellite cameras had first caught the band moving west along the coastal plateau. This had been some three days earlier. Unfortunately, Mosa'ad had been given no Samos material that would show its movements before that time. The Americans were willing enough to share their satellite information gleaned over the Peacekeeping Area, but they were less willing to supply the Israelis with photographs of adjacent Arab lands.

He and Greenblatt were now, with reason, interested instead in what the Cosmos photographs showed of the incident that had taken place yesterday off the north coast. The Russian satellite had done a first-rate job of catching the American pilot of the Shrike in the act of embarrassing Anatoly Rostov and the Soviet Navy, an incident that had the politicians in an uproar. The Cosmos photographs would be forwarded to Washington and Es Shu'uts after Mosa'ad had evaluated them. There was, as both men knew, a tacit understanding among the intelligence communities of the Soviet Union, Israel, and the United States that this kind of material should be leaked back and forth freely. The subterfuge of its being "stolen" made it possible to cut off the pipeline at any time the exchange of information was inconvenient. This was seldom done, though, because it was, in a practical sense, vital that each side should know what information the other side possessed and was using to make what otherwise might appear to be hostile strategic and political decisions.

Greenblatt, a frail young man with glasses and receding

curly black hair, bent over the magnified photograph of the waters off Es Shu'uts with calipers, making minute measurements. "This is something they can argue about forever," he said, studying the vernier scale on his instrument. "The *Allende* is exactly fifteen kilometers from the nearest land. The wake is closer, but there's a current there that sets toward the shore." He looked grim. "The American is hovering a hundred meters from the ship with his ordnance exposed. It's beautiful."

He bent again to make other measurements, this time of the visible features of the Soviet vessel, which was of a type not well known to Western intelligence agencies.

Bar-Sharon, while interested in both the incident and the ship to a degree, was a landsman and an infantry officer. His attention went to the photographs that had accompanied the frames of the confrontation off Es Shu'uts. He shuffled through the set until he found the photographs of the terrain between the Gulf of Suez and the foothills of Mount Sinai, and then began to search for the Bedouin band that had appeared in the recent American satellite films.

The definition and clarity of the Russian work were excellent, he thought, every bit as good as the American material. The Americans were more sophisticated in detecting and recording electromagnetic and thermal intelligence, but the Russian photographs were as sharp and clear as any he had seen. The sky over Sinai had been cloudless when this particular series was taken, and it was possible to identify objects on the ground as small as six inches across. That these pictures were taken from orbit, hundreds of kilometers above the earth, filled him with a sense of wonder.

The color was clear and true, and the satellite had produced a band of images that swept diagonally across the peninsula from the Strait of Gubal to the north coast. Offshore in the gulf could be seen the shapes of reefs below the surface of the clear water; near the African shore a dhow had been caught and recorded on paper and emulsion so sharply and clearly that Bar-Sharon could make out the seams in the decking fore and aft, the coils of rope at the stem, the nets hanging across the reefed sail to dry in the sea wind. A sailor or fisherman could be seen sleeping near the tiller and another man, in a white breechclout, squatted amidships mending nets. It was a feat of technology that Bar-Sharon found thrilling. What would those Arab dhow men think if they knew that they had been so clearly seen by an invisible eye hundreds of leagues in the sky? He could imagine their awe; he shared it.

At the edge of another print, the coastal plateau and the foothills of the Sinai massif, he could make out the steep scarps and near-vertical ravines that surrounded the holy mountain. On the next frame should be the Monastery of St. Katherine and the rock habitations of the herdsmen who had lived around the monastery for a thousand years. A faint smile touched his lips. Men such as these might better be able to accept the fact that they were under surveillance. Christians tended to feel that they were always under the eye of God.

He clipped the photograph to the light table and lowered the magnifying lens. There were his Bedouins—the same band he had been following in the American photographs. But they had turned away from the coast, he noted. Until now, their progress had seemed purposeful. Indeed, it had been this mild anomaly that had first aroused his interest in their movements. He had followed them—assisted by Samos—across the bottom tip of the heart-shaped peninsula. They had moved compactly—more compactly than was usually normal for nomads—toward a point on the coast south of El Tor. There was little in that area to attract them: the grazing was poor to nonexistent, and there was little chance of water. Occasionally Bedouin bands approached the coast for salt for their animals, and he had assumed that this might be their purpose. But this photograph showed that the band had turned away from the gulf toward the mountains. He knew that the sectors set up on each side of thirty-four east were totally ignored by these people who had roamed the area since Biblical times, but he noted that this particular band was moving out of the Russian sector toward the DMZ. The sabra in him tended to argue with the soldier, saying that arbitrary political lines of demarcation meant nothing to Bedouins. Why should they?

He looked through the magnifying lens with a feeling somewhat akin to omniscience, peering down on the images of his fourteen unknowing subjects.

Fourteen? Had he miscounted? He was certain that he had not. On the trek across southern Sinai there had been fourteen riders and some half-dozen pack animals. Now there seemed to be fifteen riders and *five* pack camels, heavily laden.

He frowned, turned the magnification on his viewer higher. Of course there was nothing particularly sinister about the fact that this band of nomads had added one man to their number somewhere along the coast—except that Bedouins were supremely clannish and simply did not pick up stragglers in the desert. He examined the photograph with renewed interest, his frown deepening.

"Moshe."

Greenblatt, bent over his own work across the light table, was too engrossed in his measurements of the Soviet missile ship to reply.

"Moshe." Bar-Sharon spoke with a note of urgency that alerted Greenblatt. He looked up.

"Come here a minute and see this," Bar-Sharon said.

Greenblatt put down his calipers and came around the broad table.

"Look at this frame."

Greenblatt sat down at the magnifier and studied the images on the print: the rock-strewn coastal plateau, the rising foothills and dry wadis, the russet-colored flanks of the swiftly rising mountains. It was very like the photographs he had seen of the moon, vertical elevations of a land without kindness.

Having just been concerned with clear blue water and white beaches, it took him a moment or two to attend to the details that Bar-Sharon was obviously interested in.

The Major said impatiently, "The riders. The Bedouins. Don't you see it?"

"What should I see?" Greenblatt asked.

"Well, to begin with, there are fifteen riders—not fourteen. *But look at the rider in the lead.*"

Greenblatt cranked the magnification up to the maximum. The face of the Bedouin seemed to leap upward at him, or, rather, he seemed to have plunged through the clear air until he was looking down at the upturned features from a distance of two or three meters. The man was hulking, powerfully built. He held his kaffiyeh in his hand, probably having removed it to let the sun strike his face and head—a thing that Bedouins almost never did. The man's broad cheeks and heavy mustaches were most un-Arabic, as was his pale skin. Now that his mind was alerted to anomalies, Greenblatt got the impression of camouflage cloth showing through openings in the man's robes, and the feet were shod, not in the felt shoes of a desert nomad, but in calf-height para's boots.

"Good God," he breathed. "We have trouble, I think."

"He is no Arab, that's certain."

"Definitely not an Arab," Greenblatt agreed.

"Then it follows that what we have there is not just a band of Bedouins."

Waiting no longer, Bar-Sharon reached for a telephone and placed a call to Military Intelligence.

Greenblatt said, "Hadn't we better notify the Americans?"

"That can wait," Bar-Sharon said, all soldier now.

Greenblatt was about to protest, and then thought better of it. This information came from a Russian satellite photograph. Therefore the Russians knew about it and knew that the Americans would receive the intelligence through the pipeline. If they had planned matters this way, it would do no harm to let the Yankees wait for a short time while the information was digested by Mosa'ad and the Israeli General Staff. But the Americans should be told that the Russians had definite evidence of a guerrilla band with a European (Russian?) adviser moving through the Soviet Sector toward the Demilitarized Zone.

Bar-Sharon concluded his telephone conversation and said, "They want to see for themselves. They'll send someone. Then if they agree with our appreciation, they will notify Washington and Es Shu'uts." Noticing Greenblatt's worried frown, he said, tapping the photograph, "Whoever he is, he's been in Sinai at least two days. Another half hour won't mean the end of the world, Moshe."

Greenblatt did not reply. He was busy setting up a copier, so that the face in the photograph could be measured for a computer run and, with some luck, an identification. He thought of the meeting about to take place at Zone Center, and of the important people who would attend it. Of course, security would be extremely tight. There would be soldiers by the battalion swarming over the ground near Zone Center. To imagine a guerrilla attack on such a meeting was next to impossible. Still, the mere fact that an act was outrageous and without hope of any practical success had never before stopped the fanatics of the guerrilla movement. Guerrillas had struck in Munich, in Khartoum, in London and New York and Paris. Even the outbreak of fighting that had resulted in the Cyprus Accord, a scrambled air-and-land engagement that was sometimes called the Near War, had been triggered by terrorism and murder. Anything, anything at all, was possible. Greenblatt, filled with a rising sense of urgency, shivered.

Anatoly Rostov, seated behind the armored glass of his staff car, fretted with impatience. He disliked traveling by automobile anywhere, and he most particularly disliked having to travel by car because of some senseless and arbitrary prohibition against aircraft inside a restricted area. When the Cyprus Accord had originally been signed, he, Anatoly Borisovich Rostov, had been a new member of the Politburo and unwilling to expose himself to criticism by attacking any of the provisions of the agreement. But even then he had foreseen that the prohibition of aircraft belonging to the four occupying powers in the DMZ would be, at best, an inconvenience, and it was possible to hypothesize situations in which the prohibition could be far more serious than a mere bother.

He had been riding, it seemed to him, since dawn. He had, quite properly, been flown as far as the town of Suez, and crossed the canal there. But then the motor trip had begun, made both necessary and tedious by the irritating fact that there were no suitable Russian bases between the head of the Gulf of Suez and thirty-four east at this latitude. Soviet strength had been heavily concentrated along the north coast of Sinai and near the populated areas of the Nile delta. The reasons for this were obvious, even to the opponents across thirty-four east: Soviet forces were in the Sinai only partially to help the Americans keep the peace between Arab and Jew. An equally strong motive for their presence was to carve a place for themselves as a strategic power in the Mediterranean. And one did not do this by scattering limited troops through a barren wasteland.

The result of this decision was that there were wide areas of Egyptian and Russian responsibility in the peninsula that were left unguarded and undeveloped. A secondary result, at present more annoying to the Deputy Premier, was that one could travel two hundred kilometers across west-central Sinai—over an abominable road built by Egyptians—without finding a place to stop and stretch one's legs and drink even so much as a glass of tea.

Now the long, heavily guarded convoy had come to a jolting stop some twenty kilometers from the western boundary of the Demilitarized Zone. The trucks carrying the first

KGB companies had emptied the moment there was a pause, the troopers scattering into an alarming display of guardianship around the limousine carrying Rostov and General Ulanov. Rostov, peering through the thick windows, could see absolutely nothing but a wilderness of sand and small boulders dotted with an occasional bush of *spina Christi*. There was no real cover within a kilometer on either side of the road, and no possible place where danger could hide. That blustering sot Novotny could only be putting on some sort of idiot display of vigilance in the mistaken notion that it would erase the bad impression he had made during the reception in the wardroom of the *Allende*.

Rostov turned to Ulanov, who sat stolidly beside him, and said, "Go see what that fool is up to, Ulanov. We'll never reach Zone Center on time at this rate."

Ulanov left the car with the young officer serving as his aide and walked toward the head of the stalled column. Rostov lit a cigarette and spoke to Captain Zakharov. "What force do the Americans have down here?"

The naval officer shrugged. "Very little more than we have. A battalion of parachute infantry at El Thamad. The Jews keep an air squadron at Eilat, just outside their sector. There is little point in stationing men in this part of the Sinai, Comrade Deputy Premier."

Rostov grunted agreement, looking again at the empty landscape around the stationary convoy. He shifted his weight uncomfortably on the seat and let his carefully controlled sense of history stir him. Though there was little of interest to see but desert and milky sky, this land through which he was traveling was interesting. It was a palimpsest of man's past. Alexander of Macedon's troops had marched through the Sinai on their way to Egypt, and so had the legions of Rome. Before them, Assyrians and Babylonians had driven their chariots across these wastes. Five thousand years of armies marching and countermarching had left a spoor of man's futility on the land, a thing that could be discerned by one sensitive enough to detect it. He allowed himself to wonder if five thousand years in the future the marks of Russians and Americans on this earth would be as faint. It was a most un-Marxist thought, and it made him uncomfortable.

Ulanov came lumbering back from the head of the column and thrust his head through the open door. "The point has picked up a wounded man, Comrade Deputy Premier. He seems to be a monk—an old man—and in a bad way, it seems."

"A monk? Here?" Rostov's skeptical tone encompassed the empty landscape.

"He isn't making much sense, but apparently he is one of the fathers from the Monastery of St. Katherine."

"But that's a long way from here," Zakharov said.

"A fair distance," Ulanov agreed. "Nevertheless—"

Rostov cut him off. "Wounded, you say?"

"His hand is badly hurt. By gunfire, I'd guess. Novotny agrees."

Rostov turned to look enquiringly at Zakharov.

"I've never heard of the Bedouin attacking the monks, Comrade Deputy Premier," Zakharov said. "But it is possible, of course."

"What shall we do about him, Comrade Deputy Premier?" Ulanov asked.

"What does the medical attendant say?"

"He's dressing the hand—or what's left of it. But the man will need more attention."

"Can he talk?"

Ulanov shook his head. "He's raving. In Greek. About Saracens and the charnel house."

Rostov looked again at Zakharov for an explanation.

"The charnel house is the ossuary at St. Katherine's. At the holy mountain, Comrade Deputy Premier."

The use of the word "holy" to describe Mount Sinai did not escape Rostov. Zakharov was known to hold archaic crypto-Christian notions. Such leanings were still to be found among children of the old aristocracy, even after fifty years of Marxism.

"He is out of his head," Ulanov said, "but when he speaks of a battle it is worth listening, Comrade Deputy Premier. His Saracens could be a bandit gang."

Rostov thought for a moment and then said, "That Egyptian—what's his name? Suweif. Where is he?"

"At the head of the column, bothering the medic and shouting Arabic at the patient," Ulanov answered.

"Get him," Rostov said to Ulanov's aide. The young officer trotted off.

"What's all this about Saracens?" Rostov asked.

"To a monk of St. Katherine's, anyone with weapons could be a Saracen," the old General said.

"The last 'Saracens' to attack the community of Mount Sinai were Haroun-al-Raschid's men," Zakharov said.

Ulanov shrugged. "A matter of definition. This old man is a Macedonian peasant, who has probably spent fifty years or more tending saints' bones in a monastery. If there are any so-called Saracens about, I think we should get the Deputy Premier to Zone Center without any further delay."

"Agreed," the naval officer said.

Rostov looked from one man to the other. "You aren't suggesting we haven't enough force to handle a band of Bedouin hooligans, are you?"

Before either could reply, General Suweif, still wearing the medals he had displayed at the reception in the wardroom of the *Allende,* came hurrying down the line of vehicles. "This is very distressing, Comrade Rostov," he said breathlessly. "The old monk has been brutally injured—and in the Soviet Sector."

Rostov frowned. "Your indignation is noted, General. It might be more useful, however, if you could venture an opinion as to who might have shot him."

The Egyptian gestured extravagantly. "Why, Bedouins, of course. The desert people are notoriously lawless. If the Soviet government would take its responsibilities more seriously, Comrade Rostov—or if it were more generous with matériel, so that we could patrol these areas regularly—"

"Thank you, General. As you say, it took place in the Soviet Sector, and it is therefore a purely Russian matter." Having gone through the motions of consulting with his Egyptian liaison, Rostov dismissed the distrait officer without further comment. He turned to Ulanov. "When can I talk to the monk?"

"The medical attendant has given him morphine, Comrade Deputy Premier. But perhaps when we reach Zone Center the old man may be ready—"

"The man is obviously dying," Suweif said, unwilling to be dismissed.

"We can do little for him out here," Ulanov said, ignoring the Egyptian pointedly.

Rostov turned suddenly back to Suweif. "What guerrilla activity has there been on this side of thirty-four east, General?"

The Egyptian was taken aback. "Why, none. Absolutely none, Comrade Rostov. When the government of the UAR signed the accord, it was understood that the Arab Front and the other liberation fighters would not be allowed access to the Sinai."

"From time to time those liberation fighters have taken another view of the situation, I believe," Zakharov said.

Colonel Novotny, his thick figure festooned with field equipment and weapons, jogged across the road and saluted Rostov. "My men have scouted the area, Comrade Deputy Premier, and found nothing. May I radio to Suez and have an air search conducted?"

"How far could the monk have come with that wound, Novotny?"

"It is impossible to say, Comrade Deputy Premier. He is very old, but these monks are like tough leather. It could have been a long way."

Rostov came to a decision. "Never mind the air search. The aircraft could not cross into the DMZ, and we have had enough incidents during my visit here. Let's get under way and get the monk to Zone Center. Perhaps we can unravel the mystery there."

"I will call my men in at once, Comrade Deputy Premier," the KGB man said. Rostov watched him trot away toward the head of the column. Why were the State Security forces always run by such blusterers? Was it a natural development of the endlessly proliferating bureaucracy the Soviet state had become?

"Should we radio the Americans and tell them about the monk?" Ulanov asked.

Rostov was about to assent but remembered that Ulanov seemed to feel what was, in his opinion, a dangerous friendship for the American commander. Co-operation was fine, in its place, but it could be overdone. He, personally, would tell the American Vice President about the wounded monk when they met at Zone Center. It would be interesting to test Bailey by seeing what his response would be to the suggestion that guerrillas were operating in southern Sinai, under the very noses, as it were, of the occupying powers. There was always some advantage to be gained by probing at one's opponents with unsuspected bits of seemingly irrelevant information. "No, Comrade General. Time enough for that when we finally reach our destination. If we ever begin to move again. Perhaps, General Suweif," he added, "it would be safer if you were to ride back here with General Ulanov and me."

The Egyptian accepted the offer with alacrity. Another fool, Rostov thought. The world was filled with them.

Father Anastasius saw his rescuers through a film of pain and feverish delusions. They had given him something that dulled the throbbing of the blackened flesh and bone at the end of his arm. The pain was still omnipresent, but he felt it as a separate reality, not connected to his immortal soul except by tenuous filaments of sensation.

At times it seemed to him that he was a youth again, drifting oddly over the rocky hillsides of Macedonia like a ghost, searching for the dusty fleeces moving on the trails between the sun-warmed stones. At other times he seemed to have slipped farther backward in time, so that he became one of the martyred monks of antiquity whose chronicles had been the sole intellectual pleasure of his monastic half-century of isolation. He dreamed, half waking, of the steep rock passages that ridge the spine of the holy mountain and imagined that he flew, like the corpse of the blessed St. Katherine, from a field of martyrdom and torture, through the high still air next to heaven, toward a place saved for him among the bones of the holy dead in the ossuary below the mountain.

There were lapses during which he either slept or fell into unconsciousness, and he could not measure the passage of time because the sky that he could see, from time to time, through a window whose movement he was too sick and confused to understand, remained white and milky with the timeless light of the desert.

Then there were voices, and these would come and go. He had even heard the accents of his childhood, some angel, perhaps, speaking to him in the Greek of his stone-terraced hills. The Greek had a Russian accent, but he could do no more than wonder why, if he was actually hearing the voices of heavenly angels, they could not speak his native tongue perfectly, as they must do everything. Perhaps heaven was not as he imagined it.

He wanted more than anything to ask the voices to warn the monastery that the Saracens had come again. The monks of St. Katherine's should look to its defenses; the house of Christos Pantokrator was in danger. Then he shivered with a sudden sick horror, wondering if he was in the hands, not of angels or even of Christians, but of devils who served Antichrist and who might quite easily draw from him the knowledge of the secret, silent way into the charnel house so that they could fall upon the monks of St. Katherine all unsuspecting. He moaned with despair at the thought.

The Russian medic, a fair-haired young man in the uniform of the KGB, laid a gentle hand on the leathery, dust-dry brow of the sick old man, and said softly, "Easy. Easy, little father."

Anastasius opened his eyes, milky blue with age and glassy with buried pain and drugged fatigue. He did not understand the words, but surely this broad-cheeked, kindly young face was not that of a demon.

Into Thy hands, Father, he thought. Thy will be done. Then the light faded and he slipped again, more deeply now, into an opium dream.

Bill Tate banked the helicopter away from the vanishing convoy and headed north toward Es Shu'uts. Through the open side window he could see the jumbled land of the Demilitarized Zone, a boulder-strewn and tortuous shambles of little wadis, sharply cut hummocks and small hills, abrupt slopes and talus slides, and plateaus of packed sand littered with stones. It was a lunar landscape—and as difficult of access. The accord presented its prohibitions as a kind of cosmic space into which aircraft and armor and armed men could not penetrate.

For a short time Tate allowed himself some personal reflections on the people in that motorcade now crossing the DMZ toward Zone Center. First in his mind was Deborah Zadok. He could not shake the notion that somehow last night had been a farewell and that he would not see her again. This was intuition, not sense, and it was not his habit to let emotion color his judgments. Yet the idea plagued him and brought with it a chilling sense of loneliness. Then there was Jason Seidel, upon whom the arrival of the vice-presidential party had worked some subtle changes. It was as though the Judge (and Tate realized he had come to rely heavily on the older man) had been given some special knowledge that could not be shared—at least not with his military commander. And this knowledge, whatever it was, had erected a barrier between them that was undefinable in any terms a professional soldier could understand. To be so subtly divided from his adviser increased his feeling of isolation.

And finally there was Talcott Bailey himself—a man committed to political ideas completely at variance with Tate's own; one whose every utterance rang with the hollow clang of self-righteous retreat and national exhaustion. He had come into the sterile arena of the Peacekeeping Area bearing the infection of politics, and he would now proceed to pour the virus into the irritating wound opened by Dale Trask, while the soldiers looked on helplessly.

At ten minutes after five, Captain Elizabeth Adams received a call in General Tate's office. The face on the television screen was Sam Donaldson's. He was calling from his office in the Glasshouse.

"Something has just come in here, Liz. It's rather important. Has the General landed yet?"

"No. He's still flying." Liz's voice was thin from the strain of a bad day. Her imaginings about Tate and the Jewish girl had plagued her bitterly, and the routine work in which she had tried to submerge herself had not served to dull her jealous fantasies.

"Let's scramble," Donaldson said, and his image dissolved into racing patterns.

Liz pressed the scrambler button, and Donaldson's image reappeared.

He said, "I just got something from the Israeli Liaison Group that the General should know about. It may be nothing at all, but we'd better make sure it's passed on to Sergeant Robinson and the General."

"What is it?" Liz had difficulty keeping the irritation out of her voice and she did not try very hard.

Donaldson was too preoccupied to notice. He said, "They tell me there might be a guerrilla unit in the area of Zone Center." He glanced away to read a message form. "Here's what they say. 'Cosmos photographed suspicious activity in grid two niner slant three four zero eight hundred. Possible Front terrorists. Copy of film to you by special courier soonest.' Got that?"

Something lurched slightly in Liz's mind. A movement took place that was out of context with her firm skepticism and common sense. For all of her adult life, she had been suppressing what was actually a volcanically emotional personality under a veneer of cold propriety. Her fantasies concerning Bill Tate had been warnings that her control had begun to falter, that the shell containing her dream-life was breaking up. Last night's jealous shocks and the taunts of Trask had weakened her inhibitions to the fail point. Now, for the barest blazing instant, her imagination flared and she trembled with an almost sexual pleasure as she imagined the Vice President's convoy—and Deborah Zadok with it—running into a terrorist ambush. The guerrillas not only killed, they also raped, and tore, and defiled—

"Did you get that?" Donaldson said again.

"I have it," Liz said in a calm voice. "Send a confirming copy and I will see to it that General Tate knows as soon as he lands at the helipad."

"Don't you think you ought to radio him?"

"There is nothing he can do without confirmation, Mr. Donaldson," Liz said coolly. "And we don't want to put him in the position of having to violate the DMZ on the strength of an unsubstantiated report. There has already been one incident. We don't want another. Send the photograph when it arrives."

Donaldson hesitated, not wishing to antagonize the General's military secretary. Tate was already annoyed about the discussion earlier that day. He said, "Tell him that I am passing this report on to Washington."

"I'll do that," Liz said, and broke the connection. Then she sat motionless, thinking about what she had done.

At 1700 hours, the Abou Moussa Commando was well north of Zone Center. The UN troops that Enver Lesh had thought he might meet were totally absent. With a sudden insight into the ways of eternally and perpetually neutral military men, Lesh suspected that the Swedish general in command at Zone Center had called in his patrols to form some sort of honor guard to greet the arriving dignitaries. The idea filled him with wry delight. One of the purest pleasures in the life of any true Bakuninite was the constantly reinforced knowledge that his opponents were fools, and that neutrals were the biggest fools of all. The Swedes had not fought an engagement since the time of Charles XII, and so quite naturally they considered themselves authorities on the techniques of modern guerrilla war. Lesh gave thanks for their fatuousness.

The commando turned east for a time to follow a branch of the great Wadi el Arish, then north again to intersect the narrow macadam road from El Thamad.

By 1740, Leila Jamil had found a suitable site for the coming action. The road in this place ran between two low hills, rounded, Lesh thought with controlled but rising excitement, like a woman's breasts. As a matter of fact, he noted, the terrain resembled in more ways than that a supine female body. The road ran between the breasts and curved sharply downward into a low ravine, the sides of which formed the thighs of the reclining woman, rubbled with rock slides and some few stands of desert thornbushes.

This narrow pass and the shape of the land around it formed the only usable cover near the road. Lesh did not concern himself too much about the noises of battle: the commando was now a full forty kilometers from Zone Center, and it was unlikely that the Swedes in the compound would be alerted by any faint wind-borne sounds.

He rode his camel to the rounded tip of the northerly breast and surveyed the lay of the killing ground. He turned to Jamil, who had followed him, and said, "Excellent. It will serve very well."

The woman's dark face remained unreadable as she said, "I am happy it pleases you."

Lesh consulted his map and looked to the southwest, back at the russet peak of Ras el Gineina. "We will have to go back that way again, and in the dark, with our hostage—if we have luck. Can we do it?"

"There is a new road that runs south to Mount Sinai fifteen kilometers east—just there, this side of Ras Keitat." She indicated a somewhat smaller mountain visible off to the northeast. "Wouldn't we do better to travel that way, and give Zone Center a wider berth?"

"That road would be in the U.S. Sector."

She nodded.

"They could use aircraft against us."

"But it would be night, wouldn't it?" she replied. "And don't you expect them to use aircraft against us in any case?"

"They will. But not immediately. There will be delay and arguments about violating the Demilitarized Zone. They'll do it eventually, of course, but not before we have time to travel some distance."

"Travel where, Lesh?"

Lesh's yellowish smile showed under his drooping mustache. "Are you so resolved to make this a suicide mission? I am not."

"I am prepared to die," Jamil answered.

"And so are we all. But I am not certain that we must die, handsome one. Think. With the American Vice President in our hands, who will attack us?"

She shrugged. Lesh recognized her Arab fatalism, an acceptance of kismet that was like the tangible feel of death under one's finger tips. It served its purposes, but it did not serve Lesh's *present* purpose. He said, "Some of us will live. Some of us must—to make our struggle live. Think about this: with Bailey as a hostage we could empty all the jails in Jewland."

"The Israelis will not release our people. It has been tried, Lesh."

He grinned eagerly. "Have you ever held the Americans' vice president before?"

The dark eyes under the kaffiyeh were unreadable. The woman was tired, of course, Lesh thought—bone weary of an endless bloody struggle that seemed to lead nowhere but into the grave or the dungeon. But she must find some new resources now. It was imperative.

"We will take him, Jamil. I promise you. We will take him and hold him and turn the world upside down for the struggle. *It will happen,"* he said fiercely.

"We will try," she replied, and turned her animal down the hill, calling for Rifai and Abdullah and the others to come up and hear the foreigner make his tactical dispositions.

"We'll be landing in Palm Springs in ten minutes, Mr. President."

Captain Wingate stood in the doorway of the President's private compartment, bracing himself on the bulkhead against the motions of Air Force One's descent through the turbulent air east of the San Bernardino Mountains.

The President peered over his reading glasses at the officer and nodded absently, his mind on the sheaf of National Security Council reports before him. Beyond Wingate he could see Ames Dickinson dozing in the next compartment.

Wingate said, rather hesitantly, because he was awed by the actual presence of the President of the United States, "It's going to get a bit bumpier, sir. There's a lot of clear-air turbulence over the San Jacinto Valley."

"What's the weather like in Palm Springs, Captain?" the President asked.

"Clear and windy, Mr. President."

The President nodded and readjusted his glasses before returning to the reports.

Wingate cleared his throat, glanced at the President's secretary, and withdrew, closing the compartment door behind him.

"I think the Captain would like you to fasten your seat belt, Mr. President," Helen said.

The President looked up distractedly and then grunted. "Why didn't he say so then?" He buckled the belt across his lap and twisted around to look out the window behind him. The air was sparkling and clear, with an early-morning sun brightening the snow on the peaks of the San Bernardino range with a dazzling white intensity. He could see the brown-and-dull-green fields of the flat country to the south and the distant silver slab of the Salton Sea half hidden in the slight ground haze. The mountains directly below were patterned with dark-green forest and patches of snow and ice. Air Force One's motions were swaying yaws interspersed with the soft jolts of a large aircraft in turbulent air.

The President grinned. "I hope the staff have good stomachs." He himself had never been airsick, even in the roughest weather, and he was secretly rather proud of it.

Helen Risor, who had been with the President for seventeen years and knew all his small vanities, said, "Breakfast was Dramamine and scrambled eggs for all this morning."

The President removed his reading glasses and rubbed at the corners of his eyes. He turned again to look at the scene below, its details magnified by the crystalline air and scoured by the winds. "It is a beautiful country, Helen," he said thoughtfully. "We forget that sometimes, don't we?"

"Yes, Mr. President."

She watched him, aware, as she sometimes was, of the almost sensual love of the American land that was so much a part of his personality. It was this quality of spirit, she often thought, that made him so formidable a politician. There were others more brilliant—Talcott Bailey, for one; others more charismatic. But the President's deep love for the United States was a bridge between him and the voters. They *knew,* somehow, that in an age when cynics denigrated love of country, he embodied their own inarticulate devotion to this broad American earth. And this obviously sincere response touched hidden chords even in one as experienced and sophisticated in politics as she.

The President looked away from the window and glanced at the bulkhead where a series of brass chronometers had been mounted to give him the time in various places throughout the world. The instrument marked "Pacific Time" read 0730 hours. The sun had just risen here. Air Force One had raced it across the continent, with the sun gaining only slowly. In Washington, under that murky and depressing gray sky, it was now 1030. He thought about Bailey. It was 1730 in the Middle East, and the Vice President should be close to arriving at the UN compound in Zone Center. The President thought, Luck to you, Judge. I've given you the word and put you in the way of seeing how your rival-to-be handles himself and the Russians. Part of the education of a future president—whoever he might be.

A momentary depression came over him as he thought about the disease that was even now slowly destroying his life and his usefulness to the United States.

"Shall we go on, Mr. President?" Helen asked.

"Yes. Yes, go on with it, Helen," the President said.

She began reading aloud once more from the report before her, aware that her chief's mind was elsewhere. This was just as well, because as Air Force One descended toward the San Jacinto Valley, the turbulence increased, and though she would die rather than admit it, her stomach was not so strong as the President's.

On the flight deck of Air Force One, Colonel Dayton

tapped Campbell on the shoulder and indicated that he, Dayton, would now fly the airplane, from the left-hand seat. Wingate, who had settled into the copilot's chair on returning from the passenger cabin, made a small adjustment in the autopilot, reducing the rate of descent from cruising altitude, and helped Campbell out of the restraining shoulder harness.

Dayton settled into the Major's seat and ran a quick check of the instruments. The big Lockheed was running perfectly: temperatures and pressures stood exactly on the prescribed operating readings. Only the flight instruments swung and oscillated with the rocking turbulence. Ahead lay the purple-brown flanks of San Jacinto Peak, lightly dusted with snow in the ravines as yet untouched by the low sun behind them.

"Contact Riverside Center and ask for a slower letdown," Dayton said to Wingate. "I don't want to ruffle the Man. How is it back there?"

"Some tail-wagging," Wingate said, "but the President doesn't seem to mind."

"Let's give him a smoother ride if we can, just the same," Dayton said. Actually, he could use a smoother ride himself, he thought. He felt a bit uncomfortable, with a slight pinging pain in his chest. He had eaten breakfast despite a lack of appetite, and was sorry now. He felt stuffy, as though he had to make some special effort to breathe comfortably. Thinking that perhaps the problem was a touch of indigestion, he had taken some Gelusil. He was a great one for self-doctoring, according to his wife; when in doubt, he took two aspirin and as many Gelusil as happened to be in his pocket. Not, she often said, the best way for a man Dayton's age to medicate himself. But the habit dated back to his service in the Korean War, when flight surgeons kept the F-86's flying by prescribing aspirin and a pat on the head for the fighter pilots who met the MiG trains coming down from across the Yalu.

"Riverside says go, Colonel," Wingate reported. "We're clear to use all the air we want."

"That's one of the advantages of working for this company," Dayton said with a thin smile. "Okay, let me take it." He placed his hands on the control wheel and his feet on the rudder pedals. Wingate reached across the throttle console and shut off the autopilot. Immediately, Dayton started to work hard. Air Force One was a large aircraft, and though the controls were strongly boosted by a maze of hydromechanical systems, it was still a handful in rough air.

He banked gently to the north, heading directly up the San Jacinto Valley, and reduced throttle. Already his arms and shoulders ached with the effort of keeping the big airplane on even keel. It simply would not do to give the President a bashing about, even in these conditions of hard and gusty winds. He had never flown that way with the Man on board, and he certainly was not going to start today. Pilots of the President's Flight were chosen, not only for their knowledge and prudence, but also for the smoothness of their stick-and-rudder technique. Airplanes changed—grew big as an office building and three times more complex—but the basic task of a presidential pilot was to give the Chief Executive a safe, comfortable ride.

"Passing ten thousand," Wingate said, reading the altimeters.

"Let's have a touch of brakes," Dayton said. He could feel the sweat forming on his back, turning his shirt clammy.

Wingate moved the air-brake lever until the short spoilers extruded themselves from the fuselage and then moved it back to neutral. Campbell strapped himself more tightly into the third pilot's chair as the high winds buffeted Air Force One and jolted the floor of the flight deck. Wingate glanced back to make certain the Flight Engineer was also strapped in. Craigie was holding on to the edge of his console. Pencils and logbooks slid off his desk to the deck, and he grinned and shook his head, mouthing silently: "It's a rough mothah."

After nodding agreement, Wingate turned his attention to Dayton, working hard at the controls. The Colonel's face was sheened with a light film of perspiration, and the edge of his collar was wet. Wingate considered offering to do some of the flying, but decided against it. Dayton probably didn't want anyone else at the knobs at a time like this, with the Boss in back.

The early-morning sun now slanted harshly through the right-hand windows of the flight deck and struck the instrument panels. Squares of light moved violently up and down and back and forth as the airplane lurched through the bumpy air. The glare and the oscillating patches of sun were distracting to Dayton, who tasted a dry bitterness in the back of his throat. His chest felt cottony, and each time he filled his lungs with air there was this tiny pinpoint of pain that he could not quite localize. He really felt bad, he thought, as though he wanted to purge himself of gas with a mighty eructation. He swallowed some air, trying to clear himself, but it only made him feel worse.

"Passing through nine thousand," Wingate intoned.

Several jolts made the giant aircraft shudder, almost as though it had been stopped in mid-flight. The Santa Ana winds were blowing here—great streams of air that raced through the funnel formed by the mountains that edged the Los Angeles basin and collided with the winds blowing west and south of the Great American Desert of California, Nevada, and Arizona. The result, in the San Jacinto Valley, could be a churning invisible maelstrom of winds that could gust to eighty knots.

Dayton remembered once, long ago, flying a C-45 through the San Jacinto pass in turbulence so strong it kept snapping toggle switches closed on radio and generator panels. It had been a day much like this one—clear and bright as crystal, the sky scoured of cloud and bird.

"Passing eight thousand," Wingate said.

Dayton nodded as the wheel tried to twist itself free of his grasp. "Raise the control boost," he said.

Wingate increased the hydromechanical advantage of the controls on the surfaces, lessening the effort needed to fly the plane but increasing the sensitivity of the system, so that Dayton had to increase proportionately the quickness of his responses.

"Call the tower."

Wingate called Palm Springs tower for landing instructions.

"Air Force One, this is Palm Springs." The voice of the tower operator, customarily impassive and purely professional, held a note of self-importance because he was addressing the President's aircraft. "You are cleared for a straight-in approach to runway one niner. No local traffic. The wind is one eight five degrees at thirty knots with gusts to four zero. Altimeter setting is two niner niner seven. The President's party is standing by on the ramp. Riverside Center and Continental Air Command have been notified of your arrival. Over."

Wingate looked at Dayton for approval and received it with a curt nod of the head. He spoke into his mike boom: "Roger, Palm Springs. Air Force One descending through five thousand now. Touchdown in five minutes."

Dayton sucked air into his lungs with some effort and came to a decision because of the way he felt. It would be better not to risk giving the President a rough landing. "Take it, Wingate," he said. "You make the landing."

Wingate, slightly startled, put his hands on the wheel. "I have it, Colonel. Are you okay?"

"Just a bit queasy," Dayton said.

Campbell spoke from the third seat. "Want me to sit in for you, Colonel?"

Dayton considered a moment, conscious of the increasing discomfort each time he inhaled. A series of turbulent movements decided him against shifting from the left-hand chair to the third seat. "It's all right, Major. Wingate and I will handle it," he said. He tried to swallow the thickness in his throat as he took over the copiloting duties. "Passing three thousand."

Wingate, well schooled by thousands of hours of flight and hundreds of hours in Lockheeds, called for the checklist.

Dayton began to read from the unrolling list that appeared in a rectangular window above the throttle and mixture quadrants at the touch of a button.

"Fuel-air ratio one hundred per cent."

"One hundred." Wingate thrust the handles of the mixture controls full forward.

"Spoilers out."

Wingate moved the switches that controlled the stubby fences that now extended from the wings to change the flow of air over the ailerons and give better low-speed response. "Spoilers out. Check."

"Air speed to two hundred and fifty knots."

"Coming down," Wingate said, pulling back on the throttles and raising the nose of the airplane slightly, sloughing off speed to permit the lowering of the undercarriage.

"Two fifty," Dayton said, pressing at his chest with his finger tips.

Wingate, intent on the view ahead, where Palm Springs airport was coming into view in the neck of the valley below San Jacinto Peak, did not notice the gesture. "Gear down," he ordered.

The flight deck vibrated softly to the sound and feel of the undercarriage extending. Wingate retrimmed the plane and was aware that the jolts of the turbulent air were now less abrupt, less violent, as speed was reduced.

"Two twenty-five knots," Dayton said. "Gear down. Four green lights."

From behind them, Craigie, monitoring his own instrument panel, said, "Four greens here."

"Gear down and locked," Dayton said.

Wingate spoke to Campbell. "Tell Palm Springs we are on final approach." He was a bit nervous, because this was his first landing with the President actually aboard, and he did not want to be distracted by radio chat.

Campbell spoke into his mike. "Air Force One on final, Palm Springs."

"Air Force One, you are number one and clear to land. Wind is gusting to forty—some blowing dust."

"Air Force One, roger."

Dayton's chest pains grew suddenly sharper, a small spear of discomfort each time he drew a breath. He had a moment of concern that almost reached the level of fear. What the hell was happening? His back and shoulders ached from the effort he had made hand-flying the plane, but that couldn't possibly account for the strange and frightening stabs of pain in his chest. He forced himself to concentrate on the flying.

Wingate said, "Give me full flaps, Colonel."

"Flaps—coming—down," Dayton said with an effort.

Wingate reduced the rate of descent to one hundred feet per minute. Through the left-hand window he could see the highway that bisected the San Jacinto Valley and the clutter of hotels and resorts nestled against the base of the San Bernardino range. The green of the golf courses and lawns was brilliant in the wind-swept sunlight. Turquoise-colored swimming pools dotted the populated land below.

Dayton, he realized, should now be calling off the air speed as the descent continued, but he was not doing it. He glanced across at his commander and was startled to see him sitting motionless, his hand pressed against his chest, his eyes wide behind the metal-framed sunglasses.

"Colonel! Are you all right?" His alarmed voice alerted Campbell and Craigie. The Major leaned across Dayton's shoulder to look at his face.

Air Force One passed through one hundred feet, and Wingate automatically began to flare the glide as they crossed the airport boundary. The tire-streaked runway stretched ahead.

Dayton was in severe pain now. The intima of the aortic arch was tearing, cell by cell, along the line of division, collapsing as the rift on the artery opened as though along a microscopic fault line. An unbearable pressure seemed to be building up under his breastbone, and he unlatched the shoulder harness with clawing hands. He could hear Campbell shouting something in his ear and he wanted to warn them that he was having an attack of some kind and that they should abort the landing and go around again to give them time to remove him from the pilot's seat, where he was swiftly becoming a danger to the safety of the aircraft. But he could say nothing at all because the pain had grown so great that it was blinding him, reducing his movements to spasms, paralyzing his throat and lungs so that he could make only soft, hollow animal sounds.

The rip in the aortic intima reached the junction with the pericardial sac. There was a resistance there for a fraction of a second, and then the stress caused by the surge of arterial pressure tore the tough membrane and blood, fresh from the ventricle, spilled into the space between the pericardium and the heart itself. The result was a cardiac tamponade—the pressure building almost instantly in the interstice between heart muscle and pericardial sac. This had two results: it stopped the action of the heart and ripped away thousands of tiny arteries, veins, and ligaments on the surface of the heart. Ira Dayton was, to all intents and purposes, a dead man at that moment. But his dying came in a thrust of white-hot agony. He made a nasal, gasping sound in his spasming throat and pitched forward, arms stiffly out. His clutching, insensate hands struck the control column with surprising force, catching Wingate by surprise.

The group of officials on the ramp who had gathered to greet the President included personal friends, some staff members from the Palm Springs White House, the Governor of California, and some local functionaries of the President's party. Members of the press waited inside the terminal building, restrained by Secret Service men until such time as it became known whether or not the President wished to discuss what was on most of the newsmen's minds—the *Allende* incident. In a half-second, the *Allende* incident ceased to be news.

The dignitaries and the news people, each from their particular vantage points, had watched the presidential plane approach the airport from the south. They had seen it cross the airport boundary and begin to flare for what appeared to be a routine landing. Now they were stunned to see the giant aircraft pitch forward at an altitude of no more than fifty to seventy-five feet. The angle of descent steepened to perhaps forty degrees, and the airplane struck the concrete runway nose first at a speed of one hundred and seventy-five knots. Later, witnesses would have conflicting stories about the crash of Air Force One. What actually happened would be lost in a welter of well-intentioned but hopelessly inaccurate and shocked reports from unqualified observers.

The airplane struck the runway, collapsing the nosewheel gear as though it were made of straws. The fuselage split aft of the flight deck, and the right wing broke away, spilling jet fuel over a wide area. The fuselage broke again at the wing root, and the tail tumbled to the right at an angle to the path of the disintegrating debris. Fire broke out only after the right engine disintegrated, but since the area and the tumbling wreckage had been liberally soaked with fuel, the fire was intense and widespread.

The first impact with the ground took place one hundred and sixty feet from the end of runway one nine. The last major fragment of the plane—the tail assembly and engine and the President's private compartment—came to rest one and one-tenth miles away, near the airport's north boundary. This part of the wreckage escaped the fire.

Killed instantly by the crash impact or other causes were the crew members on the flight deck. Dayton and the Flight Engineer were ejected from the disintegrating wreckage onto the runway. Campbell and Wingate were crushed against the cockpit bulkhead. In the main cabin the Secretary of Defense, two members of the White House staff, the stewards, and the warrant officer assigned to carry the nuclear codes died. A Secret Service man died in the fire that flashed through the tumbling main cabin. A second Secret Service man, new to the presidential guard team, was discovered fifteen minutes after the crash at a distance of two hundred yards from the flaming main cabin. He died within one hour of severe burns and injuries, but was reported by medical personnel at the airport to have said that there was "an explosion" aboard the aircraft immediately before the crash. This report was subsequently denied by the public-information officer of the Palm Springs Medical Center, who suggested that the statement had originated with members of the press who witnessed the accident. The "explosion" statement gained wide circulation, however, in the hours after the first reports appeared on the wire services to stun the nation and the world.

Helen Risor survived the crash but sustained, in the words of the Medical Center public-information officer, "life-endangering injuries." She was found in the wreckage of the tail section.

The President, too, was found in the shattered rear compartment. First reports reaching the public stated that he had been killed outright. These were almost immediately corrected, and overcorrected, by news media representatives who had opted for speed of reporting over accuracy. For two hours after the accident, radio and television stations across the United States carried eyewitness reports that the President had been injured slightly, but had survived the crash.

These reports were untrue. The President had, in fact, survived. But examination at the Palm Springs Medical Center, to which the President and Helen Risor had been rushed, showed that he was the victim of a depressed skull fracture, broken right arm and leg, crushed chest, and severe internal injuries, including a ruptured spleen and damaged kidneys, as well as multiple lacerations of the face and upper body. Though the prognosis given by the Palm Springs staff prior to the arrival by military jet of Major General Raymond Marty, the President's personal physician, was "guarded," it was unduly optimistic. The President of the United States was comatose and dying. This information, temporarily classified, was imparted to the Pentagon and the Joint Chiefs of Staff within twenty minutes of the crash of Air Force One.

At 1805 hours, Sinai time, word of the accident was received via the hot line at United States Component headquarters at Es Shu'uts. General William Tate's gunship had just touched down at the helipad. Deputy Premier Anatoly Rostov's motorcade was approaching the outer compound of Zone Center, a blaze of lights and flags in the deepening twilight. And Vice President Talcott Bailey's party, lightly guarded and running late, was approaching two rounded hills that, against the faintly rose-colored western sky, resembled the breasts of a reclining woman.

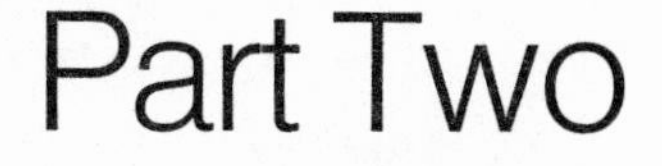

In the Case of the Removal of the President from Office, or of his Death, Resignation, or Inability to discharge the Powers and Duties of the said Office, the Same shall devolve on the Vice President, and the Congress may by Law provide for the Case of Removal, Death, Resignation, or Inability, both of the President and Vice President, declaring what Officer shall then act as President, and such Officer shall act accordingly, until the Disability be removed, or a President shall be elected.

—Constitution of the United States, Article II, Section I, Paragraph 6

Be it enacted by the Senate and House of Representatives of the United States of America in Congress assembled, That (a) (1) if, by reason of death, resignation, removal from office, inability, or failure to qualify, there is neither a President nor Vice President to discharge the powers and duties of the office of President, then the Speaker of the House of Representatives shall, upon his resignation as Speaker and as Representative in Congress, act as President.

—July 18, 1947 [S. 564] [Public Law 199]

15

For the last hour, as the afternoon waned and dusk began to well up into the sky from the darkening desert, Sergeant Major Robinson had been growing increasingly concerned and impatient. Once the party had crossed into the Demilitarized Zone, it seemed to him, the pace had slowed, with pauses, hesitations, a frequent transferring of civilian bodies from one vehicle to another as the news people and members of the Vice President's staff grew restless from the long, dull journey.

The entire operation offended his sense of military propriety and discipline, and yet he was powerless to get the gaggle of vehicles and people into anything resembling soldierly order. The General had warned him that this would be the situation, had, in fact, told him quite bluntly that the Vice President had specifically stipulated that the motorcade to Zone Center was to be a civilian operation and that the presence of soldiers of any kind would be tolerated only because it would be impossible to move inside a military zone without them.

Robinson appreciated the General's frankness, and understood, too, that the General was simply doing the best he could in a bad situation. Long experience of the Army told him that he had been assigned as troop commander on this trip because he was the best soldier available with a low-enough rank to suit the Vice President's puzzling antimilitary prejudices. He was not particularly angry or even displeased at being saddled with his present task. Being a soldier, he took things as they came, saving his anger for the enemy—wherever and whenever he was encountered. He was, however, concerned at the way the civilians were behaving, treating a land movement through rough and possibly dangerous territory as some sort of political lark.

They were almost a half hour behind schedule, he estimated. They should be within sight of Zone Center, but were, instead, at least forty kilometers from the place. It was growing dark, and the convoy carried no antipersonnel radar, no heavy weapons, and only a single squad of troopers from the Special Forces detachment. These, although they were good soldiers, could not help but be infected by the Sunday-stroll atmosphere that had invaded the convoy the moment it had passed into the Demilitarized Zone and out of General Tate's immediate jurisdiction.

To Robinson, anything that was unmilitary was automatically suspect. He remembered the disorder of his childhood in the ghetto—the slovenliness and lethargy, the deprivation and humiliation of living on welfare. The Army had changed all that for Crispus Attucks Robinson. Not that he hadn't run into white racism in the Army; that was to be expected. But he hadn't run into any he couldn't handle by the simple expedient of outsoldiering any chuck who gave him trouble. Since Vietnam, things had been good, what with the Medal and a tough commander who treated a man absolutely straight. The beautiful thing was that it was easy to pay one's way by being the best trooper in the command, and when a man paid his way he didn't have to step aside for anyone, white or black. Robinson might never learn to love or even understand white people, but he was grateful to them for having created the Army, because the Army took care of a man who was a good soldier.

It was this appreciation of the Army and of his own place in it that was disturbed by the situation in which he now found himself. He knew how to be a soldier, but it seemed to him that the Vice President and the people around him didn't have any respect for soldiers. That didn't seem right, and as he rode beside the driver of his jeep at the head of the column, he wondered if the General had realized this, too, and if he did, what he expected a black sergeant major with the Congressional Medal of Honor to do about it.

The radio light on the dashboard began to flash, and Robinson picked up the handset. "Troop Commander."

"Sergeant Robinson, this is Lieutenant Islin in the commo van. We are getting an Olympus message from Echo Sierra Control. We had better pull up until I decode it."

Olympus messages were communications intended directly for the Vice President. Islin, the Air Force cryptographer in the communications truck, would have to run it through the on-board decoding computer before delivering it to the Vice President. After decoding, the message would be in the form of a paper-and-pencil cipher that would have to be further decrypted by the Vice President's military aide.

Robinson changed communications channels and called the Vice President's car. "Colonel Crowell, this is the Troop Commander."

"Go ahead, Sergeant."

"We have an Olympus message coming in from Es Shu'uts. I'm going to stop the convoy until it is decoded." Robinson surveyed the terrain swiftly in the fading twilight. To the driver he said, "Stop up there, between those two hills."

Crowell's voice came through the radio set. "How long will it take, Sergeant? We are running late."

Robinson suppressed a twinge of irritation. No one in the Vice President's party needed to tell him that. "I know, Colonel. We'll be as fast as we can."

The line of vehicles, headlights on now, crested the flat defile between the two bare hills and stopped. Almost instantaneously, the gunmen of the Abou Moussa Commando opened fire.

At Es Shu'uts, the news flash of the accident involving the President's airplane produced a stunning effect. Though highly classified, it was immediately leaked by shocked communications technicians working at Echo Sierra Control, and though it arrived after normal working hours, within minutes a garbled version was being passed among the soldiers and civilians of the component.

Those news people who had not gone on the Vice President's trip to Zone Center set about "interviewing" almost anyone who could be enticed away from his or her duties for a minute and a half, and many of the television segments that eventually found their way onto the networks were the result of this hasty effort. Since those few persons who had hard information were not talking, and those who talked had none, the value of these quasi-interviews with clerks and riflemen was almost immediately recognized as minimal.

At least one enterprising newsman was able to rush out of the U.S. Sector by automobile as far as Gaza, there to place a telephone call to his bureau chief in Cyprus, with the result that within the hour rumors had begun to spread through the headquarters of the Cyprus Commission.

It was generally assumed that in the circumstances Vice President Bailey had been notified and that he was even now returning to Es Shu'uts by the swiftest means available. Yet this was not the case. General Tate, greeted at the helipad by the news of the Palm Springs tragedy, immediately alerted a squadron of helicopters to prepare to airlift the Vice President's party out of Zone Center. But since this would entail a clear violation of the terms of the accord, he hesitated to do so without authorization from Bailey himself.

At his headquarters, still in his flying clothes, Tate set about forestalling an impending crescendo of chaos. He opened a direct line to the Pentagon, to be ready to receive orders from the Joint Chiefs of Staff, and was told that Admiral Ainsworth was airborne, en route to Palm Springs aboard a Strike Force Mobile Headquarters airplane. The Pentagon technicians were ordered to patch in a link to the aircraft at once. Tate's experience warned him that "at once" could entail a delay of twenty minutes or more, since it had never been considered necessary to provide the Americans in the Peacekeeping Area with a secure radio link direct to the Strategic Air Command.

Tate dispatched his pilot, Captain Beaufort, to stand by Sam Donaldson, who was using his CIA communications net to obtain more information on the President's condition. He next closed the checkpoints between the American and Israeli sectors to all but specially authorized personnel. Unfortunately, this move came too late to catch the newsman who had raced for Gaza and an open telephone line at the first rumor. He then asked the Israeli Liaison Group to notify the command of the Israeli Component that the Americans were going on full alert, taking it upon himself to supply the Israelis with such official information as he had so far received from Washington.

Liz Adams functioned in a state close to shock. She remembered with vivid clarity that terrible day in November 1963 when similar news, and confusion, had come out of Dallas. The thought of a president once again clinging to a fading life drove almost everything from her mind, and her responses to the machine-gun stream of orders emanating from Tate's office were dulled and automatic.

"Captain, get me Hunter at Echo Sierra Control." Tate's voice was steady and authoritative, and she did as she was told.

Tate, his troop commanders about him, looked up at the row of television screens across from his desk. The harried face of Major Hunter, the senior communications controller, appeared. Behind him could be seen the swarming activity of the center, on whose expense Reisman had commented unfavorably to Seidel.

"What's going on with the Vice President's party, Major? Have you any word?"

Hunter said, "They acknowledged receipt of the Olympus message, General. But no reply yet."

Tate fought down a surge of impatient irritation. The purpose of the Olympus net was to pass highly classified information to the Vice President. The traffic required tedious decoding and decrypting, and took, in his opinion, entirely too much time—particularly for an information flash that need not be, again in his opinion, classified at all. He had no hard evidence, but it was almost certain that the news of the Palm Springs crash had been classified by none other than Admiral Ainsworth. Tate was sorely tempted to break security and radio Sergeant Robinson in clear language that he should turn the convoy around immediately and return to the U.S. Sector. The lights in the Glasshouse and the flurry of activity among the lower-level news people at the Falasha and in the streets of Es Shu'uts made it quite clear that the information had already leaked.

Hunter interrupted his half-angry thoughts. "The acknowledgment came in fifteen minutes ago, General. Islin will have to decode, deliver the message to the addressee, and then it will have to be decrypted. Then once Bailey is able to get his shit together—"

"You're talking about the Vice President of the United States, Major," Tate said coldly. "Possibly the President by now."

"Yes, General. I'm sorry."

"Then the whole process will have to be reversed. Is that right?"

"That's the Olympus procedure, General."

Tate regarded the chronometers on his wall, then reached a decision. "Wait for a reply for another ten minutes, Major. If there's no Olympus reply by that time, send a message in the clear to Sergeant Robinson. Tell him he is to bring the convoy back to El Thamad without any delay. Regardless of what the Vice President or any of his people say. Tell him it is a direct order from me."

"Yes, sir." Hunter's figure left the telescreen, but the scene at Echo Sierra Control remained.

Tate turned to his troop commanders, four field-grade officers in combat dress. "I want your units on full alert, with twenty-four-hour surveillance on the line of the DMZ. See to it."

"There's no chance the Russians and the Gyppos would take this as an opportunity to jump us, is there, General?"

Tate thought of Yudenich and Novotny, and he could readily imagine them suggesting some such move to the Kremlin. But he remembered Russian history and thought about old General Ulanov, who had seen a kind of war most of the men here were too young to have known. "No, they wouldn't do that. But we still had better take precautions." He thought about Talcott Bailey, too, and added, "Those we are allowed to take."

Despite the efforts of the Pentagon to classify news of the President's air crash in Palm Springs, a great deal of garbled information managed to spread swiftly throughout the world.

By 1850 hours in the Middle East, a spy in Cyprus had picked up the story from the correspondents milling about the information office of the UN Commission and telephoned it to Damascus. In this version, Air Force One had been sabotaged by black enlisted air force crewmen in sympathy with the people's liberation movements throughout the world. The excited informant declared categorically that the American President, much hated in Damascus as a friend of Israel and coarchitect, with his predecessor, of the Cyprus Accord, had been "blown to bits by explosives placed in his aircraft by black freedom fighters." Uncertain how to respond to these glad tidings, the Syrian Military Command ordered a shelling of the Golan Heights. Kibbutzniks in this disputed territory, already in their bunkers for the night, counted fourteen rounds landing in their fields before the shelling stopped.

In Moscow, where the time was one hour later than in Damascus, an extraordinary session of the Executive Committee of the Politburo was called and a series of high-priority messages dispatched to the Soviet Embassy in Washington demanding information and clarification of the confused situation.

In New Haven, Connecticut, where a group of graduate students (including one William Tecumseh Sherman Tate III) was busy planning a demonstration against the Cyprus Accord on the anniversary of the original signing, the only word was a short radio report that Air Force One had been involved in "a minor accident" while landing at Palm Springs.

In both Peking and Tirana, there were only fragmentary reports of a rise in coded radio traffic among some NATO units and ships of the Sixth Fleet. Through their Canadian Embassy, the Chinese received a report of the death of Secretary of Defense Dickinson. Unaccountably, perhaps due to excessive caution by members of the embassy staff, the President was not mentioned until some hours later.

In Washington, a frustrated press corps was reduced to releasing cryptic reports of activity among congressional leaders. Television programing continued the normal daytime routine except for the periodic appearance of well-known commentators delivering one-minute statements that contained little or no real information.

Fowler Litton Beal, Speaker of the House of Representatives, asleep between the pillowlike breasts of his good friend Terri MacLean, former GS-3 secretary in the typing pool of the Department of Urban Development, and now a resident of Rockville, Maryland, heard none of the early reports.

At Zone Center, Deputy Premier Anatoly Rostov fretted at the failure of the Americans to arrive exactly at the time specified. His reception by General Eriksson and his Swedes had been as punctilious and correct as anyone could have wished, but the fact that Vice President Bailey's party had not yet arrived made Rostov wonder if the breach of diplomatic etiquette was not deliberate, perhaps some subtle "signal" on the part of the American meant to indicate that he was preparing to make some troublesome demands, or to shift the onus of the *Allende* incident to the Soviet side.

Well, he would not be allowed to do such a thing, Rostov thought, and began considering how he himself might inject some delays and diplomatic gambits into the basically simple and straightforward business they were meeting here at Zone Center to conduct.

He had managed to rid himself of the company of General Suweif by dispatching the Egyptian to see what information could be extracted from the wounded monk they had picked up.

Neither Washington nor Moscow had as yet decided to inform the United Nations—and, in consequence, the people at Zone Center—that there had been a significant air accident on the other side of the globe.

The first man in the Vice President's party to die was Air Force Lieutenant Islin. The convoy had stopped, nose to tail, just short of the center of the ambush laid for it by Enver Lesh and the Abou Moussa. The headlights of each vehicle neatly illuminated the vehicle in front of it, making it almost impossible for the gunmen of the guerrilla commando to miss.

The communications van came under fire immediately. A fusillade of Kalashnikov automatic fire turned the vehicle and its contents to scrap metal. Islin and his two technicians died instantly, and the driver almost as quickly. The two hundred or more rounds that turned the truck into a slaughter pen also reduced the communications gear, the computer, and the classified equipment in the vehicle to rubble. The thermite devices intended to destroy the secret contrivances ignited, and within seconds the van was a holocaust, the combined gasoline and magnesium flames gouting into the air and flooding the entire scene with infernal light.

If the thin overcast that had covered the Sinai Peninsula throughout most of the day had not been dispersed by the evening winds, the glow of the burning communications van might have been seen by sentries on duty at Zone Center. But full night had fallen by this hour, and the sky was clear and starry. There was no sky glow, and the wind blew south to north, carrying the popping sounds of gunfire away into the empty barrens of central Sinai.

With his forces committed, Lesh stood on the crest of one of the low hillocks, an assault rifle cradled in his arms. From his vantage point he could see Leila Jamil directing the fire of the fire team nearest the road. She had four men with her, and they were pouring a flanking fire into a vehicle that appeared to be loaded with soldiers. It was only from this vehicle that any return fire was coming, but Lesh was gratified to see that it was ineffective. As far as he could tell, not one of the guerrilla gunmen had yet been hit.

He shouted a command to the fire team across the road, ordering them to break cover and close in on the bunched vehicles. He had located the staff car bearing the Circle and Arrows flag of the Peacekeeping Force, and he began to jog in that direction, his weapon held high across his chest. A line of miniature explosions erupted in the dust across his path, and he automatically dropped to the ground, rolling into firing position and searching for the source of the well-directed shots. In the firelight he could see a tall man with a gleaming black face. He was raking the ground near him with an M-36, firing full-automatic, but in short, well-spaced bursts. Lesh felt a flash of angry admiration for the black soldier. It took more than just courage to stand exposed in the tracer-streaked confusion down among the vehicles and fire at a shadowy target on the high ground. Lesh raised his weapon to fire back, but even this small movement brought a stream of M-36 bullets that made him grovel into the dry, dust-smelling earth.

After crawling backward until he lay hidden behind a low clump of desert thorn, he took aim again on the tall soldier. The movement was instantly detected, and the bush above his head exploded into bits of flying debris. He retreated farther and lay for a moment, grinning breathlessly. The black was good. He had to be killed. But when he moved forward once again, he could not find the marksman. Soldiers were jumping from the personnel carrier and rallying back toward the staff car, firing blindly at the muzzle flashes beyond the light of the burning communications van.

At the rear of the convoy Lesh could see what seemed to be a number of men without weapons spilling in panic from a car and two trucks. As he watched, one of the guerrillas ran forward and lobbed a grenade. The weaponless runners were cut down in mid-stride, and one truck began to burn.

Lesh stood and signaled to his reserve fire team to follow him toward the staff car. The night seemed inordinately bright now, with a vehicle burning at each end of the stalled convoy. He felt a great and familiar surge of pleasure at the scene. The AK muzzle flashes were like red-orange blossoms in the shadows, the few tracers from the return fire by the Americans like threads of gold. The terrible beauty of the moment clutched at him as he ran. The sights and sounds of the killing ground and the acrid stink of cordite filled him with an almost unbearable joy. To have a woman now, he thought, to have a woman here and now—that would be magnificent.

Dov Rabin did not survive the first moments of the ambush. Almost at the same instant that the communications van exploded into flames, a volley of automatic fire starred the windshield of the Israelis' command car, killing the young officers in the front seat and ripping away the back of Rabin's skull. He fell sideways across Deborah Zadok's legs, and the girl, reaching out to steady him, felt her hand touch a warm mass of blood and brains that had an instant before been part of a living man.

She suppressed the scream that wanted to well up in her throat, opened the rear door of the command car, and fell to her knees on the ground, retching. For a time she could do nothing to stop the waves of bile that spilled from her mouth. Each gasping breath brought a spasm of her throat, and she thought she might die there, choking on her own regurgitus.

Presently the spasms lessened and she was able to lean against the wheel of the command car and look about her with streaming, blurry eyes. What she saw was a scene from hell. Behind the command car and the car assigned to the newsmen, a truck was burning, and she could hear someone screaming in the blaze. The ground appeared to be littered with bodies, though in actual fact there were only a half-dozen dead and dying, brought down by the thrown grenade that had ignited the truck.

The vehicles of the convoy were jumbled together, as though some of the drivers had made an effort to pull out of line and escape when the shooting began but had not been able to get themselves or their vehicles clear. There were soldiers crouching in front of the command car, near the car in which Vice President Bailey had been riding. They were firing over her head into the uncertainly lit shadows. The tracer bullets were making gold-red rips in the darkness. She turned and saw Rabin's body half spilling out of the open door of the car. His face was unmarked and his eyes and mouth were open, but his head was shaped peculiarly, and the back of his uniform glistened wetly. Through her shock she realized that he was dead. Looking down at her skirt, riding high on her thighs, she saw that the cloth and her knees gleamed with blood; it was as though she had been wading in a black-red river. Though the bile rose again in her throat, there was nothing in her but a foul and bitter-tasting emptiness. She reached out and disentangled Rabin's Uzi from his body. With jerking hands she tried to wipe the blood from the stubby stock and the webbing sling.

Nearby she thought she could see running human figures, and she was certain she could hear Arab voices. Still crouched on her knees against the bullet-shredded tire of the command car, she raised the Uzi and began firing at the spectral shapes beyond the flames.

Of all the passengers in the Vice President's car at the time of the ambush, it was Talcott Bailey who retained the most presence of mind. Never—before this moment—had he been physically attacked, or even endangered. But there was nothing whatever wrong with his intelligence. His mind was quicker than most, and he was not a physical coward. He was capable of learning, under stress, very swiftly.

Therefore, while the soldiers in his party, Crowell and Seidel and the enlisted driver, reacted by trying desperately to locate the attackers and bring some neutralizing pressure on them; and while the civilians, Reisman and Bronstein, were totally frightened and disoriented, Bailey remained reasonably cool and clear-thinking.

He knew almost at once that his own life was not in immediate danger. Since arriving in the Sinai he had discounted as military paranoia the notion that there were desperate people active on the peninsula who were capable of insanely rash actions. Tate had tried to convince him of this and had failed. Now, in the fiery light and confusion, he realized that the General had, after all, been right. From this distasteful fact evolved another. It was the same truth that Enver Lesh had worked out for himself some hours earlier: the Vice President of the United States would be a hostage beyond price.

It was possible, of course, and Bailey knew it, that whoever had ambushed the convoy was simply intent on murder. But what was far more likely was that the ambush had been set to take prisoner an important American: himself. With his thoughts again paralleling Lesh's, he knew that as a hostage he could be used to enforce an almost unlimited number of demands. The Israelis, for example, had resolutely refused to free terrorist prisoners held in their jails under this kind of pressure. But could they remain as steadfast when the hostage was the second-ranking politician of their strongest ally? And that was only one of the series of even more outrageous demands that could be made. It was conceivable that he could be used to force the Americans—and the Russians, for that matter—out of the Sinai completely. And while he firmly believed that the United States had no business attempting to act as international peace officer, he had no wish to be used as a weapon against the established policy of his own country. Political opposition was one thing; becoming a pawn in an international blackmail scheme was something else entirely.

The logic of these swift thoughts drove Bailey to a clear—though distasteful—value judgment. He weighed himself and his value to the terrorists against the few soldiers of his escort. It was agonizingly clear that the men of the escort could not win this fight. They were far too few and they had been taken by surprise. He was tough-minded enough to realize that he himself had to some extent created this situation. That same, seldom used, tough-mindedness led him to the decision that he must, at all costs, not be taken prisoner. He must escape, even if it meant deserting his would-be protectors. A physical coward would have no difficulty making such a decision, and a moral coward could not have made it at all. Talcott Bailey was neither, and the need to hide from the battle was only painfully acknowledged. They were, after all, in a patroled demilitarized area under United Nations control. Bailey had always had an almost childlike faith in the United Nations. Therefore, he felt certain that UN soldiers would hear the battle and come bravely. So he needed only to avoid the attackers for a short time, perhaps a matter of minutes only, and all would be well. Then the guerrillas who were responsible for all this could be dealt with on an orderly and reasonable basis, without further bloodshed.

But even Bailey's faith in human decency was rocked when

he saw a man in an Arab headdress run from the darkness and lob a grenade into the carload of civilian reporters at the rear of the column. He wanted to cry out in outraged protest as the newsmen's truck burst into flames. And when those few who had escaped the grenade and the flames were wantonly cut down by automatic-weapons fire, his conviction fragmented.

He could see a group of soldiers, not more than five of them, being led back along the line of stalled vehicles by General Tate's tall black sergeant. They moved in crouching rushes, singly, as others fired their weapons into the desert. From behind his car he could hear the high-pitched, quick popping of a machine pistol. A small soldier knelt near the front of the Israeli command car, shooting at unseen targets. Then Bailey realized that it was a woman, the Israeli officer who had been riding with Brigadier Rabin. In the light from the burning truck he could see that her skirt was drenched with blood. She had lost her beret, and her black hair hung tangled and sticky to her shoulders. There were muzzle flashes out in the shadows, and once he had the crazy notion that he saw a camel shambling by out beyond the circle of brightness made by the burning vehicles.

Emerson, his Secret Service bodyguard, had a stubby revolver in his hand and was trying to force the Vice President away from the rear window. *"Get down, sir! Get down!"*

Bronstein had thrown himself to the floor in the front. The driver had an M-36 in his hands and was stooped low to the sill of the left-hand front window. Seidel was calling to the black sergeant to fall back to the car with his men, and Crowell, the radio handset in his fist, was trying to call the communications van on the short-range transmitter. Bailey could see fire at the head of the column and realized that the commo van had been the first vehicle hit. "It's no good, Benjamin," he said, amazed at the steadiness of his voice. But Crowell kept trying, intermittently cursing the radio, the darkness, and the UN for not securing the Demilitarized Zone.

Bailey decided that now was the time to move. As soon as

the black sergeant had his men in place around the car, he would order Crowell and Seidel to escort him in a dash across the open ground and into the dark hills on the south side of the road. There had been no firing from that direction. He would take the Israeli girl and the Brigadier, if he could be found. The UN troops would surely appear quickly; they had had a long time to see the flames and hear the gunfire. Actually, the time that had elapsed since the convoy had stopped between the two rounded hills was no more than six minutes, but to Bailey, a stranger to the fog of war, it seemed much longer.

He caught Crowell by the arm and told him the plan. In the uncertain light, Bailey could see scorn and amazement spreading on his military aide's face. Even in their present extremity, Crowell's contempt stung badly. "You will come with me, Colonel," Bailey said. "I am ordering you."

Crowell nodded slowly, his shining black eyes fixed on the Vice President's face. There was a flat, brittle splatting sound inside the car. Crowell's expression changed slowly to one of vague surprise. His mouth opened to show his white, even teeth. He leaned slowly against Seidel, who turned in time to see a dark stain spreading just below Crowell's service ribbons where the bullet that had starred the side window had entered his chest.

Colonel Benjamin Crowell had not been a particular friend of the Vice President. Talcott Bailey did not make friends of professional soldiers or seek their good opinion. But his former coolness could not spare him the knowledge that this familiar and competent officer was dying before his eyes, struck by a stray bullet fired somewhere in the darkness by some unknown, ignorant, and angry man with no more conception of what he was doing than a marauding tiger.

"Benjamin—"

"He's dead," Seidel said.

In the front of the car, Bronstein made a frightened sound. His experience of violence was exactly what the Vice President's had been: nonexistent. Even during his student-activist days he had always managed to absent himself when the demonstrations turned to confrontation and fighting with the police. He had managed to give to his contemporaries the impression that he was, or had once been, an old street fighter. But the truth was that despite his associations with the Black Panthers and the would-be revolutionaries of Venceremos, and the Arab student groups in America, he had never seen a man killed, or even seriously injured. The reality of what he had, as a university student, so often advocated was literally overpowering. He, too, could think only of escape—but for reasons different from Talcott Bailey's.

"Do you want to make a run for it?" Seidel asked the Vice President.

"Have you a better suggestion?"

Seidel shook his head.

There was more shadowy activity on the slope to the north of them, and the five soldiers led by Tate's sergeant had taken cover at the front of the car. Bailey saw Robinson smash the headlights, to extinguish the light that exposed them to guerrilla fire.

Seidel called to the driver.

"Sir." The soldier did not turn his head, but kept watch on the northern hill, where Bailey remembered having seen, or having imagined that he saw, the shambling camel.

"We're going to try to break away and find some cover. Tell Robinson to cover us and then follow if he can."

"Sir!" The driver opened the door, rolled to the ground, and crawled across the sandy earth toward the remnants of the squad of soldiers.

"We can try to reach that little wadi just there where the slope levels out," Seidel said. "Then work our way around the hill." The tone of his voice was flat, noncommittal. "Robinson will keep them busy while we get away."

Bailey said, "What else can we do, Judge? I can't let them take me hostage."

"I know." He leaned across the seat and grasped the back of Bronstein's shirt. "Get up. *Up,* damn you. Get ready to make a break for the hill."

"I can't, Colonel. I just can't do it," Bronstein whimpered.

Seidel turned to Emerson and said, "Get him moving. We have to get the Vice President out of here."

The Secret Service man hauled Bronstein to a sitting position and began to speak to him in a low, threatening voice.

Seidel said to Bailey, "The girl—Captain Zadok—she comes with us."

"Of course." Bailey listened to the slackening sound of gunfire from the head of the convoy. Apparently, to judge from the tracers being fired from the American M-36's, the only return fire was now coming from the group digging in in front of his car.

Seidel opened the rear door and crouched before rolling to the ground. He held an issue forty-five-caliber automatic pistol in his hand. It looked new, and the Vice President thought, with a curious detachment, that of course it was new, that Judge Seidel, a man in his fifties, a judge, a former congressman, a staff officer—and probably completely untrained in the use of weapons—was about to risk his life in an attempt to protect the Vice President of the United States.

Seidel crawled along the ground toward the Israeli command car. As he drew near, Deborah turned and pointed the Uzi she had been firing directly at him. Her eyes looked immense and dark and cavernous, the eyes of a slightly mad woman. "Captain Zadok—Deborah! Don't shoot. It's Colonel Seidel."

She wavered, lowered the machine pistol, and closed her eyes, leaning back against the tire of the command car.

"Rabin?" Seidel asked.

She moved away so that Seidel could see the Brigadier's body.

"Is he dead?"

"Yes."

"Come with me. We are going to try to reach the wadi."

She said listlessly, "There are Arabs on the high ground."

"How many? Did you see them?"

She did not reply, shrugging her shoulders instead and making a pathetic distracted movement to brush her tangled hair back from her face. Her fingers left streaks of Rabin's blood on her temple.

Seidel asked, "Are you hit?"

"No."

"Come on, then." He led the way back to the rear of the car and tugged at Bailey's coat to make him crouch down in the open door.

Bailey left the car, followed by Emerson and Bronstein. The light from the newsmen's truck was less intense now, and Seidel began hoping that they might, perhaps, actually get away from their exposed position.

"Where is the UN?" Bailey asked suddenly.

Deborah said, "The *what?*"

"The UN soldiers who patrol this area."

The girl began to laugh silently, near to hysteria. "God, you'll never learn, will you," she said.

To forestall further useless talk, Seidel shouted to Robinson. "Can you cover us, Sergeant?"

"Go when we start to fire, Colonel," the deep voice came back strongly.

Someone else, one of the soldiers, said, "I'm down to two magazines, Sarge."

"Use 'em, soldier."

The massed M-36's of the squad's survivors opened up with the high-pitched ripping sound of full-automatic fire. Robinson had the satisfaction of hearing someone far out in the tracer-ripped darkness utter a shrill shriek of pain.

Seidel struck the Vice President on the back, not gently, and pointed. "That way. Go now."

Bailey ran with surprising agility. There were some shots from the direction of the head of the convoy, but they were suppressed by the prodigal expenditure of ammunition by Robinson's soldiers.

"Deborah. Reisman. You next. *Now.*" The girl stood, staggered, and almost fell. Reisman steadied her. Then they ran through the firelight, Reisman blowing hard, the girl's legs flashing white.

"Bronstein—*now.*"

The bearded young man knelt, head to the earth. "I can't."

Emerson pressed his stubby revolver against the base of his neck and said harshly, "Run, you son of a bitch, or I'll shoot you myself."

Bronstein ran, stumbling.

"Now you, Colonel," Emerson said.

"Together," Seidel said. "I'm not as fast as I used to be."

"All right. Ready? Now, then, let's go."

The two men ran heavily for the cover of darkness. The noise of the M-36's behind them was slackening as the troopers exhausted their ammunition. But the Vice President had made it, thank God, Seidel thought, sucking air into his laboring lungs as he ran.

He heard movement ahead of him. The fire fight was a hundred yards or more behind them. By God, he thought, by God, we are going to get clear—

He ran headlong into Bronstein's back, and would have shoved him into motion again, for they had not put nearly enough distance between themselves and the ambush. But Bronstein screamed for him to stop, not to shove. And as Seidel's eyes became accustomed to the darkness he saw with a sick disappointment that Bronstein stood with a weapon at his chest—a Russian assault rifle held by a man wearing a kaffiyeh. And standing in a half-circle within the wadi were perhaps a dozen other Arabs with guns leveled at the people from the convoy. Deborah lowered her Uzi, hesitated while she calculated the odds, and then let it fall to the sand.

Bailey said in English, "Who is in command here? Who is responsible for this act of banditry?"

Seidel almost smiled, despite his despair. A nice try, Bailey, but the voice of authority is unlikely to impress anyone here now. He heard Reisman, still panting from his run, mutter, "Oh, shit."

Two figures stepped out of the mass of shadowy gunmen. To Seidel's vague surprise, he saw that one of them was a woman. The other, a bulky man with a Balkan accent to his English, said in a smiling voice filled with irony, "You are prisoners of the Abou Moussa Commando of the Arab Front for the Liberation of Palestine, gentlemen. And lady," he added with a slight inclination of the head toward Deborah. "This is Leila Jamil. And I am Enver Lesh. Throw down your weapons and tell your soldiers to surrender at once or you will all be shot."

16

Sam Donaldson stared across Bill Tate's desk in disbelief, his thick fist clenched above the photographs spread before him. His face was as red as the flowers on his gaudy sports shirt, and he said again, "Are you telling me you haven't seen these Cosmos pictures yet? Is that what you're saying?"

The row of television screens behind him showed a variety of scenes: Echo Sierra Control, where the communicators were trying without success to raise Sergeant Robinson; the commo room at Zone Center, where a Swedish UN officer was standing by for the arrival of General Eriksson, who had been summoned for a teleconference with the American commander; and the global War Room at the Pentagon, where could be seen a row of military controllers engaged in opening the communications network to the various American commands throughout the world. A fourth screen, alive but blank, awaited a contact with Admiral Ainsworth, now somewhere above the southwestern United States, returning from Palm Springs.

"These were delivered to your office at least two hours ago, General," Donaldson said. "Captain Adams signed for them. I personally told her that you were to be notified on the helipad."

It seemed inconceivable to Tate that Liz Adams could have fallen down so badly in a critical situation, but perhaps it was the situation itself that was to blame. Since the news of the President's crash had arrived in Es Shu'uts, the balance of the U.S. Component headquarters had rocked on an unpredictable edge. The failure to raise the Vice President's party by radio, either in response to the Olympus notification or in clear language, had added a note of hysteria to the confusion. Everyone with access to the knowledge that Talcott Bailey had neither replied to the urgent radio calls nor arrived at Zone Center now performed his assigned task with a grim face. The elaborate precautions built up over the years to protect the succession of power in the United States seemed to be crumbling moment by moment as the Vice President remained unreported.

Tate had started air searches along the demarcation line of the Demilitarized Zone with helicopters and Shrikes, and he had resolved that if the convoy remained unreported for thirty minutes longer he would order the air search extended into the proscribed air space. So far the search had been hampered by darkness, and the hope faded that he could continue to abide by the terms of the accord and keep American aircraft out of the DMZ. Much depended on what Eriksson and the Swedes were willing or able to do. So far, they had done nothing but hold consultations with Cyprus, the UN in New York, and their own government in Stockholm.

And now Donaldson had stormed into his office with a Cosmos series about which Tate had been in complete ignorance.

Donaldson shoved the glossy prints across the desk top and pointed to a group of objects circled with red marking pen. "These pictures were taken during the first pass of 623 early yesterday. One shows our flyboy Trask buzzing the *Allende,* right?"

Tate looked and saw that this was so. The Shrike and the destroyer were plainly visible.

"Now look at this one." Donaldson pushed another print across. "That group that looks like a Bedouin band is a guerrilla team, General. See that man looking up? The Israelis have tentatively identified him as Enver Lesh, an Albanian officer." He laid an open file of computer print-outs beside the photographs. "This is from our data bank in Virginia. We know a few things about Colonel Lesh. Korea, Vietnam, Bangladesh, back to Indochina to advise Khmer Rouge. Then Libya, Syria, and Iraq. The son of a bitch has been a thorn in our sides for twenty years and *there he is*. With an Arab commando. A hundred klicks from the Vice President. And that was early yesterday." He scowled and clenched his fists on the edge of the desk. "I don't think you are going to find Talcott Bailey, General. Not alive."

Tate studied the Russian photographs while a hard knot tightened in his stomach. If Donaldson's information was right—and in these matters he did not make mistakes—the implications were enormous.

Donaldson put them into harsh words: "Remember, General, these are *Russian* photographs. They had all this information yesterday morning. Now hear this—" He ticked off his points on stubby fingers. "Two days ago a Samos satellite saw a submarine wake off Shadwan Island in the Strait of Gubal. We couldn't get a sound-print from the screws because the Navy doesn't have the money to keep an ASW squadron in the Red Sea any more. But the sub was conventional. The Albanians still have a dozen old Russian diesel subs. For that matter, so have the Russians." He folded another finger down, glaring at Tate with red-rimmed eyes. "Thirty-six hours ago Mosa'ad reported a possible intrusion into the Sinai by what their informant claimed was the Abou Moussa Commando of the Arab Front for the Liberation of Palestine. There was a conflicting report yesterday, but Mosa'ad discounts it. They think *that*—" he rapped hard on the photograph—"is the Abou Moussa." He folded down another thick finger. "Point three. Major Paris reports from Zone Center that the Rostov party picked up an old monk on the west coast–Zone Center road. He's half out of his head, raving about Saracens and crusaders—but it looks as though he was caught in some sort of fire fight and wounded. And point four. The Syrians are bragging that the President's airplane was sabotaged. I'd discount that because the Arabs are congenital liars and the guerrilla outfits are always claiming credit for things like that. But I received word from Virginia that one of the stewards said there was an explosion aboard before the crash. Maybe there was and maybe there wasn't. Things get pretty crazy when there's a serious accident. But even so, we can't afford to discount the report.

"So what do we have? Four indications that none of this is coincidence, General. First the President's plane goes down and now the Vice President is missing." His tone grew harsh and thick with anger and suspicion. "I think it's goddamn strange that the Soviets had this Cosmos information yesterday and did nothing about telling us there was a commando moving toward Zone Center. And stranger still that they did nothing at all special to protect their man Rostov. Maybe I'm paranoid, General. But it *is* possible we are looking at a conspiracy. And I'm not going to be the only one to think that if Bailey doesn't turn up healthy in the next few minutes."

He slouched back in his chair, his face redder than before and his eyes hard and glistening as polished stones. "Now, General, suppose you let Captain Adams come in here and explain why in hell she delayed getting this material to you as she was ordered to do."

Tate said, "I'll handle Captain Adams, Donaldson."

"I told you this morning—I warned you that you were sitting on a land mine with that one. You can't ever tell about the quiet type. Since Vietnam, you never know where their sympathies are."

Tate looked up angrily. "Are you suggesting that Captain Adams is disloyal?"

"Shit, General," Donaldson said. "Right now I don't know what I'm suggesting. I only know that we're all in trouble here—and you are in worse trouble than any of us." He heaved himself erect and lumbered toward the door with weary steps. Turning back, he said, "I'm sorry if I've offended you. But right now I wouldn't give a quarter for your career if Talcott Bailey becomes president. That's a shame. But I wouldn't give half that for the safety of the United States if Stuart Ainsworth takes over—" He leveled a finger at Tate. *"And he will if this turns out to be a conspiracy."* He departed, leaving the door to the swarming outer office open.

Bill Tate rubbed a hand across his cropped hair and down his cheek, across the stubble starting there. He felt unbelievably tired, the effect of the last two days' tensions. And now this suggestion of a plot to eliminate the high officeholders of the government. If Donaldson, who for all the brutality of his trade was a sensitive and intelligent man, could see a Communist plot here, it was a certainty that Admiral Ainsworth, with his deep hatred of the Soviets, would be even quicker to accuse. And act? Was that possible? Donaldson had made it plain that he believed the naming of Speaker Fowler Beal to be acting president would be essentially the same thing as naming the Admiral. The Speaker of the House was a party hack, a wheel horse, accustomed to doing as he was told. If the President or the Vice President was not around to give him orders, he would take them from someone else. It was common knowledge in Washington that Beal was heavily influenced by the military. It was unreasonable to expect that he would not take whatever action the dynamos of the Pentagon demanded. The Joint Chiefs—the submariner Chief of Naval Operations, the iron-ass Marine Commandant, the missile genius of the Air Force, and the near-to-retirement Army Chief of Staff—were military thinkers, accustomed to solving problems by the threat of application of military power. And they were all accustomed to the restraining hand of the President. Prodded by Ainsworth and uncurbed by the White House, how would they respond to any complicity by the Soviets or the Chinese in a murder-sabotage-kidnapping plot intended to decapitate the United States?

The Constitution provided for a succession, and Congress had long ago defined it. *Fowler Litton Beal, Acting President of the United States.* But the indistinct image of an indistinct man seemed to flow and waver—and behind it emerged always the angry, militantly righteous features of Admiral Stuart Ainsworth, with his hand (or was it Beal's?) on the nuclear trigger.

Tate shivered as though a cold wind had brushed him. He pressed the intercom button on his console. Liz Adams's frightened face appeared on the small screen. She had seen Donaldson go in with the Cosmos material and now she waited for the inevitable. Tate was tempted to subject her to the questioning and discipline her lapse deserved. But the failure was not really hers. It had been his own. His affair with Deborah Zadok lay at the root of Captain Adams's breakdown. He thought about Deborah and considered the possibility that she might be dead, or worse, in some night-shrouded wadi far to the south. He didn't want to think much about that. There were degrees of personal loss, which began with simple deprivation and extended to bereavement. A soldier dared not dwell on any of them—not the loss of his woman or of his commander in chief—lest he cease to be a warrior and become only a grieving man.

"Captain," he said in a flat, hard voice, "the air search is to be extended into the DMZ. All pilots." He broke the connection before she could reply or even suggest that she would prefer his punishment, his anger rather than this bleak formality that could only mean she was to be sent away from him, as far and as quickly as the present emergency allowed.

She could hear, in the General's office, the accented voice of one of the Swedish UN officers coming from the television screen, saying with ponderous formality that General Eriksson, Commander of the United Nations Observer Force in the Sinai and Commandant of Zone Center, was now ready to speak to Major General Tate of the United States Component of the Peacekeeping Force.

Liz was overwhelmed with guilt. The military consequences

of her dereliction had been obvious to her even in the confusion that followed the breakdown in communications between Es Shu'uts and the Vice President's party. She could be court-martialed for what she had done—or, rather, for what she had not done. Her frantic jealousy of Deborah Zadok had made any such consequence bearable, as long as the Jewish girl did not return. But now, at least partially through her delay with the Cosmos information, a situation had arisen that forced General Tate to violate the terms of the Cyprus Accord—the bible people lived by, along thirty-four east. The end result for him must be disastrous, because with characteristic decisiveness he had acted on his own.

She heard the thin voice of the Swedish general coming from the telescreen, then the angry steel-shod step of Tate's paratroop boots on the vinyl floor, and finally the slamming of the door to his office.

Aboard the supersonic airplane designated as Airborne Strike Force Command Headquarters Two, Admiral Stuart Ainsworth and his personal staff had just concluded a briefing conducted over television relay by an officer of the Defense Intelligence Agency. This presentation had consisted of a detailed discussion of Russian army and air force doctrine and of Soviet first-strike capability as of this date. The numbers involved in this evaluation of military strength were impressive but not alarming. The provisions of SALT I and SALT II, according to Samos, Midas, and Skylab information, and to material obtained from covert operations within the Soviet Union, had been carried out to the letter.

An earlier briefing, restricted to Ainsworth and his aides, had been delivered by a Yale psychologist, a specialist in the "gaming" of Soviet intentions and reactions to hypothetical situations. For years the Department of Defense had made a practice of positing every conceivable combination of social, military, and political situations to the games computers on a "what if" basis.

One of these thousands of hypotheses had been the subject of the psychologist's appreciation. Case Headless had been written first by the Rand Corporation in 1961, and modified yearly. The original scenario attempted to determine how the Soviets would react to a situation in which both President and Vice President of the United States died. During the civil disorders that followed the assassinations and attempted assassinations of the 1960's, the scenario had been modified. With this addition, the probabilities of a Soviet pre-emptive strike had risen from the original one in sixty to one in twenty. The Nixon visits to Peking and Moscow had sent the probabilities sharply downward, to one in two hundred. The signing of the Vietnam peace agreement in Paris in early 1973 had reduced the odds to one in three hundred and fifty. The Brezhnev summit meeting in Washington had so reduced the chances of conflict, even under the terms of Headless, that the scenario became, according to most games psychologists, almost moot. Almost, but not quite. The Yom Kippur War and the worldwide American alert it provoked gave the odds a seismic spasm, and the Kissinger initiatives again reduced the odds to nearly nil. The signing of the Cyprus Accord and establishment of the Peacekeeping Area in the Sinai—which any layman would have assumed lowered the odds to a minus value—had actually revived Case Headless. The rationale for this was that now Soviet and American forces—the components of the Peacekeeping Force—actually faced each other across thirty-four east. (For gaming purposes, the psychologists tended to ignore the DMZ and the United Nations presence there.)

Ainsworth's staff psychologist, Dr. Emmett Brown, would not have been a member of the Admiral's personal brain trust if he had not shared, to a great extent, Ainsworth's suspicion of Communists. Therefore, his personal reading of the much revised Case Headless probabilities was alarmingly high.

Now Ainsworth sat alone in the conference compartment, pondering the heavy responsibility that seemed to be falling upon his shoulders. General Tate's preliminary report from Es Shu'uts had stated simply that the Vice President had failed to arrive at Zone Center at the time scheduled for his meeting with Anatoly Rostov. But the implications were staggering, and unless communication with the Vice President was re-established very soon, the conditions of Case Headless would come near to being fulfilled.

The President was dying. Major General Marty, looking haggard and grief-stricken, had made that quite clear. The facilities of the intensive care unit at Palm Springs Medical Center were excellent, and they were being used to the fullest to keep a semblance of life in the ruined body of the President. Ainsworth had been shocked by the discovery that the President had been an ill man, one weakened by Parkinson's disease. Marty had imparted that information privately and confidentially, believing that the Chairman of the Joint Chiefs should know all the factors that were conspiring to kill the injured President.

After receiving Tate's report on the loss of contact with Vice President Bailey, Ainsworth had radioed New Haven for an update on Case Headless, and Dr. Brown had appeared with commendable swiftness at the New London Naval Telecommunications Center to brief the Admiral and his staff by satellite relay. His conclusions: *If in fact the United States was left without executive guidance for a period longer than seventy-four hours, the temptation to launch a pre-emptive strike against NATO and the continental United States would force the probability of such a strike to one in five.*

Congress was not in session, and the death of Secretary Dickinson eliminated, temporarily, one level of authority between the military and the now uncertain civilian-political leadership. Congress could conceivably act quickly to confirm the Speaker of the House as acting president, but swift action was not a notable characteristic of Congress. Furthermore, the President was not yet dead, and the Vice President was only unreported. Fowler Beal would be far too spineless to expose himself to charges that he had become involved in an unconstitutional usurpation of power.

So the legalities must be preserved, Ainsworth decided—not only for immediate and practical reasons, but also for the good and future of the republic. The proper forces must be set in motion and time allowed for them to function. But simultaneously, measures must be taken, and at once, now that Case Headless seemed so near to becoming a reality.

A light showed on his control console, and the voice of Captain Kraft, his aide, said: "We are ready with the War Room, Admiral."

Ainsworth swiveled his seat to face the television screen on the rear bulkhead. General Armando Rivera, the acting chairman, appeared on the color screen. He was a swarthy, thin-faced officer, handsome in air force blue, chest ablaze with decorations, shoulders glittering with silver stars. Ainsworth's Calvinist tendency toward intolerance of Latin Catholics disturbed him from time to time. He had no right to think of Rivera in such terms. Immediately, he swept the shadowy prejudices from his mind and said, "General, on my authority we will go to Yellow Alert status."

Without a moment's hesitation, Rivera said, "Computer tapes are running, Admiral."

"Call the others to the War Room and have them there when I arrive in Washington."

"The deep shelter, Admiral?" The handsome face showed no change of expression at the ominous order.

"Not yet. Send a car for the Speaker of the House. If you can't find him, try the address in Rockville. I want an armed guard with him at all times until further notice." If Rivera deduced from his concern for Beal's safety that a conspiracy was suspected, well and good. It was a time for performance under extreme pressures. Beal imagined that his nest in Rockville was secret. That was a measure of the man's naïveté. A foolish man. But foolish or not he was suddenly near to being *de jure* president of the United States.

"We have an open line to Es Shu'uts, Admiral. General Tate has ordered the component to full alert. There is still no contact with the Vice President's convoy."

"I am in touch with Tate's communications center at Echo Sierra Control," Ainsworth said.

For the first time, Rivera showed some slight tension as he spoke. "The Agency has received the Cosmos photographs the Soviets plan to use as a basis for their protest on the *Allende* incident, Admiral."

Ainsworth waited, composed and silent, for Rivera to go on. He was just aware of the muffled sound of the jet engines.

Rivera said, "We got them through the Moscow-Tehran-Jerusalem pipeline, the way we customarily receive Cosmos material. But I find it puzzling, Admiral. They usually screen the stuff so carefully that we get only what they want us to have—"

Ainsworth said, a trifle impatiently, "Yes, all right. Get on with it." Intelligence evaluation did not fall within Rivera's area of responsibility.

"Along with the *Allende* material came the tail strips taken over southern Sinai on the same pass. They show what the Israelis claim is an Arab terrorist unit on the move. They have even identified one of the men. His name is Enver Lesh, an Albanian. We have him in our data banks, and the Cosmos picture shows him with the Arabs, all right."

Ainsworth frowned deeply.

"Yes, exactly, Admiral. If the Vice President is in trouble down there, there is only one conclusion we can draw. That is that the Russians knew in advance he might run into guerrillas and did nothing to inform us. Then they let this stuff leak through the pipeline when it is hours old."

Ainsworth felt a strangely pleasurable confirmation of his suspicions. For years he had known the United States was on the wrong track with the Communists. They could not be trusted in the Stalin days, and they could not be trusted now.

As he considered what Rivera had been saying, it seemed to him that it implied far more than the General realized. Rivera was accusing the Soviets of a sin of omission. Ainsworth suspected that something darker and more apocalyptic might somehow have taken shape in the minds of the men in the Kremlin. Quietly, he asked, "What percentage of the missile force is on the line, General?"

"Eighty per cent of the Minutemen, Admiral. Eighty-six per cent of the Poseidons are at sea and on station."

"Very well. Do not screen our Yellow Alert call. I want the Russians to know about it. Get the Deputy Chiefs aloft in ASF Command aircraft. Let's just see what happens."

Rivera, seated at a U-shaped control console back in Washington, looked searchingly at his superior. Ainsworth could almost feel the pressure of his scrutiny through the television and satellite circuitry that connected them. Rivera was thinking that a Yellow Alert was well enough, but that anything further required presidential approval—or what the law would accept as such approval. "Very well, Admiral," he said.

Ainsworth broke the connection and was rubbing at his eyes wearily when Kraft came into the compartment.

"Where are we, Captain?" he asked.

"Over St. Louis, Admiral."

With the present winds, still an hour from Andrews Air Force Base. Ainsworth suppressed his anxiety and impatience. What could be done was being done. He could not order events further—not until matters became clearer, more precise.

The commo light flashed, and the communications officer spoke through the console grille. "Brussels, Admiral. NATO Command."

"Put it on the screen."

The television screen that had earlier shown Rivera in the Pentagon War Room now showed a scene half a world away and the drawn, worried face of Lieutenant-General Sir Alexander Clayborne, the NATO deputy commanding general. "We have a Yellow Alert signal," he said without preamble. "Is that confirmed?"

"It is, General," Ainsworth said.

There were few matters pertaining to command that troubled Stuart Ainsworth, but he did find himself a trifle annoyed that at this particular time the American commander of NATO forces, General Julian Muller, should be on leave—in, of all places, Hawaii—leaving Clayborne in command.

Clayborne brushed his carefully trimmed Guards mustache with a finger tip in a gesture that betrayed his uncertainty. He said, "Stuart, I know that you are in a flap over what has happened, and I couldn't sympathize more. It is a terrible thing, as all of us here realize. But a Yellow Alert, Stuart—that puts a warlike face on things, doesn't it?"

Ainsworth said evenly, "It is a precaution, Alex. At the moment. There is some slight evidence that our friends across the line may have been involved. It is our feeling that we had best give them pause with some degree of readiness."

Clayborne looked vaguely perplexed. "Evidence, Stuart?"

"There's talk that Air Force One was sabotaged."

The British officer looked shocked, and Ainsworth's annoyance was increased by what he sometimes thought of as the Sandhurst Syndrome: the upper-class Englishman's traditional reluctance to believe that someone—even an opponent—might not be playing the game. It seemed to the Admiral that peacetime infected the British with this weakness; once at war, they were as tricky and nasty as anyone on earth.

"Under the circumstances," Ainsworth said, "I think it best to take some precautions."

Clayborne said uneasily, "You say the Russians could have been implicated. Have your crash investigators made a finding so soon?"

"I did not say 'Russians,' Alex. But there has been a report—not yet confirmed—of an explosion aboard the airplane before the crash. The press has picked it up, and Lord knows what the public reaction will be. The majority of the people are going to be very angry and very suspicious."

"Yes, of course. I can see that. But—"

"There is something else. You'll get this on the command net within the hour, I should imagine, but I will give it to you personally and now. Bill Tate has lost radio contact with Vice President Bailey."

"What?"

"Precisely. The Vice President crossed into the DMZ at about 1615 hours Sinai time. Now he cannot be reached by radio. He failed to respond to an Olympus message, and his escort still can't be raised."

"Good God."

"It is worse, Alex," Ainsworth said dryly. "I won't get into details, but we have come onto some information that indicates the Soviet government knew that an Arab terrorist unit has been operating in that area. The Russians had hard evidence thirty-four hours ago at least." He leaned forward to stare into the camera eye immediately above the screen. "Putting the mildest possible interpretation on all this, we must consider their failure to warn us an extremely hostile act. When you couple this with what has happened in Palm Springs, a very ugly set of possibilities emerges."

"Yes, of course," Clayborne said. "I can see that."

"The fact that Rostov is sitting down there at Zone Center waiting for the Vice President suggests to me some typically Communist cynicism. I am reminded of Kurusu and Nomura smiling in Washington while Jap airplanes were bombing hell out of Pearl Harbor."

"What is Tate doing, Stuart?"

"Running air searches in American-controlled territory. But his forces are limited and his hands are tied by the accord. When it gets light in Sinai, I certainly wouldn't be surprised to find that, if the Vice President is still unreported, he is going to begin to ignore the restrictions. That is one more reason for bringing our forces to readiness."

"Can't you prevent that, Stuart?" Clayborne asked. His tone was anxious. No doubt he was imagining a series of escalations leading to a direct confrontation between the forces of NATO and those of the Warsaw Pact.

"Bill Tate's command is controlled directly by the Commander in Chief. And I am not so certain I would try to stop him even if I could. *The President is dying,* Alex," he finished grimly.

"Has Tate spoken to the Russians?" Clayborne asked, flushing slightly. "I know that sounds absurd, Stuart, in the light of what you have been telling me. But it is possible, isn't it, that they would be willing to help?"

"The way they helped by warning us about the terrorist unit?" Ainsworth made no effort to dull the edge of his sarcasm.

"I simply find it difficult to believe that the Soviets would embroil themselves in something as dangerous as this. These are not Stalinist times, after all."

"They are *Communists,*" Ainsworth said. "They have been fighting us for thirty years. A handshake from Rostov does not alter that simple *fact.*"

"I only meant," Clayborne said, recoiling imperceptibly from the flash of naked, implacable hatred, "that Tate could use some assistance—from whatever quarter." He finished lamely, "I find it almost unthinkable that a man like Yuri Ulanov would lend himself to an attempt by terrorists on your Vice President."

"Your faith in General Ulanov is touching, Alex," Ainsworth said. "I even hope you are right about him and about his countrymen. So far the weight of the evidence is on the other side of the scales. You have your orders. Follow them."

"I will have to notify Whitehall, of course."

"That is being done. Also Athens, Bonn, and Ankara.

General Muller is being recalled to Brussels. But for now, I repeat, you have your orders. Carry them out."

"Yes, Admiral," Clayborne said reluctantly. "As of now, all NATO air, ground, and naval forces are on Yellow Alert status."

"Thank you, Alex," Ainsworth said. "We appreciate your co-operation."

17

After his men had completed the round-up of the surviving Americans—and not until then—Enver Lesh surrendered himself to a savage exaltation. He had not yet bothered to identify all of his prisoners, but the tall man who managed to look aristocratic even in these circumstances was, beyond a doubt, Talcott Quincy Bailey, Vice President of the United States. Lesh knew him by sight, though it had been some years since he had actually seen him. In the middle 1970's Bailey had attended a conference on World Peace in Shanghai and had addressed the delegates, one of whom had been Comrade Lesh of the People's Republic of Albania. The American was much aged, but the imperious manner that had antagonized so many of the socialists at Shanghai remained intact. Only a born aristocrat could carry on in so arrogant a manner under the threat of so many guns in the hands of his enemies. The others, the soldiers, the two civilians, and the Jewess, had had the sense to recognize the precariousness of their position. The Arab Front was not known for humanitarian restraint when dealing with hostages.

Within minutes of the round-up, Lesh had given orders that the wounded be shot and the fires put out. There was no point in giving any would-be rescuers beacons to follow, though he was reasonably confident that his operation could continue undisturbed for a time yet—certainly enough time to commandeer the two still-usable vehicles, disperse that part of his force he could not load into them, and strike for the road south. The Russians, who would have arrived at Zone Center by now, were not likely to send out searchers for the tardy Americans, nor were the Swedes garrisoning the UN post. By this time it was possible, and even probable, that the massacre of the shepherds at Feiran would have been discovered and the attention of the Russians, Egyptians, and UN constables focused on the oasis to the west of Mount Sinai. With luck, Lesh decided, or even without it, the Abou Moussa and the hostages could cover the necessary seventy-odd kilometers by road before dawn. He had decided on his destination. The strength of his position plus the ironic fitness of his choice of fortress filled him with delight. Bakunin would have been proud of this operation.

He heard the last shots fired as the Arabs finished off the American wounded, and two of their own who had been hit too badly to travel. The big black soldier had been responsible for the Arab losses. He had been the only American to put up effective resistance. Under his leadership, the few Special Forces soldiers had managed to kill six of the Abou Moussa before their ammunition ran out. Perhaps it was a streak of sentimentality unworthy of a socialist, he thought, but he had given orders that the black was to be spared and kept with the other prisoners, all of whom were now in one of the American vehicles, their elbows wired behind their backs, and under guard.

Leila Jamil approached him out of the dusty, diminishing firelight. It seemed to him that her eyes were much brighter and her manner more animated than at any time since he had met her on the gulf shore. He grinned at her and said, "A little success makes the heart warmer, no?"

"Everything is ready," she replied. "But where do we go?"

Lesh spread his map on the ground and used his pocket torch to light it. His blunt finger traced the road back toward the U.S. Sector, then down the demarcation line to Gebel

Katherina. He tapped the black square indicating the Monastery of St. Katherine at the base of Mount Sinai. "There. Just there. We will ask sanctuary," he said, amused with the idea.

Jamil stared at him and then began to laugh. It was the first time he had heard her do such a thing, and it startled him. He had not imagined she had any sense of the absurd, of the fantastic. It was a small revelation to know that she had this sort of audacity.

"It is a stone fortress. It would take artillery to drive us out once we are inside. And no one will go so far as that. The place is almost a thousand years old," he said.

"It is perfect," she said. "I congratulate you, Lesh. Now I see why you were the Silent One, alone with your thoughts."

He placed a hand on her shoulder, feeling the thin bones through the loosely woven robe. He was conscious of a rank animal smell that came from her, and he remembered how much he had wanted a woman while the fighting was going on.

She disengaged herself and stood. "But we have to travel through the Americans' sector."

"What can they do to us? We have *him.*" He indicated the back of the captured truck. "They might risk the others, but never Bailey." He grinned again. "If they had tanks, they could stop us, box us in, perhaps, wear us down. But they have none. They agreed not to bring any into this place. They have some aircraft, of course. But what can they do with them? They can watch us, that is all. And as for the monks of St. Katherine's—well, they can be persuaded to offer us sanctuary." He patted his slung Kalashnikov rifle.

He stood up and said, "Gather the men who will ride with us. The rest are to scatter and come by their own choosing to St. Katherine's on camelback. We go now."

The hubris that Lesh attributed to Vice President Bailey had largely vanished now. He sat in the back of the captured turbotruck, the wires holding his arms drawn back already sending sharp pains through his shoulders. The vehicle was traveling fast—as far as he could tell, back along the road to the U.S. Sector. Across from him sat the Israeli girl. She sat hunched forward in silent despair, the blood on her clothing cracking and flaking, her legs bare and dust-streaked. Beside her sat Tate's giant black sergeant, his face a mask of sullen anger and frustration. The Arabs had had to use their gun butts on him to take him alive, and there was blood on his face and on the front of his once-impeccable uniform. Seidel and Reisman had been forced to the floor of the truck to make room for the dozen or so armed guerrillas who had crowded in, and Bronstein huddled against the side of the vehicle beside the black soldier, shivering as though from an attack of fever.

The Vice President now had some time to consider his situation and the causes of it, and his reflections were far from arrogant. They were, rather, bleak and perplexed. He realized that he had made a serious mistake in not allowing General Tate to supply him with a stronger escort, but his perplexity stemmed mainly from the fact that he was in the hands of people whom he had never harmed, and whom he had, in fact, striven to help.

Now, and with shocking force, he remembered the killed men scattered about the ruined vehicles. If he had been safe in Washington reading about an assault such as this one, he would have intellectualized about the manner in which violence begets more violence. But there was no urge to intellectualize now. There was only the memory of recent wanton death, and he found that it sickened him and assaulted his lifelong belief that *reason* could deal with any wickedness.

Seven thousand miles away, in the equipment-cluttered and crowded intensive care unit of the Palm Springs Medical Center, a bright green line that had been moving in ever shallower and gentler waves across the phosphors of an EEG machine flattened to lie inert, an unmoving diameter across the face of the cathode-ray tube. And at that moment, in a truck crowded with killers who called themselves soldiers of a liberating army, among the shocked survivors of his mission, and when his cherished convictions were most seriously threatened, the Dove, Talcott Quincy Bailey, became, unknowing, the thirty-ninth president of the United States of America.

Fowler Beal, naked except for his lisle socks, sat on the edge of the round bed he had bought for Terri. A soft and rumpled face above a paunchy sixty-year-old body greeted him from the full-length mirrors that lined the walls of the pink-and-mauve room. Sweat matted his longish gray hair to his forehead in spiky ringlets, and as he looked down at his protruding abdomen he could see the labored beating of his heart between the womanish breasts. The girl, he thought bleakly, was going to kill him. She was going to screw him to death one day, and he would be found here, amid all her fluff and mirrors, a soft mound of old flesh sacrificed on the altar of a twenty-four-year-old's sexuality.

He could hear her now, splashing about in the bath, quite ready to spend the rest of this murky day touring Rockville's stores looking for pink negligees and country-and-western music records. She would do this just as soon as he was able to gather himself together, dress, and depart with weary steps, he thought, for his office, where he could rest. He could hear the radio in the bathroom playing the loud music that so delighted her.

He rubbed a palm across his mouth, feeling the soft flesh under his hand shift on the bones of his face. He wondered why he, who had had what any rational man would consider a successful career, should suddenly feel so low in spirits. In spite of his complaints about Terri's young appetites, he had always had someone much like her to fill his leisure hours, and he had usually enjoyed them. He had always been a sensual man, and he remained so at an age when most of his contemporaries had acquiesced to the imperatives of tired blood and enlarged prostates. But recently his ability to perform in bed had begun to pall. He wondered if it was because his feelings of intellectual and political inadequacy were on the rise once more.

Fowler Litton Beal had come to Washington as a young congressman from Idaho twenty-six years ago. In those days he had thought of himself as forceful, concerned, dedicated. That was so long ago that he found it hard to identify that young man with the man his constituents had long called, with scornful tolerance, "Old Fowler." Young Fowler Beal had come east with ambitions. A few terms in the House, then a move to the Senate, and from there—who could tell? The White House, possibly. And on arriving in Washington it had seemed to him that the way a young freshman got ahead was by being co-operative, acquiescent to the powers of the great party that had put him in Congress. There was nothing wrong with this philosophy. Hundreds of elected officials had traveled the same route to greatness in the course of the history of the republic. But for Beal, somehow co-operation became compliance; loyalty became a need to be dominated. "Old Fowler," the party leaders said, "never makes waves." His vote could always be counted in advance.

He was rewarded, of course, with party tasks: majority whip, caucus chairman. He became too valuable—and not valuable enough—to be taken out of the House of Representatives. And his farmer constituents co-operated by sending him back to the House again and again. "Old Fowler," *they* said, "might not be much, but the wheels and bigwigs trust him—and he isn't about to pull any surprises on them, or on us."

They were right. More and more, recently, he realized just

how right they were. He was Speaker of the House now, a party man. A lawmaker with a record that was either liberal or conservative depending on the cast of party doctrine in any given year over the last twenty-six. He was a man who could be told what to do and who would then do it—not brilliantly, but willingly and well enough, as any man could who long ago (privately but with secret relief) had abandoned independence of mind.

Yet there were times, such as now, when he regretted not having been more nearly the man he once imagined he would be. For years, ever since his wife, the daughter of a sophisticated political family, recognized his failings and closed her bedroom door to him, he had sought the mindless company of a series of "Terri's"; Washington was filled with them. Sometimes potency in bed made up for impotence in the Capitol. But sometimes it did not.

Early that morning he had left Admiral Ainsworth at Andrews after the President's departure. He had intended to go to his office, but somewhere between Andrews and East Potomac Park he had realized that he had, in actuality, little real work to do. And rather than spend a sterile morning in a silent office, he had gone on across the city to Rockville and Terri.

Terri, who had been selected with care because she was young, not so handsome as to encourage competition from younger men, voluptuous enough to appeal to a somewhat jaded man past his fifties, and slothful enough to be both grateful and almost always available, had been his mistress for over a year. There was no scandal about it, or even much gossip. The times were permissive enough for frontal nudity and sexual intercourse on stage and screen. The fact that the Speaker kept a mistress did not exactly add to his stature, but it did nothing to diminish it.

Even this, however, was vaguely disturbing to Beal on this day. He was a man to whom dependence had become a way of life, and his long record of absolute obedience had caused the party leaders—even the President—to take him for granted. It was natural in the circumstances that he should develop loyalties elsewhere. He needed leadership and guidance. Over the years he had become addicted to it. Stuart Ainsworth supplied it. The stern Admiral was the perfect father figure for the rumpled, sixty-year-old boy who had never grown fully into manhood. Ainsworth, Beal knew, did not approve of his liaison with nubile young girls; he was still a moralist, still a Calvinist crusader.

It was partially because of this that Beal had come to Terri MacLean's apartment with a certain stealth. It was because of this that he had fallen upon her gluttonously, exhausting himself in the abundance of her muscular young body. And it was because of this that he had shut himself away from the outside world for the heart of the day, pulling the telephone jack from the wall socket and refusing to let her play the radio in the bedroom.

Now, in the bath, she had turned on her transistor set in mild defiance of the old man who kept her and who secretly disgusted her, but whom she treated with considered respect and false prurience because he was generous and she was bone-lazy.

Beal knew that he should not be sitting here on the edge of Terri's ostentatious bed, naked but for socks, reviewing his career. But he felt lethargic, unwilling to return to the rainy, cold world outside this perfumed warmth.

He recalled his interview with Ainsworth the day before. The Admiral had taken him into his confidence to give him the information about the *Allende* incident before it became public knowledge. He had felt then, and he still felt, that Ainsworth's action had somehow committed him to something as yet left unspecified.

The door to the bath opened, and Terri appeared. She made a smirking, half-ironic gogo-girl entrance, nude and holding her transistor in an extended hand. The cacophonies of a rock tune were erupting from the small plastic cube. Terri's favorite station was a small independent located somewhere in the North Carolina back country. Its programing, as far as Beal could tell, consisted of commercials for acne salves and hemorrhoid reducers, incomprehensible talk, and trendy music.

The radio had a cord loop, and Terri, pointing her toes and swiveling her hips, draped the receiver around her neck so that it hung to the level of her deeply indented navel. She grinned mockingly at Beal and said, "Too tired to dance with me, Daddy?"

He regarded her through soggy, bloodshot eyes. She was a large girl, with a narrow waist and broad hips. Her thighs were muscular as a halfback's, and her breasts, swinging now in time to the music, were full, white, and traced with blue veins. She ran her hands up the inside of her thighs to the sparsely haired but prominently mounded pubis, making her way across the fluffy synthetic-animal-hair carpet toward the bed. In spite of himself, Beal felt the stirrings of new desire. He knew she was mocking him—she often did. But once she was under him in the rumpled bed they so often shared, her mockery was apparently consumed in a heat that he would not have believed possible to simulate.

Abruptly the noisy music stopped, for a full five seconds of dead air. Terri ceased her foolish gyrations and shook the radio, muttering, "Come *on*—"

The twangy, down-from-the-hills announcer–disc jockey came on. The man was obviously trying to sound serious, but he owned a clown's voice, which gave his words an obliquely shocking impact that a more portentous tone could not have achieved.

"We interrupt this program to bring you an update on the situation in Palm Springs. Reporters on the scene of the crash of Air Force One have learned from reliable sources that there are one, and possibly two, survivors. It is not known whether or not the President is among them. . . ."

Fowler Beal, stunned into a frozen immobility, heard someone behind the announcer saying something about Helen Risor, the President's secretary, and then the sound of a single teletype machine starting up, stopping, starting again. The announcer was saying: "The crash took place at approximately ten-forty-five this morning, Eastern Standard time, seven-forty-five o'clock Pacific time—"

Beal lurched for his watch amid the powdery confusion of Terri's dressing table. Ten-forty-five? My God, that was hours ago, he thought. He found the watch and studied the face as though it could tell him how it was that he had spent so long in sweaty sex without ever knowing that the President of the United States had crashed at an airport three thousand miles from this room. It was now three-thirty in the afternoon. Anything could have happened between then and now, he thought desperately, anything at all.

He ran clumsily across the room to the television set, in whose reflecting blank eye he had watched himself fucking Terri an hour—was it an hour?—ago. The picture flickered into smeary, colored life—a scene before a low glass-and-fieldstone building, the lawns and walks crowded with standing, silent people and batteries of television cameras. Beyond the building he could see palm trees whipping in a strong wind and the steep, purplish slope of a brilliantly sunlit mountain. A CBS correspondent was saying: "The announcement was made personally by the President's friend and physician, Major General Raymond Marty. The President died at 12:16, in the intensive care unit of this small, but modern, hospital. Needless to say, the press corps—representatives of which you can see standing silently before the hospital—was stunned by the news. It is very quiet here, ladies and gentlemen, since General Marty went back inside. No one speaks. The only sound is the wind blowing. The weather is clear and cold—"

The correspondent's voice thickened with emotion, and he seemed unable to continue. Then he said, "And so it is once again our sad duty to inform the American people that their President—" He stumbled, and went on, "That the President of the United States has died while in office. We all here remember that terrible day in Dallas—and now, it seems, it has come again—" The camera zoomed in on the solemn face. "Once again, the people of the United States, it seems, must learn to accept tragedy." He looked away across the blowing palm trees toward the mountains, swallowed, and drew a deep sighing breath. "From the Palm Springs Medical Center, this is Art Melcher returning you to CBS in New York."

Terri MacLean began to cry. She stood in the center of the room and her large breasts heaved with her weeping. "It can't be," she said. "It just can't be. Not the *President*. Not *again*."

Beal struggled to get himself dressed. There was a taste like rusty iron in his throat. He could half hear the voice of the CBS anchor man in New York saying that the Vice President was being recalled to Washington, that already expressions of sympathy were flowing into the capital from heads of state all over the world, and that business was at a standstill in New York and Washington.

Terri continued to howl—at least it sounded like howling to Beal. It was grief on a broad and shallow scale, and he found suddenly that it—and she—revolted him. He crumpled her dressing gown in his fist and threw it at her. "Here," he said, "get dressed."

She thrust her arms into the sleeves without protest, but continued to sob loudly. Beal fastened his trousers around his waist and changed channels. NBC was saying essentially what CBS had said, that the Vice President would be flown back to Washington at once to take the oath of office. Beal put on his shirt and coat and then searched for his shoes. He felt confused, fearful, and almost angry with the President for having done this thing.

He remembered having heard Ainsworth say once that if

the day ever came when Talcott Bailey moved into the White House, the nation would be in deadly danger from his liberalism, his isolationism, and his willingness to trust our enemies. Would it be like that, Beal wondered.

He was shocked into alertness by a hard, insistent knocking on the door. He looked at Terri. Her expression matched his own. "Were you expecting someone?" he asked over the sound of the television. Then he knew what a totally asinine question that was as the knocking became a hammering. He shuffled across the room into the entryway and opened the door a crack. Four armed men of the Air Police stood in the hallway. Their leader, a hard-faced master sergeant with white webbing and a gigantic-looking pistol, said: "Congressman Beal?"

"What is this—what do you mean—" Shoeless, disheveled, and without dignity, he floundered while searching for his lawmaker's aura of inviolability. Down the hall he could see open doors and fearful people looking.

"Are you Congressman Fowler L. Beal?" the Sergeant demanded again.

"Yes. Yes, I'm Congressman Beal."

"You will come with us, sir."

"Where? Why, I didn't send for—"

The Sergeant pushed the door open gently but firmly. The other three air policemen stared at Terri without a change of expression. She stood stupidly, gown drawn tight, belly and thighs outlined. Beal felt a hot flash of humiliation. "Go in the other room and find my shoes," he said to the girl. *"And cover yourself."*

"We have orders to escort you to the War Room, Congressman," the Sergeant said. "Immediately, sir."

"The War Room?" Beal heard his voice trembling and the sound of another field correspondent in Palm Springs describing the scene in front of the Palm Springs Medical Center for his television viewers. "Why the War Room? And by whose orders?"

"By order of Admiral Ainsworth, Congressman. We are to escort you to the Pentagon at once."

Ainsworth. By God, Ainsworth. Of course, Stuart would see to it that he was fully informed at once. A flood of relief shook him. Terri appeared with his shoes, and he put them on with as much dignity as he could muster.

"What's happening? Where are you going?" Terri wanted to know. She sounded confused and quite frightened.

His relief was diluted by the girl's fear and by the expressionless professionalism of the air policemen. He said, "I'm ready."

He allowed himself to be guided into the hallway. Terri tried to follow, but the air policemen closed the door on her before falling in behind him. They marched down the stairs, ignoring the elevator, to the parking area. There he was surprised to see a turbojeep, with four more AP's, these armed with automatic rifles, waiting behind an air force staff car.

They rode in silence through the streets of Rockville, onto Interstate 70 South, past Burning Tree. When the staff car turned onto Interstate 270 and began to parallel the river, the driver turned on his red light and hooter and increased speed to one hundred thirty kilometers per hour.

Beal, an armed airman on each side of him, had the uncomfortable and frightening feeling that he was a prisoner, and he wondered what the sergeant in command of his escort would do if he should demand to be taken to the Capitol rather than to the Pentagon. He did not want to find out, and so rode in mute dishevelment until the car and jeep swept into the Pentagon grounds and he was escorted, still under heavy guard, through the crowded outer rings toward the Command Center and the War Room.

Operations were not being conducted from the deep shelter, he noticed, but the heavy blast doors to the lift shaft were ajar, as though the War Room personnel might make that move at any time. The entire vast building, with which, as a member of the Armed Forces Committee, he was so familiar, seemed different somehow from the way it was on his last visit. The tight-lipped stillness of the personnel he passed might be accounted for by the news from Palm Springs. But there was a deeper tension running here, a *professional* intensity of purpose that he found quite chilling.

The War Room was teeming. The consoles were all manned: row on row of them, connecting the communicators and duty officers to SAC, to the fleets, to Norad inside Cheyenne Mountain, to NATO, and to the Americans in the Sinai.

He was escorted past the rings of consoles and computer stations, across the floor of the Pit, up the ramps to the five levels of communications stations, and into the glassed-in ring of offices facing the wall displays across the great bowl-shaped room.

At a steel door marked "Command and Control Beta," the escort halted. The Sergeant rapped twice on the door, opened it, and stood aside. Beal stepped through, and the Sergeant shut the door behind him.

At a desk that more closely resembled the flight deck of an airliner, or even the bridge of a nuclear carrier, sat Air Force General Armando Rivera. He stood when the Speaker came in and walked around the bank of television screens to his right. The General's military neatness made Beal even more conscious of his own rumpled, uncombed, and dampened appearance.

Rivera said, "I am pleased they found you so quickly, Mr. Speaker."

"Where is Stuart?" Beal asked, a trifle belligerently. "I understand it's by his orders I was brought here."

Rivera essayed a small and quite mirthless smile. "Admiral Ainsworth has been to Palm Springs and almost back today, Mr. Speaker." He glanced at the complicated golden chronograph on his slender dark wrist and said, "The Chairman will be at Andrews in less than an hour."

"Then perhaps you can tell me why it was necessary to

bring me here under guard, General. I should be at the Capitol—"

"As I said, Mr. Speaker, it was Admiral Ainsworth's personal command. The first consideration must be for your safety."

"Why should I be in danger?"

"Please sit down, Mr. Speaker."

Beal automatically did as he was told and settled into one of the gray metal chairs facing the complex desk. Rivera reached across the uncluttered surface to press a switch. The face of an aide in army green appeared on a telescreen. "Smith, I am not to be disturbed for a few moments. I've handed C and C over to General Brandis until the Admiral arrives. He will operate from C and C Delta."

"Yes, sir." The image on the telescreen faded.

In spite of himself, Beal was both disturbed and impressed. It was unusual for two of the Joint Chiefs to be on duty in the War Room at one time. Yet here were Rivera, of the Air Force, and Brandis, of the Marine Corps. And were the others here? He had the uneasy feeling that they were indeed present somewhere in the maze of offices and observation posts overlooking the Pit.

The tragedy in Palm Springs might account for it, but Beal sensed something more, something that struck him as ominous. His political instinct was warning him that matters were not as well in hand as they appeared to be.

"Mr. Speaker," Rivera said, "I am about to give you highly classified information. Have I your word that it will remain with you and *only* you, until the situation is clarified?"

Beal was accustomed to such warnings and provisos. He was a known friend of the military and he was trusted by the generals and admirals far more than any other member of his party.

"You can be certain of my discretion, General Rivera." He felt much better on this level. This was political, a feature he recognized in the familiar landscape of the country of *quid pro quo*. But he was not prepared for the shock Rivera delivered so suavely and efficiently.

"At approximately 1415 hours Greenwich Mean time, Vice President Bailey entered the Demilitarized Zone around thirty-four east en route to his scheduled meeting with Soviet Deputy Premier Anatoly Rostov. At approximately 1630 hours GMT, an Olympus message was forwarded to his convoy to inform him of the accident involving Air Force One." The smooth, saturnine face betrayed no emotion whatever. The dark eyes remained fixed on Beal's own.

"No reply to the Olympus message was received," Rivera continued, and Beal felt his heart give a slight lurch of apprehension. He had a terrible premonition that he knew what the General intended to tell him in this impromptu briefing, and why he had been rushed to the War Room under such heavy security.

"When no reply to the Olympus message was received by Echo Sierra Control in Es Shu'uts, General Tate attempted to contact the Vice President's escort by ordinary VHF radio and in plain language. No reply to this message was received either."

Beal's mouth felt dry. A tight griping had seized his stomach muscles.

Rivera went on. "At 1730 hours GMT—1930 Sinai time—General Tate ordered an air search of the Vice President's route. In so doing he violated the terms of the Cyprus Accord, by the way, and General Eriksson, of the Swedish Component of the Peacekeeping Force, has already filed a protest with the Cyprus Commission of the United Nations. He was joined in his protest by the Egyptians, Syrians, Libyans, and Iraqis—but not the Russians—"

Beal felt a release of some of his tension in outraged anger at the pomposity, litigiousness, and insensitivity of the Swedes and the Arabs. "Damn them—and damn the UN, too. What did they expect Tate to do—" He broke off, his concern recentering on the single important fact he now knew: Talcott Bailey was *not* on board a fast jet returning to the United States.

Rivera said stonily, "I will shorten this, Mr. Speaker. At 2100 hours GMT, just a short time ago, a Shrike jet fighter of our component picked up heat on its infrared sensors and made a closer investigation, illuminating the source of the radiation with paraflares. The pilot has reported that he is hovering over the Vice President's convoy—*or what is left of it*. There is evidence that there was a fire fight, Mr. Speaker. Casualties are scattered about, and there are many wrecked vehicles—the source of the infrared that attracted the Shrike pilot's attention. The fact seems to be, sir, that the Vice President has been attacked and possibly killed. *There are no apparent survivors.*"

Beal, though instinctively forewarned that it might be something like this, found it difficult to cope with the reality. Coming so soon after the shock of the announcement of the President's death, it only added to a numbness, to an already overloaded perception. But Rivera had not finished. Beal wondered at his ability to keep his cold composure.

"That is not all," he continued. "We have evidence that the Russian government had knowledge that an Arab terrorist group—an outfit calling itself the Abou Moussa Commando —was in the southern Sinai *two full days ago*. Admiral Ainsworth suspects that the Soviet government may be implicated in the attack on the Vice President. And it follows that there is the possibility—I might say even the probability—that the KGB had something to do with what happened this morning in Palm Springs."

Beal felt suddenly very ill, shaken with a nervous nausea that was half fear and half anger. His hands trembled and he clasped them together to hold them steady.

"Are you familiar with a scenario called Case Headless, Mr. Speaker?"

Beal nodded. "It was presented to a few members of Congress by some Yale psychologist, last year, I think it was."

"Then, sir, you'll understand," said Rivera quietly, "why it was so necessary to ensure your personal safety. If the conditions of Headless are actually met, *you,* sir, may be the acting president of the United States."

18

In the glare of the hastily assembled floodlights, the medical teams and investigators worked through a scene resembling some surrealist hell. Outside the immediate area of illumination, the American helicopters—including Tate's—rested like sleeping insects, casting long black shadows across the lunar-like landscape. The moving men crossed and recrossed the lights, their voices low and filled with suppressed rage at the carnage left by the Abou Moussa ambush.

A team of communications technicians was setting up television cameras and a parabolic transceiver antenna, collecting equipment from the cargo helicopter parked on the edge of the light. Heavily armed patrols of parachute infantry brought in from El Thamad patrolled the perimeter, and from time to time the night was disturbed by the whining roar of a Shrike overhead.

The medics had gathered the bodies, which now lay in a long row at some distance from the bullet-holed and burned vehicles. They had searched in vain for a single survivor. The commanding officer of the medical team had reported to Tate what he had already suspected: the wounded had been machine-gunned where they lay. Even the Arab bodies had been riddled with bullets at muzzle-point range. All weapons had been taken except those damaged by gunfire.

Tate walked slowly along the line of corpses, studying the

white bloodstained faces in the brightness from the floodlights. The civilians, he thought, looked surprised. He stopped, recognizing the features of Abel Crissman, the Reuters correspondent. Crissman's eyes stared at the dark, predawn desert sky. Tate walked on down the line of the dead, noting each of the dozen or so men who had arrived at Es Shu'uts only yesterday to accompany the Vice President on his mission of peace to Zone Center.

Newsmen had died in guerrilla war before this, he thought, and quite possibly they would again. But this wasn't war. It had been a massacre, with overtones to remind one of the murders at Lod Airport. He could see that at least one grenade had been thrown at the vehicles carrying the newsmen and their equipment. One of the dead men still carried a camera, now smashed, around his neck. Had he tried to take pictures, Tate wondered, when the fight began?

He had found Dov Rabin's body near his command car, and the shattered corpses of the other Israeli officers. But not Deborah. He had momentarily succumbed to a flood of relief that broke through the wall of deliberately nurtured insensitivity with which he had surrounded himself since he'd learned of the ambush. Yet the knowledge that Deborah was not among the dead was a piece of information to be received with mixed emotions. If she was not dead, then she must be among the hostages taken by the Arabs. The thought of how they were apt to use an Israeli woman soldier made him burn with anxiety and anger.

More important to the world, if not to him personally, was the discovery that the Vice President's body—no, that was wrong, he corrected himself—the *President's* body was not among the casualties. He wondered, with a chilling sense of the insanity of the situation, if Lesh and the men of the Abou Moussa realized the importance now of the man they had taken. They had aimed high, those terrorist killers. Did they know already how much higher they had managed to strike? The enormity of the dangers that flowed from this was almost mind-numbing. What crazy wave of panic would sweep the world when it became known that the President of the United States was a hostage of a band of revolutionary psychopaths?

He turned away and stood watching the technicians adjusting their cameras. At least, he thought, they apparently had not killed the Judge, or Jape Reisman, or even that bearded feather merchant Paul Bronstein. The body of Secret Service Agent Emerson had not been found either, so the Vice President—no, damn it, he told himself, making himself face the terrible reality—the President, Talcott Quincy Bailey—the President was not alone.

It had surprised Tate to find the bodies of his Special Forces men without finding Sergeant Robinson's. But he remembered that he had told Robinson that the safety of the Vice President rested with him, and so it was probable that Robinson had managed to stay alive and with Bailey.

He glanced at his watch. It was now 0430 hours. Two hours to sunrise. His patrols and air sweeps were covering all of southeastern Sinai, but they were few and the land was broad and rugged. And what, he asked himself, can I do if I find what we are searching for? The Arabs had shown on many occasions that the murder of hostages was not beyond them. On the contrary, to *fail* to kill hostages when attacked was to render incredible the primary weapon of their way of fighting against superior force. No, even if they could be found before they went to ground with their captives, there was little that could be accomplished with military power. He would have to wait for them to make their demands and then see what could be done—though the scope of those demands, given the strength of the terrorists' bargaining position, could literally be world-shaking.

Across the area, Tate could see the small detachment of UN troops gathered around General Eriksson's white-painted vehicle. The blue UN flag hung limply from the radio whip, limply, and ineffectually.

The Swede had actually complained to the Cyprus Commission that the Americans were guilty of massive violations of the Demilitarized Zone with aircraft and light armored vehicles. This was so outrageous and incredible, given the circumstances, that Tate had had to avoid Eriksson for fear of losing command of himself and punching the son of a bitch in the face.

The communications officer had reported earlier that a Soviet party consisting of Anatoly Rostov, Yuri Ulanov, and some army medics was coming up from Zone Center to offer assistance. There was, of course, no real assistance the Russians could give. There was nothing here in this hell of sand and broken machines except the angry and the dead. But the stunning series of events that had, in two hours or less, shocked the United States of America seemed to have shaken the Kremlin almost as much as it had Washington. The fact that the United States had immediately gone into a condition of nuclear readiness appeared to have badly frightened the Soviet leadership. There were rumors circulating already about possible sabotage of Air Force One, and there was that damning Cosmos print that seemed to prove the Russians had prior knowledge of a commando in southern Sinai.

Tate, knowing the Russians as he did, and aware that the traditional Russian gloominess was only one facet of a Slavic emotionality Westerners seldom recognized, had a suspicion that the proximity of the *Allende* incident's capture on film and the almost incidental disclosure of the Albanian adviser on another picture of the same series had caused a blunder in Moscow. He suspected that the Soviets were so worked up about having caught the Americans in the act of harassing their ship off the Sinai coast that they had failed to evaluate the entire film strip before "leaking" it to the Israelis. Donaldson had once told him that intelligence services make small mistakes by the thousands, and occasionally gigantic ones, as in the case of the Bay of Pigs and the U-2 incident. The KGB or the GRU, or whosoever's responsibility it had been to evaluate the Cosmos 623 film, had probably done just that—

made an error. Whether it was to be a small one or a world ball-breaker remained to be seen.

Now, in a rush of apprehension, the Russians were seeing the results of their oversight: the United States at Yellow Alert, and every ancient Cold War suspicion reborn. Therefore, naturally, they must come to sympathize, to offer help. And to snoop.

And Mosa'ad—what about them? Had *they* made a mistake in sending Dov Rabin and Deborah Zadok out to Zone Center with the American Vice President? Yet how could they have known that the American commander would lack the courage to insist, against any threat of opposition from the Dove, that the party have a really adequate escort? This was the result, he thought, looking about him at the carnage. And this was the private hell he would wander for the rest of his life. There would be temptations to blame others: Trask, for blunderingly creating the *Allende* affair, which masked so much happening elsewhere; Liz Adams, for delaying information that could have been vital in forestalling the ambush; even the airmen of the President's Flight, for failing to deliver their precious cargo safely to a sunlit California city. And Talcott Bailey's blind liberalism, his inability to see that good will was no defense against the intent of evil men. He could try hard to evade the responsibility for this disaster and let someone else take the blame. But in the final analysis this had been a military failure, and this single fact identified it as his personal defeat—his and no other's. It had been his job to keep Bailey and the others safe. He had not done it.

A communications officer reported, saluting crisply. "The cameras are set, General. We can begin transmitting pictures any time." In the flurry of movements triggered by the discovery of the battleground by the Shrike, Tate had received specific orders from the Joint Chiefs of Staff to establish a television link between the scene of the ambush and the War Room in the Pentagon. The order had come directly from General Brandis, on duty as command and control chief.

It was nearly quarter of five now, 2145 hours in Washington. It must be a somber, subdued, and probably frightened Washington: a city that had just been told by its highest military officers that unseen enemies were plotting, that these same enemies were somehow involved in the death of the President, and that it was considered prudent to take precautions against a possible nuclear attack. It was, Tate thought, as though the whole damned world had begun to go mad in neat, segmented increments. What would President Bailey think about having been inadvertently, partially, and *involuntarily* responsible for an ominous Yellow Alert?

"Start transmitting when you are ready, Lieutenant," he said. He had misgivings about telecasting this emotion-rousing, bloody, and outrageous scene into the sterile unreality of the Pentagon's War Room in living, crimson color, but he had his orders.

He walked slowly across the road and up the gentle slope of the hill on the western side of the killing ground, leaving the bright glare of the floodlights. Twice before he reached the crest he was challenged by soldiers of the Special Forces detachment and once held for close scrutiny at gunpoint. The men of the detachment here were ready to kill, and the slaughtered bodies of their comrades and the civilians down by the wrecked vehicles were all the justification they needed. Tate felt the same way his men did—frustrated, angered, sickened, and hungry for some form of retribution. But against whom? And at what price? Already, in Jerusalem, the government of the State of Israel was debating its response to the stunning demands that were certain to come.

Tate walked past the line of hastily posted sentries on the hill and looked back at the scene below. From this distance the shot-up vehicles looked like broken toys. On the Vice President's car, the Circle and Arrows placard was barely recognizable, a symbol lost in the ruin and destruction.

For a moment Tate surrendered to his own bitterness against Talcott Bailey, whose self-righteous arrogance had led to this bloody hour. Once again he thought of Deborah in the hands of the Abou Moussa, and a cold premonition settled into the pit of his stomach.

A message was coming in to the radio on the edge of the lighted area below. The sound carried clearly through the predawn darkness. One of the helicopter detachments had a convoy under observation and was investigating. He felt a flash of hope that it might actually be the Abou Moussa, but then he heard the pilot of the gunship reporting that it was a detachment of Russian vehicles moving up from Zone Center, and asking should they be stopped.

The question carried with it a chilling overtone of suspicion and hostility. It was hardly surprising in the present circumstances, but it drove personal thoughts from Tate's mind, and he jogged back down the hill to the message center to order the gunship pilot not to interfere with the newcomers.

Within minutes he could see the lights of the approaching vehicles, four of them: a Russian jeep, a staff car, and two thin-skinned personnel carriers filled with soldiers. They stopped abruptly thirty meters from the wreckage of the convoy. The American soldiers formed a loose ring around them, M-36's pointed inward. From the slope Tate could see that the Russian personnel carriers were being covered by at least one section of Special Forces troops armed with antitank weapons. An angry tension seemed to crackle in the desert air.

A stocky figure dismounted from the jeep and crossed in front of the headlights. It was Grigory Novotny. His meaty face showed mingled anger and apprehension at the hostility of the reception. What did the man expect, Tate wondered as he strode down to the road to meet him. From the other side of the road, Eriksson trotted toward the Russian vehicles, gesticulating for the American troops to get back, to lower their weapons. The soldiers ignored him.

Novotny saw Tate and made a gesture approximating a salute. He said blusteringly, "Are we going to have still another incident, General? Do we have to defend ourselves against you?"

Tate returned the salute correctly and said, "Keep your men in their vehicles, Colonel Novotny, until our dead are removed."

The KGB man looked across the lighted area to where the bodies were now being put into plastic bags. He started to speak, and then thought better of it. From the staff car came the bearlike form of Yuri Ulanov. When he reached Tate he stood looking at the dead before he spoke. "William," he said heavily, "I am sorry. How many did they kill?"

"Twenty-six," Tate said in a flat tone. "There were no surviving wounded. They were shot."

"I must speak to you," Ulanov said, looking meaningfully at Novotny. When Novotny made no move to retire, he jerked his head angrily and said, "I will speak to General Tate alone, Grigory Konstantinovich." Novotny retired reluctantly.

"Idiot," muttered Ulanov. "Why are spies and policemen always such fools?"

Tate did not reply. He stood facing the Russian, trying to analyze the cold anger and distrust he felt for a man he admired. Even if the Soviets were in some way implicated in the series of disasters that had overtaken the United States in the last hours, he felt almost certain that the old General bore none of the responsibility. Yet the possibility that his countrymen might be capable of such fantastically dangerous treachery smeared Ulanov, diminished him, in Tate's eyes.

Ulanov said, "Must we stand under the guns of your soldiers, William?" He was a proud man, and Tate understood that it cost him something to make what could be regarded as a submissive remark, a plea for a lessening of the tension between them and their respective detachments.

Tate turned his head and said sharply, "All right, you men. These people have my permission to stay in this area. There will be no mixing with the Russians. They will stay in their vehicles." The last of his order was given distinctly and deliberately, and for the purpose of making it clear to Ulanov that, for the moment, judgments were in abeyance.

Eriksson came up and said protestingly, "We are in the Demilitarized Zone, Generals. Neither of you has a legal right to issue orders here."

Tate wheeled swiftly and said, "General Eriksson, return to your men and don't interfere, or I will place you in arrest."

The Swede began to complain to Ulanov in Russian, but the old General cut him off. "I would do as he says, General, if I were you."

"The commissioners will hear of this, too," Eriksson said, and marched off stiffly.

Ulanov said, "He is right, you know, William. Neither you nor I has any authority here. You have violated the terms of the accord by bringing in aircraft."

"I will bring in an armored division, if it will find our President," Tate said.

Ulanov nodded slowly. "So would I, if it would help."

"How easily you say that, General. You might have helped earlier."

Ulanov frowned at Tate's tone and said, "I swear to you that we did not know there were terrorists nearby."

"I saw photographs that suggest otherwise, General," Tate said coldly. "You made one hell of a row over Trask and the *Allende*. If you had been as quick to respond to what else those photographs showed, we might have been able to prevent this."

"I learned of it only two hours ago. That is the truth."

"I've had twenty years of dealing with Leninist truth," Tate said. "But never mind that. What I believe isn't important. It is what is believed in Washington that counts, and the military there is being more skeptical than usual."

Ulanov's eyes veiled. "Your strategic forces have been alerted, William. We do not understand such an act of hostility. At whom can such a threat be leveled?"

"The KGB may have missed the Abou Moussa on its own photographs, but I would guess it has heard that there is talk Air Force One might have been sabotaged. And now this—" He gestured at the wreckage and the dead. "You had better return to Zone Center, Yuri, and let me get on with what I have to do."

"We have had to bring our own forces to alert status," Ulanov rejoined. "We do not wish to do this, and we understand that you are disturbed and angered by what has happened, but we must take steps to discourage any threat against our own land."

He sounded so mournful, so genuinely concerned and moved by the rapid series of events, that Tate was touched in spite of his suspicions.

"We come back to the same thing. Why didn't you warn us there were Arab guerrillas here?"

Ulanov said in an angry tone, "The spies, William, the stupid spies. They could only have been so overjoyed at having caught your airman insulting our Deputy Premier that they failed to evaluate all the films until it was too late. It was the Jews who identified the man Lesh, not our fine KGB or GRU." He looked intently at Tate and asked, "Did your CIA do so much better? Could they not have warned you that Lesh was in the Sinai?"

It was a telling point, Tate conceded. The fact was that intelligence agencies had a fatal tendency to fail when they were most relied upon. In his own military career he could not count the number of bad decisions that had been made on the basis of faulty or misinterpreted intelligence. But this time, the failure was of such a magnitude that the consequences were impossible to predict. Already, the two major nuclear powers were tense and suspicious, ready to forestall any pre-emptive move. Even in this place, surrounded by the debris of horror, one could sense the greater dangers looming beyond the horizon.

"Let us help you," Ulanov said. "At least let us show that we are not to blame for this."

Tate stared hard at the General. All of his adult life had been lived with Cold War realities. The years of so-called *détente* could not eliminate those realities. He had seen his soldiers and friends killed by Communist bullets while apologists argued. Yet Ulanov was a man he thought he knew, and knew he admired. He was a soldier's soldier, a man with a deep love for his country that paralleled Tate's own for America. This love did not mean that one must agree with all that one's politicians did. Often the contrary was necessary, though dissent was more dangerous for a Ulanov than for a Tate.

Ulanov seemed to read his thoughts, in that disconcerting way he had. "We know one another, William," he said. "We are the new sort of soldier, you and I. I am old and you are young, but in one way we are of the same mind. We believe that if the politicians cannot keep the peace between us, then we must do it. We have our differences. But there is no ideology in a graveyard." He laid a heavy hand on Tate's shoulder. "I say it again. Let us help you if we can. What we do here is vital. You know that is so."

Tate said slowly, "Unless we can find the Abou Moussa and take their hostages, Yuri, the choices will be made in Washington and Moscow, not here."

"This thing that has happened, how will it be resolved in Washington?"

"If Talcott Bailey is dead, the Speaker of the House—a man named Fowler Beal—becomes acting president."

"What sort of man is this? Is he strong?"

Tate shook his head regretfully. "He is not strong. He is—a man who can be influenced."

"By the fascists in your government?"

Tate's anger flared, and, exasperated, he said, "For God's sake, Yuri. One minute you begin to make sense and the next you talk like an agitprop fool. Simply because a man distrusts the USSR doesn't make him a fascist. You have given us reason enough to be wary over the last thirty years."

"But still," Ulanov persisted, with Slavic stubbornness, "there are many such men in the Pentagon."

"You had better understand this, Yuri: very few Americans anywhere trust the Soviet government. That is a fact of life. Learn to live with it."

"The Chairman of your Joint Chiefs of Staff is such an American."

"Yes."

"And he would influence this man Beal?"

"Very much."

"But if Beal is a weak man, how will he become your president?"

"The office does not go to the strongest, Yuri. The succession is governed by law. And though you people may think of us as a nation of hooligans and gangsters, there are laws we keep. The Constitution is such a law, and it tells us that if Talcott Bailey is dead, or unable to act, the Speaker of the House of Representatives becomes our president. This has never happened before, but the law binds us just the same."

Ulanov sighed and raised his eyes to the eastern horizon, where the first faint light had begun to show in the sky. He said heavily, "We had such hopes—some of us." He shrugged his thick shoulders inside his greatcoat. "I think I shall never really understand Americans," he said. "But if you tell me that this is the way it must be, I believe you. Come with me, William. There is someone waiting to speak with you in the automobile. Perhaps the fact that he is here will reassure you."

"Rostov?" Tate asked.

Ulanov nodded.

"It proves nothing, Yuri."

"Speak with him anyway. There are things you should know, and he would prefer to tell them to you."

Tate nodded briefly and followed the Russian over to the big dusty staff car.

Anatoly Rostov opened the door to the rear seat and said in thickly accented English, "Come inside, General."

Tate entered the car. The driver and an aide eyed his side arms uneasily, but Rostov motioned them away impatiently. His eyes fixed on Tate like pinpoints of black metal, probing. "This is a disaster, General," he said without preamble. "For all of us. We must do what can be done to make it less dangerous. Do you agree?"

"I agree to that, Mr. Deputy Premier," Tate said noncommittally.

"But little else, I suppose," Rostov said. "Well, one can't blame you for that." He shifted his weight on the seat, and Tate felt that the man was frightened—and certainly not for his own safety, despite the presence of so many angry American troops. "We should have warned you about the Abou Moussa," Rostov continued. "Or we should have taken action ourselves. We would have done that if we had realized. Do you believe that?"

"What I believe doesn't matter right now, sir. The *fact* is that you did neither of those things."

"Well, General, whether you believe it or not, if the fools at GRU headquarters had done their work properly, we would have ignored that idiot's game our intelligence plays with yours and warned you at once that Lesh was in the Sinai. He is a known Maoist, a wrecker, an enemy of peace and of the Soviet and American peoples. He might as easily have attacked me as your Vice President." The bright eyes narrowed. "Why was your Vice President so lightly protected, General? Surely you knew that there are always chances for guerrillas to slip into the Peacekeeping Area?"

Tate took the thrust in silence. Why had Bailey been so lightly protected? Why, indeed? To understand that, Rostov would have had to have a far better grasp than he did of American politics and the antimilitarism of a Talcott Bailey. Clearly, no Russian accustomed to the autocracy and discipline of a Communist state could even begin to understand the forces that influenced the decisions of a man like the Vice President.

"In the Soviet Union," Rostov said cruelly, "whoever was responsible for the security of Mr. Bailey would most likely be shot, General."

"Americans handle these things differently, Mr. Deputy Premier," Tate said. "But the end result may well be the same."

"Then," said Rostov, "it is to your advantage to co-operate with us."

Tate's voice became colder. "Don't bargain with me, Mr. Deputy Premier. My president is dead; the man who should take his place may be dead and is certainly in danger. My men have been attacked and murdered. For the moment that is what concerns me—and only that. If you think you can help, I will accept your aid. If not, I suggest you get out of the Demilitarized Zone as quickly as you can. There could be incidents that would make matters worse than they are. I have already violated the terms of the Cyprus Accord by bringing aircraft into the DMZ and—" his tone became more uncompromising—"I intend to violate it as much and as often as I must to get our people back. I hope that is very clear."

"It is clear enough, General. And I give you my assurance that the Soviet forces in the Peacekeeping Area will co-operate with you in every way possible," Rostov said. "Of course, you realize that General Eriksson has already filed a protest with the Cyprus Commission, and the attitude of the commission will influence the response of my government." He raised a blunt-fingered hand to forestall comment. "But until such time as I receive instructions from Moscow to the contrary, I shall order General Ulanov to offer every assistance. Already I have commanded Colonel Yudenich to begin air searches over our sector, and General Suweif has been instructed to pick up all suspected guerrilla partisans in his area." He peered outside at the garishly lighted patch of desert where the medical teams were now loading the bodies of the dead into helicopters. Shaking his head slowly in disbelief, he said, "This has been the act of madmen, General. Of criminals. We had no part in it. The Soviet government would not involve itself in such a thing."

"So General Ulanov tells me, sir," Tate said, still uncommitted to Rostov's claims of innocence, though he suspected the Deputy Premier was telling the simple truth.

"There is something that has happened that you may not know about, General," Rostov said. "It may have some significance or it may not. At the moment I do not know. But on the way to Zone Center we picked up a wounded man. An old monk from the Monastery of St. Katherine at Mount Sinai. He had been shot. Monks seldom get shot, General—at least in this part of the world. The man, as I say, is very old. Remembering something about the ways of monks from my childhood, I would guess he was on retreat somewhere else in the massif. He raved about Feiran, about the oasis there, and about being attacked by Saracens. Saracens have been rare in the Sinai since the eleventh century. But guerrillas are not, as we both know to our cost. I ordered Yudenich to airlift a unit of soldiers to Feiran to investigate. They found a massacre there, too, General. Native Bedouins—about thirty or more—all killed and left at the oasis. Apparently they were ambushed by men with automatic weapons—"

"With Russian weapons, Mr. Deputy Premier?" Tate asked deliberately.

"The weapons may have been of Soviet manufacture," Rostov said. "Let that go for now. Later we can investigate. Perhaps Novotny can explain how Soviet weapons reached a murder gang inside the Peacekeeping Area. I fear that we must attribute this great battle and victory to the Abou Moussa Commando. In addition to this—" he nodded at the scene outside—"they attacked and killed a party of Bedouins armed with knives, shepherd's crooks, and jezails. They must have needed their animals—or perhaps they simply attacked them as a testing exercise or for their campsite near the water.

From what we know of the man Lesh, he would kill many more for much less. That is one of the reasons that you must allow us to help you, General. If your people are in the hands of such a man, the danger is very great. Even the Arab people would not wish anything more to happen to Mr. Bailey, who has always been known as their friend, even though Americans are traditionally pro-Israel."

Tate ignored the political remark and asked, "The monk saw the attackers?"

Rostov shrugged. "Who knows? He was near enough to be shot, far enough away to escape and wander north to the road where we picked him up. But I have been asking myself: where would Lesh and his gang of hooligans seek shelter now? Where in all this wilderness would they be safe, and even comfortable, while they formulate the demands they will surely make?"

"The Monastery of St. Katherine?"

"Of course. There is nothing else in the south of the peninsula—and surely they dare not move north. Even the Egyptians would not give them shelter. It must be the monastery."

"Did you act on this assumption?"

Rostov shrugged and shook his head. "*We?* No, General. We have not brought aircraft in to violate the Demilitarized Zone. I cannot order such an action without permission from Moscow. But you—"

But I, thought Tate, have already broken the terms of the accord and bear the responsibility on my own head. He could almost smile at the cynicism of the Russian. He offered help, but it would be of a highly equivocal kind, intended only to proclaim Russian innocence to the world. He could do without that sort of aid.

"If and when I require assistance, Mr. Deputy Premier," Tate said, "you will be among the first to know." He moved to leave the car, but Rostov restrained him.

"A moment, General." Rostov's tone carried a note of warning. "You will be reporting to Washington, of course. I ask that you caution your superiors against any rashness. The Soviet government is guiltless in this affair, and we will take whatever measures are necessary to prove it. But we will also take precautions to safeguard ourselves. We will not allow this tragedy to become the excuse for imperialist adventurism."

"Mr. Deputy Premier," Tate said, "for thirty years the Soviet government has abrogated agreements, supported subversion, subsidized murder and armed revolutionaries. Wherever there has been mischief in the world, the government of your country has encouraged it. It may be difficult to convince my countrymen you've had no part in this. *I* believe you—because I think such an act would be too dangerous, even for you. But, Mr. Deputy Premier, it would never have happened without everything that's gone before—all those years of Soviet troublemaking. So you are just going to have to sweat it out, sir, like the rest of us."

He stepped from the car and walked past Ulanov without speaking, back across the battleground toward the communications team that was telecasting the scene to the Pentagon's War Room.

He returned to his helicopter, where Beaufort waited, and said, "Get a flight of helos down over St. Katherine's, Captain. I want it under observation until further notice."

"Do the helos attack if they spot the commando?" Beaufort asked.

"Under no circumstances. The choppers are to locate, observe, and report. Nothing more than that except on direct orders from me."

"Yes, sir." Beaufort climbed back into the helicopter to use the command-net radio.

Ulanov had followed Tate across the road to the aircraft. In the harsh light his greatcoated figure was massive and shapeless as a boulder. "William," he said in Russian, "you spoke with the Deputy Premier about the old monk?"

"Yes."

"I listened to the old man myself. He is—or was—the

keeper of the ossuary of St. Katherine's—the charnel house where they bury their dead."

"How does that help?" Tate asked.

"I'm not sure. But I believe I once read that one can enter the monastery from underground at the ossuary. One might assault the place in that way."

Stalingrad again, thought Tate. The old General had never forgotten the battles fought underground in the sewers of that ruined city.

"I will have the medics question him," Ulanov continued. "I would do it myself, but I have no Greek." He placed his hand on Tate's shoulder. "This may not be the time—but I will say it anyway. You have my sympathy. For the loss of your president. For the death of your soldiers."

"I thank you, Yuri," Tate said. *"Do svidaniya, tovarishch."*

Ulanov lumbered away, back to the line of Russian vehicles. Tate watched them reverse and roll away toward Zone Center. Eriksson and his men followed.

A lieutenant from the communications section appeared. "Sir, we are transmitting to the War Room. The Chairman is there and wants to talk to you."

It was a conversation—no, a confrontation—that Tate would readily have avoided just now, but it was impossible. He looked again at the sky. It was growing light swiftly. Whatever was to be done must be done soon. He left the helicopter and joined the technicians at the television transceivers to make his report to Admiral Stuart Ainsworth.

For Deborah Zadok the last hours had been a chaotic horror. She was tortured by the remembrance of the explosive violence of the ambush, the bad death of Dov Rabin, the flight of the Vice President's party, and their quick capture. She had sat dully through the hours in the back of the captured American truck smelling the dusty sweat of the Arabs, the sickening odor of the blood on her clothes, and the stink of recently fired weapons. Jammed in among the guerrillas, she had endured the proddings and petty cruelties of the men, who seemed to derive some childish pleasure from inflicting pain on an Israeli woman soldier: pinches and twisting of flesh, groping hands on thighs and legs, gun muzzles shoved against her breasts. When the Americans had tried to intervene, they had been threatened with shooting, and on one occasion Sergeant Robinson had been struck in the face with a rifle stock.

Talcott Bailey had seemed stunned into silence by the quick reversal of his situation. He appeared to be having difficulty understanding that he was in the hands of people who had not the slightest conception of what his station in life demanded in the way of respect and good treatment. He had the look of a man who was experiencing true violence for the first time.

The young man called Bronstein had been thrown into a state of shock. Each movement by an Arab guard had made him flinch, and even in the gloom of the truck she could see the terrible, staring fear that was fixed on his bearded face.

Colonel Seidel had taken the capture as well as anyone could—with some dignity, some controlled anger, but with an over-all self-possession that had, apparently, impressed the Arabs. At least they had avoided offering him personal offense or physical abuse. Even their threats were presented in a sort of decorous silence; weapons were pointed at him with a peculiarly Arabic formality that clearly implied they would kill him quickly enough, but with regret.

The stolen vehicles had run east for a time, then south along the road to St. Katherine's, speeding nose to tail without lights. Once, Deborah had heard the sound of a jet aircraft flying low, but either they had not been seen or the pilot had not known what, if anything, could be done to stop them without risking harm to the hostages.

She had not been able to look outside, but her knowledge of the peninsula and of Arab terrorist tactics suggested that the Abou Moussa was heading for the Monastery of St. Katherine. It would make a splendid strong point from which to announce their intentions: it was a dramatic location and it was completely defenseless by its present residents, a quality that would make it peculiarly attractive to guerrillas.

They had arrived just before dawn, and the European, the man who called himself Lesh, had turned out all but a pair of guards, who remained behind to cover the hostages. Shortly thereafter there had been shouting and some gunfire and the sound of a Bedouin woman wailing.

The Abou Moussa had broken into the monastery with ease. Until the nineteenth century, access to the place had been limited to a single opening cut into the granite walls some five meters above the ground. Travelers had been lifted to it in a basket—but then only after the monks had assured themselves that the strangers would neither threaten them nor disturb their monastic quiet. But this was no longer the case. The walls had been pierced by doors and gates in a number of places to accommodate tourists and visitors and pilgrims. One of these gates had been opened willingly enough by the monk assigned to care for visitors. He had paid for his Christian charity with his life—shot down where he stood yawning and blinking with sleep. The noise had alarmed the monks sufficiently to bring them rushing from their cells and into the guns of the Abou Moussa. Eight more had been murdered before Lesh called a halt. Deborah and Robinson, who, of all the hostages, were the only ones who had heard the sounds of guerrilla actions before this day, knew what was happening. The others understood it when the lamentations began inside the walls. Listening to the grieving, terrified cries of the monks, Deborah had thought dully that the sounds were only an echo of the sounds that must have been heard in places like Dachau and Treblinka. Slaughter was slaughter, and dressing it up as an act of racial purification or as a people's war did nothing to alter its character.

It had taken little more time to round up the surviving monks, most of whom were old and terrified, and put them under guard to serve as expendable hostages. The Abou Moussa was in command of the monastery and the rock-bound valley below. As the prisoners were transferred to the walled enclosure, Deborah heard again the distant sound of jet aircraft. They were flying somewhere east of the valley, but she could see nothing in the sky except the fading constellations.

Now she was separated from the others and confined in a cruciform stone room that was part of the massive walls. A single high window that had once been simply an arrow slit allowed the gray light of morning to enter the cell. If she stood on the single article of furniture the cell contained, a splintery wooden table, she could look out across timbered roofs to the church, beyond that to the far walls, and past the walls to the still-twilit mass of the stone cliffs against which the monastery had been built.

The Church of the Transfiguration was a strange building, half sunk into the earth, looking ominously like a fortress. Once, during the quasi peace between the Six-Day and Yom Yippur wars, when Israeli soldiers were touring the Sinai in triumph, she had visited the monastery with a group of sight-seers. But she had seen it then in sunlight, the gardens and courtyards within the perimeter of the walls blooming in the fullness of a desert spring. It seemed very different now, gloomy and shadowed, huddling against the rubble of granite slopes and the riven rock cliffs of the massif. Directly below her window, two of the Abou Moussa Arabs were prodding the black-greenery of the gardens, looking for anyone who might have hidden and so escaped from the first, swift search.

The monastery was still deep in shadow. But the eastward-facing mountains that rose precipitously beyond the wall were beginning to redden with the faintest touch of the sun, a pale and lifeless light moving from the sky to the earth. Here and there in the creases of the ancient rock could be seen an occasional thornbush of *spina Christi* or a stunted tamarisk. A line of cypresses, dark green against the lighter color of the cliffs, rose above the far wall. Beyond those trees were the shelters and workshops, Deborah remembered, where the Bedouin dependents of the monastery spent their days. In the morning stillness she could hear faintly the sounds of shouts and curses as the Arabs drove away the confused and bewildered tribesmen. Far up the valley, on the impossibly steep slopes of the massif, could be seen the sheep the Bedouins herded, frightened away by the gunfire, but too foolish to do more than run partway up the sheer escarpments and pause there, looking for nonexistent forage.

Deborah sat down with her back against the ancient stones of the wall. She tried to force herself to think clearly, as the Army had trained her to do in difficult circumstances. She tried to locate herself within the monastery, attempting to recall what she could of the ground plan of the place. The section of the wall in which she was confined overlooked an interior garden known as the Garden of the Holy Bush. Every nook and cranny of the four or five hectares within the perimeter had a name. She could remember few of them. Between the garden and the church lay a triangular court. Near the end of the court and within the wall, she remembered, was the tiny Chapel of St. George. She recalled it because it abutted against the only gate she could remember in the western wall. She closed her eyes and tried to reconstruct the drawings in the tourist guides, but it was hopeless. The place was a jumble of open courtyards, enclosed gardens, chapels, shrines, hospices, monks' cells, sacristies, and hundreds of unused and probably forgotten rooms similar to the one she now occupied. The monastery had been under construction almost since the time of the Emperor Justinian, and it had become an absolute maze. Even the thick walls were honeycombed with rooms and passages. It would be impossible, her army training told her, for a force of fewer than a thousand men to occupy the place effectively. And she was sure that the Abou Moussa had no more than two dozen men here, if that many. But it was as certain that a few determined people, armed as the terrorists were, with automatic weapons, could control any one part of the monastery almost indefinitely. It would take artillery or bombing to blast them out, and such action was clearly impossible. Not only did the Arabs hold the American Vice President as hostage, but the Americans had never quite recovered from the psychological trauma of having destroyed, in World War II, the Abbey of Monte Cassino—as it turned out, for nothing.

The Americans would come, or they would not. She had no really clear idea what they would be willing to risk. If they came with men and light weapons, many would die, and they would have no assurance at all that they would recover their vice president alive. All this became inevitable, she thought, the first time a hijacker commandeered an airplane and succeeded. It was too much to think about, too absurdly horrible to be believed. Yet it was true. She closed her grainy-feeling eyes and tried to sit calmly. She was burning with thirst, but no one had offered water. Beyond the heavy planked door stood an Arab with a Russian assault rifle. From time to time he opened the door, looked inside, and spat. He was a good-looking youngster, not more than eighteen, long-haired and lightly bearded. When she had asked for a drink, he had told her that there was no water for Jewish whores and slammed the door closed.

She tried to guess where the others had been taken. From the window she had seen Bronstein and Reisman herded into the basilica. There were a half-dozen small chapels in the sunken building. Perhaps Lesh derived some sort of gallows humor from confining his prisoners there. He seemed the sort of man who would enjoy risking gunfire in rooms containing priceless religious art.

There was more shouting outside, and she heard the distinctive whack-whack-whacking noise of a helicopter. She rose to the window but could see nothing except a patch of slowly lightening dusty-blue sky. The sound of the aircraft grew louder; there was more than one, she thought. With some effort she pulled herself higher, trying to lean across the stone sill for a better view. But she could see nothing. The helicopters must be approaching from the east. The beating sound grew stronger as the machines overflew the monastery, and then began to fade swiftly, until at last she could hear it no longer.

The departure of the aircraft plunged her into deeper despair. Unable to sustain her weight on the sill, she released her hold and fell back onto the table, scraping her knees on the wall. A sense of abandonment and defeat such as she had not felt even as Rabin died in her arms overwhelmed her. She thought of Tate, but he seemed incredibly remote, astronomically distant. She could not analyze her feelings; she was too tired and frightened for that. But her sense of alienation and abandonment centered on Bill Tate, and the silent finality of their last love-making came back to add to her despair. It seemed to her now that she had, in some way she could not escape, come to this situation naturally: that she belonged here, in this ancient stone pile with dusty Arabs at her door; while *he* belonged elsewhere, in a bright land of green hills and temperate rains, in a country of free cities founded by his well-born ancestors to express their disdain as Anglo-Saxon Protestants for the swarming, sweating, jostling importunities of Europeans, Asiatics—and Jews.

The half-formed thought was so desolating that she began for the first time to weep, her head resting back against the old stones while tears cut runnels through the dust on her cheeks. He will not come for me, she thought. Perhaps he will come for his vice president, who is the same sort of creature as himself. But not for me. It was totally irrational, and she knew it, this sudden excess of Semitic grief. It made no sense, because no matter how impregnable the position of the Abou Moussa might appear to be, they could not be allowed this particular victory. And so Tate and his men *must* come; there was no other choice. But if that was so—as it had to be—then why was it that she, Deborah Zadok, was so certain she would die in this alien Christian place?

The door opened suddenly, and the Arab woman, Leila Jamil, came into the room. She had put aside her Bedouin robes and stood dressed in camouflaged military fatigues. For the first time, Deborah could see how slender she was, her body so leaned by sun and deprivation that it had lost its femininity. The black hair, cropped short, was streaked with gray, though her face was still young. The high, flat cheeks and narrow brows, the thinly aquiline nose and dark widely spaced eyes showed clearly her Semitic heritage. She had left her weapon outside with the Arab sentry. Now she stood looking at Deborah, her expression oddly neutral for one whose hatred of the Jews was said to be legendary.

"You need not be afraid," she said in careful Hebrew.

Deborah stared back at her and answered in clear Arabic. "I am not afraid of you."

"I forgot," Jamil said ironically. "You are a sabra, aren't you?"

Deborah did not reply.

"I came to tell you that the Americans are coming. You heard the helicopters?"

Deborah held her silence. Let the woman have her say. She sensed a peculiar tension in her. It hovered about her like an aura.

"One of the helicopters landed up the valley, near the road. We expect this. They will come and stand in front of the walls, but that is all they will do. Lesh is trying to contact them with one of the truck radios. If they do as they are told, no one will be hurt."

"Excluding the dead, of course," Deborah said.

Jamil shrugged. "There are always casualties in a war of liberation."

Deborah's expression showed clearly how she regarded that statement.

"We are willing to die for our beliefs," Jamil said. "Aren't you?"

"You say that to a Jew? That's very funny."

"I may set you free to tell the Americans and the Jews what we want. What would you say to that?"

"I don't believe you."

"We want all Arab Front prisoners in Israel set free—"

"They will not do it," Deborah said.

"They will this time. There has been an air crash. *That man we have down in the church is now president of the United States.*"

"I do not believe you."

"It is true. The American President died yesterday. We have the man who is to take his place. We can do anything now. *Anything*. There is no limit."

Deborah sat quietly, feeling the heavy beating of her heart.

"All Arab prisoners will be released. All Arab lands will be restored. We will want reparations—the amount of five hundred million American dollars."

"You're insane."

The Arab woman closed her eyes for a moment, and Deborah saw that she was reeling with fatigue. "All Americans, Russians, and Jews will get out of the Sinai, leaving their vehicles, weapons, aircraft, and military equipment."

"Absolutely insane," Deborah whispered, and it was true. The woman had been fighting too long, losing too often, spending herself in a hopeless cause for so long that she was no longer rational. She felt something that was weirdly akin to sympathy for her. No person should have to spend a lifetime the way Leila Jamil had spent hers, in hijacking, bombing, murdering, and always, always, running.

Jamil seemed suddenly to sense what Deborah was thinking. It appeared to infuriate her. She stepped forward and struck Deborah across the face with all her strength. Deborah stumbled from the table to her knees in time to avoid another blow.

The Arab in the passageway opened the door and thrust his rifle inside. Jamil turned and screamed at him to *get out, get out!*

She caught Deborah by the hair and tried to strike her again, but Deborah fought back. The Arab woman felt like a knotted mass of corded leather. She was making thick animal sounds as she struck out. It was as though a lifetime of bitterness and days of privation were being released in a display of physical violence.

Then as the two women grappled, something happened that Deborah could scarcely credit, something that made her feel sick. Jamil thrust her hand inside Deborah's shirt and found her breasts, and with shocking suddenness her anger was transformed into a gasping, starved passion. She pressed her mouth against Deborah's neck, biting and sucking. The thin, iron-hard fingers clutched Deborah's breasts painfully. Deborah stared at her assailant with disbelieving eyes. She knew that homosexuality was common among Arabs, but she had never before encountered it in a woman. Her revulsion started as a deep, convulsive shudder and grew to a racking feeling of disgust as the Arab woman tried to force her to the floor.

She summoned all her failing strength to push away the hand that had reached under her skirt and was bruising her thigh, searching to enter her. Catching the Arab woman's hair, she pulled her head back.

Then as suddenly as she had begun, Jamil stopped and leaned against the wall. Somehow she had managed to open the buttons of her fatigues, and Deborah could see her bony, heaving chest and small hard breasts, dark nipples erect and distended. The widely spaced dark eyes were unfocused, wet, and glistening under the straight black brows.

Abruptly, Jamil buttoned her clothes, and took a deep breath. Her face was taut, lined with the effort of suppressing her wild tension. She gradually brought herself again under control. Her eyes focused on Deborah, who felt the cold malevolence in them like a physical blow.

"No," Jamil said, as if to herself. "It will not be you. I will not send you."

Then she was gone, the thick door closing behind her, and Deborah let herself slide to the floor, where she huddled against the wall and shuddered in reaction. Unexpectedly, her stomach turned over, and she vomited on the stone floor. When the spasms had stopped, she wiped her lips and crawled onto the table, numb with despair.

19

The War Room, so protected by layer upon layer of military security and protocol, had always before seemed to Fowler Beal the ultimate in havens. Though he had an imperfect understanding of all the activities taking place in the protected room, and in others like it at places like Omaha and Cheyenne Mountain, he had always been impressed by the air of calm, almost grim, competence displayed here by high-ranking officers of the Army, Navy, Air Force, and Marine Corps.

On previous visits, usually guided by Stuart Ainsworth, he had noted with genuine approval the apparent skill with which the many incomprehensible, to him, tasks were performed during practice alerts and exercises. It had always given him a feeling of safety and well-being to know that such an organization stood between himself and the threat of nuclear extermination.

But now, as he sat guarded in the room mysteriously labeled "C and C Beta," his remembered sense of well-being refused to materialize. To begin with, the hours since the death of the President had not lessened his feeling of shock and bereavement. The President had always been a man upon whom he could rely for guidance, leadership, and support. The realization that he was no longer there to perform this function frightened him.

He had never liked Talcott Bailey; secretly he had always

felt the Vice President was a snob. He accepted him because the President had accepted him. As a political animal, he understood that Bailey had been necessary to the election of the party ticket because his aristocratic liberalism still appealed to voters needed to form a plurality.

On a few occasions, Beal had pondered the possibility that Bailey might, in some circumstances, become president. He had found that the notion, though disturbing, appealed to some hidden remnant of his own early populism. He had decided that he could live with the idea of a President Bailey. He had, of course, never dared mention these idle speculations to Ainsworth, whose opinion of the Vice President was well known to Washington insiders.

But upon learning that Bailey was not available to step into the President's place, that, indeed, his present whereabouts and situation were unknown, Beal was near panic. Never in the history of the republic had a situation quite like this one existed. A succession that the Congress had ordained (but never imagined as an actual possibility, Beal was sure) seemed about to drop the awful power of the presidency on one who feared it, felt unsure of his capacity to wield it, and did not want it. To add to his sense of impending doom, a warrant officer now sat outside the steel door to C and C Beta holding a locked briefcase containing the nuclear codes. Like a uniformed angel of death, he had materialized (presumably at Ainsworth's command) soon after the news of Bailey's encounter with the Arab terrorists reached the War Room.

Three television screens, activated for his benefit, brought him news of the world outside the Pentagon. By this time all three networks had canceled their regular programs to devote themselves entirely to the national reaction to the death of the President in Palm Springs. Beal was frightened by the intensity and swiftness of the American people's response to the news. He was even more shaken by the speculations that were being freely aired by the men who selected the news to be seen on the nation's television screens. The sabotage theory, adding as it did to the already nerve-snapping sense of drama inherent in the story, was being freely circulated. Helen Risor was not yet able to answer questions about the crash, nor had the results of an autopsy on the bodies of the flight crewmen been released. In the absence of hard news, the radio and television people were indulging in increasingly lurid speculations.

Beal was politician enough to sense that an angry swing in public opinion was taking place. Mingled with the grief and sense of loss caused by the death of a popular president flowed a hidden fury. If he read the national mood correctly, the reaction to any suggestion that Arab terrorists had ambushed and possibly killed or kidnapped the Vice President would be savage. And what if it should be believed that the Soviets knew of it, that they were implicated? He shivered, having a vision of himself faced with the shattering disturbances that would result, the demands for action. *What* action? he asked himself. How did one reply to such an act of treachery? He knew, deep inside himself, what Ainsworth would reply, and the thought was chilling.

On ABC, a senior correspondent was describing the spontaneous gathering of citizens in mourning at the Lincoln Memorial. On the screen could be seen perhaps ten thousand people standing bareheaded in the light rain. They were silent, for the most part, but here and there some speakers were addressing small segments of the crowd. These were not the experienced protesters: they appeared to be ordinary citizens asking one another how they might petition their government for information on how the tragedy in Palm Springs really happened. There had been a few official announcements, but these had been incomplete. No vice president had, as Lyndon Johnson did in Dallas, swiftly taken the reins of government.

"Since we were told that Vice President Bailey is returning from the Middle East," said the correspondent soberly, "there has been no official word on his whereabouts—"

A White House correspondent, perplexed and grim-faced,

appeared in the ABC studio. He shuffled papers and said: "It takes only some eight and a half hours, at most, to fly here from the Sinai Peninsula. Yet there has been no word on the Vice President's arrival time in Washington. There is a growing uneasiness about this all over the capital."

The ABC correspondent in Cyprus could supply no certain knowledge of the Vice President's whereabouts. "It's very mysterious here," he reported. "The Public Information Officer for the UN Commission, Mr. Ravi Singh, has said that there will be no statements by any of the Commissioners here for at least twenty-four hours. I have spoken with the *Pravda* correspondent and he informs me that Deputy Premier Rostov is still at Zone Center. But he did *not* say that the renewal of the accord had been signed. This is considered significant here. No one really wants to speculate about Vice President Bailey's—or perhaps I should now say President Bailey's—movements."

The anchor man cut in to ask how the people of Cyprus were taking the disquieting news.

"Several hundred people have gathered in the streets around the barracks of the Knights of St. John, where the United Nations Commission for the Implementation of the Cyprus Accord has its headquarters, in spite of it being early morning here. The crowd is orderly—but one senses a great deal of uneasiness, even fear. That's really all I can tell you."

Beal shut off the ABC sound and switched to CBS. Their screen showed their Cairo correspondent standing before a brightly lighted Cairo Hilton Hotel. Beal listened to him with a growing sense of apprehension. He was the first of the television correspondents to have picked up a rumor of terrorist activity. "Sources near to the outlawed Arab Front for the Liberation of Palestine are suggesting that they may know more than they are saying about the delay in the Vice President's return to Washington. CBS has learned that a guerrilla organization known as the—" The screen went abruptly blank, and then the anchor man, at his New York desk, appeared, saying that the Cairo transmission seemed to be encountering some sort of technical difficulty. This sudden censorship was alarming to Beal. If the government of the UAR had cut the correspondent off the air, it implied a knowledge and complicity that would demand a reply—and soon.

Through the outward-slanting windows of C and C Beta, Beal caught sight of Admiral Ainsworth, surrounded by a group of officers of all the services, coming across the floor of the Pit. On the computer displays covering the far wall, Beal could see the map lights showing the state of readiness of the nation's nuclear forces. As he watched, the cluster of lights identifying the Minuteman squadrons turned from yellow to red, indicating a full alert. Only orders from the president were now needed to launch the entire intercontinental ballistic missile force. The Speaker's throat felt dry and furry. He had no idea Ainsworth had carried matters so far. His eyes sought the computer displays indicating the real-time intelligence being received from the Midas and Samos satellites now over the central Asian land mass. All the known Soviet strategic bases, their Bear squadrons and SS-9 and 11 missile installations were shown as being at Second Degree Readiness, which was comparable to the Americans' Yellow Alert. On a third computer display he could read the track of the Soviets' Cosmos satellites, the nearness-to-launch condition of their fractional-orbit weapons systems, and the constant tracking of the American satellite-killers' radar.

The cumulative effect of this information and the intentness of the uniformed legions in and around the Pit, serving their machines and computer consoles and communications gear, was terrifying. He regretted now not having read carefully the heavily technical section of the Case Headless material, which had been delivered to him by officer courier the day after his briefing by that Yale think-tanker. He had simply not done it:

the columns of figures, the projections of "megadeaths" and "interdictions," had been too intellectually taxing. Now he had to rely exclusively on Ainsworth and his officers to tell him what, exactly, could be expected to happen if indeed the Russians had prodded the Arab gunmen to provoke the United States. From what he could see in the Pit, the preparations looked mightily like preparations for war. He had a momentary urge to run, to find his way back to Terri's pink bower in Rockville, there to smother himself between her heavy breasts, hiding from the awesome fate that seemed about to overtake him. But that was impossible, of course, and he must follow the next most compelling course. He must do what needed to be done, for himself, for all the mourning, angry, puzzled people across the country, and for the United States. The problem was that he had long ago forgotten all but the forms of leadership. Now he knew with sinking heart that he must rely on someone else to guide him.

Admiral Stuart Ainsworth came into the room. He looked tired after his rushed journey across the country. His customarily impeccable uniform was wrinkled slightly, and there were shadows under his eyes. But his jaw was set and his expression was cold. "The telecast from the Peacekeeping Area is coming in now, sir," he said. "I want you to see it."

Beal noted with a chill the formality of the Admiral's address. He had not called him by name, or by his old title.

Ainsworth spoke into an intercom. "Pipe the satellite transmission from Sinai in here. Screen Two." The networks were cut off, and a new scene appeared on the center screen: a clutter of burned and damaged American military vehicles nose to tail on a narrow road in a rock-strewn desert. The scene was harshly lit by floods, though the sky showed the dusty-blue tinge of dawn. The camera was focused on a group of American soldiers wearing the blue beret of the U.S. Component working to sack bodies in plastic bags, which gleamed wetly in the lights.

Ainsworth said harshly, "That's the convoy. It was hit no more than forty kilometers from Zone Center. Inside the demilitarized area. So much for the goddam United Nations."

The camera's eye zoomed in on a bullet-pocked staff car, a large one. The glass was starred and shattered by gunfire. On one fender it carried the insigne of the Peacekeeping Force, the Circle and Arrows and the mocking "Peace" in four languages. On the other standard was the vice presidential seal.

Ainsworth raised the sound level, and a young voice, that of one of the component officers documenting the event on the scene, came into C and C Beta: "Colonel Benjamin Crowell's body was found on the floor of the rear seat of the Vice President's car. The car's driver was found on the road beside the vehicle. The main body of the Vice President's military escort was apparently killed in the first attack. Four of them never made it out of their vehicle near the head of the column. The rest were killed in front of the Vice President's car. Of the military escort, only the body of Sergeant Major Crispus Robinson has not been found."

The camera panned to the burned-out communications van. "The bodies of one officer and three technicians were found in this vehicle," the young voice said inexorably. Again the camera eye moved, this time to the rear of the column, where the tangled, burned wreckage of television and film equipment lay scattered about. "All civilian correspondents who were listed as traveling with the Vice President have been identified and accounted for."

"He means they are dead," Ainsworth said grimly.

"A number of the civilians were apparently wounded by grenade fragments and then shot at close range," stated the bitter voice.

The view changed again, to show the command car behind the car carrying the standards. "All members of the Israeli Component party except the Liaison Group commander's military secretary are accounted for. Dead."

Beal's stomach turned slightly at the sight of the blood

spatters on the bullet-starred windshield of the command car.

"Missing are the Vice President; Colonel Jason Seidel, the component chief of staff; J. P. Reisman, the President's press secretary and special envoy; the Vice President's appointments secretary, Paul Bronstein; Sergeant Robinson; and Israeli Captain Deborah Zadok." The scene flipped as the technicians in the Sinai desert changed cameras, and Beal now could see the officer who had been speaking, a young captain wearing the blue beret with the Circle and Arrows insigne. "That is our preliminary report, sir. We will continue taping, of course, until we get this mess cleaned up."

Ainsworth took a hand microphone from a clip under the large screen and spoke into it. "Is General Tate on the scene, Captain?"

"Yes, sir. He's coming now." Then the officer added, with a hint of disapproving hostility in his voice, "He's been conferring with the Russians, who arrived about twenty minutes ago."

Ainsworth's mouth tightened into an angry, thin line. When Tate stood before the camera and sound pickups, he rapped out his displeasure. "What the hell are Russians doing there, General?"

Tate, his face lined and showing some strain, peered up at the camera eye, and Beal had the uncomfortable feeling he was looking straight into C and C Beta. "General Ulanov came to offer what help he could, Admiral," he said. "The Deputy Premier came with him."

Ainsworth said, "Get them the hell out of there, General." His voice was frigid with controlled hostility.

"They are leaving now," Tate said. "Ulanov's people think the Abou Moussa has moved south to the Monastery of St. Katherine. I have sent a helo section down to do a recce. I am expecting their report momentarily."

"You have taken this action on information offered by the Reds?" Ainsworth asked, frowning.

"I have, Admiral."

"One moment, Tate." Ainsworth cut his microphone and turned to Beal. "Well, sir?"

Beal was confused. "Well what, Stuart?"

"Do we mount an attack on the old monastery if Tate's information is correct?"

"My God, Stuart. Why ask me? I'm not a military man."

"The decision must be yours, sir. You are acting president."

There it was then, Beal thought with a stab of panic. This was the moment he had been dreading. He temporized. "Wait. Congress has taken no action yet. We don't know that Talcott Bailey is dead—"

"*I* think he's dead, sir. And even if he is not, he is certainly unable to act. The conditions of Case Headless are fulfilled."

"Stuart, I can't just declare myself president. The Constitution—"

Ainsworth's eyes were merciless. "The Constitution and the law are your authority, sir. Do I have to quote them for you? You *are* acting president. Make the decision."

Beal's breath seemed to catch in his throat. He felt a clammy sweat on his back and in the palms of his hands. "Stuart—" he said faintly. "Stuart, I *can't*—"

"Then, sir, since the National Security Council is not convened as yet, I will decide in your name. As you say, it is a military decision, and not political."

Beal found himself nodding wordlessly, relieved and shaken at once.

Ainsworth opened the voice link to Sinai and said, "General, if your helicopters find those Arabs, you are to assault the monastery with whatever force necessary to get our people back—those who are still alive."

Tate stared at the camera lens.

"Acknowledge that order, General," Ainsworth said.

"Admiral, if we do that, they will certainly kill the hostages."

"We must accept that possibility."

"They have the President," Tate said, accenting his words carefully.

"We don't know that, General. We have no way of knowing whether or not any of our people are still alive."

"They would hardly have taken them along if they were not, Admiral."

"In any case, Talcott Bailey is *not* the president. Not yet. And very possibly not ever."

Beal noted Tate's swift change of expression. He could not read it, but he could imagine what was going on in the General's mind as Ainsworth disclosed the substance of his intention.

After what seemed a long time, Tate said, "I do not accept that, Admiral."

Ainsworth said, "It appears we are going to interpret the law differently, General. Let me offer you one chance to reconsider. Even if Mr. Bailey were known to be alive and had taken the oath as president, his present position would make it impossible for him to fulfill the duties of that office. Therefore, the presidency falls to the Speaker of the House of Representatives—who is in this room with me at this moment—*and by whose authority I order you to find and attack the Abou Moussa.*"

Tate spoke slowly and with great caution. "Sir, my purpose in the Sinai is to help keep the peace, not destroy it. I have already been forced to violate the terms of the treaty that authorizes my presence here. I request you to reconsider what you are asking me to do."

"I am not *asking* you to do anything, General Tate. I am *ordering* you to kill or capture those who have insulted the flag, killed our soldiers, and connived with our enemies to endanger the security of the United States. I do so on the authority I hold as chairman of the Joint Chiefs of Staff and as military representative of the Acting President of the United States."

Beal could see that Tate was struggling to contain his anger. "I repeat, sir," the General said, "I do not accept the authority of an acting president. Talcott Bailey is the president unless and until we know that he is dead."

"Or unable to act, General," Ainsworth said. And there, Beal thought with sinking heart, the Chairman's position was technically and legally correct. Young Tate must know that. Why was he challenging his superior? Why, indeed? he thought bleakly. Because Tate knew, of course, that President Beal was no president at all. Because it was clear to him that if he accepted the Admiral's orders, the power to make war or save the peace would rest in the hands of Stuart Ainsworth. For the first time, Beal realized how the new breed of soldier differed from the old. The new men were peacekeepers, rather than simply warriors; convinced of their right to question, intellectualize, satisfy their consciences, rather than simply obey.

Ainsworth understood this distinction too well, and it infuriated him. "General Tate, I am relieving you of your command. You are to return to Es Shu'uts at once and place yourself in arrest until you can be flown back to Washington."

The Speaker was amazed to see Tate actually smile. "I regret that I cannot accept that order either, Admiral. My command derives its authority directly from the Commander in Chief, not the Joint Chiefs of Staff."

Ainsworth's face grew red with anger. He turned to Beal and said, "Validate that command, sir."

Beal floundered. "Admiral—this is a purely military—"

"*Sir.* This is vital. I insist that you, as commander in chief, support me." The voice had a cutting edge. Beal knew that without Ainsworth he was lost. He nodded soundlessly, and Ainsworth handed him the microphone. "I—General Tate—this is the Speaker of the House—"

"The *President,*" Ainsworth hissed.

"This is the Acting President," Beal said, stumbling over the words.

Tate said evenly, "I'm sorry, Mr. Speaker. I recognize no acting president of the United States at this time. I cannot accept Admiral Ainsworth's orders and I cannot accept yours, sir."

Beal looked at Ainsworth helplessly. The Admiral snapped a switch, and the picture from the Sinai went dark. Ainsworth spoke into an intercom. "Put Echo Sierra Control on Screen Three here. I want Component command headquarters."

Screen Three came to life at once, showing the officer of the day at Es Shu'uts. "Captain Baring here."

"Captain, this is Admiral Ainsworth. Locate Colonel Dale Trask at once and get him on this link. I want a military secretary with transcribing equipment, with him as witness."

The Captain, an air force officer no more than twenty-three or twenty-four years old, looked startled to be suddenly face to face with the Chairman of the Joint Chiefs. "Yes, *sir*. Right away, sir."

Ainsworth spoke into the intercom again. "Put General Shackleford and General Rivera on this net." To Beal he said, calmly and with deliberation, "This concerns the Army and the Air Force, sir. As well as you. I want you to tell the generals that the orders I am about to give carry your approval. I want no more argument about who controls our component in the Sinai." He nodded. "They are on, sir. Tell them."

Beal said in a strained voice, "Gentlemen, the Chairman has my approval for the orders he is about to issue."

Ainsworth nodded curtly. "Thank you, Mr. President."

The disfigured face of Colonel Trask appeared on the Es Shu'uts television link. Behind him could be seen a WAC captain, whom Beal vaguely remembered as being Tate's long-time military secretary.

Trask looked puffy-eyed and slightly rumpled, as though he had been only recently awakened. Beal thought of the stories he had heard about Trask's heavy drinking. Everyone near to Ainsworth knew Trask's background—his terrible mistreatment at the hands of the Vietnamese. This was the man who had caused the *Allende* incident, the officer the Russians had been demanding be demoted and punished for endangering the renewal of the Cyprus Accord.

"Trask," Ainsworth said, "get this recorded and make certain that girl with you takes it down. I'll send confirmation by special courier at once."

"Yes, sir," Trask said thickly.

"I have relieved General Tate of his command—"

Trask's mouth opened in surprise. Then a hard light came into his eyes. "Yes, sir." The girl behind him looked stunned.

"I have relieved him for insubordination and for failing to provide proper security for Vice President Bailey," Ainsworth said. "I am promoting you to brigadier general. This is subject to confirmation by the Senate, but you are to take rank from today. I am placing you in temporary command of the United States Component. You are to take a platoon of Air Police into the DMZ at once and place General Tate under arrest. Is that clear?"

Trask now seemed fully awake. "Yes, *sir*. It is perfectly clear."

"Then you are to take whatever force you need to the Monastery of St. Katherine and call upon the terrorists holed up in the place to surrender at once. If they do not, you are to go in and take them. Understood?"

"Yes, sir. You said whatever force necessary. Does that include air bombardment?"

"It means what I said, General Trask. Whatever force is necessary. We do not make deals with Red terrorists. Move out at once, and report to me by satellite net as soon as you are in position."

"Yes, sir." Trask looked triumphant. Beal wondered what ill feeling had so swiftly developed between Tate and the air force officer to make this terrible thing so pleasurable a duty.

Just before Ainsworth broke the television link, Beal caught a fleeting glimpse of the expression on the WAC Captain's thin face. It was one of absolute dismay. Was she loyal, then, to Bill Tate? But what, after all, could a WAC captain do to alter the moves of the major pieces that were being shifted so desperately on a board that encompassed the whole world? Within moments, Beal had forgotten Captain Elizabeth Adams.

In Moscow the starlight shone thinly on the blanket of snow that covered the city.

Lieutenant Colonel Gukovsky, of the GRU, came out of heavy sleep, disturbed by the insistent banging on the door of his apartment on the Leninskij Prospekt.

Beside him, his mistress and secretary, Irena Malenkova, was waking, too. She rolled against him, her voluminous warm breasts heavy on his arm. "What?" she said muzzily. "What is it?"

The Colonel sat up and fumbled for a light. The knocking on the door continued. He looked at his Swiss wristwatch on the night table and saw that it was five o'clock in the morning. He frowned and shook himself, trying to achieve some sort of true wakefulness. He was growing angry.

The banging grew louder, and he shouted, "All right! All right! I'm coming!"

He sat up, found his greatcoat where he had thrown it last night on the floor near the bed. He thrust his beefy arms into the sleeves and shambled to his feet. Irena was sitting up, her yellow hair hanging in tangles to her heavy shoulders, her naked breasts exposed. "Cover your tits, woman," he said.

When he opened the door, he was startled to see there two officers, a full colonel and a senior lieutenant. Behind them stood two KGB noncoms armed with machine pistols.

"Lieutenant Colonel Gukovsky? Of GRU Dezinform?"

"Yes. I'm Gukovsky. What do you want?"

"You will come with us, Comrade Colonel."

Gukovsky felt a sickness in the pit of his stomach. "Is it permitted to ask the reason, Comrade Colonel?"

"You are under arrest, Comrade Gukovsky. Get dressed."

From behind him came a panicky wail. Irena Malenkova sat in the rumpled bed holding the bedclothes against her chest. The KGB Colonel asked, "Is that your secretary, Irena Malenkova?"

Gukovsky's voice had turned scratchy. "It is."

"She is under arrest, as well. Get dressed, Comrade Malenkova. At once."

Irena scrambled from the bed and ran to the wardrobe across the room on thick legs, buttocks ajiggle, her broad white back creased by the bedclothes.

The KGB officer turned to Gukovsky. "I said for you to get dressed. Do so without further delay."

Gukovsky did as he was told. His face felt bearded and gritty, but he did not think it a good idea to ask if he might wash. As he dressed, he racked his brain, desperately trying to think what offense he could possibly have committed to occasion this disaster. And why Irena, too? Were they rounding up all his office staff?

He had his answer when he and the big blonde girl followed the KGB men down to street level. The early morning was bitterly cold but clear and starry. They walked to a black sedan standing at the curb before the new apartment house. When the door was opened for Gukovsky and Irena, he saw, sitting miserably in the front seat next to the driver, his clerk, Sergeant Kamenev. "It's those damned Cosmos pictures, Colonel. There was something in them you should have seen." He sounded almost hysterical. "Tell them, Comrade Colonel! Tell them I'm only a clerk—a messenger boy! Colonel, please tell them—"

"Be silent!" the KGB officer said.

Gukovsky looked at him and asked, "Is that the truth? Is that why we are being arrested?"

The KGB man stared at him. "You are being arrested for negligence in the performance of state duties. Thanks to you, Gukovsky, we may all be blown to hell within the next twenty-four hours."

Gukovsky fell silent. Irena wept. Kamenev shuddered.

Some half hour later, the frozen-faced KGB man said, "You will be flown, under arrest, to El Arish and then to wherever Comrade General Ulanov is. The Comrade General hopes that when the Americans see what sort of incompetent idiots hold responsible positions in the GRU, they will accept the possibility that a grown man claiming to be a military intelligence officer could miss whatever it was you missed in the photographs pipelined to the Israelis." He drew a deep breath and blew it out. "The Americans are very nervous, Gukovsky, and when they are nervous they are very dangerous. I hope, for all our sakes, that you can convince them that you are a fool."

Talcott Quincy Bailey opened his eyes and saw before him a sight that half convinced him he had died and been transported to some medieval materialists' version of paradise.

A vast and shadowy chamber, lighted by gold and silver lamps descending from a high ceiling decorated with sprays of golden stars, lay before him. On either side of the long room stood rows of carved columns. He could see, too, a series of darkened arches opening onto what appeared to be small chapels. The row on his left glowed with reflected colors, and he realized that this was the eastern wall and that the light came from the rising sun piercing stained-glass windows.

He had not imagined that he would be able to sleep, yet when the Arabs had brought him into the rear of the church after herding him, with the others, through a maze of courts and gardens in the predawn darkness, he had stretched out on the stone floor and fallen into a sleep of exhaustion.

Three Arabs cradling automatic weapons squatted against

the nearest columns. They were motionless, and in the weak light he could not be certain whether or not they were awake. He surmised that at least one of them must be watching.

Beside him, leaning against the wall, was Jason Seidel. The Judge was dozing fitfully, his mouth working in tiny twitches as the memory of last night's ambush and flight disturbed his sleep. Beyond the Judge, Bailey could see a pair of dusty paratrooper's boots. They belonged to the black troop commander, Robinson, who lay at full length along the wall, sleeping soundly. Bailey wondered how it was possible for him to rest so peacefully after what they had all been through. But that was one of the things said of professional soldiers: they could fall asleep anywhere and under almost any conditions. It was almost a cliché of military life.

Bailey returned to his scrutiny of their surroundings. This must be the church at St. Katherine's. Sometime during his academic career he had read of this place. He had never imagined that he would see it under circumstances like these, but his restless mind had the ability to catalogue and recall so many things that he found he could identify much of what lay before him.

The gilded screen that separated the altar and the sanctuary from the rest of the church was, he remembered, called the iconostasis. It was covered with pictures of saints dating from the sixteenth century. He knew little about religious art, but the opulence of this place was impressive, so much so that it rather offended his Yankee puritanism. He had an urge to smile at his own peculiar resilience. In the last hours he had experienced outrage, disgust, fear, revulsion, despair, discomfort, and anger. And yet now he found himself sitting on a stone floor considering works of religious art under the eyes of Arabs who would, he felt certain, as readily kill him as say good morning. Not for the first time in his life, Talcott Bailey's veneer of righteous indignation cracked to allow some of the strangeness of life to penetrate.

He raised his eyes to look at the mosaic above the altar. A strong, rough Christ gazed down in what he could almost imagine was stern disapproval of the use to which His house was being put.

He looked again at the sleeping soldier and at Seidel, who was stirring now, waking to this singular gilded scene. For the first time that he could remember, Bailey was succumbing to serious doubts of his own wisdom. It was painful to admit, even to himself, that the values by which he had tried to live his life and govern his political career were totally worthless here. Such concepts as peace, reason, and tolerance had one meaning in America, safely surrounded by the awesome power of a modern industrial state. One could speak of beating swords into plowshares and the brotherhood of all men easily enough when one was not faced directly with the hatreds of the real world. Security brought its own fantasies. And he, Talcott Bailey, who should have known better, had tried to transform those fantasies of trust and brotherhood into reality by dispensing with the very security that made them possible. How could he have been such a fool, he wondered. For years he had been the self-righteous enemy of the soldiers, saying in effect: "Why buy a gun when the price of it will feed a child?" Who, having never needed a gun, could argue with such idealism? But here and now—what? The bitter answer was that he would willingly risk the hunger of many innocents for the force to break free. For the first time he could recall, he genuinely understood, with a visceral certainty, that his pacifism had created a situation capable of destroying not only himself, but also all pacifists. To indulge his convictions, he had caused half a hundred deaths and made himself into a pawn in a chess game played by madmen.

He rested his narrow gray head against the ancient stones of the wall and looked at the Judge with veiled, thoughtful eyes. He wondered if Seidel knew that he was aware of the President's hope of substituting him for Bailey as his successor.

Would he have made a good president? Would either of them ever have been able to achieve the delicate balancing of forces that made the President great? He put it to himself in this way because he had the dull feeling that neither he nor the Judge, nor any of the others, would get out of this situation alive. He tried to consider dispassionately what their murders would mean, eventually, to the world. He had always disapproved of the deployment of American soldiers in the Sinai. Thirty-four east had always been, to him, simply one more of those dangerous lines drawn on the earth to proclaim: "Cross at your peril." He had sympathy enough for both Jew and Arab, but he had never really believed it was an American responsibility to keep them apart. The line of history had placed them there, however. And so, ironically, he had become the instrument that might now destroy the balance in this wilderness—and quite possibly, even probably, across the world.

If the Arabs held him hostage for any practical reason other than senseless hate, what could they ask? He had to admit that they could ask—could *demand*—a high price. The release of terrorist prisoners, certainly. Perhaps a great deal more: the removal of American troops from Arab lands, possibly. And would the blackmail succeed? Somehow he doubted that it would. They had stolen a valuable counter in the person of the Vice President of the United States. But not quite valuable enough to buy a complete reversal of American foreign policy. And so it is almost certain, he thought, that we shall all die here. And it would not end with that. There would be a terrible retribution.

He heard the sound of nailed boots on the flagstones. The Judge opened his eyes, and Sergeant Robinson sat up, making the transition from sleep to full wakefulness as swiftly as a cat.

The Arab guards stirred and stood. Across the open chancel came the man Lesh and the woman who called herself Leila Jamil. Bailey had the fleeting thought that Leila, in Arabic, meant "night." She was like that, dark and silent, beautiful and threatening. Both carried weapons; it was as though they were incomplete without them.

Bailey brought himself to his feet with an effort that he dissembled for the sake of his challenged dignity. He watched Robinson do the same. The Sergeant seemed coiled, poised, and ever-vigilant, like a man waiting only for a chance to strike. But of course it was hopeless, Bailey knew. If Robinson made a move, the guerrillas would shoot him down as self-righteously as they had butchered the monks who let them into this place. He wondered why he had thought of their act in quite that way. Self-righteousness was not an attitude one customarily associated with murder. And yet the description was both apt and familiar. Self-righteousness had been, after all, a mark of radicals, reactionaries, of protest movements all over the world in olden as well as recent times, movements to which these terrorists belonged, heart and soul.

Lesh had shed any semblance of Arab dress and was now displaying the stars of a Communist-bloc colonel on his camouflage fatigues. Bailey's encyclopedic mind produced a memory of military staffs at some Washington reception, and catalogued the insigne: Yugoslav, or possibly Albanian. Most probably the latter, given the situation. It was almost an absurdity, he thought, to be the captive of a man from such a grimly melodramatic state.

Lesh's heavy face was exultant, Bailey noted. The man carried himself with an air of excitement and triumph. He stationed himself before Bailey and said, "I bring you important news and congratulations, Great One."

Bailey, taller than Lesh by almost half a head, looked down at him, frowning. The man was quite obviously unbalanced, he thought. There had been a time—and not too long ago—when he would have been certain that the proper way to deal with such persons as this one was with patience and understanding. This, now, was very different. This heavy, mustachioed, cold-eyed man had the power of life and death over all Bailey's people. In the last few hours Bailey's world had become so circumscribed and so endangered that he had come to think of the hostages in that way—as *his* people. His was the responsibility, and therefore to speak his angry mind to this Lesh would be to risk punishment for all.

"I do not know what you hope to gain by this, Colonel," he said quietly. He glanced at Jamil and added, "There is no advantage to your cause in what you have done."

Lesh said to the Arab woman, "Perhaps he is not interested in his good fortune."

"Stop this, Lesh," she said. "Do not make a Bakuninite game of it. Tell him."

Bailey noted that the woman looked worn, as well she might be. But she seemed troubled by more than the obvious situation. Perhaps she was afraid that she was losing command of her own people? The Arab Front had always made a great deal of their willingness to put women in positions of danger and responsibility—but it was a basically un-Arab attitude, a borrowing from their Marxist doctrine.

Lesh said, "I congratulate you, Mr. Bailey. Or perhaps I should now say *President* Bailey."

Bailey felt the blood draining from his cheeks.

"That takes you by surprise, I see," Lesh said. "I am not precisely astonished. We have all had more luck than we could have imagined." He paused, waiting for some comment from the Americans, and when it was not forthcoming, he said, "Your president was killed in an air crash yesterday. At a place called Palm Springs. I believe that makes *you* chief of state of your country, Mr. Bailey."

Bailey heard Seidel's sharply indrawn breath. Even the inscrutable Robinson murmured, "Christ."

Bailey looked at Jamil. "Is this true?"

The Arab woman nodded.

Bailey felt a sudden, surprising grief. He had always been the President's political enemy. He had often fought him and believed him wrong. He had sometimes disliked and resented him. And sometimes he had felt contempt for his ordinariness. But he *was* the president and he *had* led a confused and divided nation—if not well, according to Bailey's principles, at least with courage and deftness. He had been, after all, the president of all the people, even of those who opposed him.

Bailey was astonished to feel a dampness in his eyes and a thickness in his throat.

And then, slowly at first, but with gathering force, there came to him the international and political import of this radically altered situation. Yesterday a great crime had been committed: a high official of the American government had been attacked in a demilitarized area and taken hostage. It was a dreadful act of banditry and could be expected to have awesome reverberations throughout the Middle East and the world. But today the criminality and danger were raised to the nth power. Today insanity reigned. The President of the United States was a prisoner of a band of political murderers. It turned the world upside down.

Seidel spoke. "You must release the President at once, Colonel Lesh."

"You disappoint me, Colonel," Lesh said. "I expected something more intelligent than that from the Chief of Staff of the U.S. Component in the Sinai. I was told you had a strong legal mind."

Seidel said, "What you did yesterday was the act of a criminal—and dangerous. But if what you say this morning is true, the danger has grown incalculably. There is such a thing as holding too many cards, Colonel, in a game with powerful opponents. They can destroy you, the game, everything—if they are goaded too far."

"I am pleased to see that you, too, regard this as a kind of game, Colonel," Lesh said. "It has become much more than a simple case of *quid pro quo,* I agree. I had hoped to aid my Arab associates, of course, and plant some slight seed of suspicion between you and your Soviet friends. But a piloting error—or an act of judicious sabotage by some clever comrades—" he spread his thick hands—"and suddenly I am the most important man in the world. I find that splendid."

"Are you saying that the President's airplane was tampered with?" Seidel demanded.

"There are rumors. You know your American press. The radio accounts say that black militants could be responsible. Marxist black militants." He showed his long teeth in a smile directed at Robinson. "I congratulate you, too, comrade, on an act of liberation by your people."

Robinson spat on the floor at Lesh's feet.

"Colonel Lesh," Seidel said again, "I beg you. Release Mr. Bailey at once. Hold the rest of us, if you wish, but release Mr. Bailey *now*. You don't know what you are risking."

"But I do, Colonel. Why are you so afraid?" Lesh fixed Bailey with cold-eyed intensity. "You, an intellectual and a progressive, should understand my position, Mr. President. I have followed your political career with interest for many years. Before you became vice president you often said that you believed American society was sick and needed to be dismantled so that a new and better one could be built. You are already half a Bakuninite, Mr. Bailey. Surely you see that?"

Bailey forced himself to speak calmly, and he addressed himself to the woman, realizing that the man was lost in his personal jungle of creative destruction. "Think what may happen, Miss Jamil. Try to imagine what will come to your people because of this. You will be accused of barbarism again. But this won't be like Munich or Lod Airport or Khartoum. It won't be forgotten or forgiven. There are men in my country who will insist that you be hunted down. And it won't end there. Anyone, anyone at all, who has ever helped you, or given you weapons, or protected you will be hunted down, as well. The word 'Arab' will become a synonym for murderer. The stakes have been raised too high. The only result now will be tragedy for all Arabs, and possibly for the whole world. Think, Miss Jamil, before it is too late."

She frowned, because she was half convinced that all the tall American said was true. But the years she had spent in the struggle weighed heavily against his argument. She said, "Our friends will protect us."

"You will have no friends," Bailey said. "None."

Seidel said earnestly, "They will be too busy protecting themselves. Listen to him. What he tells you is true."

Lesh heard them in mocking silence. When Jamil did not reply, he said, "Before anything can be done, Mr. Bailey, there are certain conditions that must be met."

"Colonel Lesh," Bailey said, "believe me when I say to you that my countrymen will not bargain with you. You have gone too far for that."

"I cannot believe they will let their chief of state be killed," Lesh said. "Americans have not shown that sort of fortitude for a long time."

"You don't understand us, Lesh," Seidel said. "People of your sort seldom have. There is always another to take a president's place. Always. It is in our law."

Bailey thought of the Speaker of the House and suppressed a shiver of dismay. But what the Judge was saying was, of course, literally true, and the fact that a Balkan anarchist did not understand it, could not, in fact, conceive of it, made no practical difference at all. If—or when, he should say—it became known that the successor to the president was for any reason whatever unable to fulfill the duties of the presidency, the next in line would take his place. The Constitution and the law made it as inexorable as the turning of the earth.

"I do not believe you, Colonel," Lesh said. "Laws are not such strong things."

"To Americans, some laws are unbreakable," Seidel said.

"That is not my picture of your countrymen," Lesh said. "Arrangements and accommodations can be made."

Seidel studied the heavy, cruel face of the Albanian. Bakuninite, the Arab woman had called him, and Bakuninite he was: a disciple of chaos. Wasn't it Mikhail Bakunin who said that the passion to destroy was a creative passion? A man so destructive that he revolted even Marx, who expelled him from the First International? A disciple of such a philosopher might bargain, but he would never keep his end of any agreement. He would ask for the moon, and after getting it would betray friend and enemy alike. No matter what "arrangements and accommodations" were made, Seidel thought, we are all as good as dead.

"Would you care to hear on what terms we will release Mr. Bailey?" Lesh asked, looking from the Judge to Bailey and back again. "Let me tell you anyway. There are already three American helicopters on the ground in the valley. Your companion the fat newspaperman, the one called Reisman, will be released to carry our terms to your friends. First, the easiest thing to obtain: money. Your people will supply, at a place of our choosing, five hundred million dollars in gold—"

"Good God," Seidel said. "That's absurd."

"Not at all. We are being modest because our needs are—or will be—less than you imagine. Second, all American troops will be withdrawn from the Sinai. Third, all Arab freedom fighters held in prisons anywhere in the world will be released and flown to a destination of our choice—"

"None of this will happen, Colonel Lesh," Seidel said. "Believe me—none of it."

"Fourth, the State of Israel will withdraw from all Arab lands, back to the boundaries allotted it in the original partition of Palestine by the United Nations in 1948."

"Madness," Bailey said heavily.

"Not at all. I consider that we are being extremely generous and reasonable. We could as easily demand that the State of Israel cease to exist. That the Americans see to it that it is disbanded—by force, if necessary. So a withdrawal to the original boundaries established by partition is a mild request, all things considered."

"What is this bullshit?" Robinson spoke for the first time, his voice thick and threatening. "Who do you mother fuckers think you're talking to?"

"Be still, comrade," Lesh said. "You will play your part. Just be patient."

Robinson looked at Seidel, and the expression on his battered face made it clear that he was ready to do something about all this, no matter how many armed Arabs stood by. He felt full of a dark, killing anger. He wished the General were here. The General and a few good men like the ones he had lost back at the ambush. That was all it would take to put a stop to this talk. The guilt he felt for the death of his comrades lay heavily on him, and he ached for some action. But Seidel shook his head almost imperceptibly.

"Fifth, the Sixth Fleet will be withdrawn from the Mediterranean Sea."

"Miss Jamil," Bailey asked, "do you actually believe any of this will take place?"

The Arab woman's black eyes hardened. "It must," she said.

"Then we are all lost," Bailey said. "Every one of us."

"And there is one last condition," Lesh said. "The United States will deliver to an Arab government we shall specify one complete air squadron of Specter fighter-bombers, complete with their nuclear armament. In this way we will be in a position to ensure that all the terms of our agreement are kept."

"You have completely lost your mind," Bailey said. "None of these things will be done. I will not permit you even to put such terms to anyone as a price for my release."

"I need hardly remind you that you are not in any position to permit or prevent anything, Mr. Bailey. Those are the terms that will be taken to your countrymen by Reisman—accompanied by you, black comrade," he said, pointing to Robinson.

The Sergeant said quietly, "You call me your 'comrade' one more time and I'm going to shove that AK you carry down your throat. I'm a soldier, a United States goddam soldier, and I take no orders from you. Not now and not ever, man. You dig that?"

Seidel said, "If he'll let you go, Sergeant, do what he says. Get out of this, and tell General Tate what we have on our hands here."

"That is what I had in mind, Colonel," Lesh said. "I would not wish it said that we held an American slave against his will here." He signaled to two of the Arab guards to take Robinson from the church.

Robinson looked to Bailey for orders. He disliked him, but if he was now the commander in chief, it was for him to say what Sergeant Major Crispus Robinson should do.

"It's all right, Sergeant," Bailey said. "Don't let anything happen to Jape Reisman. There's been enough blood spilled already."

Anger and discipline clashed in Robinson. He said quietly, but with emphasis, "If we'd had enough men on this trip, most of the blood would have been *theirs*—" he raised his long jaw at the Arabs—"instead of *ours.*"

"That's enough, Sergeant," the Judge said.

"No," Bailey said. "The Sergeant is right." He said to Robinson, "Go ahead, Sergeant. Tell General Tate what the situation is here." He paused, and then put himself at a hurdle he had never believed he would be forced to cross. "The problem is in his hands. Tell him that whatever course of action he chooses to take, I will support him." He turned to Lesh. "There is no reason whatever for you to hold anyone but me. I appeal to your humanity, Colonel. Release the others."

Lesh shook his head. "One must husband hostages carefully, Mr. Bailey. Believe me, I have experience in such matters. It may become necessary to convince your people that we mean what we say."

"The dead you have left behind speak eloquently," Bailey said.

Lesh merely shrugged.

"At least let Captain Zadok go. You have no use for her."

"No." It was Jamil who spoke. "The Jewess stays."

Lesh said, "I regret, Mr. Bailey, but the commander of the Abou Moussa says no to your request." He signaled to the Arab guards. They closed warily on Robinson, weapons ready.

"You will be sent food and water," Lesh said to Seidel and Bailey. He gave Bailey a mocking salute and turned away. The Americans watched them go.

"What will Tate do?" Bailey asked.

"What can he do?"

How ironic it was, Bailey thought, that the man chosen by the President to replace him should stand at his side. The situation was bizarre, to say the least.

The thought of the President was unsettling. He felt curiously numb now that the first shock had come and gone. Seidel had been a close personal friend of the President, and yet even he seemed unable to react to the news of the Chief Executive's death with any deep emotion. Perhaps it was simply that both of them knew how close they themselves stood to extinction. In such circumstances it might well be that no man could really come to grips with the abstract death of another.

Depressed, feeling isolated from Seidel, Bailey studied the face of the young Arab guarding them. It was a handsome face, but stubbled and lined with dirt. The eyes were dark, hostile, opaque as stones. This young man's forebears had been a great people once. But that was long ago and before their children's descent into a new barbarism. With reason and sense, this man and others like him could work with the Israelis to make the desert bloom. But they preferred to fight and refight lost battles, for they had fallen in love with murder. When an Arab fought, he tried to destroy not only his enemy but also his enemy's wife and sons and daughters. He wished to burn his enemy's house and trees and slaughter his livestock. With the weapons of modern war in his hands he was a scourge—a far cry from a Saladin or a Haroun-al-Raschid.

He said, "Do you speak English?"

The Arab stared, silent and hostile.

"What is your name? Where do you come from?"

The young man stirred, and the smell of sweat and desert dust came from his clothes. He gestured with his weapon that the two Americans should sit against the wall.

Bailey did as he was told. A wave of hopelessness swept over him. How could one deal with such people? He felt old and powerless under the Arab's hostile gaze and the steady, cyclopean eye of the gun barrel.

The Judge sat looking bleak. It was evident that he did not wish to speak, preferring to be alone with his thoughts.

Bailey asked, "Do you believe what Colonel Lesh said?"

"About the President?"

"Yes."

"I believe him. The man hasn't the imagination to make it up. He's dead, all right." There was resentment in Seidel's voice. He seemed to be saying, "Yes, he's dead and you're alive and ten of you would not make one of him. So where's the justice in that?"

"It must be hell at home," Seidel went on, as though to himself. "November 1963 all over again, but worse."

Bailey thought: We need some common, human link between us. After all, men who are going to die together ought to be able to talk to each other. "I am sorry for a great many things, Judge," he said. "But mostly I am sorry that the President and I were not better friends."

Seidel said nothing.

"We disagreed on so many things."

"He was generally right, Bailey," Seidel said.

Not "Mr. President," Bailey noted. Well, of course not. Not

here and not now. Such courtesy and usages belonged to another world, not the world of ambushes and dusty Arabs. It would be a mockery here, from one powerless man to another. Besides, it was unlikely that for the time that remained to him Jason Seidel felt the need to accept another president.

Bailey found that he wished with all his heart for Seidel's good opinion and respect. In this extremity, what else was there to sustain them both? But it was unlikely that between now and the moment the frustrated Arabs stood them against the wall he would get either.

"I am trying to imagine," he said, "what Fowler Beal will say when he hears all that these people want in return for my head."

"It isn't Beal who worries me," Seidel said. "It is the Admiral. Ainsworth is almost certain to smell a conspiracy."

"Then," Bailey said slowly, "God save the United States."

"Say a prayer for the rest of the world, too," the Judge said, and turned away.

Part Three

If one looks at history and sees how often it has happened that wars have been produced by the rivalries of client states, without a full consideration of the worldwide issues . . . the overriding need of finding a solution to the problem of worldwide nuclear war becomes overwhelming. . . . This is *the* central question of our period, and it is a problem that will have to be solved either by this group of officials or by their successors. But it cannot be avoided.

—Secretary of State Henry Kissinger, 1973

Hobson's choice (hob s'nz) A choice without an alternative; the thing offered or nothing.

—Webster's New International Dictionary of the English Language

20

"Arrangements have been made for Mrs. Beal, Mr. President." The speaker was an aide to General Shackleford, the army chief of staff.

Fowler Beal looked at the assembled officers in C and C Beta in alarm. The form of address startled him, and he could not imagine what his wife had to do with all this military maneuvering. "What arrangements do you mean, Colonel?"

"Why, for the First Lady's safety, sir," Shackleford interjected patiently. "We have taken the liberty of having Mrs. Beal moved to the VIP shelter at Catoctin Mountain. She will be quite comfortable there, I assure you."

Beal sucked the dry, filtered air into his lungs. It smelled and tasted vaguely of electrical equipment. "Is that necessary, General Shackleford?" he asked. "I mean, surely there's no real possibility—"

"I'm sure not—but it is best to be certain, sir."

Beal found the old man's calm something less than reassuring. He had been inside C and C Beta for several hours now, and the activities that surrounded him were confusing, unreal. Some of the tasks being performed by the officers working in the Pit were familiar; he had watched them before, during practice alerts and exercises at which he had been an honored guest of the Chairman of the Joint Chiefs. But now it all seemed quite different. The crews at the consoles and the high-ranking men around him were behaving in an altogether disquieting manner. And to take his wife off, without a word, to Catoctin Mountain? He could imagine with what a lack of enthusiasm she must have met that peculiarly ominous surprise.

Ainsworth said in a low, if somewhat disapproving, voice: "Do you have any particular wishes concerning—the occupant of the apartment in Rockville, sir?" He had on his most Calvinist face, but it was obvious that his concern was genuine. "Not Catoctin, of course, but we could at least get Miss MacLean out of the city."

"Stuart, my God—you sound as though you actually expect something to happen," Beal said. To him, the unthinkable was, had always been, and would always be truly unthinkable.

"Precautions, Mr. President," Ainsworth said.

"I must say I don't really understand all this. Surely we can deter any threat from the other side. We have in the past."

"That is true, sir. But it must be said that this situation has never obtained before."

"What is going on outside, Stuart? I feel so isolated here." It was as near to a critical comment as he had yet made about the high-ranking hierarchy that surrounded him.

Ainsworth gestured at the computer displays flashing onto the wall across the Pit. Graphs, bar charts, incomprehensible lists made up of even more incomprehensible symbols, and changing map displays appeared, remained for a time, and vanished to be replaced by others.

"I can't make head or tail of those damned things," Beal said nervously.

The Admiral spoke into an intercom connected to one of the technicians or officers at the consoles in the Pit. "Bring up the Enemy Status display, Lieutenant."

Instantly, a large-scale map of the Asian land mass appeared on the far wall. As he watched it, Beal could see that bits of information were appearing, changing, rearranging themselves. "Explain it to me," he pleaded.

"Of course, Mr. President. It is quite complete—or so we hope. You can see that the Soviet Union's Strategic Forces have responded to our Yellow Alert with an alert of their own. This has happened before and was predicted by our computers. But there are some ancillary responses that we did not foresee. They have sixty Bear long-range bombers aloft. They have never put such a large force on airborne alert before. It indicates that they take seriously the possibility of our launching a first strike."

"I know all this is a matter of credibility, Stuart. But surely they don't really believe we would actually attack them!"

"May I once again remind you of Case Headless, Mr. President? We cannot ignore the possibility that *they* are preparing for a first strike. The Bears are now over Siberia." He turned to General Rivera. "What does Cheyenne Mountain say?"

"They confirm the Bears, Admiral. If they cross their customary airborne-alert line, Elmendorf Air Force Base will scramble interceptors."

"It is possible, of course," Ainsworth said, "that they are still only probing, trying to test our responses. They may believe we are helpless without the President or Mr. Bailey."

He turned back to look at the computer displays across the War Room. "Their ICBM force of SS-11's is already on the line. That may simply be a threat gesture—or they may mean it. Our Minuteman force is heavily targeted on their SS-11's. We are also refining our tracking of their early-warning satellites. If they bring their SS-9's on the line, we are going to have to take out some of their spy birds. We can't allow them to go on watching our preparations."

Beal's mouth felt hot and dry. "What's happening on the streets, Stuart? What are people doing?"

"The people are reacting splendidly, Mr. President. Far better than one would have expected after their behavior of the last few years."

"Yes, but what are they being *told?*"

"We must rely on the news media for that, after all, Mr. President. The press is doing what our press has always done—faking, creating, sensationalizing. Of course, in the absence of any hard information, I suppose we cannot blame them for that. In any case, it serves the nation's purpose for the time being."

"But the public must be growing apprehensive."

"I agree, sir. And when we have some confirmable facts for them, we will release them."

Rivera said, "Apparently that CBS correspondent did pick up something from Arab Front sources. The Egyptians cut him off the air, but he managed to telecast enough to start the rumors flying. The Washington *Post* service has picked it up and so have some of the other newspapers. CBS has been onto General Frierson in Public Information to confirm or deny the ambush story. He told them that Sinai and the component were White House business and that they should look directly to the administration for confirmations or denials."

"But Jape Reisman is with the Vice President—with Talcott Bailey." Beal caught himself tripping over a choice of title for the man he was replacing.

"True, sir," Rivera murmured. "However, the media's problems are not within our purview."

"Nor do I see any reason why we should make them so. It has been a long time since press and Pentagon were partners," Shackleford added.

"But *I* want to know what's happening, General," Beal said.

"Sir, no one in Washington has attended more military briefings than you have," Ainsworth said in a low, reproving voice that seemed to imply that Fowler Beal was embarrassing him before his associates.

I must get myself in order, Beal thought. I'm behaving like Old Fowler, and that will not do now. He said, "What have you done about convening the National Security Council?"

"All members have been notified. But I do not see the possibility of a meeting before tomorrow at the earliest."

"The CIA?"

"I think that for the moment we will have to rely on our own military intelligence, sir. Donaldson is on the spot and will report. But remember that in recent years the Agency has developed a lean to the left."

Beal turned his attention to the row of live-but-silent television screens monitoring the national networks. He raised the sound level on the NBC telecast. Once again there were the silent crowds in the rainy streets. The scene was New York this time, the UN plaza. A voice-over commentary was saying: "The people gathered here are not reacting as expected to the spate of rumors coming out of Arab capitals. There have been some small demonstrations of anger, and an Egyptian flag has been burned. But the obvious concern of the Egyptian delegation here at the United Nations would seem to suggest that if indeed the Arab Front for the Liberation of Palestine has interfered in any way with the Vice President's peace mission to Zone Center, it has done so without the knowledge or approval of Arab governments represented here at the United Nations. Meanwhile, along thirty-four east there have been unexplained military movements in both the American and Russian sectors—"

"As you can see, Mr. President," Ainsworth said, "the people are behaving with great fortitude."

"I know how they are *behaving*. I'd like to know what they're *thinking*."

"There have been some demonstrations; the reports are accurate—as far as they go. The Russian Consulate in San Francisco has been stoned, and the Egyptian Embassy here in Washington has asked for—and received—special police protection. I believe there have been some incidents involving academics and street people—self-styled revolutionaries. In all honesty, sir, I cannot blame the demonstrators for taking action. It is a pity the news media are circulating rumors, but then, they always have, haven't they? If I were to hazard a guess about the temper of the population, I would have to say that they are angry, and getting angrier. The President's death has affected all of us severely, and the suggestion that something may have happened to Mr. Bailey is bound to unsettle a great many people. But by and large they are behaving well and facing all possibilities with determination."

Beal had the impression that he was afloat in a sea of quicksand. "Determination" to do what? The nightmarish calm of the Joint Chiefs was more frightening than the unsettled attitude of the people.

Ainsworth returned to his interested scrutiny of the computer displays across the room. Beal looked hard at them, willing himself to understand them. It was important. It was *vital.* If he actually was the president now, he had to know. But though the light-writing on the cathode-ray tubes held him fascinated, almost hypnotized, the displays remained totally mysterious.

A commo light flashed, and Ainsworth said, "Yes?"

A disembodied voice from outside the War Room said: "Ambassador Kornilov is asking for a meeting with Mr. Beal, Admiral. The Department of State referred him to us."

"Where is the Assistant Secretary of Defense?"

"En route to Catoctin Mountain, Admiral, as you suggested."

Ainsworth paused, seeming to consider. Then he said, "Have General Frierson see Kornilov personally. He is to be told that the Acting President is not available at this time. Have him quote the circumstances—Frierson will know what to say."

"I should see him, Stuart," Beal said. "Perhaps there is a reasonable explanation for the Russians' failure to warn us about the Arab guerrillas. I really think I should see him—"

"It would not be suitable for you to involve yourself in a discussion with any foreign diplomat until we hear from

General Trask about the status of his mission. You do understand me, sir?"

The voice from outside went on, dispassionate and impersonal. "State also informs us that the UN Secretary-General has made a number of telephone calls asking for an appointment with the Acting President. Our man at the UN and the new Soviet Ambassador, Keriakin, want to approach the Secretary-General and demand that he schedule an emergency meeting of the Security Council. All of our UN people are begging for guidance."

Beal glanced anxiously at Ainsworth. The American Ambassador to the United Nations was a crusty old associate of the dead President's, a Texan named Wilmot, who was openly contemptuous of Congressman Beal, and who would readily join with Keriakin in a request for an extraordinary session of the Security Council. But even at the risk of a loss of personal prestige, Beal was ready to snatch at the chance of shifting responsibility. He said, "If you don't think I should talk to Kornilov, Stuart, all right. But surely the Secretary-General—"

Ainsworth said into the intercom, "Notify Ambassador Wilmot that the Acting President does not consider it prudent at this time to take matters before the Security Council. An extraordinary session would be premature and alarming. When we have a clearer picture of what has happened in the Sinai, the Acting President will instruct the Ambassador." He broke the connection and said to Beal, "The Russians have used the UN against us before, sir. It is not to our advantage to let them do it again at this time."

"They will call the session anyway, Stuart."

"To do what, sir? To admit they encouraged a band of cold-blooded killers to attack an American peace mission?" Ainsworth's eyes were hooded. "The news will be common knowledge soon enough, I think."

"If that happens, Stuart, I am really afraid of what the public will do."

"The people will be told everything, sir," Ainsworth said.

"This is no military junta. The Joint Chiefs of Staff won't be guilty of deception. But we will wait until you are *de facto* president—as you will be when Trask reports."

Beal had a vivid memory of the way in which Tate had resisted that idea, the almost arrogant manner in which he had said: "I recognize no acting president." Even knowing, most probably, that such a statement would cost him his command and his career, he had utterly rejected the contention that Talcott Bailey's claim to the presidency could be bypassed, overlooked, dismissed, because he was not free to act.

Legally, Tate was wrong, and he and Beal, as well as the Joint Chiefs, knew he was wrong. But it seemed to Beal that what the General had been trying to do was preserve the peace, to buy some time (for the United States? for the world?) that could be used to plan rationally. Now that chance was lost. He was—or shortly would be—under arrest and unable to affect the situation in the Sinai Peninsula.

Beal turned to Shackleford. "Don't you think that we should withhold any statement about a possible Russian involvement in the Arab attack on the Vice President?" He somehow hoped for something more moderate, an attitude less militant and perilous, from the old Army Chief of Staff. But Shackleford only inclined his grizzled head and said, "No, I do not, sir. When we know—and we should know very soon now—the people must be fully informed."

"But—everything? The Russians knowing? All that?"

"Particularly that," Shackleford said. "Otherwise our reasonable precautions become self-serving saber-rattling."

"But not until the situation at St. Katherine is brought to a satisfactory conclusion," Ainsworth said, and Beal felt a cold shiver run down his spine. The only possible conclusion to the situation at the monastery was, in Ainsworth's opinion, an assault that would result in the death of the hostages. Then, of course, there would be no possibility of a question about who the legitimate president of the United States might be.

Rivera, who was watching the computer displays, interrupted the discussion. He said quietly, "Eastern Sea Frontier reports movement of the Russian nukes at line Gamma."

Ainsworth, his naval instinct aroused, turned from Beal to study the displays. "What are they doing?"

Rivera spoke into the intercom. "Update and details on that Gamma-line contact, if you please."

A column of figures appeared over a map outline of the eastern seaboard of the United States. The figures were different from the previous displays. They were light-printed in red.

Rivera read and interpreted aloud. "Yankee-class nuclear-powered subs. The usual three on station, but they are coming to MFD."

"MFD? What does that mean?" Beal asked uneasily.

"Missile firing depth," Ainsworth said.

"They could be coming up for some fresh air," Shackleford suggested.

"Possible," Rivera said, "but I don't buy it. I think they are threatening us." He listened to a voice in the headset he had put on and said, "CNO says they are covered. One and Two are being tracked by PV-100's and Three has a hunter-killer locked onto his wake."

Beal was aware that Soviet submarines habitually prowled the American coasts, just as American Tridents did the Baltic and North Pacific. But the bluntness of the report was chilling.

"As you know, sir," Ainsworth said, "there are always eight to a dozen Yankee-class boats skulking around the one-hundred-fathom line. When they try to come to missile firing depth, we discourage them. It appears our friends are being provocative."

"Quite frankly, Admiral," Beal said, with an attempt at formality and authority, "it seems to me that it is we who are behaving in a provocative manner."

Ainsworth fixed Beal with a cold-eyed stare. "Is it necessary, sir, to brief you again on what has happened in the

Sinai? Should I remind you that the rumors about sabotage of the President's airplane may well be true?"

Beal quickly shook his head to deny any lack of faith in his military advisers. Stuart Ainsworth might be tough—even hard—but he was a fair and honorable man who had devoted a lifetime to the service of his country. Such a man could not, Beal was sure, take unnecessary risks with the security of the United States.

"Rivera, where are the nukes now?" Ainsworth asked.

"Bandit One is at the one-hundred-fathom line off Nantucket Island. Two is off Hampton Roads. And Three is twenty-two nautical miles off the mouth of the Savannah River."

"Note, Mr. President," Ainsworth said, a trifle pedantically, "how well co-ordinated their movements are. The Soviets have an excellent low-level transmission system. They use a geologic shield in eastern Siberia as a reflector. You may recall that some few years ago we asked for permission to build a similar system for our own nuclear-submarine communications over the Canadian Shield, and the environmentalists prevented it. It was claimed it would be bad for the deer in Wisconsin, or the migrating Canada geese—something of that sort." His expression clearly indicated what he thought of the priorities involved in that decision.

Beal, who had been one of the congressmen intimidated by the environmentalist objections to the naval communications system in question, felt vaguely guilty. But the idea of Russian submarines near the American coastline was unsettling. He asked, "Are the missiles these boats carry all MIRVed?"

"I believe so, sir. These particular nukes are newly arrived from the Soviet Union." He checked the computer displays and nodded. "All three carry multiple independently targeted hydrogen warheads on their ordnance. A total of twenty warheads per boat."

Beal considered the implications of that cool statement and could think of nothing at all significant to reply.

Ainsworth took a headset from a rack on the console and spoke into the microphone. "CNO, Chairman here. Tell the Venturas and the hunter-killer to give those Red nukes a warning. Just one. If they try to come to MFD, sink them."

Beal's heart felt as though it were being slowly squeezed. A trickle of cold sweat ran down his ribs. "Isn't that—rather extreme, Stuart? I mean—well—I didn't intend to suggest we should—"

Ainsworth said calmly, "I am quite sure the Russian subs will accept the warning, Mr. President, when they see how easily we have detected them."

Beal sat in silence, looking out at the teeming activity of the War Room. There were so many men and so many machines and he understood so little of what they actually did. Yet it was these very things that were the total and absorbing concern of the men about him. They should know what they were doing. But he could not suppress his feeling that each successive move seemed an increasingly angry escalation of the tension.

"Isn't there some less violent response we can make if they ignore a warning?" he asked.

"My mission is the defense of the United States, sir. If they come to firing depth, I will sink them. There is no other option." The Admiral spoke, Beal noted, with the same absolute assurance of the true believer that marked the militant leftists he so despised. To wield such power a man must be something more than certain, Beal thought.

Ainsworth seemed suddenly to reach another plateau. "Who's Looking Glass today?" he asked Rivera abruptly.

"Brigadier General Cheney, sir."

"A black officer?"

"Yes, sir."

The Admiral's prim face showed his momentary struggle with bigotry and the triumph of the military mind over it. "You are satisfied?"

"Yes, sir."

"Very well."

"Looking Glass?" Beal looked to Rivera for an explanation.

"Looking Glass is the code name for the Airborne Command Center, sir. A specially equipped jet that would take over command if for any reason you—and we—are unable to act here."

Beal said in a tight voice, "You mean if we were hit with an H-bomb."

"It would more likely be a missile, sir, in Washington. Quite probably several."

"My God," breathed Beal.

"We are *the* obvious target, after all, Mr. President," Shackleford said reasonably.

Beal felt as though an icy draught had touched him.

"And now, sir," Rivera said in a quiet tone, "I think it would be safer if we moved into the underground Command Center."

General Tate's helicopter had scarcely touched down on the rocky soil of the valley below the Monastery of St. Katherine before it was surrounded by a large crowd of lamenting, gesticulating Bedouins. Men, women, and children formed a circle hardly large enough for safety, and the babble of voices and Arabic lamentations submerged the diminishing beat of the rotor.

Sergeant Anspaugh, crouching between and behind the pilots' seats, said, "I wouldn't go out there without a side arm, General."

Tate looked across the open ground between the place where Beaufort had put down the helicopter and the monastery. The sun was up now, and the reddish rock of the walls glowed with the crimson-touched illumination from the east. On the north side of the monastery he could see cyprus trees. Beyond them a rubbled talus rose to meet the sheer riven cliffs of the mountain that blocked off almost all of the western sky.

Near the monastery wall he could see, too, a ragged procession of Orthodox monks moving across the stony ground. They were carrying a number of their dead.

The helicopters he had sent ahead to do the recce had landed some minutes earlier on his orders, and the crews were coming toward him, shoving the crowding Bedouins aside with no great gentleness.

He unfastened his shoulder harness and opened the door of the helicopter. Immediately, the Bedouins closed in about him. He did not understand their language, but it was obvious enough that these people were badly confused and asking for assistance and protection.

Beaufort unholstered his service pistol anxiously, but Tate said sharply, "Put that away, Captain. These people are frightened enough already."

He swung his legs out of the door, saying to Anspaugh, "I want you to radio Eilat and have them fly out an interpreter right away."

"Yes, sir." Anspaugh's expression showed that he was concerned about the order, but he risked no further comment.

Tate said, "I know it's a violation to call Israelis into the DMZ, Sergeant. Don't concern yourself with that. And after you've talked to Eilat, contact Es Shu'uts and have the rest of the Special Forces detachment airlifted down here. They are to bring plans of the monastery and whatever photographs we have. I want them here by 1100 hours. Beaufort, you come with me."

Tate and his pilot moved through the crowd of excited Bedouins toward the air force men. The smell and dust were overpowering. Yesterday's overcast sky was gone; today was going to be clear and hot. Tate studied the walls of the monastery from a distance. The place looked impregnable. He thought of Bailey and the Judge somewhere in that imposing pile of ancient stones—if they were still alive. It was going to be a bloody business trying to get them out. Deborah was in there, too, and that thought brought a tightening of his throat and a leaden apprehension.

The senior helicopter pilot saluted and reported. "They pitched the people out of the place—those they didn't shoot. And they shot quite a few, sir. I make it about eight or ten."

A young lieutenant, his face pale, said, "We spotted some riders on camels on the way down, General. They shot at us with automatic weapons, so we figure maybe they are Abou Moussa guerrillas who couldn't squeeze into the stolen vehicles. We notified the Swedes at Zone Center to pick them up if they could."

"Of course," the first officer said acidly, "there might be some shooting—which would mean the UN people would have to ask Cyprus what to do."

"I have sent for reinforcements, Captain," Tate said. "The camel riders won't give us any trouble here, even if they should reach us." He wondered briefly how this young man, of another service, would respond to his assurances and orders if he knew that the Chairman of the Joint Chiefs had tried to relieve him of his command. By his own refusal to accept Ainsworth's orders he had placed every man of the U.S. Component in an equivocal position. To accept an order from their commanding officer was now to risk disciplinary action from high up the military ladder. It was a nice legal problem, and one that would concern military historians of the future—if there was to *be* a future with historians of any sort in it. But what he had told Ainsworth and Beal had been neither more nor less than the truth as he saw it. His mission was to protect the peace, not to destroy it. The question, for the next few hours at least, was *how*?

"Have any of you spoken to the monks?" he asked.

The officers shook their heads.

"Let's go see if any of them speak English. Before the

Peacekeeping Area was established, this place used to be visited by tourists from all over the world."

As they made their way through the gathering of unhappy Bedouins toward the monks, a figure appeared on the rim of the wall facing the rising sun. It was one of the guerrillas, and he raised his Kalashnikov and loosed a five-shot burst into the air. The staccato noises echoed and reverberated harshly against the sheer mountain. The Bedouins scattered in panic.

Tate raised his field glasses and saw that the man was a European, with a heavy mustache, and dressed in the camouflage uniform so favored by revolutionaries and guerrillas.

The man slung his rifle on his shoulder and cupped his hands about his mouth. "Is your commander here, Americans?" he called.

Tate took several steps forward and waited. One of the air force officers warned, "They might want to set you up and grease you, General."

Tate signaled for silence.

The man on the wall shouted, "I am Lesh. I am sending you a message. Pay close attention, General. And look carefully."

Four figures appeared on the crest of the wall beside him. Tate again raised his glasses and recognized Secret Service Agent Emerson, flanked by Arabs. The agent stood stiffly, his arms tied behind him at the elbows, Vietcong fashion.

Lesh shouted, "There, at the north corner, General. Those are your people; do not shoot at them. And listen to them carefully."

Around the corner of the building came a tall black man and a heavy-set Caucasian. Tate recognized Sergeant Robinson and Jape Reisman. Robinson walked erect, his soldier's pride outraged by the helplessness of his position. Reisman stumbled awkwardly across the rock-and-boulder-strewn ground below the wall.

Tate moved forward to meet them. Reisman tripped and would have fallen, but for Robinson. The Press Secretary looked haggard and near to exhaustion.

When the three men stood face to face, Robinson saluted, his injured face bitter. "Sir," he said. "I lost the convoy. I didn't protect the Vice President."

Tate felt mingled pride and compassion for Robinson. What the Sergeant had said was exactly what he himself would have said in a similar situation. It was, in fact, what he must say, sooner or later, when called to account for his stewardship of the American command in the Sinai. Robinson offered no excuses and no evasions; he did not state the obvious—that the meagerness of the escort was primarily to blame for the fiasco on the way to Zone Center. He had spoken as a soldier to a soldier, and Tate thought proudly that it was this quality in man that the Army, imperfect as it might be, could bring forth, if it was in the man to begin with.

Reisman said, "They have the Vice President, General." And then, in a tone that belied belief and begged reassurance: "Is it true about the President?"

"Yes, it's true. I am sorry, Reisman."

Reisman's face showed his dismay. "I hoped they were lying. I really hoped that they were lying—"

"I'm sorry," Tate said again.

"Then those maniacs hold the President of the United States," Reisman said. "The world has gone absolutely crazy."

"Where have they got him? Can I be taken to him?"

Reisman shook his head and fumbled inside his shirt for a sheaf of what appeared to be old parchments. "These are their terms, General. They didn't even have paper to write them on. They tore these pages out of a book." His eyes, nested in puffy, darkened flesh, held a light of hysteria, but his voice grew steadier. "You won't believe what they are demanding, General. You simply will not believe it—"

Tate took the parchment sheets and read the angular script that someone—Lesh, to judge by the Balkan penmanship—had written there. He read the demands in silence. He did not find the items particularly surprising. Impossible of fulfillment, yes. But not really surprising considering everything.

"I was to tell you, sir," Robinson said, "that they want you to know that they mean business. They said they will give up another hostage—Colonel Seidel or maybe Captain Zadok—when you agree to their demands. And Mr. Bailey when all conditions are met—whenever that may be."

Tate looked steadily at Robinson, trying hard to separate his professional and personal feelings.

"I guess Captain Zadok is okay, General. I haven't seen her since they took over this place."

"I see."

Reisman said, "They told me that they were going to put on a demonstration for you, General. Something to prove to you that they are serious about this."

Tate felt a sinking sensation as he raised his eyes to the tableau on the wall. He had a dreadful feeling that he knew what the promised demonstration would be. Reisman, too, looked up at the wall, and then said, "Oh, sweet Jesus."

Lesh called down to Tate. "Have you received our terms, General?"

Tate shouted back, "I have. There is no need for any demonstration, Colonel Lesh. I believe you mean what you say."

"I want you to be absolutely certain, General," Lesh called back, and nodded to the guerrillas beside him.

John Emerson was pushed from the wall. He fell, without a sound, for the first half-dozen meters. Then he was jerked to a violent stop by the rope noose around his neck and hung there, swinging, heels drumming spasmodically against the stones.

A lamentation arose from the monks huddled against the wall below the corpse. The Bedouins, watching from a distance, cried out in fresh terror. And Tate heard one of his officers behind him scream in an enraged voice, *"You lousy murdering bastards!"*

Tate felt nauseated, sick with fury. His face seemed set in concrete, the expressionless grimace hardened there. He stared for a long while at the figures on the wall and at the body of the Vice President's bodyguard hanging, still swinging slightly, against the wall.

He said to Beaufort, Reisman, and Robinson, "Come along." He led the way back to his helicopter, where Anspaugh waited, white-faced.

"I am sending you back to Es Shu'uts, Mr. Reisman," he said. "Captain Beaufort will arrange transport for you back to Washington. You will have to tell the National Security Council what you have seen here and deliver Lesh's demands."

Reisman, haggard and shocked, but still basically a reporter, said, "I would like to stay and see this through, General."

"Someone who has been through it will have to go back and tell them about it," Tate said, more gently. "You are the only one available. We can't let that list of demands become public knowledge, or everyone else will start going crazy. I don't think this is covered by the First Amendment. I rely on you to stay away from the press."

"All right, General. If that's the way it has to be."

Tate said to his pilot, "Get him to Es Shu'uts fast, Beaufort. And if there is any trouble at all about his transport back to the States, take him to the Israelis. Mosa'ad will lay on an El Al airplane if they have to." He turned to Reisman. "Admiral Ainsworth relieved me of command here, and I refused the order. You'd better keep that as quiet as you can, too. Speaker of the House Beal is being pushed to declare himself acting president. He may already have done it."

"Jesus," Reisman muttered. "Every goddam thing is coming apart."

"Not quite everything. Bailey is still alive. He isn't my choice for leader of the Free World—but he *is* the President now. That might be the most important message you ever give anyone. The Joint Chiefs think the Soviets set all this up. *But Bailey is still alive*. Keep telling them that over and over again."

"I will, General."

"Take off, Beaufort. When you've delivered Mr. Reisman, come back here."

"I'd like to see anyone try to keep me away, General," Beaufort said, looking at the monastery wall.

Tate helped Reisman into the Huey and ducked clear of the starting rotors. He watched the helicopter rise and circle away in a wide turn to the east and north. Then he said to Robinson, "Are you all right, Sergeant? Do you need medical assistance?"

"I'm not hurt, General. I'm mad."

"Good. You come with me." Tate trotted toward one of the parked air force helicopters, and Robinson loped after him.

"Where are we going, General?"

"We are going to see General Ulanov. Maybe we can stop flexing our useless muscles and start using our heads for a change."

21

The message from Admiral Ainsworth to Colonel (now Brigadier General) Dale Trask signaled the collapse of Captain Elizabeth Adams's fantasy world. She had performed two acts of rebellion in her lifetime. The first had been joining the Army. The second had been her deliberate delay in transmitting to General Tate the information from Sam Donaldson, the CIA station chief—the single bit of information that might have prevented the ambush of Talcott Bailey's party.

Her first rebellion had been against a prim and sterile heritage. A heritage, incidentally, not too dissimilar from Bailey's. Because it had brought her into intimate contact with William Tecumseh Sherman Tate, she had come to regard her abandonment of her dull life as an act of bravery that had earned thrilling rewards. She had sat at the right hand of the mighty (as one of her clergyman relatives might have put it) and had combined propinquity and imagination to synthesize an imaginary romance with her young commander.

But her second rebellion had been the result of emotion and jealousy. It had been an impulsive act of betrayal, the petty revenge—as she saw it—of an emotional and unstable woman. It had led, she believed, directly to General Tate's failure to secure the Vice President's safety, and now seemed the root cause of her fantasy lover's destruction. She had heard with her own ears the order from Admiral Ainsworth putting Dale Trask in command of the U.S. Component of the Peacekeeping Force. The same dreadful man who had, by his puerile mock attack on the *Allende,* endangered all that Bill Tate had achieved in the Sinai was now to be given Tate's command and authority. And none of it could have happened had it not been for her own sinful vindictiveness. That Tate had been conducting an affair with Deborah Zadok no longer mattered. He was a man, and men were weak in matters of the flesh. She could have made allowances; she could have understood and remained steadfast. Instead, she had permitted her own disgusting carnality to overcome those very qualities that her general admired and respected in her: loyalty, efficiency, intelligence, and chastity. She had betrayed him and all those things in herself that made her different from the swarthy Jewess, or even from the whores in the native quarter of Es Shu'uts patronized by the soldiers. She had fallen beneath contempt, and it was *he*—the only man who really stood between them all and the dark mass of Asiatics and Africans on the other side of thirty-four east—who now must pay the price.

The death of the President in Palm Springs and the shock of Bailey's ambush by the Abou Moussa had stunned the component headquarters people. The flags in front of the Glasshouse and the other buildings hung at half-staff. Civilian and military personnel not on duty gathered in small groups in the barracks, in the Falasha, and in the air-conditioned offices to listen to the radio reports and watch the satellite transmissions from home. The very atmosphere had become unreal, almost mistily blurred and distorted by the great events taking place elsewhere. To this could be added a sense of impending doom, the feeling that all that had been done in the last few years to secure the peace had been, ironically, twisted into some unthinkable Götterdämmerung. Through this miasmic atmosphere, filled with self-loathing, moved Captain Elizabeth Adams, determined to set right what she had done out of jealousy and neurotic passion.

Dale Trask was in his quarters, preparing for the flight to the site of the ambush, when Liz knocked on his door. He opened it impatiently, to find her standing there, a slender figure limned darkly against the slanting morning light. She wore full service uniform with shoulder bag, as though prepared for a journey.

"Yes? What is it, Captain?" He was in a rush to get away. The Air Police were waiting at the helipad.

Liz was suddenly unable to speak. Her plans had seemed so clear only moments ago. She had prepared so carefully all that she must say to Trask: that he must not do what he had been ordered to do by men far away and not really aware of the situation in the Peacekeeping Area, that he should wait and consider what effect it would have on the men of the component to have their splendid commander arrested as though he were a common criminal and not a national hero. She had planned painstakingly to say these things to Trask in a way that would not antagonize or anger him, to say them reasonably and with every indication that she understood how important all this was to him personally. To show her understanding, she had even taken from General Tate's quarters a pair of silver stars to give to Trask as a token of her desire—and General Tate's—to be his friend.

She had planned this thoughtfully, and, to make it all right, had even thought of seducing Trask, imagining how she would go about it, saying nothing but simply walking into his quarters and undressing in that sensuous way she had heard men were always unable to resist. She would stand before him naked, perhaps with the offering of silver stars in her hand, and this would—must—distract him from the performance of what he surely understood was an odious and improper duty. Scarcely had she gathered the wreckage of one fantasy when she had begun to construct another, one of self-sacrifice and self-immolation to protect the man she loved and had wronged. She saw herself submitting to Trask, feeling his scarred face against her belly and thighs. She would do all this and more for her commander, and he would know of her shame and sacrifice and even if he did not love her he would be grateful—

"What the *hell* do you *want,* Captain?" Trask said impatiently.

Liz started, and looked at Trask as though he had appeared out of nowhere. Why, none of her plan would work, she thought. It was all the dream of a neurotic woman. There was nothing she could do, nothing at all. If she stood naked before him, he would only laugh. One did not seduce a soldier like this from his duty with a show of tiny breasts and skinny flanks.

She searched the room's hard contours with desperate eyes. She saw the flying kit on the rumpled bed, the as yet not completely unpacked luggage, the soiled uniform hanging from the wardrobe door, the bottle of whisky and unwashed glass on the nightstand. She shivered with a prescient revulsion. This scarred and angry brute of a man intended to wear her shining warrior's stars, exercise his command. How could she have imagined that she could touch him, move him to an act of understanding and nobility? Her gaze fell on the holstered service pistol on the dresser beside the open doorway, and she was filled with a soaring sense of fate. What better could she ever become than an instrument of justice? She stepped into the room and her hand closed over the butt of the heavy revolver.

She heard Trask yell *"What the hell do you think you're doing?"*

She was surprised that the weapon was so heavy. Her thin finger curled around the trigger, making the muzzle waver.

"You stupid goddam broad—put that down!"

There was a roaring, ringing in Liz's ears and the strong and acrid smell of cordite.

Trask's disfigured face was frozen into an expression of utter incredulity. His hands moved to push himself away from the wall. Something had thrown him backward against it. Liz squeezed the trigger again, and this time she heard the explosion clearly. It was deafening in the small room.

Trask slid down the wall to a sitting position, his bulging eyes fixed on her, still disbelieving. A dark trickle of blood escaped from his open mouth, and he made a liquid, sighing sound, then no sound at all.

Captain Liz Adams turned and walked slowly out into the sunlight. There were faces everywhere, but not *his* face. No matter, she thought. He will know what to do now. She took several steps across the gravel walkway between the low concrete-block buildings. The pistol dropped from her limp fingers.

Someone ran to her—several people, it seemed. She was having some difficulty focusing her eyes because the sun was so bright. The red-orange sun, the desert sun—she remembered that the sun did not shine so brightly at home. Someone put an arm about her shoulders. It was Sam Donaldson, and she wondered how it happened that he should be here, forgetting that he lived in the next building from that new air force colonel whom she did not like, did not like at all.

Someone behind her was shouting. It sounded as though he were calling "Medic! *Medic—over here!*"

Surrounded by white faces, she felt a momentary fright until she recognized the CIA chief again. "Mr. Donaldson," she said vaguely.

"It's all right, Captain," he said with great gentleness. "It's going to be all right."

But she knew that things would never be quite all right again.

"It is important to the cause of world peace that it be understood we did all we could."

Deputy Premier Anatoly Rostov stared bleakly at the Swedish General and measured his words carefully. "The fact is, General Eriksson, that you have done exactly nothing. I do not wish to be uncultured in my criticism of the United Nations, but the record—if there is to *be* a record—will bear me out."

Eriksson bridled, red-faced. "I fail to see, Excellency, how I could have prevented this unfortunate occurrence."

"I am sure you do fail to see," Rostov said.

"If you are suggesting that my troops should have kept the Demilitarized Zone clear of guerrillas, may I point out to you that the guerrillas in question came from the *Soviet* Sector."

"The record will show that, too, to our shame," Rostov said. He inhaled a puff of the acrid smoke from the Turkish cigarette in his stained fingers and frowned at the men he could see standing about in the compound beyond the windows, made of American Thermopane. The Swedish UN troops, in their blue berets and smartly uniformed, stood apart from the KGB troops of his own escort. How, he wondered, could the Americans have been such fools as to allow their vice president to travel with a single section of soldiers as security? What he knew of General Tate, and the impression he had of him from their short talk at the scene of the ambush, did not suggest slackness; quite the contrary.

He turned again to the Swede. "Has the Secretary-General been permitted to see Mr. Beal yet?"

The General shook his head and pursed his heavy lips in disapproval. He reminds me of a schoolmaster I once had, thought Rostov. He could not keep discipline either.

"The Acting President has vanished inside the Pentagon," Eriksson said. "I have received a message from Stockholm that Prime Minister Kastrup is appealing to him to exercise great discretion." There was an abrupt knock, and a KGB officer walked into Eriksson's office. "We have established communication with Moscow, Comrade Deputy Premier."

"I'll come," Rostov said, getting wearily to his feet.

The interior of the KGB communications van was crowded with electronic equipment and technicians. A lieutenant got to his feet and indicated where Rostov should sit before the camera eye and television screen. "They are on now, Comrade Deputy Premier," he said.

Rostov took his place and motioned for the technicians to leave the van. He did not wish this conversation to become the subject of gossip among the troops at Zone Center.

The scene on the screen was the Kremlin Command and Control Center, which, as Rostov well knew, was not in the Kremlin at all, but underground at some distance from Moscow.

The strong light needed for the television transmission felt hot and uncomfortable on his face, but he tried not to show his weariness or his lack of sleep. The Premier liked his deputies to appear fresh and alert at all times, regardless of circumstances.

The heavily medaled figure of Defense Minister Marshal Aleksei Morozov appeared on the tube. He conferred with an aide standing behind him about the sheaf of reports in his hand and then dismissed the man with a nod and turned to look at the camera. He seemed to be peering directly into Rostov's face. "Comrade Deputy Premier, can you see me well?"

"I can see you and hear you," Rostov said. He did not like Morozov, never had. His dislike was nothing really personal, for he did not know the young Marshal that well. But for many years, while each was rising through the Soviet hierarchies and bureaus, they had clashed again and again on spending policies and priorities. Morozov was a man who believed in rockets instead of television sets, while Rostov's concern had been the maintenance of a placid, comfortable docility among the Soviet people.

Morozov said, "The Premier will speak to you in a moment, Comrade Rostov. First, I would like to give you an appreciation of the military situation."

"Do so," Rostov said. Whatever the actual situation was, he thought, Morozov would, of course, put the worst possible face on it. For some years he had devoted himself to building up the Red Army and the Strategic Rocket Force, with the express purpose of putting the Fatherland in a position of nuclear pre-eminence. He had often pointed to Korea, Vietnam, Cuba, and the Dominican Republic as clear indications of the United States's imperialist intent. The agreements reached at SALT I and II had been signed over his strenuous objections, and he was the primary Politburo opponent of Russian-American co-operation in the Peacekeeping Area.

"First," Morozov said, "a general overview of the situation."

"Get on with it," Rostov said, unable to contain his irritation.

"The Americans are pretending to believe that we are in some way involved in both the accident that killed their president and in the kidnapping of Talcott Bailey." He paused, as though waiting for Rostov to attempt contradicting that bald statement. When the Deputy Premier made no such contradiction, he added, "They have not yet made an accusation, of course, and it is possible that they will not do so." His eyes were cold and pale blue, and Rostov tried to remember if they had always seemed so calmly inhuman. Perhaps it was the color transmission that made the Marshal seem more a part of the electronics system than a flesh-and-blood human being.

Morozov continued. "Our evaluators are now engaged in trying to synthesize their intentions. But I, personally, do not feel the need to consult academicians about this. The Americans feel they have the excuse they have always wanted and they are now working up the nerve to attack us."

Rostov felt an all-too-familiar knot in the pit of his stomach. "You are jumping to conclusions, Comrade Marshal," he said.

"I doubt it, Comrade Rostov. You are, of course, at liberty to form your own military appreciation of the situation." The sarcasm was thinly disguised. Rostov knew well enough what

Morozov and others in the Ministry of Defense thought of his service as a political officer in the Great Patriotic War.

Morozov said, "The Americans have challenged three of our nuclear submarines on routine patrol off their coast. They have scrambled interceptors over the Bering Sea. We have not as yet broken their war code of the day—though we have computers working on it. But they have alerted their Minuteman force, and the Sixth Fleet is flying combat air patrols over their carriers. If that is not a first-strike posture, Comrade Rostov, I would like you to tell me what it is."

"It is understandable that they would be jumpy in the circumstances, Comrade Marshal."

"Is it also understandable that their press is printing the foulest lies about us? Accusing us of a conspiracy with Arab bandits and hooligans?"

Rostov said heavily, "I understand, Comrade Marshal, that GRU contrived to miss a very good likeness of one Albanian adventurer, by name Lesh, on some Cosmos photographs."

"We were in a great hurry to pipeline the material," Morozov said unpleasantly, "to prove to the American war clique that *you* and the Soviet flag had been threatened by an American air pirate."

Rostov suppressed an impulse to raise his voice in exasperation. Morozov and his war hawks were more orthodox than Stalin, more Leninist than Lenin. Though he himself often used the same anti-American locutions, he never made any pretense of believing them. When speaking to a frustrated and underground Vietcong or Khmer Rouge, one was naturally expected to speak of "war cliques" and "air pirates" and even of "fascist-running-dog-bandit-aggressors." Hyperbole was the language of revolution and therefore suitable to the innocents in jungle guerrilla band or urban cell. But to hear a marshal of the Soviet Union using such idiot clichés in conversation with a deputy premier was, at this most critical juncture, cause for real alarm.

"The fact remains, Comrade Marshal," Rostov said, "that

the information was available to us and we failed to pass it on to the Americans except through an absurd spy network that almost certainly guaranteed they would believe we had screened it, and that it would arrive too late to help them. I have talked to their General Tate and know whereof I speak."

"Ah, Tate, the military aristocrat, the student of Russian history," Morozov said ironically. "Ulanov's friend."

"Just so," Rostov said. "He is here at Zone Center. I find it difficult to believe they plan to attack us while he and Ulanov are trying together to contrive some plan to obtain the release of Mr. Bailey."

"Your trusting nature does you credit, Comrade Rostov. Let me tell you that your euphoria about American intentions is not shared by anyone here in Moscow. We can *see* what they are doing."

"Let's return to the matter of the satellite photographs, Comrade Marshal. Have you sent us the man responsible?"

"Barring mishaps, he should be with you by nightfall. But I should tell you that the decision to send him and to admit any culpability was a political one. The military opposed it."

"I am not surprised," Rostov said. The military of whatever state or time was highly allergic to looking foolish. Furthermore, the error by a member of the GRU almost certainly ensured that the Red Army's military intelligence service would lose one of its zealously guarded prerogatives—the evaluation of orbital-spy data—to the Committee for State Security, the KGB. Which was, in the eyes of the higher officers of the Army, already altogether too powerful. Rostov sighed and wished for a glass of water, to ease his rasping throat, but the fool of a technician had not provided any. Then he chided himself for allowing tension and lack of sleep to distract him to the extent of growing petulant over a lack of small amenities. The world seemed to be tottering toward the brink of the unthinkable—and Anatoly Borisovich Rostov, Deputy Premier of the Soviet Union, was unhappy because a technician had not the foresight to provide a pitcher of water.

Truly, Rostov thought, the earth is populated by a race of imbeciles.

Morozov said, "The Premier is ready to speak with you, Comrade Rostov. Just one final word: in your dealings with the Americans you need not accept insult or disrespect. We are fully prepared for whatever may come."

Imbeciles, did I say? thought Rostov. Savages, robots, suicidal lunatics. How, after all, did Morozov really differ from Lesh or those hooligan Arabs? A clean uniform and eight rows of medals were apparently license to blow up the world, just as were dirty clothes, automatic weapons, and Arab Front slogans. He felt his fingers trembling and he knotted his hands together to steady them. In his lifetime, he thought, he had known only a handful of professional soldiers who truly understood their function in the modern world, which was to preserve the peace—*any* peace that permitted a nation to function reasonably and the world to survive. Ulanov had once been such a soldier, crusty old *soukin syn* that he was. And, he thought, this man Tate seemed also to be. Both the young man and the old were fighters; one sensed this immediately. They did not threaten and bluster and rattle their weapons until an opponent grew convinced that it was strike or die.

But neither General Tate nor General Ulanov controlled the really deadly powers of his nation. That, Rostov thought, was almost always left to men like Morozov or that rabid, Russian-hating fanatic Stuart Ainsworth. He did not like what he had heard from the Marshal and he liked even less what he sensed of Washington's activities. The tension seemed to be rising almost of itself. If Bailey should die, nothing would stop the Ainsworths and Morozovs, nothing at all.

"Now, if there are no Jews listening, Comrade Rostov," Morozov said, "the Premier will speak to you." Rostov suppressed his annoyance at the gratuitous anti-Semitism. The remark was a cheap gesture intended to impress the Premier, who was rumored to dislike Jews. One of our least likable characteristics, Rostov thought, is our prejudice against the Hebrews. Doubly ironic in Soviet man—whose precious revolution owed almost its entire intellectual content to Jews, Jews, and more Jews.

"Rostov?"

The Deputy Premier was shocked to see how the strain of the last hours had affected his chief. The old man's face had a waxy pallor, and his naked scalp gleamed vulnerably under the television lights. Rostov guessed that he was having troubles with the war hawks in the Politburo, and that he had slept little recently. "I am here, Comrade Premier," Rostov said.

"Things are bad here, Anatoly Borisovich. The Americans are behaving very provocatively."

"Yes, Comrade Premier." The old man sounded querulous, and this both surprised and disturbed Rostov. Any slightest indication of weakness or uncertainty in the Kremlin leadership could presage a change or a shift in the power structure. That had always been so, as formerly powerful men now exiled to power stations in Siberia or retired to guarded *dachas* could testify.

"What is it like in the Peacekeeping Area? What is the atmosphere?"

"Tense," Rostov said. "But there is hope for co-operation, Comrade Premier."

"Co-operation? How is that?"

"The American General arrived here at Zone Center a short while ago to meet with Yuri Ulanov. He came alone, with only one black soldier, Comrade Premier."

The old man showed signs of petulance. "What is one supposed to infer from that, Comrade?"

"Why, simply that he, at least, does not believe that we are guilty in the abduction of the American Vice President, Comrade Premier." He could not help but add, "I should think that would be obvious."

"You are too anxious to trust the Americans, Anatoly

Borisovich. If you were here to see what they are doing, you would feel otherwise."

Rostov accepted the criticism in silence. The Premier could well be right, of course. Tate's rather dramatic arrival at Zone Center might be a diversion to cover the Americans' first-strike intentions.

"Morozov wants us to come to a full war alert," the old man said in a thin voice. "I don't see what I can do but comply. I am ordering a partial evacuation of our cities."

Rostov listened with sinking heart. He had the feeling of being caught in the path of some immense juggernaut that many madmen—on both sides—were intent on shoving into irresistible motion. He said, "There have been no clashes here, Comrade Premier—"

The old man cut him off irritably. "There was that attack on your vessel, Anatoly Borisovich."

The sinking sensation Rostov felt increased. The remark was one of such banality, of such total inconsequence, that he began to suspect that the fearful old man had already made some dark decision. A few hours ago the *Allende* affair had been a useful breach of international courtesy that could be utilized to score propaganda points against the Americans and their allies in the Middle East. But events in the United States and along thirty-four east had completely negated any such usefulness. The incident may have served to start matters moving in a dangerous direction, but it would be the height of folly to rely on it to enlist any sympathy for the Soviet cause while the Americans were in so hostile, even paranoiac, a frame of mind.

"Sir," he said, "if you evacuate the cities, the Americans will be convinced that we are preparing to attack them."

"What do you suggest I do, Anatoly Borisovich? Should I go to them on my knees?"

Rostov said, "They are confused, Comrade Premier, as we would be if you were dead and I in the hands of Arab guerrillas."

“That’s all very well to say. But what good is it to say it? Morozov tells me that their preparations are extensive. And their press is making ugly accusations against us. I must protect the Fatherland.”

“Use the hot line, sir,” Rostov said earnestly. “Try to make them see that we are guiltless.”

“Use the hot line to speak with whom? Who is this man Beal? I don’t know him. You don’t. No one does. Morozov tells me that he is only a tool in the hands of the war party and the fascists. I cannot recognize his authority while Talcott Bailey is alive. There is no one in Washington we can deal with.”

“Then at least call for an immediate meeting of the United Nations Security Council, Comrade Premier. Appeal to world opinion to stop this dangerous escalation.”

“We are doing that,” the old man said testily. “Keriakin has his instructions, and there will be a Security Council meeting in the morning. All very well, Anatoly Borisovich, but what will that accomplish? What has the organization ever been except a place where old men insult one another?”

The old Premier squinted into the camera eye, and Rostov was struck again by the querulousness of his manner. He was being overborne by younger and more militant men. Rostov remembered the fall of Khrushchev after the ignominious retreat of the Cuban missile affair. The Premier, too, would be remembering this and resolving that he must not take one single step backward from the developing confrontation with the Americans lest he follow in the steps of the late Premier. But the alternative was so appalling to contemplate that Rostov shivered at the image of world-wide destruction it engendered.

“I still believe that you must speak with the Americans, Comrade Premier,” he said. “Offer them all our assistance in recovering Mr. Bailey, and promise them that we will help in every possible way to bring his abductors to justice. I am prepared to do that here. In fact, I have as much as done it.”

"Don't be a fool. You know that Bailey is as good as dead. No amount of force can free him from those lunatics."

"I simply suggest that you should make the offer, Comrade Premier." He paused, steeled himself, and plunged on. "And you should make it clear to them that our military is standing down, that we are making no move of any kind that they can possibly consider hostile. It is that or tragedy, Comrade Premier."

The old man was silent, staring emptily at something outside the camera's field of view. Presently he said slowly, "I cannot do that."

Rostov bit his lips. Of course he could not. Morozov and his warriors would never permit it. Yet it seemed to him that nothing less would slow the American preparations for war. A wave of Slavic fatalism swept over him. The juggernaut was in motion, and it was gaining momentum. It was probably too late already to stop what must be. He said, "I understand, Comrade Premier. Do you wish me to return to Moscow?"

"Stay where you are." The old eyes seemed suddenly to burn into the camera lens as though to transmit a desperately important message that could not be spoken aloud before the others standing nearby in the underground Command and Control Center. "Do what you can, Anatoly Borisovich," the Premier said.

Father Anastasius opened his eyes to a white ceiling, a pale room, and a cold light. He felt weak and uncertain, but at least the wild mental images that had been deviling him were gone, for which thanks be to God.

He lay in a high bed in what he correctly assumed to be a clean and modern hospital room still smelling faintly of new construction. The walls were white-painted concrete brick and the floor was of shiny vinyl tiles. He had seen such a room once, long ago, on a pilgrimage from the monastery to the city of Jerusalem. The bustling Jews had herded the monks through one of their new buildings in the part of the city they took from the Arabs of Jordan.

The nightmarish dreams of Saracens and slaughter were gone, though he recalled them with a quiver of his emaciated frame. Yet there had been some sort of fight, or massacre. The aching pain of his injured arm served as an ample reminder. Now he remembered clearly that he had been on retreat high in the mountains and had come down to seek the waters of Feiran and the companionship of the Bedouin shepherds there and had found horror. His old man's mind firmed on that, and he chided himself for letting his imagination run away with him. There were no Saracens in the Sinai Peninsula now, nor had there been for many centuries. The moldering bones of generations of monks in his care were proof enough of the passage of time.

But someone had killed the shepherds and someone had shot away most of his wizened hand; so if there were no Saracens, there were certainly devils.

He twisted his narrow head on the hard pillow to look at the room in which he lay, and saw that he was not alone. There was a young man, blond, broad of face, wearing a uniform of some sort. Seeing that the monk's eyes were open and clear, the young man smiled and said something in a language that was not familiar but sounded vaguely like the Russian that one of the monks sometimes spoke at St. Katherine's.

Anastasius replied in his native Macedonian Greek, faintly but with a firmness that both pleased and surprised the Russian medic. "I thank you for what you have done for me. The blessing of Christos Pantokrator be upon you."

The young man smiled again and went to the door to admit two men in uniform and a third in nonmilitary dress. One of the soldiers was old and wore many medals. The other was younger and was dressed in a suit of spotted, patterned cloth that made Anastasius uneasy, because he remembered having seen something like it in the fire-streaked twilight of Feiran.

Both soldiers wore the curious Circle and Arrows insigne that he recognized as the symbol of the men who had come to the Sinai, "to keep the peace of the world," they said—as though mere men could usurp God's task.

The civilian spoke gently, and in Greek. "How are you feeling, Holy Father?"

Anastasius said softly, "I am not a priest, my son. I am only a monk of St. Katherine's."

"Very well, Father. But how are you feeling?"

The old man on the bed drew a deep breath and said, "Better, thanks be to God. I am grateful."

The civilian spoke to the soldiers in English. The monk could pick out a word or two. Then the civilian turned back to ask, "Are you strong enough to talk with us now?"

"Yes," Anastasius said. "I want to speak with you. Someone attacked a band of monastery shepherds. It was at Feiran. I walked a long way—"

"It is known, Father. It was General Ulanov, here, who brought you to Zone Center."

"The dead must be given Christian burial," Anastasius said. "The Bedouins of St. Katherine are followers of the Lord Jesus."

"It will be done."

"These are new Russians?"

"This man is. And so is the young man who treated you. The other is an American."

Anastasius frowned with some effort. "The new Russians drove the Church out of their country," he said sternly.

The Greek-speaking man turned and translated the monk's remark with some asperity. Ulanov shrugged and said something in Russian.

"You are Anastasius?"

"That is my name in Christ."

"You spoke while you were delirious."

The monk sighed and closed his eyes for a short time. These

people had performed an act of charity, but they had not respected his privacy. Well, that, perhaps, was to be expected from men who would drive God from their homeland.

"I am a civilian member of the United Nations Observer Team here," the civilian said. "I am a Cypriot."

"A Greek Cypriot," Anastasius said, wishing to show these men that though he was a cloistered monk he was not unaware of what took place in the world outside monastery lands.

"Yes, a Greek Cypriot," the man agreed. "Now please listen to me carefully, Father Anastasius."

The monk nodded, aware that the bed on which he rested was shamefully clean and comfortable, but aware, too, that he was desperately anxious to return to his familiar cell near the ossuary inside his beloved St. Katherine's.

"The men who attacked your shepherds have invaded the monastery and have committed other crimes."

Anastasius felt a surge of alarm, and the young medic spoke sharply to the civilian.

"I am sorry if I am upsetting you, but you must know what has happened so that you can help us."

Saracens in the house of God! No, *not* Saracens—he must remember that. But barbarians, and of a new sort, who killed simple Bedouins for little reason, or for no reason at all. The Antichrist still commanded dark hosts, even in this modern age, Anastasius thought. Christos Pantokrator, Master of the World, strike them down.

"Now, listen to me very carefully," the Cypriot said. "It is vital—absolutely vital—that these soldiers learn of any way not generally known to enter the monastery. Is there such an entry through the ossuary? Some passageway from outside?"

Father Anastasius thought with dread of soldiers passing through the ancient rock-carved galleries under the walls and into the charnel house, disturbing the bones of monks which had lain in the dry darkness for half a thousand years. He had a mental image of men with weapons divesting the mummy of

St. Stephanos himself of his *megaloschemos,* tumbling his venerated corpse into dust.

As caretaker of the ossuary, he had taken an oath to the dead, and it was as sacred as the seal of the confessional. What right did these new men have to penetrate the house of God's devoted dead and disturb their sleep of centuries?

The American spoke to the Cypriot in quiet tones.

"What does he say?" Anastasius asked.

"He promises that he will go in himself, with a single companion, and that your dead will not be disturbed."

The old monk looked at the American soldier with astonished eyes. How could he have known that it was the desecration that troubled him? Was this then some sign from heaven that he should render to the new Caesars that which was Caesar's?

The old Russian spoke, in halting, clumsy Greek. "We found you, and you were near dead. We did not think you could live, monk. But we did our best, and you are alive. Your business is miracles. That you are alive is a small one. We need another. Help us."

Anastasius lay silent.

The Greek Cypriot said desperately, "In the name of God, Father. The men in the monastery hold a prisoner. His death surely means war. In the name of peace, help us."

"God's will be done," murmured Father Anastasius.

Fowler Beal's nerves were beginning to fray badly. For the last hours he had been surrounded by "his" military advisers; decisions had been made in "his" name; and by "his" authority the United States had been placed virtually on a war footing.

Though the man who had come to be known to his constituents as "Old Fowler" before he was in his forties was not a forceful man, and had forgotten, if he had ever known, how to be brave, his intelligence, even overlaid with a patina of congressional malleability, was not negligible. And his intelligence told him, more clearly with each passing hour, that

Admiral Stuart Ainsworth was not—by any definition suitable to a nuclear age—completely sane.

What had come about through a series of ironic happenstances now appeared to have become a license for the Admiral to cleanse the world of Communism. The thought terrified Beal.

His terror was not lessened by his escorted trip into the underground Command Center. The massive blast doors, spring-supported floors, armored glass, and triple-purified air systems conveyed, in terms even he could not ignore, the eventual conclusion of the current of events. If his surroundings had not been enough to frighten him, the network broadcasts, which were continuously piped into the deep shelter, would have done as well. Since the death of the President, the civil government of the United States had been in a state of paralysis. This became increasingly evident as the hours passed and no Vice President appeared to assure the people of the calm transference of power. The lower echelons of government—the bureaucracy—functioned well enough to maintain a certain order; but the failure of any discernible civilian leader taking the reins and conducting the business of the nation had a shocking effect on the mass of American citizens.

Their confused emotions were, not unexpectedly, soon lashed into a storm. The information services circulated each new rumor by extra editions and special television reports. Many stories were vague, some were irresponsible invention, and the Pentagon news officers, while releasing no official word, appeared to leak hints of desperately serious and grimly imminent threats to the nation. The result was the emergence of a need for one simple, well-defined enemy. The Arab guerrillas, whose complicity in the absence of Talcott Bailey was now suspected everywhere, would not do. As a political force in the world they were simply too inconsequential to be worthy of massive American outrage. Viewed from the American perspective, almost every conflict and confrontation for a full generation had originated with Soviet ambitions. It was both logical and satisfying to blame the Russians for the death of the President and the rumored death, or worse, of the Vice President.

Now Beal was treated to on-the-spot coverage by television of riots and demonstrations against Soviet agencies and citizens in almost every major American city. What frightened him most deeply was the unacknowledged but easily recognized psychological bond that existed between the angry people and the Chairman of the Joint Chiefs of Staff. Within a short time, if the situation remained unrelieved, the people would demand war, and it was growing increasingly clear that Stuart Ainsworth intended to give it to them.

In the underground Command Center, Beal had been escorted with some ceremony to the Presidential Communications Room and deposited there, his door guarded by armed military policemen. He had the uncomfortable—and understandable—impression that he was virtually a prisoner of the Joint Chiefs. Perhaps, he considered restlessly, not of the entire Joint Chiefs' establishment. Of Stuart Ainsworth, of course. And Armando Rivera. They were the firebrands who clearly saw this as an opportunity to force the Russians to retreat or to end forever the threat of Communist power. And quite probably Brandis, the Marine, agreed with them. That left the Chief of Naval Operations, who owed his advancement mainly to Ainsworth, and the Army Chief of Staff, old General Shackleford, as the only possible proponents of moderation.

Beal turned off the television screen on which he had been watching CBS's anchor man emeritus deliver an epigrammatic, but not very significant, commentary on the dangers of even a day's delay in bestowing the executive power on *some*one; the man seemed to be suggesting anyone who could handle it, even the mysteriously unavailable Speaker of the House. He pressed an intercom button and said, "I wish to speak with General Shackleford."

An aide's voice replied, "I'll see if he is available, sir."

Beal nerved himself and said sharply, "Tell General Shackleford that the Acting President wants him here—*and immediately*." Before the young voice could reply and possibly confirm his suspicion of his status in the Command Center, he broke the connection.

Smoking nervously, he wondered what his wife was thinking now, buried somewhere below Catoctin Mountain. And what was happening to Terri MacLean? Her scented, oppressively female bedroom lingered in his mind. He felt rather ashamed that at the very moment he was called upon to exercise his constitutional duties he should have been sweating away between her thighs. It was like him to be there at such a time, but it did little for his self-esteem. God pity my country, he thought, to have such a man as me to control the Stuart Ainsworths and Armando Riveras.

Shackleford appeared, his ruddy face composed into a noncommittal mask. What did the old man really think about what was happening? Somehow, Beal would have to know that if he were to affect the events of the next few hours.

Shackleford said, "You asked to see me, sir?"

Beal studied him before framing his reply. Shackleford was near to retirement age. Beal recalled that young Bill Tate had been scheduled to take over his post on the Joint Chiefs. Stuart had never openly opposed the appointment, but he had intended to work against it. Shackleford, however, was a cautious supporter of the young commander of the U.S. Component of the Peacekeeping Force.

Under Beal's scrutiny, the General shifted his weight. He was a portly man, a handsome and well-connected officer who had served his country long and, if with no great distinction, at least with competence.

"General," Beal said at last, "I am not satisfied with the way in which matters appear to be developing. We are giving the Russians no opportunity at all to answer our charges."

"I don't believe we have made any charges, Mr. President," Shackleford said neutrally.

"That is exactly my point. We've made none and yet we are convicting them of conspiracy out of hand." Beal gestured at their surroundings. "We are provoking them with all this. The alert. The business of their submarines. Frankly, General, I'm getting really frightened. They aren't going to sit still for all this, and we both know it. Stuart knows it better than either of us."

Shackleford said, "Sir, if they allowed themselves to become involved with the Abou Moussa Arabs, they were surely aware of the risks—"

"That's precisely my point, General. *If* they did. We have no real evidence that they did."

"We have their Cosmos photographs, Mr. President."

"That isn't conclusive and you know it, General."

"If you have such strong doubts, sir, why don't you present them to Admiral Ainsworth?"

"You know the answer to that as well as I," Beal said. "I don't think we can pretend any longer that I am in control of the situation here. The Russians are quite rightly demanding a session of the UN Security Council, and we are not co-operating. I have the feeling that Admiral Ainsworth has no intention of trying to handle matters in an orderly, peaceful way."

"The Secretary-General has announced that there will be a meeting as soon as the members can be notified and assembled, sir. But I, personally, have no faith in the United Nations any longer—"

"And neither has Ainsworth," Beal said. "All right, that's as may be, General. But these are civilian matters, which should be handled and decided by civilian members of the government—not by anyone here in the Pentagon, surely."

Shackleford remained tactfully silent, and Beal noticed a slight discomfort on the man's face. He was, after all, an American soldier, and anything that smacked of military usurpation of civilian power could not help but make him uneasy. Beal, calling on his years of experience in political dealings and accommodation, felt a glimmer of hope. "All I want, General, is a little time to resolve the situation. A few days could easily make the difference between, well, peace and war. I am certain that if Stuart would take the time to consider he would agree with me." He paused to order his thoughts into the most telling arguments for use on this professional soldier. "You are near to retirement, General, after a long and honorable career. Couldn't you see your way clear to recommend a few days'—a few *hours'*—time for us to stop and consider what we are doing here? It seems to me that Stuart is determined to push this thing to the bitter end—and what will any of us have then? Can we be sure there will *be* any then? Any afterward?"

"I have never made it a policy to act rashly, Mr. President," Shackleford said.

Though it was the last thing he felt like doing, Beal managed a rueful smile. "You see, General? We don't even know that I *am* the president, do we?"

"You are assuredly the *acting* president, sir."

"According to the law, perhaps. But can you deny that Stuart and Armando are the ones making the decisions?"

"They are *your* representatives, sir." The General, Beal noted with dismay, was not about to accept responsibility for either peace or war. The attitude was so terribly familiar to him that it made him want to grimace with psychic pain. It was his own attitude, nurtured over many years in his congressional sinecure.

"General," he said, "I want you to come with me to Stuart and help put a stop to all this—or at least a *brake*," he said pleadingly as he saw Shackleford bridle. "A little time to make sense of all this. The nation hasn't had time to recover from one tragedy, let alone another one so monstrous it could mean the end of the United States."

"Sir," Shackleford said with a touch of unsuspected temperance, "no soldier wants war. Least of all this kind of war."

"Well, then?"

The General frowned and looked uncomfortable.

"Stuart doesn't want it either," Beal said, giving the lie the full benefit of his politician's sincerity. "He's angry and, God damn it, so am I. What American wouldn't be? But are we going to risk blowing up the world because we're angry with the Reds? At least we should let them talk." He added shrewdly, "That is really all Tate wanted to do, and Stuart relieved him and ordered his arrest. That, when you think about it, General, is not the act of a completely rational man. Why, General Tate was more or less scheduled to be promoted over a hundred or so names in the Army List so that he could take your place when you retired. The President himself told me that, General."

"Perhaps you are right, sir," Shackleford said. "Perhaps we are plunging ahead a bit too fast."

"I am relieved to find you see it my way, General," Beal said, rising quickly, before Shackleford could retreat. "Now please come with me to Admiral Ainsworth."

But the Admiral was, an aide on the floor of the Pit said, engaged in talking to Echo Sierra Control, and would the Acting President care to wait in the Admiral's own communications area?

Shackleford, looking less certain of his attitude with each passing minute, led the way to Ainsworth's position on the deck overlooking the Pit. Fretting at the delay, Beal watched the computer displays across the room. He could see the red lights coming on across the map of the Soviet Union as the Samos and Midas satellites recorded activity at each of the Soviet ICBM sites. He found that he almost could not swallow.

On the floor of the Pit, Ainsworth and Brandis appeared out of a communications room. The aide to whom Beal had spoken pointed to him and Shackleford on the upper gallery of the War Room. Ainsworth nodded and strode across the floor of the Pit between the consoles, speaking to Brandis as he moved. Presently Brandis turned away toward his own complex of communications equipment.

Beal said to Shackleford, "I am relying on your support, General. It is absolutely vital."

Shackleford gave no indication of having heard. His attention was fixed on the increasing number of warning lights on the computer display of the Asian land mass.

Ainsworth appeared, and Beal was immediately taken aback at his appearance. The rock-hewn face was red with anger.

"Mr. President," he said, "I am sorry to have to tell you that Dale Trask has been murdered. Yes, I said murdered, sir. And by General Tate's military secretary. He was shot down in cold blood by one of Tate's officers. The unsavory and dangerous possibilities this suggests are almost beyond imagining. Apparently the woman—she may even have been a Soviet agent—decided that she must prevent the implementation of the orders I gave Trask to arrest Tate and storm the monastery." His eyes were cold and furious. "Accordingly, sir, I have told General Brandis to contact the Sixth Fleet, put a full battalion of its Marines on helicopters, and attack the Monastery of St. Katherine without further delay. They are to recover Talcott Bailey, dead or alive, and they are to take General Tate the same way."

Beal saw his carefully nurtured plan crumble. He would get no support from Shackleford now.

Ainsworth said to Shackleford, "Tate ordered the balance of his personal Special Forces detachment down to St. Katherine's and then made off to Zone Center to *confer with the Russians.*" His tone made it clear that this, at last, was solid evidence of treachery in the highest echelons of the U.S. Component. "There is a possibility his troops might try to resist the Marines when they arrest him. That would be grotesque. Even he must see that. I want you to contact him at Zone Center and tell him that the Marines are coming and that he would do well to place himself in arrest, as I ordered, *before* they arrive. It may mitigate the punishment at his court-martial."

The Admiral turned back to Beal. "And now, Mr. President, as you can see by the display over there, the Soviets are bringing their entire ICBM force on the line. The situation has grown very tense in the last thirty minutes, and I believe you will be safer in the quarters assigned to you."

Before Beal could protest, he felt the presence at both elbows of military policemen. Even the pretense that he was in command here was now gone.

22

Paul Bronstein had never in his life imagined that he would find himself on the wrong end of a gun. The experience had been unnerving. He found that to be the victim of acts of terror was a knee-shaking, bladder-emptying experience.

At the whim of the terrorists, he had been confined alone in a small room not far from the cell containing Deborah Zadok. For a time he had considered the possibility of attempting to reason with Lesh and his guerrillas, but his own reason convinced him that reason had no place here. Terrorists were terrorists because they enjoyed committing acts of terror, and not, as they claimed, because they were desperate men seeking redress of grievances. Whatever the wrongs they claimed to want righted, men who committed violent political crimes—whether they were IRA gunmen, Weathermen, Vietcong, or Arab Front thugs—acted as they did because they thrived on violence.

In another time and place, Bronstein might not have made such an admission, even to himself. But he was close to death, and this, he realized, was no time for self-delusion. Truth had rammed an ugly spear into the body of his carefully constructed life style. The walls around him, the Arab gunmen, the terrifying night, and grim prospects for the future could not be denied.

He heard the sound of boots in the corridor outside, and his heart began to pump frantically. When the sounds stopped before his door, he forced himself to stand, wanting above all not to present a picture of resistance or arrogance, yet at the same time not wishing to show the dread that sluiced like ice water through his veins.

The man who called himself Colonel Lesh came in and stared at Bronstein. The thick face and yellow teeth struck terror into him. Lesh said, "Your name is Bronstein?"

"Yes." Bronstein was relieved that his voice didn't tremble. He even began to hope that his long hair and beard, his "Movement image" as he called it in his undergraduate days, might establish some sort of rapport with the Albanian.

"Am I supposed to know you?" Lesh asked. "Are you important?"

Bronstein felt himself wilting under the ironic stare. "I am the Vice President's appointments secretary, Colonel."

"Then," said Lesh with heavy humor, "you are not important at all. I have already had my appointment with your employer." He shouted something down the corridor, and a pair of Arabs came running.

"Bronstein. Bron-stein." Lesh mouthed the name with mock thoughtfulness. "You are a Jew?"

"I—I have always been sympathetic to the Arab cause, Colonel."

"I didn't ask you about your politics, Bronstein. I asked if you were a Jew."

Bronstein tried to stare Lesh down. He could not do it, and the effort left him shaking, but he was timidly proud that he had tried. "Yes," he said. "I am a Jew."

"So that is settled. Zionist?"

"No."

"How is that possible? All Jews are pro-Israeli Zionists."

"I am an American Jew, not a Zionist. Many American Jews feel sympathy for the Arabs who have suffered here in the Middle East, Colonel."

"Sympathy."

"Yes." He tried to harden his tone. "We condemn the violence and terrorism, but we sympathize—"

"Condemn, Bronstein?"

Bronstein could do no more than nod his head. He was talking like a fool, hardly realizing what it was he was saying. This brute savage couldn't be reached.

"Bronstein. *Brronnschtein—*" Lesh rolled the name about until it became a disgusting sound. "We hate Jews in Albania. Did you know that, Bronstein?"

Bronstein swallowed hard and said nothing. He felt a fearful bursting hatred of himself, an unmanning, revolting, loathsome hatred that made his knees watery.

"But you are not important, after all," Lesh said. "You are an appointment—" He raised his eyebrows.

"Appointments secretary."

"You are a disgusting Jew."

Bronstein now felt sick.

"And you have sympathy, I think you said, for the Arab people."

"Yes."

"Excellent. You can be useful then."

"The Vice President values my advice, Colonel Lesh," Bronstein said with an effort. "I could be useful in any negotiations."

"I intend that you shall be," Lesh said abruptly. He shouted to the Arab guards and prodded Bronstein into movement with the muzzle of his automatic weapon.

Feeling a new wave of apprehension, Bronstein was led through a stone corridor in the walls, around a corner, and up a narrow flight of stairs. At the top he could see the sky, white and clear with the full force of the desert morning.

They emerged onto the broad parapet atop the wall. Bronstein was dazzled by the brilliance of the sun and conscious of the massive loom of the mountains behind the monastery. As his eyes became adjusted to the light, he could see, in the flat valley stretching to the east, a pair of blue-painted U.S. air force helicopters bearing the Circle and Arrows insigne of the Peacekeeping Force and, beyond them, a trio of large troop-carrying machines. American soldiers wearing the blue component beret were deployed in a wide semicircle across the valley. Overhead, a single Dragonfly observation helicopter patrolled across the sheer, riven rock face of Mount Sinai.

At some distance from the wall, amid a stand of tall cypress trees, the monks of the monastery stood over a number of black bundles on the stony earth. Bronstein realized that they were praying over their murdered dead. Some American medics had begun to treat the wounded.

Lesh said, "Your countrymen have surrounded the monastery. But so far they have wisely chosen not to assault us."

Bronstein was militarily uneducated, but even he understood that the troops could take the monastery at any time. It was equally clear that if they did so they would find the hostages dead.

"You see what the situation is, then, Bronstein?"

"Yes, Colonel. I can talk to the American officers and—"

Lesh cut off his hopeful suggestion with a shake of the head. "Your officers have been informed of everything they need to know. It is that they may need a reminder from time to time, and in this you will be of great service to us."

"Anything I can do, Colonel. Anything at all—"

"Excellent, Bronstein." He prodded his captive along the wall to a spot from which two more guerrillas could be seen. A rope, secured to the inner parapet of the wall, stretched across the stones and down the outside surface. Bronstein could not see the end of the rope, but something heavy obviously hung there, for at a word from Lesh the Arabs began to haul whatever it was to the top of the wall. Bronstein noticed that the soldiers facing them in the valley stood to watch silently.

Lesh grinned at Bronstein. "As a good negotiator, Bronstein, you will of course agree that from time to time it is necessary to administer a strong and impressive lesson."

"Of course, Colonel," Bronstein said faintly.

"Then come along."

Prodded by a guerrilla's gun muzzle, he followed Lesh. The Arabs ahead hauled at the rope, and presently Bronstein was horrified to see the broken-necked body of Secret Service Agent John Emerson bump over the edge of the wall. Lesh stooped, loosened the noose from around the neck of the corpse, and draped it over Bronstein's head. The touch of the rope was nauseating, and bile trickled from Bronstein's lips. He would have fallen, but the two Arabs with Lesh supported him.

The man who had guarded him pulled off his wristwatch. Lesh smiled regretfully and shrugged. "A gift from one Arab sympathizer to another, Comrade Bronstein," he said. "You don't mind."

Bronstein began to breathe in dry, racking gasps. The bright morning turned gray all around him, the russet color of the mountains and the cornflower blue of the sky losing tone and depth until everything appeared etched in lead.

"Now you will be of service to us, Bronstein," Lesh said.

He rolled the corpse of the Secret Service man to the edge of the wall and over. One of the soldiers, a small and doll-like figure in the distance, made an angry sound, but Bronstein could scarcely hear it for the rushing sound of his pulse in his head.

Lesh said, "You will stay here with Hassan and Rifai, Bronstein. If the troops come too near, you will be assisted off this wall to discourage them. In this way you can serve the cause of peaceful coexistence." He turned away.

It took Paul Bronstein some time to realize that he was not going to be thrown off the wall immediately, but must wait—noose around his neck—and rely on the discretion of the soldiers in the valley.

In the Command and Control Center of the Soviet Strategic Rocket Force, at some distance from Moscow, General Igor

Mikhailovich Krasnov spoke to the televised image of his immediate commander, the Minister of Defense.

"All warheads are now armed, Comrade Marshal. May we proceed with fueling of the rocket force?"

"I have not received permission for that," Morozov said. "But I expect to very shortly. Stand by."

"Yes, Comrade Marshal." Krasnov suppressed a feeling of anxiety. The American ICBM force, most of which was targeted on his own weapons silos, was composed of Minuteman missiles, which were solid-fueled "touch-and-go" systems. The Americans did not need to spend three-quarters of an hour filling their missiles with volatile hydrogen and liquid oxygen. This forty-five minutes could be critical in the event of a first strike.

He glanced around his command center. The crowded room was amazingly silent considering that it was filled with technicians and machines. The faces of his people were uniformly pale and guarded. He wondered how many of them were afraid, certain of their own destruction despite the tons of steel and concrete over their heads. He decided that he did not wish to know of their fears. Nor did he wish to think of his wife and daughter, innocently vacationing on the Black Sea coast. Or of his son, a captain in the Air Force on the Chinese Amur River border. And he most particularly did not wish to think that all his memories—of spring in Leningrad, of winter ballets in Moscow, of the dusty sweetness of Ukrainian summers—all might well vanish in fire storm before another sunrise.

At Suez, on the shimmering, sunlit waters of the canal, General Anwar Suweif reported to General Ibrahim Hassani, the excitable commander of the UAR Component of the Peacekeeping Force.

Suweif had been hustled from Zone Center by his Russian escort with specific orders from Anatoly Rostov to impress upon the Egyptian commander the need to round up, without mercy or delay, all known Arab guerrillas operating within the Egyptian Sector of the Sinai. But on arrival at the bank of the canal, the dusty and sleepless Suweif was appalled to see the confusion and anxiety that had transformed Suez from a routine-numbed military base into an overturned anthill of men and machines.

General Hassani received Suweif's instructions in a state of sweaty panic. "I can't imagine how Rostov and Ulanov can tell us to spend our time rounding up guerrillas, General. The Israelis are mobilizing all along their border. This terrible business of the American Vice President has totally destroyed the effectiveness of the Cyprus Accord. The Jews are organizing one of their notorious pre-emptive attacks."

"You *know* this, Hassani?"

"Thank God for our intelligence service, General. At least we are warned."

"But the Jews would have to cross the American and Soviet sectors as well as the Demilitarized Zone to strike us, General," Suweif protested. "I have just come from Zone Center. There is no indication there of any of this. The Americans are extremely angry and suspicious, but there is no talk of any Israeli movements. If we do our part, by rounding up the guerrillas—those known to be in our sector—at least we will have contributed something useful, something to help keep the peace."

"Peace? There is no peace, Suweif," Hassani exclaimed. "None at all. An Israeli gunboat was seen not two kilometers from Port Said! We shall be at war by morning—and dead by nightfall."

Suweif thought bitterly about the Abou Moussa. For many years, the Abou, the Black Septemberists, all the terrorists of the Arab Front had been the heroes of the Arab world. We are all responsible for this, he thought. How true were the words of the Holy Koran: "If God should punish men according to what they deserve, he would not leave on the back of the earth so much as a beast."

He turned away from the panicky component commander and stepped outside the command post. Beyond the dust clouds raised by frightened soldiers, beyond the iron glimmering of the waters of the old canal, he could see the sandy dunes of the Sinai shore, and against the sky the black shapes of kites soaring. He breathed in the smell of his native earth and the taste of the dusty sun. A vast and fatalistic sadness overtook him, and he walked slowly back to his waiting vehicle filled with a sense of his own futility.

In the photo-evaluation section of the Samos/Midas Satellite Systems Control Center, a major of the United States Air Force studied the latest pictures of the Greater Moscow area. He spoke to his assistant, a WAF lieutenant, in an awed voice. "Come look at this, Lieutenant."

The girl joined him at the photo table where the high-resolution images lay illuminated. She seemed to be looking down from a great height on the Russian city. She could see clearly the ring roads around the city center, the barges on the serpentine of the Moscow River, the web of boulevards radiating outward. The parks and open spaces of the city gleamed white with fresh snow and winter sunlight. But the avenues leading outward to the suburbs like the spokes of a wheel were black.

When the Major changed viewing lenses and increased the magnification, the Lieutenant drew in her breath sharply. The roads were black with *people*. People walking, people riding in vehicles of every sort and description. Thousands, tens of thousands, were jamming the avenues out of the Soviet capital.

"They are evacuating the city," she said in a thin voice.

"They are, indeed," said the Major, gathering the films and stuffing them into his briefcase. "This is something for the Joint Chiefs—and I mean *now*."

23

At the controls of the helicopter, Bill Tate flew down the spine of the massif from Zone Center toward St. Katherine's. Beside him sat Sergeant Robinson, a grim black giant with a bandaged face and cold murder in his eyes. And behind, in the troop seats, sat Yuri Ulanov and two Russian soldiers.

He had not wanted to bring the old General along, had argued with him against it, in fact. Novotny, blustering fool that he was, had done all that he could—even verging on outright threats and insubordination—to prevent Ulanov from accompanying Tate back to the monastery. But in the end it had been Anatoly Rostov who supported the old man and who made it impossible for Tate to refuse to take him. "I may be old and next to useless, William," Ulanov had said, "but my place is there. It is important that a Russian take part in this."

It could not be denied, though Tate was not sanguine about the hoped-for effectiveness of a show of Russian-American cooperation.

He was working now against a time limit. He had been almost ready to return to St. Katherine's when General Eriksson had informed him that General Shackleford was on the radio link from Washington. Without ground-to-satellite communications at Zone Center, it had been impossible to watch the Army Chief of Staff's face as he delivered Admiral Ainsworth's message and ultimatum. Tate had the impression that

Shackleford was uneasy about how far and how fast matters had gone. He suggested—though he did not actually say so—that the Speaker of the House was virtually a prisoner in the underground Command Center in Washington, and that Ainsworth had given orders for a battalion of the Sixth Fleet Marine force to fly to St. Katherine's and attack the monastery. The Admiral, it seemed, wanted the matter of the presidential succession resolved quickly and finally. The Chairman of the Joint Chiefs would never frankly defy a president, Tate thought bitterly, but he would willingly order an attack that was certain to kill one.

As for Tate himself, Shackleford told him he was to consider himself under arrest. And then, hedging, as he often did, he had said, "The Marines will arrive at St. Katherine's by early afternoon, General. When they do, you are to report to the officer in command, who has instructions to take you into custody. What you do between now and then is your affair, of course."

Of course, Tate thought grimly, by afternoon—and certainly by nightfall—the United States and the Soviet Union could be at war and reckoning their casualties in megadeaths. All the years of work by presidents and premiers, secretaries and ministers, ambassadors and commissioners, and hundreds of thousands of anonymous civil servants could have evaporated like dew in hot sunlight, and four hundred million people might find themselves back at the beginning, with the Cold War reborn—and all because an American politician thought military nakedness was moral. I could kill the son of a bitch myself, Tate thought with cold fury. Talcott Quincy Bailey might well go down in history as the last of the hundreds of men of peace who brought war to the world. Only, there would be no one to write such a history, and no posterity to read it—not in Russia or in America, at least.

He swung the helicopter low over the serrated ridges of rust-colored rock, sand, and thorn. In a way it was fitting that a kind of Armageddon should take place here on this barren, holy earth. From this place came the Decalogue—and it was men's failure to heed the admonitions carved on those stone tablets that had brought matters to this, possibly last, crisis.

A dozen kilometers south of their position, the mountains rose steeply to form the saddle-backed projection known as Mount Sinai. Tate, putting the helicopter's nose on that rising horizon and holding it there, considered the nature of his adversary, the Albanian soldier Enver Lesh. It was odd, he thought, that they had never met. They had fought in many of the same wars, in much the same way. Vietnam, of course, and in Thailand. And how many times had their paths crossed as each traveled about the world on the military business of his country? They would meet now face to face if Tate could contrive it. But if Lesh managed first to kill Talcott Bailey, to what end would the two soldiers meet? It would all become a meaningless joust amid the falling ruins—the bitterest kind of battle.

Ulanov leaned forward and spoke into Tate's ear. "How much longer?" he asked.

"Ten minutes."

Now in the near distance he could see a Dragonfly buzzing nervously about at the base of the steep, bare mountain. Below it, in the shallow valley, he could see the cypress trees and green patches of cultivated ground north of the monastery.

He flew once down the valley and back to locate the positions his troops from Es Shu'uts had taken. The detachment had broken up into seven teams and had isolated the monastery. But these were mere copybook tactics to prevent any reinforcement of the guerrillas. There could be no more than a dozen armed men inside the monastery. Their strength was not in numbers.

As he flew across the monastery proper, he saw that Emerson's body had been removed from the wall and that someone else stood as he had, between guards. He had a griping fear that the expendable hostage might be Deborah, and he banked steeply and flew once again across the valley at the height of the top of the wall. But it was not Deborah standing with a noose about her neck. It was a bearded man—Bailey's secretary, Bronstein.

He hovered at some distance from the stone buildings and then put the blue helicopter down in a flurry of dust. His junior officers came running, hunched against the blast, to greet him.

Their eyes widened on seeing the Russians in the back, but they retained enough composure to salute and make no comment. Instead, they crowded around their commander.

Tate asked for the plans of the monastery and the Israeli interpreter. This turned out to be a balding young part-time soldier who taught archeology at the Weizmann Institute. He saluted with the Israeli's deliberate military awkwardness and introduced himself as Captain Elman. "I speak Greek, Russian, Amharic, English, and, of course, Hebrew."

"Have you worked here in Sinai?"

"Specifically here at the monastery? No, General, I have not." The dark eyes were animated. "I would be grateful for the opportunity, though. I can't think of a better place for a dig. This place dates from the reign of—"

"Yes, Captain—Justinian. That's fascinating, but what I want you to do is this: take a set of these plans to one of the monks and ask him to indicate for you all above-ground entrances to the monastery's charnel house. Then ask him if he would be good enough to supply me with two monks' habits. One large enough for this soldier." He indicated Robinson. "That may not be easy to come by, but do the best you can."

"Yes, General," Elman said. He hurried away across the valley to where the monks had gathered their dead.

To his assembled officers Tate spoke quietly, first introducing General Ulanov. "The General is here as an official observer for the Soviet Component and to offer us whatever assistance he can." He swept the hostile young faces under the blue berets. "I believe, gentlemen, that is what we are supposed to be doing here along thirty-four east, is it not? Co-operating with the other occupying powers?"

The officers had the grace to look slightly sheepish. Ulanov, in the manner of Soviet soldiers, saluted them gravely.

Tate looked at the wall. "They have Bronstein up there. Have they offered any messages?"

"None, sir."

"Let's hope for his sake they don't feel the need to impress us again with their firm intentions," Tate said. "Now listen to me carefully. There are two things you should know. The first is that a battalion of Sixth Fleet Marines will be here, probably before 1400 hours, to storm the monastery and to arrest me—"

The Special Forces men looked stunned, then angry.

Tate continued as calmly as before, though he could feel his heart beating with the suppressed excitement of coming battle. "The Marines have been ordered here by the Chairman of the Joint Chiefs. He took this action when I refused a direct order to attack the guerrillas and retrieve Mr. Bailey and Colonel Seidel."

"We can do it, sir," a platoon commander said. "We can take the place in fifteen minutes."

"And they will kill the President of the United States in five," Tate said. "No, we can't do that, gentlemen. So Sergeant Robinson and I are going into the monastery alone—if we can find the way and use it before the Marines arrive."

"No jarhead is going to arrest *you,* General," the same platoon officer said grimly. "Not while my team is around."

Tate said, "I don't want Marines and Special Forces fighting each other, Lieutenant. The world is going a bit crazy, but not that crazy. By the time the Marine troop helicopters arrive, Robinson and I should be inside that place finding the President. But you hear this: even if there is shooting inside, you are not to rush the Arabs. Every minute we can buy for Mr. Bailey is more important than I can tell you. You have probably heard that Admiral Ainsworth and the Speaker of the House are almost convinced that the Soviets are responsible for what has happened. If Mr. Bailey dies—or if the people at home convince themselves that he is dead—" he glanced at Ulanov, flanked by his Red Army escorts (or were they guards?)—"I don't think we need to speculate on what might happen. We are trying to take a very rough tiger by the tail, gentlemen. I know you are all fine soldiers. I want you to be smart ones now. Lieutenant Carson?"

The fiery platoon commander came to attention. "Sir."

"Site your men along the slope of that talus behind the monastery wall. Have them get up high enough so that they can cover the top of the walls and the roofs of the buildings inside."

"Yes, sir."

"Lieutenant Gough?"

"Sir."

"Take a team through the Bedouin houses and see if you can find some robes to cover your uniforms. When you've done that, work around the north side of the walls and see if you can get some sort of field of fire that will let you cover anyone coming out of the north gate. If any of this works, Sergeant Robinson and I will try to bring the hostages out that way."

"Yes, sir."

"Move out, both of you," Tate said. He turned to the senior troop commander, a captain wearing the wreath-and-rifle insigne of a combat infantryman. "I want you to station your two best marksmen here at the choppers, Captain O'Neill. If there *is* any shooting inside, I want those people on the wall greased before they can pitch Bronstein over."

Ulanov spoke up. "What you need for that, William, is a long-range, extremely accurate weapon."

"What I need is a death ray, Yuri," Tate said. "I don't happen to have one."

"Let Soviet technology serve," Ulanov said calmly. He spoke to the KGB men in swift Russian, and they hurried back to the helicopter, from which they emerged with three largish metal cases, which Ulanov unlocked and opened. Inside the first was an extremely long-barreled rifle with a bipod. The second contained a large telescopic sight. Ulanov unlocked the third box and extracted a magazine of cartridges fully six inches from base to point. These he handed to one of his soldiers.

"The latest Soviet infantry weapon, William," Ulanov said. "A sniper's rifle accurate at more than fifteen hundred meters. The bullets are explosive. It is not inconceivable that if we all survive this day, I shall be shot for showing it to you—or even admitting that it exists—" He smiled bleakly. "It is a beautiful toy, is it not? We could have used it at Stalingrad."

Tate felt a genuine smile creasing his face. "Or Borodino, Yuri Dmitrievich?"

"Borodino, too, my friend."

Tate put his hands on the old man's shoulders. "My thanks, Yuri. And—you know I shall have to tell our weapons people about it."

"Of course, William. Perhaps it will create more respect among them for Soviet science. And if we fail here today, what use will it be?"

Tate watched the Russians site the weapon.

"They are marksmen. You will see," Ulanov said.

After looking again at the wall, Tate turned to Captain O'Neill. "You can deploy your men at the south wall, then. Keep them under cover unless you hear firing at the north gate—then come like hell."

"Yes, sir."

"One thing more—" Tate took O'Neill aside and said, "It may not be possible to hold the Marines back once they arrive. They have direct orders from the Joint Chiefs, and they may not be willing to hold back just because the Arabs will kill Mr. Bailey if they don't. If the worst happens and they do assault the monastery, I want you to follow Robinson and me inside. I am going to try to locate a line of old galleries cut through the rock from the ossuary to the ruins of the old burial garden near the southwest corner of the walls. If I find it, I'll mark it on a plan of the place and get it to you. Then if the jarheads absolutely insist—come running. We will need help very badly if that happens."

"Yes, *sir.*"

Tate watched the Captain trot off to rejoin his men, and then spoke to Robinson. "What do you think, Crispus?"

"If we can get in, we can get Bailey, General."

"We'll need to be quiet inside."

Robinson produced his throwing knife and held it gently in his open palm. "This is as quiet as a thing can be, General."

He glanced across the open ground toward the mourning monks. Captain Elman was loping toward the parked helicopters, a black bundle and a rolled plan in his hands.

The figures on the television screen in Admiral Ainsworth's Command Center were all familiar. He watched the assembled group with anger. The program was being carried on all the networks, and it had been scheduled without the approval of the Joint Chiefs.

Secretary of State Ramsey Green, a man so elusive and inconspicuous that not a third of the American people were sure of his name, had apparently been chosen as spokesman. Behind him in the studio were ranked five members of the President's Cabinet: the secretaries of Interior, HEW, Agriculture, Transportation, and Labor. Seated with him at a table were the Senate Majority Leader and Minority Leader and the elderly Chairman of the Foreign Relations Committee. It was obviously, Ainsworth thought, a quickly recruited cabal of civilian leaders determined to fill the vacuum of power created by the absence of both President and Vice President. It was difficult to know exactly what information these people had. Whatever it was, it must have come through the CIA and State Department agencies, and would therefore be essentially nonmilitary in nature. It was typical of the indiscipline of the men the dead President had gathered around him that they should have chosen to disregard the right of succession of Fowler Beal the moment it became known that he had been escorted to the Pentagon.

There was no one in the gathering, Ainsworth was pleased to see, from the Department of Defense. Of course, the Secretary, who might have joined the cabal, had died with the President in Palm Springs. The Assistant Secretary, appointed to pay off old political debts, was in his quarters in the VIP shelter at Catoctin by now, and receiving such information as the Chairman of the Joint Chiefs thought necessary and proper.

The Admiral rubbed at his eyes. He glanced at the line-up of wall chronometers. It was now 0245 in Washington. The day and half of the night had gone. It was difficult to realize in this timeless place that less than a full twenty-four hours had passed since the crash of Air Force One. At one-thirty or two, the extraordinary session of the Security Council had been scheduled to convene in New York. It would be, as always, too little and too late.

In Sinai it was 0945, full daylight for the Marine operations he had ordered. He had received notification from the USS *Sikorsky,* the Sixth Fleet's new nuclear helicopter carrier, that the Marines were airborne and approaching the north coast of Sinai escorted by a squadron of Shrikes. No matter what the Secretary of State took upon himself to tell the people, the assault on St. Katherine's would be concluded by early morning in Washington—at which time Fowler Beal could emerge and inform the nation that the United States had a new, and undoubted, president.

Ainsworth centered his attention on the screen. The ABC anchor man had made the announcement that the Secretary of State would address the nation. He listened with growing anger and irritation.

"My fellow Americans," the Secretary, white-haired and distinguished in appearance, began. "Gathered here in the studio with me are some of the men the late President most relied upon to help him guide the course of this nation—"

Missing, of course, thought Ainsworth, from the conspiracy of liberals was Talcott Quincy Bailey—whose death the Marines would confirm within hours. And Fowler Litton Beal, who would be with them had not he, Ainsworth, had the foresight to sequester him in a place where his wispy character could be supported by the will of strong and dedicated men.

"We who knew him and worked with him share the nation's sorrow and grief." The Secretary's thin voice quavered and broke momentarily. "But you, the citizens, have the right to know how it has come about that Vice President Bailey has not appeared before you to take the oath of office and assume the responsibilities of leadership." He shuffled the papers before him, and as he lifted them Ainsworth could see that his hands trembled badly. The man was clearly afraid, and perhaps even startled by his own temerity in convening his cabal to challenge the nation's military leadership at this moment of crisis. Ainsworth's lips thinned to a straight, hard line. Only a year ago he had put before the National Security Council an enabling regulation that would have allowed the nation's television networks to be pre-empted by the Joint Chiefs in a national emergency, and his suggestion had been greeted with cries of horror by some of the men now sitting in the Washington studio with Ramsey Green. If his suggestion had been adopted it would now be possible to cut this display of temerity and weakness off the air.

"As you know," the Secretary went on, "the Vice President was sent to the Sinai Peninsula by the President to meet with Soviet Deputy Premier Anatoly Rostov to sign the renewal of the Cyprus Accord. I now must tell you that some of the many rumors that have been circulated during the last hours are true."

By God, Ainsworth thought, the man was a fool. He was going to admit that Bailey was being held by guerrillas. Was he so out of touch with the temper of ordinary Americans that he didn't understand the fury such an announcement would arouse?

"There has been an incident in the Demilitarized Zone," the Secretary said.

An *incident?* Was that the line this gaggle of appeasers was going to take to minimize the clear and present danger to the nation?

"The Vice President's party encountered a band of Arab nationalists who—unwisely, but acting *entirely on their own*—I must emphasize that point, *entirely on their own initiative*—have detained the Vice President and are now presenting certain conditions for his release."

Ainsworth sat bolt upright, his face flushing. Somehow Green and these civilians had learned something he himself did not yet know.

"We have received a message from Mr. John Peters Reisman, who was with the Vice President's party, and who has been released by the nationalists, informing us that the Vice President is alive and well, and that he is carrying to us, and to the American people, the terms of the nationalists."

How typical, Ainsworth thought, to use words such as "nationalists" and "terms" rather than speak the simple, hard truth. It sounded like Bailey himself speaking. And that whimpering assurance that the Arabs had acted on their own initiative—who with any intelligence could believe that, when the very bullets in their guns and the clothing on their backs came from Communist factories?

"Ordinarily," the Secretary continued in an almost pedantic tone, "in the situation in which we now find ourselves, the Speaker of the House would assume the duties of acting president until such time as Mr. Bailey is able to act. In this case, however, we—" he indicated his associates with a gesture—"in consultation with members of the National Security Council, have concluded that it is not necessary to formalize an acting presidency. I say this because I am personally certain that through the good offices of our many friends throughout the world—who are, of course, outraged by this illegal detention of the Vice President—and through the efforts of the United Nations and the Cyprus Commission—a body devoted to maintaining the peace in the Middle East—the situation will soon be regularized."

Ainsworth had an impulse to voice a sharp, angry laugh. It was really incredible how swiftly civilians could lose contact with reality. He wondered if Green and his friends actually knew the "terms" the Arabs were likely to set on any release of an American president? They would demand the earth, and possibly the moon with it. It was in the nature of revolutionaries to overplay their hands, and he hadn't a doubt that they would have done so now. So Reisman had been turned loose to carry the ransom note? That meant that Bill Tate *knew* the terms and had withheld the information. It was an act close to treason. He would answer for it, as well as for his insubordination.

"And so, my fellow Americans, we ask that you remain calm and rely on your government to bring the nation through this time of tragedy and crisis."

Damn them all, the Admiral thought triumphantly. It was too late for all that. They listened, but did not hear. They looked, but did not see. All around them a shocked and curious nation boiled, and they offered *this* sort of weaseling pap. Thank *God* Americans were tougher than that.

An intercom light flashed, and the Admiral said, "Yes?"

"The Soviets are starting to fuel their missiles, sir."

Another light, another voice. "General Clayborne, sir, at NATO."

"Put him on Screen Two."

The General appeared, looking harassed and startled. "Admiral, we are getting some very alarming indications here. The Soviets are putting juice into their birds, and we've had at least a half-dozen submarine contacts—subs moving through the Skagerrak. It looks as though they are putting every Yankee-class they have to sea."

"I know," Ainsworth said. "Our antisubmarine units are tracking them."

"Frankly, I'm at a loss. General Muller hasn't even had time to return, and here we are moving to a virtual war footing."

"That is exactly what you should be doing. I would recommend you British get your nuclear subs to sea and the V-bomber force airborne."

"Good God, is it as bad as that?"

"It is," Ainsworth said grimly.

"I don't understand it, Stuart. The governments of the NATO countries are alarmed. They keep coming to us for advice and information, and no one seems to know what's happening in Washington and Moscow."

"The Reds are evacuating Moscow," Ainsworth said. "I think that gives you some indication of their intentions. They think we are helpless without the President or Bailey. I assure you, Alex, we are not."

"I heard the Secretary of State's broadcast. I don't know what it means—do you?"

"I doubt that he does, Alex. He is apparently trying to convince our people that the Soviets had nothing to do with Bailey's ambush. Not many will buy that. Certainly no one here."

"This is fantastic, Stuart. The NATO governments are buzzing and yet the people in the streets know nothing—they have no idea of what is happening."

"It is just as well."

"Stuart, tell me if you can: *are* you contemplating a first strike? We *must* know."

"It is the policy of the United States never to attack first."

"That isn't what I asked you, Stuart," Clayborne said.

Ainsworth leaned forward toward the screen and said with emphasis, "Alex, there is only one thing you, as a British soldier, must be told, and I am now telling it to you in the most unequivocal terms at my command. *Get the RAF's V-*

bombers aloft and the missile subs at sea. It is my belief that the Soviet Union will launch a pre-emptive attack at us in less than six hours. It may even come sooner. Your responsibility to NATO is one thing; your concern for Britain quite another. I believe the Reds will attack not only the United States, but also every other nation possessing nuclear weapons. They would be dangerously remiss to do otherwise."

"Stuart, I find it difficult to believe—" Clayborne began.

"That is precisely the trouble with our defense posture, Alex. We *all* find it difficult to believe. The fact remains that the United States has already, in a sense, been attacked. You may believe *that*. I recommend to you that you conduct yourself accordingly. If an exchange takes place, it will surely involve NATO. But Britain, France, and the Red Chinese will be prime targets, just as we are. Therefore, take what precautions you believe best. The United States will defend itself to the utmost."

Clayborne's face seemed to collapse inward, cheeks, lips and eyes drawing back until what remained was a skull covered by tightly stretched skin. It seemed to have aged years in the space of moments. "Yes, Admiral," he said in a thin voice. "I will do as you suggest."

"Good luck to you, Alex," Ainsworth said.

Several intercom lights began to flash. He opened the first circuit and said, "Yes?"

"Elmendorf Intercept reports that the Bears have reached their alert line. They are on the edge of U.S. air space."

"If they cross, shoot them down."

He touched the switch under the second light. "Yes?"

"The Ambassador to the United Nations is on the green phone, Admiral. He wants to speak to the Acting President."

"Negative," Ainsworth said, and touched the third communicator switch. "Yes?"

"CNO here."

"Go ahead."

"Pit reports Bandit Three is at missile depth off the Savannah River."

Ainsworth considered for only a moment before he said, "Sink him."

He picked up a gold telephone. On the other end of the scrambled line was the Command Center of Norad, inside Cheyenne Mountain. He asked briefly, "What Red birds have you in orbit?"

The impersonal voice on the other end spoke with computerlike precision. "Two Cosmos overhead and a third coming onto our ak-radar at oh two Greenwich."

"Alert Spartan to take them out."

"Roger."

Ainsworth waited briefly and then tapped out a code on the keyboard of the same gold telephone.

A voice, speaking over the muffled sound of jet engines, said, "Looking Glass."

"Cheney?"

"Sir."

"We will be going to Red Alert in fifteen minutes."

There was a long and pregnant pause. Ainsworth could imagine Brigadier General Cheney, in his immaculate blue flight suit, sitting in the midst of his consoles, while, outside, the dark night at fifty thousand feet glistened with steel-bright points of starlight. Looking Glass was flying over central Kansas at this moment, and below the lonely jet and its fighter escort lay an ocean of unseen clouds.

When Cheney's voice came back, it carried none of the soft cadences of his usual speech—no—what did they call it?—*soul.* It was the voice of a pure soldier. Rivera was right, Ainsworth thought. There was no need to be concerned about Cheney's professionalism.

"Right, sir. Red Alert in fifteen minutes. Looking Glass is on station, sir."

The Admiral stood and looked down into the Pit. We are

all doing what we must, he thought, and doing it according to plan. The safety of the United States rests with men like those below, and others all across the world in ships and airplanes and lonely, dangerous places. Very soon it would be in the hands of Almighty God. He felt a chill of exaltation at the realization of how close to the stern and Calvinist deity of his youth he was at this moment. *Dies Irae*.

He left his place and made his way down to the Presidential Communications Room. When the military policeman had passed him through the door, he found Fowler Beal watching a group of television network commentators do one of their instant commentaries on the Secretary of State's speech.

Beal turned down the volume and looked up fearfully. "Stuart," he said, "Shackleford brought word that Helen Risor is conscious and able to talk. There was *no* explosion on the President's airplane before the crash. And General Marty's autopsy on Colonel Dayton seems to show that the Colonel had some sort of arterial accident—"

Ainsworth appeared not to have heard. His face was composed, almost peaceful, the face of a man with his decisions made at last. Beal felt himself slipping inexorably into the nightmare, the dark night of his own indecision and vanished strengths, as he heard Ainsworth say firmly, almost loftily: "Mr. President, it is time to open the nuclear codes."

"Irony, Judge," Talcott Bailey said. "I hope you can appreciate it."

"In Congress I was said to be ironic to a fault," Jason Seidel said. "I've lost most of my taste for it in the last few hours."

Bailey's thin, patrician face broke into a meager smile. "It is a cliché that politics makes strange bedfellows. It is also true that it makes strange cellmates."

Seidel rubbed his grimy palms along the new, but soiled cloth of his desert fatigues in a futile effort to clean them. Vaguely he was aware of a new fact: captivity was a dirty business—actually physically dirty.

"Doesn't it strike you as ironic that the President's successor and the man the President actually wanted to succeed him are sitting here while someone totally different exercises the powers of the presidency?"

"How long have you known what the President had in mind?"

"Longer than you, I suspect, Judge. There were rumors—"

"I know those Washington rumors."

"There were rumors that the President was a sick man. That he wouldn't seek another term." Bailey's voice grew strained. "It was obvious to me from the beginning—from before the beginning—that he didn't want me in the White House."

"Well, it is academic now," Seidel said. "The people may have voted for you or for the President—but what they get now is Fowler Beal, a bowl of jello if ever there was one."

"Beal and the soldiers," Bailey said.

"Your hobbyhorse again, Bailey. There is nothing wrong with American soldiers, but by God they have to be led. That's the way it has always been with Americans."

"I didn't mean there was anything wrong with our soldiers, Judge. It's the generals and admirals who frighten me."

"You have to lead the generals, too. They are good men, mostly, but you have to let them believe in something real or they go bad. You can't ask them to believe something that their entire experience proves to them is wrong. You destroy them when you do that."

"Are you suggesting I have destroyed our arrogant young Tate?"

"Quite probably. And the rest of us into the bargain. This was no time to display your populist grandstanding dislike of the military."

Bailey had the grace to remain silent and accept the accusation. It galled him, but its truth was undeniable. He gave some thought to Ben Crowell, who had died so senselessly in the ambush. The others, the soldiers and the news people, would come back to haunt him through as many hours as he had left of life. But he had known Crowell, and, despite the fact that he was a soldier, had been as fond of him as was possible for so cold a man.

"What will happen, Judge, do you think?"

"To us?" Seidel made a shooting gesture with thumb and forefinger. "To the rest of the world? I don't know, but I have a bad feeling about it. Fowler Beal is not the man to lead the United States of America. God knows he will try a little, because the job brings out whatever toughness there is in a man. But there isn't very much in Fowler. He gave it up a long time ago."

Bailey lifted his head and listened, holding his hand up for silence. He could faintly hear the sound of helicopters.

"Do you hear them?"

Seidel nodded. He looked coolly at Bailey and said, "You know what will happen to us if they storm this place?"

"I know."

"I am very glad that you do," Seidel said. "That's realistic, at least."

Though the early-morning sun had not yet topped the roofs of Rome and had only just begun to touch the dome of St. Peter's, the square before the great church was filled with a silent throng. Bareheaded in the cold wind, the people, drawn to the great square by a dark fear and by the power of their faith, stood mutely looking at the balcony from which the Holy Father customarily delivered the *Deo gratias* and his blessing. The wind whipped the white-and-yellow flags at the Bronze Gate and fluttered the plumes of the Swiss Guards.

Within, the hastily assembled quorum of the Curia sat in murmuring controversy while Monsignor Emilio Guindani, of the Secretariat, read again, over the sound of muffled quarrel and argument, the appeal from Josef Cardinal Czernin, of Hungary.

Presently the Holy Father, with a rare expression of impatience, said, "We take it then, *amici,* that there is no unanimity here, no consensus as to what shall be done?"

Luigi Cardinal Pavoni, an eighty-year-old Calabrian who closely resembled the late, beloved John XXIII, expressed the doubts of the majority when he said, "Holy Father, we can only suggest that you speak personally with the American Ambassador and express to him your most grave concern."

The Pope, a thin, ascetic man of intellectual, rather than compassionate, gifts, frowned. "That will be done, of course. But have we nothing to say to the men who are responsible for this current danger? Have we no moral force to apply against the terrorists and those who have supported them? Cardinal Czernin assures us that there are still hundreds of thousands in the Communist world who hear our words. I ask for advice, *amici,* and you reply with diplomatic platitudes."

Pavoni gestured helplessly. "It is in God's hands, Holy Father."

The Pope said, "It is in men's hands, Cardinal Pavoni. And the hands are on their weapons."

A papal secretary hurried into the high-ceilinged room and whispered in the Pope's ear.

The Pope spoke in a thin voice edged with resignation. "The Americans have alerted NATO for an imminent attack from the Warsaw Pact nations. The Minister of Defense has notified the Papal Nuncio that Italy's air defenses are being mobilized."

There was a stunned silence among the men gathered at the long carved table. A first beam of early sunlight penetrated the arches of the high windows and illuminated a section of the Raffaello friezes above the Renaissance moldings. The angels and cherubim seemed to burn and glow in the suddenly violent light.

The Holy Father looked away with a hidden shudder. "Nothing, *amici?* No word of comfort or advice?"

The assembled princes of the Church stared at the burning angels or at the green baize surface of the table. Pavoni crossed himself and shut his eyes.

"Then," the Holy Father said, "I thank you." He rose from his seat, a thin and somehow tragic figure. "People have gathered in the square. I will go to them and offer what comfort I can." He paused, and then spoke quietly and firmly. "The Church has survived for more than one thousand nine hundred years, brothers in Christ. Pray that she survives the next twenty-four hours." He turned to Monsignor Guindani and said, "When I have done, Emilio, send my confessor to me. I feel the need to make my peace with God."

24

Deborah Zadok hurriedly got to her feet when the door to the room in which she was confined crashed open. She was trembling still from fatigue, but she had heard the helicopters and had begun to hope that assistance might come in time. When she saw the drawn face of Leila Jamil and the grinning faces of the three Arabs with her, she realized that was not to be.

Jamil said, "I came to you before as a friend." The words seemed to choke her.

Deborah felt a hopeless despair. But she said, in pure Arabic, "I am sorry. I am not a lover of women. Not even to save my life."

Jamil said to her companions, "Let her be a lover of men, then. Take her."

Two of the guerrillas caught Deborah by the arms and forced her back on the table. She struggled in grim silence, knowing there was no help for her in this desecrated house of God. The third Arab caught her by the legs and spread-eagled her on the table top. She could hear the men's hard breathing and excited laughter. Oh, God, she thought, let me die now. She felt hands ripping at her clothes, buttons tearing free, the tough khaki resisting as she struggled. Jamil stepped forward and swung at Deborah's temple with her rifle barrel. Deborah felt something break inside her head. Her joints went weak, flaccid.

Jamil leaned against the wall and watched, clammy and trembling, as the men took turns between the dying girl's legs. The Jewess's Circassian eyes, turned aside from the bearded faces, were fixed on her own. She found them terrifying—pupils dilated into the blue irises until they seemed no color at all, but black bottomless holes. The dark hair, so like hers, was matted and stuck to her forehead and temple. As she stared at the depression in the thin bones she had made with her furious blow, her thoughts tumbled and swirled. Why had she come here? She had wanted only to strike at the Americans and kill and then run as she had always done. It had all gone wrong, almost from the moment Lesh met them at the edge of the sea. He commanded now, not she, and this was what men did in war. Never before had she seen another woman used in this fashion, and it was as though her own suffering femaleness shone in the Jewish girl's glazing eyes. She felt the thick pain of guilt engorging her throat and belly and loins and knew that she could stand this no longer, that if it went on and she stayed, she would die of shame for what she had done. She turned away and stumbled through the door, past others of her men, who had gathered there like brute creatures drawn to the scent of rut and blood.

She shoved into the passageway gasping and gagging. She was vaguely aware that the men around her were calling to their companions, announcing their leader's sanction of rape. They suddenly terrified her.

"You stupid fool." Lesh, seeming gigantic in the narrow confines of the stone passage, blocked her way. He took her by the shoulders and shook her until her head rolled. "What have you done, you Arab bitch?"

"Stop them," she whispered.

"*Stop* them? Do you think I want to get killed? Leave them now. They'll finish soon enough and go back to their duty." He looked at her at arm's length and then slapped her hard across the face. "Wake up, you heroine of the revolution! Come to, goddam you!"

She tried to focus her eyes on his big, sweating face. "Get your Arab ass up on the wall and away from here," he yelled, "or you'll be next. I will attend to Bailey and the other one." He looked at her with a drawn expression. "Do you think the desert dries men's balls?" He thrust his hand into her crotch and squeezed her until she moaned with pain. "Did you think it dried *mine?*" He released her abruptly and shoved her toward the stairway leading to the top of the wall. From the cross-shaped room down the passage she could still hear the ugly laughter of her men. It was the sound of jackals swarming over a helpless, doomed deer.

In the South China Sea, on the bridge of the Soviet missile destroyer *Juan Bosch,* sister ship of the *Allende,* Captain Aleksandr Fedorovich Akimov and his radar officer watched the bank of green-lighted instruments. Under their feet the deck throbbed as the nuclear turbines worked the ship up to a speed of forty knots.

"She has not yet turned into the wind, Comrade Captain," the radar officer said. He watched the image of the USS *Nimitz* maneuvering at speed through the tepid waters some ten nautical miles ahead of the *Bosch*. "She is receiving a great deal of radio traffic from Japan, but she has not spotted her bombers for launching."

Akimov pondered. He was uncertain of his proper course of action. He had always known it would come to this one day. The highly placed ones in the Kremlin and the Ministry of Defense could write sweeping directives on reams of paper on the subject of procedures. But in the end it would always come to a command decision by one standing on the bridge of a ship or sitting in the cockpit of an aircraft.

It was his assignment to trail one carrier of the U.S. Seventh Fleet—recently the *Nimitz*—in order to be in a position to launch a nuclear-tipped missile at her in the event of war. He, the *Bosch,* and the three hundred men who served in her had this one single duty to perform at the proper moment. It was not expected that the *Bosch* would survive to fire a second missile, since the Americans were perfectly aware of the ship's location and assignment. On one radar screen he could see the eight Specters of the *Nimitz*'s Combat Air Patrol orbiting the *Bosch* at a mean distance of three nautical miles.

It presented a nice problem in ballistics, psychology, and politics, Akimov thought. Given: that war between the U.S. and the Soviet Union is imminent. Given: that the *Nimitz*'s H-hour assignment is to strike the far-eastern cities of the Soviet Union. And given: that both the *Bosch* and the orbiting Specters, as well as the *Nimitz,* are manned by dedicated patriotic madmen. Then: compute the number of absolutely useless deaths that will result when carrier, missile ship, and aircraft launch X to the nth power megatons at their respective targets simultaneously—

"Comrade Captain." The radar officer's voice sounded thin in the humming, crowded steel cave. "She is turning into the wind."

Without hesitation, Captain Aleksandr Fedorovich Akimov, age forty-three, father of four children at present attending school in the heavily targeted city of Kronstadt, gave the order: "Bring ship to General Quarters. Open the missile launchers and stand by."

The passageway began in a thorn thicket inside the wall of the burial ground beyond the north gardens. It had been built during the *dikonate* of the Patriarch Marelios, in the first years of the Ottoman oppression. The purpose had been both to provide a hiding place for the monks and to serve as a repository for the bones of the holy dead, of which, through those horrible years, there had been a surfeit, more than could be contained in the ossuary.

A pair of underground galleries had been carved secretly from the red granite under the thin topsoil, pillared, and roofed with rock. At no place was the distance from floor to ceiling greater than one meter, and sometimes less, while in other places the chambers had collapsed and filled with rubble, leaving a shallow depression in the earth above. It had been these unexplained depressions in the ground near the monastery wall, in fact, that had first attracted the attention of a young Anastasius and set him to searching the musty records of the Monastery of St. Katherine for some possible explanation. It took the monk many years of work in the old books to find the accounts of them, written by scribes beginning in the reign of Murad IV and reporting the work complete in the year 1640, when the feeble-minded Ibrahim I came to the throne of the Ottomans.

Anastasius had been keeper of the ossuary for five years when he, alone at first, began the work of clearing and exploring the rubbled chambers beneath the walls and gardens. It was he who had gathered the hidden bones of those monks who had died in the persecutions of the Turks and returned most of them to their rightful place in the charnel house guarded by the mummy of St. Stephanos.

It had been thought, before the coming of the Peacekeeping Force, that one day the funerary chambers might become another of the monastery's attractions for the faithful. Cleared and lighted, they could become another shrine, such as the Garden of the Burning Bush, or the well where Moses was said to have first met the daughters of Jethro. But the partition of the Sinai had stifled the tourist trade and inhibited the journeys of the devout, and so the charnel chambers under the wall remained now as Anastasius had left them, partially freed of debris and still populated by the dry skeletons of unknown and unnamable monks missed by Anastasius in his candlelit explorations of the shallow rooms.

He had closed off the entrance to the true charnel house, the ossuary, with a thick but unbarred door. The thorn growing along the low stone walls of the outer gardens had reclaimed the outside opening, once closed with a stone slab but for long years presenting simply a rubbled, narrow hole under the tangle of branches.

Because Anastasius had worked alone, and because the work was uncompleted, the linked chambers showed on no plan or archeological drawing of the monastery.

Staying low behind the stone wall, Tate's soldiers had cleared away some of the branches that blocked the opening. Now Tate and Sergeant Robinson, dressed in the dusty black habits of monks, lowered themselves into the narrow pit.

Tate said, "I have the opening into the first crypt. It's going to be tight for you, Sergeant."

Robinson, braced against the sides of the vertical wall to give Tate room to move, said, "Go ahead, General. I'm right behind you." He glanced up for one last look at the faces, black against the white sky, two meters above his head. He did not like dark and confined places, and the thought of crawling inside the earth brought a coppery taste into his mouth. The knife in his sleeve, the pistol in his belt, and the flashlight hanging around his neck seemed rather useless instruments with which to tempt the powers of the dark.

He was not consciously aware that the dark confined spaces he was about to enter plucked at childhood memories of ghetto tenement cellars and the chirping squeal of rats. He did not know that he was afraid and that following Tate through the narrow opening into the underground chambers made a greater demand on his courage than had the night battle that had won him his Medal of Honor.

Tate moved on hands and knees, the dressed stones of the chamber's ceiling brushing his back. In the pencil beam of his flashlight he could make out piles of fallen rock, some closing off shadowed corners of the narrow underground crypt. He had the sensation that he had been buried alive and that the stones overhead were pressing down on him, soon to crush him inexorably into the stones beneath. He slowed his forward movement and almost immediately felt Robinson close behind him and heard the giant black man's whispered "Is anything wrong, sir? Is the way blocked?"

Tate swallowed his claustrophobic fear and said, in a

voice that sounded choked to him, "It's all right, Crispus. Catching my breath, that's all."

He moved on through the narrow space, and now the dust swirled as his borrowed black robe brushed the stones. It smelled of desiccated bones. Ahead in the thin light beam he could see more fallen rubble, some of it directly in his path. Between the piled dirt and stones and the roughly chiseled masonry of the ceiling there was an opening no more than twenty centimeters wide. It seemed impossible that a man could crawl through so narrow a space and not be hopelessly trapped, but there was no other way to go. Beyond must lie the second burial chamber, and beyond that the wooden door to the ossuary within the monastery walls.

The ceiling pressed ever more heavily on his back as he was forced to crawl over a thickening layer of ancient debris. He thought of the monks laboring to build these crypts, and probably hiding here when Ottoman horsemen appeared in the flat valley under the loom of the mountains. These coffin-like spaces must have heard many a Kyrie eleison as the holy men prayed that the Turks would depart from the house of God above without searching for priests or pilgrims. No wonder old Father Anastasius had dreamed, in his delirium, of Saracens and St. Stephanos.

"It's getting very tight for me, General," Robinson said.

"Do you want to go back, Crispus?"

"I can still make it, I think, sir. If it doesn't get too much narrower."

Tate reached to shine his light through the wide crack into the second chamber. The thought of pushing himself through that tiny space made his belly tighten. There were only two or three yards of dirt and rock above, he told himself. It wasn't the whole world pressing down on his shoulders. But two meters of earth was enough to bury a man. He thought of old Anastasius working down here by candlelight, and alone. That took courage—or the sort of blind faith that convinced a man he was never really alone, even in this horrible darkness.

"This opening is narrow, Crispus," he said, breathing heavily, and not exclusively from exertion. "I'll have to try to widen it. Stay where you are for a minute."

He pushed forward again. Now he could not rise fully, even on hands and knees. The sensation of trapped confinement grew, but he forced himself to disregard it and inched ahead. He pulled at the loose debris half blocking the way and managed to enlarge the hole by a few centimeters. The dust coated his mouth and gritted in his eyes.

A sudden fall of rock pelted down from the ceiling, burying his hands and snuffing out the beam of his flashlight. He lay for a moment, stunned by a stone that had struck his forehead. He felt the clutch of real fear. The fallen detritus covered and pinned his arms, and he had the frightening sensation that the fall would continue and bury him here below the wall of St. Katherine's.

Behind him, Robinson said softly, "You okay, General?"

As a blessed beam of light pierced the dusty air, Tate could see his own shadow on the swirling cloud of dust motes that rose ahead of him in the second gallery. Carefully, and at the cost of some lost skin, he pulled his arms free of the piled rubble. His light had gone, and he called for Robinson to pass his up to him. When his hand closed over it, he dragged it forward ahead of his face and directed the beam into the next chamber.

This gallery had been partially cleaned by Anastasius. It was dusty, but there were no piles of stone and dirt fallen from above. Tate saw with a queasy shiver that the walls were lined with gray skulls and fragments of human bones. Each of the skulls had been carefully placed so that the empty eye sockets were turned upward, looking through two meters of stone toward the blessed, open air, and, presumably, toward God as well.

He began to move forward again, through the broken portal between the galleries and then along the uneven floor. The light beam leaped and danced along the floor, against the

walls, and over the upward-grinning skulls of dead monks—monks, Tate thought, who may have been killed by other soldiers in other times, paying the price the meek have often paid for assuming that, as they had been assured, they would inherit the earth.

At last, in the light's beam, he could make out the far wall, beyond which should be the stone stairs to the ossuary that Anastasius had described. For one bad moment he could not make out the wooden door. He had expected it to have a different color and texture from the wall, but even at a distance of only a few meters the wood appeared the same grayish-red as the floor and pillars of the gallery. He realized that trees were so scarce in this wilderness that Anastasius must have fashioned the door from wood as ancient and as petrified as the mountain itself.

He reached the door and paused to gather himself and wait for Robinson. The gallery was three meters wide here and relatively higher, so that the two men could crouch, with their heads brushing the ceiling.

"Okay, Sergeant?" Tate asked softly.

"Okay, General. But let's not come back this way."

Tate thought of the stories Deborah told of the Golem, the giant of mud and earth made by the magicians of the Cabala to stalk the enemies of the righteous. Here and now were not the place or the time to think about Deborah, and yet he could not drive her image from his mind. He knew that he would never be able to continue his life as he had led it up to the day before yesterday, that ordered existence of the career soldier. His anger and bitterness against Talcott Bailey would make that impossible now. What remained, then? If Robinson and he were successful and could take the hostages from the Abou Moussa to safety, and if the world did not crack apart, what then, William Tecumseh Sherman Tate? He saw clearly how adrift he would be, without career or purpose. To face that sort of life a man needed something, some*one*. Buried in the earth, he dreamed of the sunlight, and it came to him with startling clarity that what he needed in order to face the future—if future there was to be—was Deborah Zadok. He thought, almost with amazement and happiness: I *love* her.

"General?" Robinson's voice was a hoarse whisper.

"Yes. Let's try the door now." He leaned his weight against the old planks, but they resisted his efforts.

"Let me try," Robinson said, and spread his palms against the door and shoved. The barrier shrieked as dry wood scraped across the stones. In the earth-drowned stillness, the sound was hideous. The two men waited tensely for any indication of movement in the chamber beyond. There was none.

"Let's go, Crispus," Tate whispered.

He crawled through the low doorway into a shaft dressed with mud brick. From somewhere above came the smell of incense and candle wax. They were through, into the ossuary. A flight of brick stairs rose toward a dim light. He stood and drew his revolver. Robinson straightened up behind him. He could smell the robes they were wearing, musty with age and sweat. Now, with the underground galleries behind them, he felt more like a soldier. "Up," he whispered.

They climbed the steps to ground level and found themselves in the charnel house proper. It was a long building, beamed with hewn rafters that looked petrified. High windows admitted a pale light, and they could see that the walls were lined with shelves and cubicles, each containing a dusty pile of bones and a grinning, yellowish skull.

"Jesus," breathed Robinson. "More of them."

"Let's move out," Tate said, and led the way to the small chamber near the gate to the inner garden. He paused at the doorpost and listened. The only sound that came to him was the continuous fluttering beat of the Dragonfly that still patrolled back and forth across the face of the mountain. He signaled to Robinson, who moved swiftly past him into the antechamber of the ossuary.

The Sergeant stopped abruptly, and Tate raised his weapon and charged into the smaller room to see what had startled him. He almost fired at the figure seated at the charnel-house gate before he realized that he was looking at the fabled mummy of St. Stephanos, the Watcher of the Ossuary. The parchment face was piously downcast, the narrow skull wrapped in a white headcloth. The saint wore the angel robe of the highest monastic rank, purple-black and stiff with age. Behind the upright mummy, on the stuccoed wall, was a parchment ikon of the crucified Christ. From under the *megaloschemos,* St. Stephanos's naked, desiccated toes protruded.

Robinson stood staring at the apparition until Tate prodded him into motion. They moved out of the ossuary and into a narrow garden of tamarisk. Tate studied the surrounding buildings. He could detect no movement anywhere. The sun, higher now, slanted over the monastery wall to etch sharp black shadows on the ground. To their right stood the mosque. After studying the plan, he decided to chance a movement across the narrow stretch of open ground between the ossuary and the church. He thrust his revolver into his belt and adjusted the cassocklike garment that covered his uniform.

"There," he said to Robinson. "Walk with your head bowed. And *slowly,* Sergeant. As though we belonged here."

"Yes, sir."

They stepped from the ossuary and walked deliberately across the tamarisk garden toward the church. They had reached the shelter of the wall before they heard an Arab voice cry out at them from the top of the monastery wall.

At forty-seven thousand feet above the Bering Strait, the starlight was so bright that the point sources were reflected in the mirror-bright surfaces of his Tomcat's sharply swept wings. Inside the cockpit the green glow of the radar screen illuminated the pressure-masked face of Captain Willis Dahl, USAF.

A small voice in his headset spoke calmly. "The target is a Bear. Your vector is zero one zero degrees. Time to intercept is three niner minutes. Report when you acquire the bandit."

Dahl said to his wing man, "Rushmore Two, this is Rushmore One. Going to afterburners—now."

High above the arctic ice, unseen by any human being except, perhaps, some seal hunter shivering near his meager fire, two trails of flame marked the track of the hunting aircraft. All along the polar frontiers of North America, similar actions were either taking place or impending.

Admiral Ainsworth said, "Mr. President, I have prepared a statement for you to read on national radio and television from the studio in the deep shelter." He handed a single sheet of paper to Fowler Beal.

Beal read it in silence. It was short and to the point.

My fellow Americans. It is with the deepest regret that I must inform you that yesterday, without warning or declaration of war, a deliberate attack was made upon the security and safety of the United States. On that day our President and Vice President were victims of a conspiracy so monstrous that it will be remembered as long as the United States endures.

It is doubly bitter for me to tell you that the authors of this conspiracy were the very men with whom we have, since the establishment of the Nixon Doctrine, sought most sincerely to co-operate.

I mean, of course, the Red dictators in the Kremlin.

Acting by the authority granted to me by statute and by the Constitution, I now assume the responsibilities of president of the United States.

I have instructed the armed forces to respond to the attack upon us in terms that will unmistakably prove to the aggressors that the United States cannot be frightened, intimidated, or subverted.

I ask that you remain calm and devote your total energies to the achievement of quick victory and the blessings of peace. With the strong aid of our armed forces and the help of Almighty God, we shall prevail.

Beal, shaken, looked up at the Admiral and said, "When will the people hear this, Stuart?" He spoke carefully, forming each word as though it were new and strange to him.

Ainsworth's face was gaunt, with both strain and determination. He said, "We will tape it now, Mr. President. It will be broadcast the moment we receive word from Sinai that the Marines have assaulted the Monastery of St. Katherine."

"It is Baikonur Center, Comrade Marshal."

The Minister of Defense picked up the telephone. "Morozov here," he said.

"The Americans have destroyed Cosmos satellites 549, 302, and 160, Comrade Marshal," said the voice, thin and distorted by the scrambling device. "We are receiving no information from North America."

"Yes," Morozov said. "Very well." He picked up a second telephone. "Connect me with Severnaya Zemlya Center."

There were electronic-key noises on the line as the communications computer coded the Minister's call through to the Fractional Orbit Bomb Launch Complex on the arctic island. When the voice of the launch control officer came through, Morozov spoke slowly and distinctly. "Cassandra, your eyes are like tigers, / with no word written in them."

There was a short pause while the launch officer consulted his code for the day and then responded: "You also have I carried to nowhere / to an ill house and there is / no end to the journey."

Morozov broke the connection and sat very still. The attack code for this twenty-four hours was taken from a poem written by the dead fascist Ezra Pound, who was not, of course, published in the Soviet Union. Like many Soviet citizens, the Minister of Defense was a lover of poetry, and he had often idly wished that he might freely read the poems of the mad Pound. But now, of course, that would never happen. In fifteen minutes six nuclear devices would rise into polar orbit. In ninety minutes more they would approach the United States from the undefended south, accept a command from a trawler in Central American waters, and fall on six American cities. How many copies of the *Pisan Cantos* would be destroyed in the holocaust, he wondered.

The Marine troop-carrying helicopters approached out of the north with a great whacking beat of rotating wings. They made no effort at concealment, but landed in the valley before the monastery on the far side of the Wadi el Deir, where there was sufficient ground for assembly. The Marines landed in assault order, dropping from the choppers while the machines still hovered a few feet above the ground. They quickly dispersed to whatever cover could be found, then formed a skirmish line and advanced across the wadi, showing every intention of charging directly at the monastery's north gate without a pause.

Captain O'Neill, in command of Tate's Special Forces detachment, stood up and shouted at the Marines to halt. This order was first ignored and then directly countermanded by the commander of the assault battalion, who had been briefed on what might be expected from General Tate's component officers. Within minutes, a fire team of Marines had reached the north gate and was huddled there, taking cover against whatever action the defenders might attempt. This consisted only of a rush along the top of the wall by four men in Arab headcloths in an attempt to open a field of fire against the men at the gate.

Near the blue air force helicopter, General Ulanov stood, with field glasses raised, watching the one remaining guerrilla standing with the noosed hostage on the east wall. As yet the Arab, at this distance slender as a boy and fine-featured, had done nothing. But as Ulanov watched, he began to prod at Paul Bronstein with the muzzle of his Kalashnikov. The General glanced away and saw that the American Marines were rushing the gate, and that a detail was jogging across the open ground toward the position where his marksmen manned the sniper rifle.

He weighed the possibility of traversing the weapon to cut down the approaching Marines. That was exactly what Novotny would do in a similar situation, he thought. It would be the predictable action of a Soviet soldier faced with a deteriorating situation and a secret weapon in danger of capture. The old General looked again at the pair on the wall, and then did what he had promised William Tate he would do. He gave his gunners the order to fire.

The new rifle made a strange flat sound as it fired. The blast suppressor on the end of the long barrel muffled the discharge. But the bullet, traveling at twice the velocity of an American M-36 slug, covered the fifteen hundred meters between the weapon and the wall in milliseconds. As the point of the long projectile penetrated Leila Jamil's forehead an inch above her right eye, a small gelignite core was detonated. The resultant explosion would have disabled a medium tank, since it was for use against such targets that the weapon had been designed. Her head, neck, and upper body to the base of the sternum vaporized into a reddish mist. Microscopic needles of bone stung her prisoner's face. The headless body collapsed at his feet, the thoracic cavity hissing and steaming from the extreme temperature created by the combined force of the exploding charge and the bullet's velocity.

Paul Bronstein screamed, and kept on screaming.

25

Tate and Robinson heard the cry above them and the sound of the Marine helicopters almost simultaneously. They broke into a run across the remaining open ground to tumble down the rock slope to the wall of the half-sunken church. In less than a minute they heard the Marine gunfire beyond the wall and the shouting of orders and counterorders. Tate raised his head and craned to see the top of the wall at the north gate, but his view was blocked by the corner of the church.

"We have to make it now, Sergeant. That shooting can finish Bailey," Tate said. His heart had begun to pound hard, and he wondered if he had not grown too old for this commando game. Robinson was not even breathing heavily.

There was more shooting outside. Tate guessed that the Arab who had seen them had been distracted from a mere matter of two monks, overlooked and left within the monastery, to the real business of an assault from outside. He consulted the plan once more and saw that they would have to round the corner of the church and enter from the north. There were doors on the east side, but none on the west, where they now were.

"Cover me," he said, and turned the corner. He faced a corridor formed by the north façade of the church and a high garden wall built parallel to it, forming a narrow alleyway. "All clear," he said, and signaled Robinson to follow. He sprinted down the chute toward the main door. As he ran, he heard someone on the wall begin to scream. It was a sound barely human, a demented repetitive cry of horror that made his flesh crawl.

Turning into the dark interior of the church, he was momentarily blinded by the sudden change in the light. Seeing movement along the wall, he threw himself to the stones with a warning cry to Robinson as a blast of gunfire crashed and reverberated in the echoing space. Stone chips stung his face, and he could hear the ricochets whine away from the tiny row of explosions that chewed at the floor near his head. He rolled into the cover of a thick stone doorway, closely followed by Robinson.

"Are you all right?" he asked breathlessly.

"I'm not hit."

Tate could hear the noise of boots, then running footsteps and muttered words in some language he didn't understand. He searched for his pistol and found that he had lost it.

Robinson said softly, "Take mine. I have this." His throwing knife was in his hand. He whispered, "Do you think they've moved our people from the church?"

Tate shook his head. "They are in here."

Up near the front, candles were incongruously burning. The thick sick-sweet smell of them was in the air.

Tate gestured for Robinson to remain put while he worked around the building toward the front. He moved out, darting from doorway to doorway until he had a view of the passageway leading to the rooms behind the altar. He saw movement and charged hard. The sound of the Kalashnikov was deafeningly near. A line of bullets blew holes in the wooden panels behind him as he ran. He heard Judge Seidel's voice yelling, *"Here! Beside the altar!"* There was the sound of a blow being struck, and then he could see the Judge sprawling, Bailey standing nearby, and a thickset man in camouflage uniform holding the rifle. He could not fire for fear of hitting Bailey, but he came on in a pounding run. In slow motion, it seemed to him, the man in camouflage raised the weapon. Tate had the terrible feeling that he had seen this all before: a man in fatigues with a too-familiar Russian weapon in his hands raising the muzzle to blow him into bloody shreds. The setting was different, because the last time it had been the dark of an overrun A-camp in the Vietnamese highlands, but the rest of it was the same, even to the bullet that ripped into his side, spinning him around and setting his chest on fire.

He lay on his back and he could see the gun muzzle raised again, this time at Talcott Bailey, who stood fascinated by it, his long pale face etched with the strain of realization that this moment—this very instant—was going to be the last he would ever know.

Lesh grunted softly and lowered the AK. It was a slow, puzzled motion. He said one single, odd word. It was "Bakunin." Then the weapon clattered to the floor and he fell forward, onto his face, with a single great pitching motion. The handle of Robinson's throwing knife protruded from Lesh's back. The cloth around it reddened in an enlarging stain.

Tate lurched to his feet and felt at his side, where the bullet had torn through robe, uniform, skin, and muscles. He suspected that his ribs on that side were broken. Each breath seared him.

Bailey had sat down on the floor next to Seidel and was trying to help him.

"How is he?" Tate asked.

The Judge, his face swollen in eye-closing lumps where Lesh had struck him, said thickly, "I'm all right. Goddam it, I'm all right. Let's get the President out of here."

Robinson knelt beside Lesh to retrieve his knife. "Are you hit bad, General?" he asked.

"I'll make it," Tate said.

Robinson said, "This mother fucker is still alive."

Tate rolled Lesh over onto his back and looked into the broad face. The man's eyes were open—glazing, but aware. In accented English, Lesh said, "I shall be impossible—so long as those who are—" The voice faded and choked on the blood in his throat. The eyes stared.

Robinson grunted. "What was that?"

Bailey said, " 'I shall be impossible as long as those who are possible remain possible.' Mikhail Bakunin said that once. The Arab woman called him a Bakuninite—the complete anarchist."

"He's a dead anarchist now," Robinson said.

Tate was on his feet, unsteadily, holding Lesh's Kalashnikov. "Sergeant Robinson, take Mr. Bailey and the Colonel to the north gate. *Now,* Sergeant—" He freed himself of the monk's robe and pressed his arm against his side in an attempt to stop the bleeding.

Robinson said, "What about you, General?"

"There are still more hostages, goddam it. Don't stand there arguing with me. Move your ass, soldier."

The Judge said, "I think they have Bronstein and Captain Zadok somewhere inside the east wall. What's happening outside?" The sound of firing had increased as the men of the Abou Moussa tried to interdict the movement of the Marine battalion around the monastery.

"Let's get these people moved," Tate said in a tight, thin voice. He led the way back toward the double doors of the church and out into the open.

As they emerged into the bright sunlight of the corridor between church and wall, Tate ordered them to take cover. At the east end of the narrow way a gate stood open. Beyond it was a short flight of stone stairs leading to a keeper's entrance into the monastery wall. From this entrance armed guerrillas were now running. Tate fired the AK from the hip and stitched a row of bullets across the opening, forcing the Arabs back. From the top of the wall came a rattle of return fire that dug tiny craters in the earth and gravel of the walk between wall and church. Tate fired again. A man fell from the wall into the courtyard below.

On the far side of the wall they could hear the sound of running men and shouted orders in Arabic. The guerrillas were attempting to reach the end of the passage and flank them, drive them back into the church. If this were accomplished, their situation, with only one automatic weapon among them, would become desperate.

Tate heard the familiar rapid noise of M-36's. There was a short, vicious exchange on the other side of the wall, and then a line of soldiers in blue berets ran up the passageway from the direction of the ossuary. Captain O'Neill came to a stop, shot a wide-eyed glance at Talcott Bailey, then saluted Tate. "Sir. The jarheads rushed the north gate. We couldn't stop them. They are working their way down through the inside of that big wall. I told their officer he'd get the hostages killed, but he said none of that mattered because there was a goddam Red Alert declared—" He paused to catch his breath, looking curiously again at Bailey. "The Gyrenes say there was a special statement from Washington just after they opened up here. They say the Speaker of the House was on the air saying the Vice President is dead, killed by these Ayrab bastards. Shouldn't we give the word he isn't, General?"

Bailey said, "If Fowler Beal has made such an announcement, General, and backed it with a Red Alert, the United States will be at war in half an hour. Captain, how long ago was the announcement made?"

"Ten, fifteen minutes, sir. I can't say for certain. I was crawling through some bone pits."

"General," Bailey said, "how long will it take us to fly to Es Shu'uts?"

"Half an hour." The words were stony.

The Judge asked, "Is there any way to get a Shrike down here for Mr. Bailey?"

"Not here and back in less than fifteen minutes," Tate said. "Captain, send a man back to the helos. Tell them to get ready to fly the President—" The title was bitter in his mouth. He was torn by his need to look for Deborah, and his sure knowledge of what even a few minutes' delay might mean. "Sir," he said to Bailey, "I should tell you that I was personally relieved of command by Admiral Ainsworth. I refused the order. I don't believe he will cancel the Red Alert except on direct orders from you. It will have to be a television hookup. From what I guess about Ainsworth's frame of mind now, it will take a face-to-face presidential order to stop him."

There was more firing within the wall, and Tate's nerves began to jump impatiently at Bailey's seemingly deliberate, thoughtful delay in making a decision.

There was a flurry of movement at the doorway that led into the wall, and both Tate and the Captain raised their weapons instinctively. But it was a Marine major and two privates, who came at a run. The Major presented himself to General Tate and said, with breathless pomposity: "General William Tate? You are under arrest, sir, by direct order of the Chairman of the Joint Chiefs of Staff."

Sergeant Robinson made an ugly noise in his throat, and Colonel Seidel said sharply, "Major, this is not the time to be an idiot."

The Marine turned angrily, then recognized Talcott Bailey. His mouth opened slightly, and he said stupidly, "Mr. Vice President, sir—we just now heard—"

Tate said peremptorily, "Mr. *President,* Major. Now you get the President and his party back to the helicopters *on the double.*" He said to Seidel, "They will still have the television equipment set up at the ambush site. That's twenty minutes closer to us than Es Shu'uts. There might still be time."

There was one final burst of fire from inside the wall, and almost immediately another Marine appeared in the doorway to shout: "That's all of them, I think, Major."

The Marine officer said confusedly, "I can't take orders from you, General Tate. I'm sorry, but you are under arrest—"

Seidel exploded angrily. "Good God, Major, have you lost your mind?"

Bailey said, "The General is in command here, Major." He

looked at Tate, but spoke to the Marine. "He will get me to where I can reach Admiral Ainsworth without further delay."

It was a statement, an admission—and an order. Tate felt as though he were being ripped in two. Somewhere in this place was Deborah; he felt sick and giddy, with a pulsing beat of pain in his wounded side. He looked at Robinson, who read his mind. "I'll handle things here for you, General."

The code, Tate thought bitterly, the terrible, demanding code the professional soldier lived by. "Duty, Honor, Country." And, as always, *always,* Duty—that came first.

"Mr. President," he said, "let's go."

In a launch control room deep underneath the South Dakota farmland of Edmunds County, Captain Harry Middleton completed his coding and opened the door to the safe built into the thick steel wall of the room.

"I am removing my key," he said in a formal, hollow voice.

Standing at his own safe, three meters away, First Lieutenant David Epstein said suddenly, "I can't believe it, Harry. I can't *believe* it."

"Lieutenant Epstein."

The younger officer wiped his sweating hand on his air force coverall and reached into the open safe. "I am removing my key," he said.

The two men, moving with a curiously uncharacteristic military bearing, turned and walked to their seats at the firing consoles, also separated by three meters of distance, so that no one man could possibly, *ever,* turn both firing keys simultaneously.

From these consoles, underground communications lines ran to the five Minuteman silos of their flight. In other launch controls spread across the undulating, fertile lands of midcontinent, other air force captains and lieutenants were performing the same stylized, disciplined movements.

"Insert key," Middleton said.

"Key inserted."

Red lights snapped on in quick sequence across their control panels.

"Begin final countdown."

Epstein heard himself make the proper response, but inside his head a voice seemed to keep saying over and over again: *It isn't happening. It isn't true—*

Sonar Technician First Class Vladimir Suslov heard the voice of the depth technician reporting to the Captain: "Ninety meters, Comrade Captain." He was only incidentally aware that ninety meters was missile-firing depth for a nuclear submarine of the Admiral Rozhdestvenski class. He was not even conscious of the leveling of the deck beneath him as the sub assumed the proper position for launching its nuclear weapons.

But he was puzzled, and then alarmed, by the curious ploshing noise he heard in his headset—a noise that was made, in fact, by the entry into the water of an antisubmarine rocket fired from a U.S. Navy Ventura ten nautical miles away. It was not until he saw the steep, jagged traces on his oscilloscope and heard the shrieking whine of high-speed propellers approaching at more than seventy knots that his alarm expanded into terror. He turned to shout a warning, never heard, to the officers in the control room just as the ASROC found and disintegrated the Soviet nuclear submarine *Semenoff,* known to the U.S. Navy technicians working in the Pit as Bandit One.

Underwater listening stations reporting to Eastern Sea Frontier and the Atlantic ASW Force headquarters heard the explosion. A watcher on the shore saw the nuclear glow. The third atomic weapon fired in anger in the history of the world had been detonated at ninety meters below the surface of the Atlantic.

At fifty thousand feet above the Bering Sea, Captain Willis Dahl heard his controller say in a puzzled voice: "Rushmore

One, that Bear you are tracking looks phony. He might be a missile ship for his wing. I don't like the traces his radar makes."

"Rushmore One, roger," Dahl said laconically.

Almost immediately he heard his controller say: "Rushmore, start evasive action; the bastard has fired air-to-air birds at you."

Dahl, twenty-two and superbly trained and conditioned, immediately rolled his fighter into a split-S turn and dive, closely followed by his wing man.

The maneuver did not save the two interceptors from the fifty-kiloton explosion of the ATA missile that detonated at a distance of one kilometer laterally and one point two kilometers vertically from them.

The fragments of their planes fell over an area of twenty square kilometers of frozen arctic sea. When summer arrived in those high latitudes, the ice would melt and once again Captain Dahl and his wing man would have a long fall. This one would be to the black bowl of the Aleutian Basin, two hundred fathoms below the surface of the lonely frigid sea.

The fourth nuclear weapon used in earnest killed only two men: an economy of death unlikely ever to occur again.

Bill Tate, half reclining in the back of the helicopter while the medic dressed his side, watched the minutes ticking away on the instrument-panel clock.

Five of their precious minutes had been wasted in freeing General Ulanov and his men from the hostile Marines who had them under guard. Another three had been lost as the old General tried without success to reclaim his sniper's rifle from those same grim-faced infantrymen. He had finally given up and run heavily to join Seidel and Bailey in the lead helicopter.

From the medic, Tate had learned of Trask's murder, and he lay thinking bleakly, Poor Liz Adams—another casualty of this crazy battle without heroes.

He looked out at the terrain below. It had not changed one iota from what it was yesterday, a barren jumble of sand and thorn and rock. It had absorbed the blood of another score of men, but that made no difference to this thirsty ground that had been fought over for five thousand years. Thirty-four east was not a line, a border—it was nothing but an idea. A single idea that had tried to express such order and co-operation as men were capable of constructing in this latter half of the twentieth century. In the space of twenty-four hours or less he had seen the whole edifice, laboriously built on this single idea by Americans, Russians, Arabs, and Jews—and yes, by a polyglot gaggle of foreigners of every nationality—tremble and begin to fall. That was horrible enough—the terrible waste of it all. But even worse was the shock wave that the incipient collapse had sent out into the world.

He thought again and again of Deborah, fighting against the dark premonition that troubled his mind. Soldiers tended to think in romantic, almost quaint, terms. Lovelace had pleaded for soldiers when he wrote: "I could not love thee, dear, so much, / Lov'd I not honour more." God, what sort of men could feel a thrill of understanding when they read such lines? Only the duty-ridden, twentieth-century *condottieri*—the poor, bloody infantry, the Tommy Atkinses, the professionals. I'll leave the Army, he thought. If we live, I'll leave the Army and spend the rest of my life appreciating and loving her and telling her all the things I should have told her the night before last, when I had her safe and near me. She had always made what women there were before seem unimportant, and now he understood that it was simply because he had never loved before, had, in fact, not had the sense to know that he loved now. It will be different, he thought. It *must* be different now. It must *be*.

"General?" The copilot had turned to get his attention.

"Yes?"

"There. We're overtaking the Russian cars."

Below, on the road from Zone Center, the Soviet vehicles

were racing for the place where the ambush had taken place last night. Ulanov had urgently summoned them so that Rostov and Bailey could speak simultaneously to Washington and Moscow.

How far had things gone, Tate wondered. If the Red Alert had been declared more than thirty minutes ago, and the time was past that, then the missiles could be out of their silos, the nuclear bombers at their release points, the submarines at firing depth. The whole world could be dying and we not know it yet.

Ahead he could see that the helicopter carrying Bailey, Seidel, and Ulanov was letting down for a landing. He shoved the medic away and sat erect, ignoring the pain that ripped his side, as he looked to see whether or not the ground-to-satellite transmission gear had been dismantled. He could see American vehicles and among them the commo van, but he could also see that men were working on the parabolic antenna, dismantling it. "Put her down," he said to the pilot. "Get this thing *down*. And hand me the mike—on the double, soldier!"

He took the headset and started transmitting orders even before the copilot could change channels to catch the commo-team frequency.

The voice of the officer in charge of the detail below came into the helicopter: "Say again? I read you five by three. Say again?"

He made his voice urgent, but calm. "This is General Tate. Stop dismantling that dish. Set up again and get a link with the War Room. Do it fast."

"General, we were just—"

"Get cracking, soldier. I want a link with Washington by the time my aircraft is on the ground. And you are to let the Russians tap their gear into yours the moment they arrive—which should be almost immediately."

"Yes, *sir,* General. Right away."

The sweep hand on the instrument-panel clock seemed to be racing, wiping away irreplaceable seconds.

The lead helicopter was on the ground now, raising a great swirl of dust. The machine carrying Tate followed it down, hovered for what seemed forever, and then settled onto the ground beside the narrow macadam track.

The shot-up vehicles that had carried Bailey's ill-starred party were gone, hauled away back to the U.S. Sector. Except for the communications equipment, the place looked like just another stretch of desert. There was nothing there to commemorate the killings, the fact that here on this spot had been lighted the fuse that could explode the world.

Tate stepped from the helicopter and joined Bailey, the Judge, and Ulanov at the commo van. A team of technicians had once again unloaded the dish for the antenna and were remounting it on its tripod standard. Tate spoke to the startled communications officer, a captain who was staring at Bailey in the manner of one who sees a man returned from the grave. Apparently Beal's statement had reached everyone in the component. Since it was tantamount to a declaration of war against the Soviets, a certain nervousness about the presence of old General Ulanov could be expected, and Tate's order about the approaching Russian convoy would have rattled less-disciplined troops.

"What have we got for a relay?" he asked impatiently.

The Captain looked significantly at Ulanov and said reluctantly, "Midas 34 is in line of sight for the next sixteen minutes, sir. Or we could wait for Samos 60, which will be over the horizon in another half hour. Sixty is newer and would give us a better-quality image transmission—"

"Get plugged in *now,* Captain. We don't have half an hour."

The Captain moved closer to Tate and whispered, "Sir—I mean we're practically at *war* with *them*—"

"We will be, Captain," Tate said grimly, "if your people don't get off their tails and align that dish."

Seidel, speaking indistinctly through swollen lips, said, "Rostov is arriving, Mr. President."

The words "Mr. President" seemed to have a galvanic effect on the communications officer. He joined his men working on the dish and began to adjust the setting verniers.

Tate said to Ulanov, "Have your communications people put their van next to ours and tap in. Have you a satellite in the right position for a hookup with Moscow?"

"I believe so," the Russian said, and then he added with the suggestion of a grim smile, "If not—another Borodino?"

"Much worse, Yuri."

Rostov's car stopped on the road, and the Deputy Premier alighted. He walked hurriedly over to Talcott Bailey and said, "Mr. Bailey, we have the officer who failed to warn us of the danger to you at Zone Center under guard. We have his clerk and his secretary as well. When this is done, I wish you to speak with them, so that you may hear from their own idiots' mouths how this terrible thing came about. Then if you wish, it will be my extreme pleasure to have them shot."

"It is my hope, Mr. Deputy Premier," Bailey said, "that no more will lose their lives. That is why we are here, and it is also why you are here. In the hope of peace, sir."

Tate turned away from the pair. In the light of all that had happened and all that might happen, Bailey's words were pompous. But that was his way. Being president of the United States would not change his manner. Even being president of an incinerated ruin would not change it.

Tate heard Rostov say in his labored English, "I must warn you, Mr. Bailey, that it may already be too late. We have war hawks in the USSR, too." Tate looked significantly at the old General, who shrugged imperceptibly, as though to say: "Politicians."

The communications officer ran from the van and said, "We have a link, sir. I don't know about *them*." He glanced contemptuously at the Soviet technicians, who were still deploying their antenna.

"Turn the cameras out here for a wide-angle coverage,"

Tate said. "They must see that the President is under no restraint. Keep the receiver monitor under cover in the van so that only the President can see it." There was no way of telling what Admiral Ainsworth's reaction to this message might be, and Tate did not want the Russians to see it, even Yuri Ulanov. Stuart Ainsworth, for all his paranoia, was, after all, a four-star flag officer of the United States Navy, the highest uniformed commander of the U.S. armed forces. If this was his finish, he did not deserve to have it made into a spectacle for his adversaries.

From inside the commo van, Tate could hear Fowler Beal's uncertain voice. Bailey and Seidel had stepped into the vehicle for a tape replay of the statement that had been broadcast all over the world at the moment the Marine battalion started its attack on the monastery.

"—I have instructed the armed forces to respond to the attack—"

In the last analysis, thought Tate, this is exactly what we, all of us, have been tampering with since that day in 1945 when Russian and American soldiers met on the Elbe. Peace did not come easily, and it did not automatically come to those with high purpose.

"—we shall prevail."

Poor Beal. Of all the betrayals, his was the greatest and the most innocent. For years Americans had known that there was always the possibility that president and vice president might perish or be taken simultaneously. Yet the politicians could not cease being politicians even long enough to assure the nation of strong leadership when it would need it most. Speakers of the House were chosen for their longevity in office and for little else. So into that power vacuum had fallen the austere, bigoted Stuart Ainsworth. It was as natural as any act of God, any storm, earthquake, or natural catastrophe.

A Soviet technician spoke rapidly to Ulanov, whose gray face tightened. He turned to Tate and said: "There are already clashes. We have lost contact with one of our submarines. Your Air Force has lost some aircraft and has destroyed a number of our satellites."

"Can Marshal Morozov be stopped? Will the Premier act?"

Ulanov shrugged with Slavic fatalism. "What will be, will be, William." He caught a signal from the Russian communications officer and walked over to Rostov. "We are ready, Comrade Deputy Premier. But the war has started."

Bailey came out of the van and took his place before the camera. "I am ready, Captain," he said quietly to the communications officer.

Tate and Ulanov watched the monitors. On one could be seen the empty interior of the Pentagon deep shelter; on the other, Moscow's Command Center. A Russian colonel showed on the Moscow screen, speaking soundlessly to someone off screen. Tate caught a glimpse of Marshal Morozov moving past the eye of the Russian camera. On the Pentagon screen he saw Shackleford. The General discovered Bailey on his own monitor and his eyes widened in surprise.

"General Shackleford, I wish to speak with Admiral Ainsworth immediately," Bailey said.

"Yes, sir! Immediately."

Bailey turned to Rostov and said, "I will abort any further hostile moves, Deputy Premier, if I have your word that your people will do the same."

Tate was astonished and reassured by the new toughness and purpose in Bailey's voice. It had a steel edge, delicately poised.

"I will do my best," Rostov said.

Bailey turned back to the transmitting camera. Tate, standing near the monitor, could see that the studio in the deep shelter was filling with people. He caught a glimpse of the Chief of Naval Operations and the Chief of Staff of the Air Force.

Abruptly, Admiral Stuart Ainsworth's long face appeared

on the monitor. Apparently he had been warned by Shackleford that Bailey had survived.

Bailey gave the Chairman no chance to speak first. He said, "Admiral, this is the President of the United States. Can you hear and see me properly?"

"I can see you—"

Though precious seconds were ticking away, Bailey remained silent, waiting.

"Mr. President," Ainsworth added in a constricted voice.

"This is a direct order—a direct *presidential* order, Admiral. All hostile acts are to cease *at once*. Abort the *Red Alert* now."

"Sir—Mr. President—"

"Do it, Admiral."

Tate could see the severe lines of Ainsworth's face collapsing. His angry, bitter eyes showed his disappointment and his conviction that the ultimate opportunity was slipping away. He turned to an aide off screen and said, in a barely audible voice: "Send, 'Olympus says: Stand down.' "

"Thank you, Admiral," Bailey said quietly. "Now if you please, I wish to speak to Fowler Beal. You, Admiral, are to hand over your command to General Shackleford."

Ainsworth stepped away from the camera as Bailey turned to Rostov. "Now," Bailey said, "please join me, Mr. Deputy Premier. And speak to your people."

Rostov squinted up at the American camera and glanced over to the Russian van. "Am I getting through to Moscow?"

"They have received everything so far, Comrade Deputy Premier."

The Moscow monitor showed Morozov.

Rostov said, in his own harsh dialect, "You heard all that, Marshal?"

"I heard, Comrade Deputy Premier. But I do not believe it. The Americans have destroyed at least one submarine and attacked our aircraft."

An American technician, listening on another circuit to the Early Warning net, spoke to Tate and Bailey. "They have six FOB's up from Severnaya Zemlya, General. Time to impact is thirteen minutes."

Rostov heard and promptly shouted at Morozov. "Abort the nuclear satellites immediately!"

"That will be difficult, Comrade Deputy Premier," Morozov said bleakly.

"Don't say difficult to *me,* Morozov. There are trawlers on station. We both know that. Do as I say at once."

The Soviet Defense Minister was a much younger man than Stuart Ainsworth, but at this moment, thought Tate, he looked enough like him to be his twin. The same doubt, the same gray fear and anger, the same suspicion.

"The Americans are listening and watching, Morozov," Rostov shouted furiously. *"Obey your orders."*

"Very well, Comrade Deputy Premier."

On the American monitor appeared the haggard face of Fowler Beal. He said in a wavering voice: "Talcott—oh, Jesus Christ, Talcott, I am so glad to see you alive. I never wanted any of this—I swear it. I didn't know what to do—"

"It's all right, Mr. Speaker," Bailey said. "I understand."

Seidel murmured to Tate, "Understand? I'd try the son of a bitch for treason."

Bailey said across the miles, "You can go home, Fowler. We have things under control now."

"Thank you," Beal said. He started to move away, and then turned back. "Thank you, Mr. President."

Rostov spoke to Bailey. "Morozov is under arrest."

"Is that necessary, Mr. Deputy Premier?" Bailey asked.

"You have your way of doing things, Mr. President. We have ours. Will you speak to our premier?"

There was a flurry of activity in the Moscow shelter before the old Premier's face appeared on the monitor. He looked haggard, and the lights limned the deep lines in his face. "Everything is being done, Rostov," he said. Then he recognized Talcott Bailey and said, with un-Communist fervor, "Thank God. Thank God you are alive, Mr. President."

In a launch control bunker in South Dakota, Lieutenant Epstein danced and shouted to the rhythm of an abort alarm.

In the South China Sea, the captains of the *Nimitz* and the *Juan Bosch* murmured silent prayers of thanksgiving and resumed their cruising stations.

In a deep shelter near Brussels, Lieutenant-General Sir Alexander Clayborne expelled a great shuddering sigh of relief.

Off the west coast of Honduras, a Russian trawler photographed the spiraling fall of burning fragments from six destroyed objects in low orbit.

In Washington, New York, Paris, London, Moscow, Leningrad, Tokyo—in cities all over the world—the puzzled and frightened people felt the slackening of tension and waited for an explanation that would be long in coming, if it ever came at all.

Along the border of Israel and Syria, the Israeli troops noted the cancellation of the orders moving them into the Israeli Sector of the Peacekeeping Area and shrugged, turning their attention to the customary enemy.

And along thirty-four east, General William Tate began to reckon the cost.

He stood alone at nightfall near the dispensary at Zone Center. Deborah Zadok's body, wrapped in a blue-and-white flag, had been taken east by the same detachment that had collected the casualties of the ambush at the two breasted hills.

He was numb, almost without feeling. But it would come, he thought. The loss and grief would visit him every day, every morning of his life when he awoke to realize anew that she was gone and that never again would he come so close, so very close, to loving. He had spent his life, always, deliberately turning away from whatever might interfere with the performance of his duty. Then, for a little while, he had been able to have both a woman's love and his own ironbound dedication. But it had ended.

What now, soldier, he wondered.

He thought about Bailey and felt an unexpected surge of pity for him. How would he deal with those lonely wakeful hours of all the nights when the ghosts came to question? Bronstein and Liz Adams ruined, Trask and Emerson dead. Ben Crowell dead. The thirsty ground had got its fill of blood. Rabin dead. Russian submariners and American airmen lost. Lesh and Jamil dead. And the civilians—newsmen, monks, Bedouins, innocents—dead. It was sickening and empty. A soldier's life was concerned with death, yes. Deborah had known that, too. But the *kind* of death, the *way* of it, made all the high-sounding words inside sound so futile.

He felt a touch on his shoulder. It was Sergeant Robinson. He said, with surprising gentleness, "I'm sorry to bother you, General."

"What is it, Sergeant?"

"They're ready inside, sir."

Yes, of course, the ceremony. The Cyprus Accord renewal was to be signed—a little late. A Russian deputy premier, an American president designate, a Swedish general, a Russian general, now to be joined by an American sergeant major and an American general, all standing under a strange flag that claimed to mean peace with its Circle and Arrows.

"Sir?"

"Let's go, Sergeant. Let's see what we bought."

Appendix

Excerpts from The Cyprus Accord

Chapter One

Provisional Demarcation Lines and Demilitarized Zone

ARTICLE I

The primary provisional demarcation line shall be fixed at the 34th meridian of longitude east of Greenwich. Territory to a distance of 12.5 kilometers east and west of this primary demarcation line shall be totally demilitarized and shall fall within the jurisdiction of the United Nations.

ARTICLE II

Administrative and military forces of the United States of America and of the Union of Soviet Socialist Republics shall occupy territories east and west respectively of the Demilitarized Zone to a distance east and west of 25 kilometers. These areas shall be known, respectively, as the U.S. Sector and the USSR Sector.

ARTICLE III

Administrative and military forces of the State of Israel and of the United Arab Republic shall occupy the sectors respectively east and west of the U.S. and USSR sectors.

ARTICLE IV

It is agreed by the signatory powers and the United Nations that the Demilitarized Zone (DMZ) shall be absolutely and totally inviolate and that the military forces of the occupying powers shall be prohibited from entering, patrolling, overflying, or reconnoitering said DMZ under any conditions whatsoever.

Administration and policing of the DMZ shall be exclusively the duty of the United Nations Observer Force, which shall be based at a site to be called Zone Center and to be located at approximately 28° 41′ north latitude, 34° 0′ east longitude. . . .

ARTICLE V

The eastern boundary of the USSR Sector shall be a line 12.5 kilometers west of, and parallel to, the primary demarcation line of 34° east longitude. The western boundary of the USSR Sector shall be a line parallel to the eastern boundary and 25 kilometers from it.

The eastern boundary of the UAR Sector shall be the western boundary of the USSR Sector. The western boundary of the UAR Sector shall be the low-tide mark of the Gulf of Suez from a point two (2) kilometers northwest of El Tor to the eastern bank of the Suez Canal and thence to the approaches to the canal at Port Said.

The western boundary of the U.S. Sector shall be a line 12.5 kilometers east of, and parallel to, the primary demarcation line of 34° east longitude. The eastern boundary of the U.S. Sector shall be a line parallel to the western boundary and 25 kilometers from it.

The western boundary of the State of Israel Sector shall be the eastern boundary of the U.S. Sector. The eastern boundary of the State of Israel Sector shall be the low-tide mark of the Gulf of Aqaba from Ras Nisrani to the 1948 Armistice Line. . . .

Chapter Two

Military Force Limitations on Signatory Powers

ARTICLE I

The U.S. and the USSR, as primary guarantors of peace in the Sinai Peninsula, may garrison their respective sectors in the following numbers, it being understood that deployment of forces in excess of these numbers shall be *prima facie* evidence of a breach of world peace:

1. With ground forces not to exceed 5,000 men
2. With logistical forces not to exceed 2,000 men
3. With VTOL or STOL aircraft not to exceed 30
4. With fixed-wing aircraft not to exceed 15
5. Ballistic missiles are specifically forbidden, as are chemical, biological, and nuclear weapons.

ARTICLE II

The UAR and the State of Israel, as primary potential belligerents in the Sinai Peninsula, may garrison their respective sectors in the following manner:

1. With ground forces not to exceed 3,000 men
2. With logistical forces not to exceed 1,000 men
3. Air forces of any sort or description are specifically forbidden in the Sinai Peninsula.

ARTICLE III

The United Nations shall designate, as the United Nations Observer Force, four neutral nations to supply such military forces as they deem fit to garrison, patrol, and occupy the Demilitarized Zone. These forces will perform this duty consecutively, each neutral force occupying the DMZ for thirty days in turn.

ARTICLE IV

In the interests of safety, the United Nations Commission for the Implementation of the Cyprus Accord will be headquartered in Nicosia, Cyprus, rather than at Zone Center, which shall be considered the United Nations Observer Force's military headquarters. . . .

Chapter Three

Naval Force Limitations on Signatory Powers

ARTICLE I

All naval forces of the signatory powers shall maintain a distance of no less than 15 kilometers from the coasts occupied by the other signatory powers except when special permission for a nearer approach has been granted, in writing, by the military commander of the sector to be approached. . . .

Chapter Ten

Miscellaneous Addenda

ARTICLE VII

Sector component commanders shall ensure that persons under their authority who violate any provision of the present accord are suitably punished.

This accord shall be binding on all members of the armed forces or administrative cadres of the signatory powers and their respective allies. All personnel in the Sinai Peninsula shall be clearly instructed in their duties as guardians of world peace. They shall be warned to respect the Demilitarized Zone and the territory under the control of the other signatory powers, and shall commit no act and undertake no operation against said cosignatories. No military force in Sinai shall engage or participate in any blockade, incursion, or provocative maneuver of any kind whatsoever. . . .

AGREEMENT ON THE QUADRIPARTITE OCCUPATION AND ADMINISTRATION AND DEMILITARIZATION OF THE SINAI PENINSULA SIGNED AT NICOSIA, CYPRUS, BY REPRESENTATIVES OF THE UNITED STATES OF AMERICA, THE UNION OF SOVIET SOCIALIST REPUBLICS, THE UNITED ARAB REPUBLIC, AND THE STATE OF ISRAEL.

Done at Nicosia, Cyprus, in English, Russian, Arabic, and Hebrew, all texts being equally authentic.